T0358139

'With the magic of country atmosphere, a cast of incredible characters . . . true community spirit and a relatable romance, it has all the contents of an engaging read. You can smell the way of life, feel the weather and breathe in the fresh air as Karly's inviting storytelling comes to life from the pages.' —HappyValley BooksRead

PRAISE FOR *A Stone's Throw Away*

'Fans will not be disappointed and new readers are likely to be converted . . . those looking for romance, suspense or contemporary novels will all find something to enjoy.' —Beauty and Lace

'With its appealing characters, well-crafted setting and layered storyline, *A Stone's Throw Away* is an entertaining read.' —Book'd Out

'Karly Lane has delivered a wonderfully immersive novel with a highly engaging plot, gripping suspense and compelling twists. *A Stone's Throw Away* is a story of courage, resilience and a passion for the truth.' —The Burgeoning Bookshelf

'I'm always highly impressed by Lane's ability to write compelling, entertaining and emotional storylines and weave some of Australia's history through her stories . . . an absolute treat.' —Noveltea Corner

PRAISE FOR *Once Burnt, Twice Shy*

'Well written, and bravely done . . . *Once Burnt, Twice Shy* is Karly Lane's best yet, celebrating the power of community working to support one another in terrible calamity.' —Blue Wolf Reviews

'Karly Lane gives it her all in *Once Burnt, Twice Shy* . . . a story of faith, courage, strength and future prospects, Lane's eighteenth novel is a sizzling summer read.' —Mrs B's Book Reviews

'This book has a huge amount of hope after loss, a wonderful read.' —Noveltea Corner

'Heart in mouth stuff, readers. You won't be able to put the book down till you know what happens to Jack and Sam.' —Australian Romance Readers

PRAISE FOR *Take Me Home*

'Full of romance, humour and a touch of the supernatural, this is another engaging tale by the reliable Karly Lane.' —*Canberra Weekly Magazine*

'Such a fun read . . . Karly has smashed the contemporary fiction genre with *Take Me Home*.' —Beauty and Lace

'*Take Me Home* is a delight to read. I loved the change of scenery while still enjoying Karly Lane's wonderful, familiar storytelling.' —Book'd Out

PRAISE FOR *Something Like This*

'Another unmissable rural romance story of pain, loss, suffering and the power of love . . . Karly Lane is firmly on my must-read list.' —Beauty and Lace

'There is more to this narrative than rural romance; this is a multi-faceted exploration of loss, grief, families, second chances and courage . . . I loved this!' —Reading, Writing and Riesling

'An engaging story, set at a gentle pace, told with genuine warmth for her characters and setting, *Something Like This* is a lovely and eminently satisfying read.' —Book'd Out

PRAISE FOR *Fool Me Once*

'*Fool Me Once* is a guaranteed perfect light read . . . Karly Lane has woven a delicious tale of lust, love, betrayal, consequences and chasing dreams.' —Blue Wolf Reviews

'With its appealing characters, easy pace and happy ending, I found *Fool Me Once* to be another engaging and satisfying rural romance novel.' —Book'd Out

'Karly Lane's affinity for the land shines through in her stories . . . *Fool Me Once* is a feel-good story not to be missed.' —The Burgeoning Bookshelf

Karly Lane lives on the beautiful mid-North Coast of New South Wales, and she is the proud mum of four children and an assortment of four-legged animals.

Before becoming an author, Karly worked as a pathology collector. Now, after surviving three teenage children and with one more to go, she's confident she can add referee, hostage negotiator, law enforcer, peacekeeper, ruiner-of-social-lives, driving instructor and expert-at-silently-counting-to-ten to her resume.

When she isn't at her keyboard, Karly can be found hanging out with her beloved horses and dogs, happily ignoring the housework.

Karly writes Rural and Women's Fiction set in small country towns, blending contemporary stories with historical heritage. She is a passionate advocate for rural Australia, with a focus on rural communities and current issues. She has published over twenty books with Allen & Unwin.

Time After Time

KARLY LANE

Time After Time

ALLEN&UNWIN
SYDNEY · MELBOURNE · AUCKLAND · LONDON

This edition published in 2024
First published in 2023

Allen & Unwin
Cammeraygal Country
83 Alexander Street
Crows Nest NSW 2065
Australia
Phone: (61 2) 8425 0100
Email: info@allenandunwin.com
Web: www.allenandunwin.com

Allen & Unwin acknowledges the Traditional Owners of the Country on which we live and work. We pay our respects to all Aboriginal and Torres Strait Islander Elders, past and present.

A catalogue record for this book is available from the National Library of Australia

ISBN 978 1 76147 106 3

Set in Simoncini Garamond by Bookhouse, Sydney
Printed and bound in Australia by the Opus Group

10 9 8 7 6 5 4

For Milly.

*My youngest and very last teenager. I can't wait to
see all the amazing things you go on to do.*

Part One

Chapter 1

Alice Croydon stared at her grandmother. 'You're what?'

'Leaving your grandfather.'

Of all the things she'd been preparing to hear from her gran at this family meeting, this had not been one of them.

Daisy and Verity, Alice's older sisters, swapped startled looks as her brothers, Charlie and Toby, reached for their beer bottles, seeming determined to keep their heads down and stay quiet.

'Oh, for goodness' sake, Meryl,' Kathy Croydon said, eyeing her mother-in-law with a dubious expression. 'You can't be serious.'

'As serious as a heart attack.'

'Leaving him?' Kathy added. 'As in . . .'

'As in leaving the silly old coot.'

'But why?' Alice asked.

'Because I finally realised that if I don't go out and chase my dreams now, I never will.'

'Chase your . . .' Kathy repeated vaguely before giving a confused chuckle. 'What dreams?'

'Exactly,' Gran said, sounding almost triumphant. 'What dreams? *My* dreams, Kathy. I want to finally do something for *me*.'

'I don't understand,' Alice said. Her grandparents had been married for sixty years and now Gran was saying she wanted to end their marriage?

Gran's eyes softened slightly. 'I know it must be a bit of a shock, pet,' she said, 'but it's something that's been brewing inside me for a long time now.'

'It can't be that long, we literally celebrated your sixtieth anniversary two weeks ago.' Kathy threw her hands in the air. The party at the local Ex-Services Club had been a huge event—more like a Croydon family reunion. The Croydons were Gunnindi's largest family. It had all started with Bartholomew Croydon and his wife Brunhilda, who'd carved out a life in the bush and started a dynasty. Fifteen children later, they'd gone on to help build the town of Gunnindi and overrun it with Croydon descendants.

A large proportion of the original family had branched out and moved to other towns in the region—a wise decision, seeing as they were pretty much the only gene pool in what was, at the time, a remote, largely unsettled part of the country. However, there had always been a hefty core of Croydons in Gunnindi and the name was still associated with a number of roads, bridges and playing fields around the district.

Croydons were breeders. That's what they did. Had done ever since old Bart and Hilda. Alice's parents had five children and it seemed her siblings, the eldest being ten years older than herself, were all following the tradition. Alice had twelve nieces and nephews, aged from seventeen down to just six weeks old. Baby Tabitha was currently, obliviously, sleeping in her mother's arms on the lounge.

Marriage and family had been the Croydons' life motto—until Gran dropped the mother of all announcements on them.

'If you recall, Kathy, I specifically said I didn't want a party,' Gran said now, bringing Alice back to the drama unfolding in her parents' living room.

'It was your sixtieth wedding anniversary, for goodness' sake!' Alice's mother said. 'Of course you had to have a party.'

Parties were the other Croydon speciality. They threw parties for everything, and with an endless supply of children, grandchildren and great-grandchildren, there was pretty much a party of some sort going on at any given moment.

Alice's father, Jim, hadn't weighed in, which wasn't unusual—he was a man of few words, even fewer when his wife was in the same room. He wasn't known for getting overly worked up about anything. Unless the subject involved *greenies*. The Croydons had always had ties with timber milling and farming, and both industries had a long history with changing environmental practices. It was the only subject you were certain to hear Jim's opinions on. Now, though, he leaned forward in his seat, eyeing his mother with a concerned frown.

'Mum, when did all this happen? Where's Dad?'

'Where do you think he is? Out playing golf!' she said with an impatient huff. 'Where he *always* is.'

'So you actually told him you were leaving?'

'I did,' Gran said with a decisive nod.

'And?' Jim prodded.

'And what?'

'What did Dad say?'

'He asked if I need a hand to lift my suitcase into the car,' she said dryly. 'Then headed off to his golf game. Let's just see how smug he is when he gets home and there's no dinner on the table.'

'Mum,' Jim sighed, shaking his head. 'You know what Dad's like.'

'Yes, son, I do. I've been the one married to him for sixty years.'

'How about we all sit and have a cuppa and calm down, then I'll take you home so you can talk things over with Dad when he gets back.'

'Clearly you're not wearing your hearing aids today, son. I said I was leaving him. I'm not going back.'

'Mum, you can't just—'

'I can do whatever I like. Last time I checked it was a free country.'

'But Mum . . . *leaving*? Don't you think that's a bit . . . extreme?' Jim asked, clearly picturing his mother storming down the street towing her suitcase on wheels behind her.

'No, I don't.'

'Mum, you can't—'

'Are you saying you won't let me stay here?' Gran snapped.

'I didn't say that.'

'You're not exactly being very supportive.'

'We're all in shock, Mum.'

'Then I'll just get a room at the motel.'

A collective protest went through the room before Alice piped up, 'Gran, you can come and stay with me.'

'Thank you, darling. It's nice to see there's still *some* family loyalty around here,' Gran said, eyeing her son sternly.

'Mum—' Jim said before his wife cut him off.

'Jim, how about we just take a moment. I'll go and make us all a nice cuppa. Come and give me a hand.'

Alice watched as her parents had a silent conversation through a series of narrowed eye movements in that secret language of couples who'd been together a long time. She tried to ignore the flutter of disappointment she felt about the fact she and Finn hadn't managed to master the same level of silent communication as her parents. It was probably something that came with decades of togetherness and she and Finn had only been together nine years after all.

'Gran, whatever it is that you and Grandad are going through, I'm sure it'll be all right,' Verity said, moving one hand out from under her sleeping baby to take Meryl's hand. 'You and Grandad are our rock.'

'I'm sure it's a bit of a shock to you all,' Gran said gently.

Getting zapped by static electricity was a shock—this was more like a bus sideswiping your car out of the blue, Alice thought.

'But despite what your parents think, this isn't me having some kind of senior moment. I'm completely aware of what I want.'

'But, Gran,' Daisy said, 'you've been together for sixty years.'

'Yes, we have.'

'And you're wanting to throw all that away?' Daisy sounded dumbfounded, her blue eyes troubled as she continued to stare at her grandmother. All the Croydon offspring had blue eyes—everyone except Alice. She just had plain old brown. She also seemed to be the only Croydon throwback to have red hair—everyone else had varying shades of browns or honey blonds. Although her hair wasn't red-red, it was more of a burnt copper, which Alice thought sounded better than red.

'Sometimes you have a moment of clarity and it doesn't make any sense to anyone else,' Gran said.

Alice understood her older sister's dilemma. If their seemingly happy grandparents' marriage of sixty years could suddenly fall apart, what hope did the rest of them have?

Her parents returned with the tea and, for a moment, the bombshell was almost forgotten as hands reached for cups and spoons, piling in sugar. There was a valiant attempt by Alice's brothers to change the subject by talking cricket with their father before, eventually, the elephant in the room could no longer be ignored.

'Would it help if we got Dad over here to clear the air?' Jim suggested. 'You'd have some moral support.'

'I know you're only trying to help, son, but I've made up my mind. I have to be true to myself.'

'Don't you think you've left it a bit late? I mean, jeez, you're both in your eighties.'

Alice cringed at her father's bluntness, although from the less horrified expressions on her siblings' faces, clearly it was the question they were all thinking.

'Son, my mother—your grandmother—is currently one hundred and two years old. Longevity runs in the family,' Meryl pointed out. 'I possibly have another twenty or so years ahead of me and if so, don't you think that's a rather significant time to simply while away being unhappy, waiting until I die?'

'I just don't understand why, if you were so unhappy all this time, you didn't say anything before now?'

'And when would have been a good time? In my seventies? You would still have said I was too old. I'm not here to debate anything, son. Alice, if you don't mind, I think I'd like to lay down for a bit.'

Alice jumped to her feet. 'Of course,' she said, picking up her handbag and sending her parents a wave. 'I'll take care of her,' she said quickly, trying to reassure them before hurrying after her gran, who was already moving towards the front door.

'Thank you for giving me a lift, darling. Of all the times for my car to be out of action at the mechanics.'

'That's okay Gran.'

'All things considered, that seemed to go better than I was expecting.'

'As far as dropping bombs goes, I guess,' Alice said as she reversed into the street from her parents' driveway.

'There was no easy way to do it.'

'No. I guess not.'

'I thought if anyone could understand all this, it would most likely be you.'

Alice glanced at her gran, before returning her gaze to the road. 'Why do you say that?' she asked cautiously.

'The others are content with their lot in life. They don't have any big dreams to chase.'

'I'm content,' Alice protested and when Gran didn't respond, she sent her another quick sideways look. 'I am.'

'Hmm,' Gran murmured, shifting her gaze to look out the side window.

Chapter 2

I am content, Alice told herself again silently as they turned into her driveway at the end of the street her parents lived on. Matilda Street was jokingly referred to as Little Croydonville thanks to no less than seven Croydon households living along it: herself, her parents, grandparents, a brother, two cousins and a second cousin, once removed . . . or was it twice removed? Alice wasn't sure; it all got a little bit confusing after the first generation.

The little house Alice and Finn owned once belonged to her great-grandmother, Granny Dot. When Alice had found out it was going to be sold, she'd known she had to buy it. She'd always loved Granny Dot's cottage—there was something special about it. Maybe because it was one of the oldest houses in not only the street, but in Gunnindi itself. There was an old-world charm about it that drew Alice to it, even as a child. It had been in need of some serious TLC, but it was within their budget and close enough to the main street that Alice could walk to work.

Outside, the paint was chipped and the tin roof was rusting, so stepping inside was often a surprise to most people. The house still had the original flooring, ceilings and tongue and groove walls, which gave the house so much of its character, but Alice and Finn had just finished painting the interior of the house and had installed a new kitchen and bathroom.

She smiled as a memory of a weekend spent working side by side in the garden with Finn when they'd first moved in floated before her like a vision. As a farmer, he worked long hours tending crops, but gardening simply for aesthetics was something he didn't particularly understand. She knew he'd have preferred to spend the first weekend he'd had off in months doing something he enjoyed, but he'd pulled out weeds and edged, planted seedlings and painted second-hand garden furniture because it was important to her. By the end of the second day she suspected he was almost enjoying himself. She could still see his slow grin as he'd gently wiped away a smudge of dirt from her cheek and looked down at her with that expression that always made her stomach flutter and her heart rate speed up. He'd laid her down on the freshly painted day bed, sliding the straps of her overalls off her shoulders and trailing his lips down her throat, her fingernails digging into his shoulders as he slowly tortured her with his drug-like kisses and caresses. She'd barely even put up a protest about being outside—the hedges created the perfect privacy screen to the outside world. It had always been the same—they'd fitted together so perfectly.

Alice blinked away the memory as she lifted Gran's suitcase from the back of her car and led the way to the front door.

'Look at your agapanthus,' Gran said, admiring the long-stemmed purple flowers that lined the front path. 'You've certainly developed a green thumb.'

'I don't know, I think they're just extremely hardy. Now they aren't hidden under all the overgrown weeds, they seem to be doing much better.' This was the first year they'd flowered since they'd been here.

She noticed Finn's ute parked along the side of the house and wondered how he was going to take having a surprise visitor staying with them for the night.

Was it only for the night? The way Gran was talking, it sounded as though she wasn't going back to Grandad any time soon.

'Hello?' Alice called as they walked down the timber-floored hallway. 'Gran, I'll put your suitcase in here,' she said, opening one of the bedroom doors that opened off the hall, across from her sewing room. The guest room had previously been used to store unpacked boxes, but Alice's old double bed was in there now and often got used for the occasional niece and nephew sleepover. It had never been used by a grand-parent . . . until now.

A large blue rug covered the floorboards and a set of lace curtains hung in front of the stained-glass windows. On the opposite wall was a small upright wardrobe with a mirror.

'My old bedroom,' Gran said with a smile, looking around.

'It's probably a bit different now,' Alice said, wondering if Gran was picturing the way it would have once looked and feeling nostalgic. 'I hope it's okay.'

'It's lovely, dear. This will do nicely.'

Loud steps sounded along the hallway. 'There you are,' Finn said, coming to a stop outside the door. 'Oh. Hi, Gran.' His gaze switched between the suitcase and his fiancée.

'Finn, Gran's going to be staying with us for a . . . while.'

'Everything okay?' he asked slowly.

'I've left Wes,' Gran supplied simply.

'Oh,' Finn said, sending Alice an alarmed glance.

Alice briefly shut her eyes. 'I'm going to find something for dinner. Gran, why don't you have a rest? I'll let you know when it's ready.' She took Finn's arm as she passed him in the doorway.

'I think I *might* have a little lie-down.'

Alice closed the door softly behind them and headed out to the kitchen.

'She's not serious, is she?' Finn asked.

'I don't know,' Alice said, shaking her head. 'She sounds serious. There was a family meeting at Mum and Dad's and Gran made the announcement.'

'What happened?'

'I have no idea.'

'So . . . how long is she planning on staying?'

Alice sent him a helpless look. 'Mum and Dad were so worked up about it, and Gran was getting angry. The whole situation felt really awkward and I just didn't like how everyone was treating her like a child,' she said. 'I mean, I know they were all really shocked, but still . . . she's a grown woman and she can make her own decisions. I offered our place because I think everyone needs time to calm down a bit.'

'It's not exactly . . . normal, is it?' Finn replied, still looking doubtful. 'I mean, they're your grandparents—they're old. Old people don't get divorced.'

'I don't think age has anything to do with it.'

'Sure it does,' he said, shrugging. 'It's not like either of them is going to get married again or anything, so why would you get divorced at their age and mess everything up?'

'Because they're still human beings,' Alice snapped.

'Why are you getting cranky at me? I'm just pointing out the facts.'

'They aren't facts. They're opinions. Yours.'

'I reckon they're also your parents'. Most people would think the same thing.'

'Regardless, Gran's clearly upset and unhappy. So, until she figures out what she wants to do, I said she could stay here.'

'Fine,' he said simply. 'But it's still weird.'

Alice bit her tongue as she watched him walk away, then went to the fridge to search for something to make for dinner. She had a feeling this whole thing was about to shake up a lot more than just one couple's marriage. It felt like it had already begun to shift the foundations of everything she'd believed in—and she wasn't sure if that was a good thing or not.

Alice switched on the light as she opened the door to her sewing room. Tomorrow she was planning on taking in some dresses to show her boss, and she wanted to double-check they were ready before she packed them.

Gran had been asleep when she'd checked on her for dinner and she'd decided to leave her. It had been a pretty stressful day. Finn had turned in early. She suspected he was still a bit annoyed at her, since dinner conversation had consisted mainly of one-syllable answers and the occasional grunt in reply to anything she said.

Her gaze was drawn to the mannequin in the centre of the room wearing the stunning wedding gown that sparkled beneath the bright lights like a dress out of a fairy tale.

It was perfect.

She gave a small self-deprecating smile. Was it weird that she could be so enamoured of something she had created from her imagination? She loved designing; it was the only time she felt truly complete. Over the last few years, she'd become increasingly passionate about fashion design. It wasn't just the hobby she'd had since she was a kid—sewing outfits for her dolls, then clothes for herself in high school—it had become something she craved. When she locked herself away in her sewing room, everything else ceased to exist, it was just her and her imagination. Most of her family were creative and her mother and grandmother both knitted and crocheted, as did her older sister, Verity. Alice had never quite found the same enjoyment in knitting as she did in sewing, though.

She'd been dreaming about creating her own wedding dress for years. She'd made a few before; Verity's and her sister-in-law, Steph's, a few years earlier, and ever since, she'd been itching to do more. There was something special about a wedding dress. The search for the perfect dress was the most important part of planning a wedding and every bride knew the moment when they found the one.

Alice had spent months tediously hand-stitching hundreds of beads and sequins over the V-neckline bodice and its deep V lace-up back. The ivory lace gown with long bell sleeves and an extended train had been lovingly hand embroidered with wildflower appliques then draped over a mocha underskirt. When she'd finished, she'd felt the breath catch in her chest. This was the dress she'd seen in her dream. *Her* wedding dress.

'Darling, it's stunning,' Gran said softly, making Alice jump slightly.

'I thought you were asleep,' she said.

'I was, I thought I'd go out and make a cup of tea and some toast when I saw the light on in here. You've outdone yourself with this one, sweetheart,' she said, putting an arm around Alice as she stared at the glittering gown before them. 'Absolutely spectacular.'

'Thanks, Gran. You don't think it's too much, do you? For Gunnindi,' she added.

'Absolutely not. Gunnindi won't know what hit it. You've got a gift, my child.'

Alice felt a small smile touch her lips at her gran's words.

'What's wrong?' Gran asked.

'Nothing,' Alice said, forcing a brighter smile to her face.

'It's something.'

Alice let out a small sigh. 'I don't know . . . now that it's finished, I'm not sure . . .' she said, shaking her head irritably. The truth was she honestly didn't know how to describe the lingering emotion she was feeling. She'd been planning her wedding for so long and now that it was all happening—the date set, the dress finished—it somehow felt like an anti-climax. Which was stupid. It was only the beginning. But the beginning of what?

'You'll figure it out,' Gran said after a moment of silence.

Alice turned to look at her. Her gran's words had always comforted her—she'd always given such wise advice and known exactly what to say in any situation, from squabbles with parents and siblings to the death of a beloved pet and everything in between. Gran always had the answers, only this time she wasn't offering any. She was leaving it up to Alice and the thought was unsettling.

'Gran? Are *you* all right?'

Meryl patted her arm. 'I will be, darling. We all will be. You'll see. How about a cuppa?'

Gran headed to the kitchen, leaving Alice to turn back to her dress. She gave another small sigh, switched off the light and closed the door behind her.

Chapter 3

The following morning, Alice unlocked the side door of the shop, juggling the dress bag folded over one arm, her handbag, laptop and keys.

Chic Chateau had been part of the Gunnindi main street landscape for almost thirty years and had been a source of town friction for around the same amount of time, ever since Antoinette Bonnaire arrived back in town to open her little slice of French provincial elegance. Born Annette Bonner and raised by her father, the town drunk, little Annette had fled Gunnindi at fifteen and vanished from memory until making a regal return fifteen years later to open a dress shop and start all the town gossips' tongues wagging. It could have been a page right out of a Rosalie Ham novel, except there was no exciting tale of retribution or heartache to follow—just speculation.

After leaving school and excelling at pretty much only one thing—textiles—Alice had taken a job at Chic Chateau, planning to save enough money to head to Sydney to complete a Bachelor of Design in Fashion and Textiles.

Six years later, she was still here. She'd never followed through on her dream of studying at the University of Technology in Sydney, but she had done a TAFE course and a number of online courses over the last few years and while it wasn't a degree from UTS, it *was* something. Her life hadn't been a complete failure and she hadn't settled—no matter what Gran thought about the matter.

Alice switched on the shop lights and took a deep breath, taking in the familiar new-fabric smell that she loved. It was mixed with the exotic scent of perfumed reed diffusers that cost almost a week's salary, but which Antoinette stubbornly refused to stop ordering. 'Darlink, we must strive for perfection,' she'd always tell Alice whenever she tried to convince her boss to switch to a less ridiculously priced company to supply their diffusers. 'This is our signature scent, mon chérie,' she'd say in the French accent she insisted on using. Alice knew it was fake because whenever Antoinette got angry, her accent mysteriously vanished and was replaced by something that sounded a lot less French and a lot more *Kath and Kim*.

She had to admit, though, Antoinette did know how to make a statement. Stepping into the little boutique, you could almost imagine you were somewhere in Paris. The classy black and white striped awning out the front, complete with the antique bike with its basket of bright flowers that was cemented outside the front window along with the little cafe table and chair all screamed Parisian chic and stood out quite prominently amid all the other businesses in Gunnindi.

When the local mine had first opened and brought with it families with disposable incomes, the little business really picked up. But the shop was now also a drawcard for their small town, attracting people from the more affluent surrounding districts on weekends to peruse the array of fashion on display. Antoinette had a savvy business mind and she catered for all occasions, from formal attire and bridal wear to casual styles, and had recently also added a homewares section that had become a huge hit with the visiting tourists.

Alice glanced at the table in the centre of the room with its display of woven baskets and linen tablecloths and a bubble of something warm and fuzzy rose inside her. She *did* love her job. She hung the dress bag up out the back and nervously brushed out the fold marks. She'd been working on the three evening gowns for the last few weeks, hoping to convince Antoinette to have another look and hopefully take on a few of her designs to sell in the shop.

She hadn't brought the subject up with her boss for over a year and she hoped that this time, actually seeing the gowns she'd created would change Antoinette's mind. Alice had asked a number of times over the last few years, but Antoinette had been insistent that she only wanted to stock brand-named clothing. She wasn't interested in dealing with an unknown designer, despite having hired Alice to do alterations for customers and knowing about her love of design. Alice had stopped asking as her pride and confidence began to wane and life got in the way.

She should be grateful for all the things she had instead of secretly pining for more, but creating something beautiful was where she stopped being Alice the daughter, or Alice the fiancée, or Alice, one of the Croydon girls, and became, well . . . Alice! The designer! She didn't even have to become famous and have her own boutiques in New York or London, she just wanted to create beautiful dresses right here in Gunnindi.

For a while, she'd managed to satisfy her creative urges by making the occasional dress for family and she had been working diligently on her wedding dress, pouring all her energy into it. Now though, with her wedding dress completed, that desire to create hadn't diminished at all—in fact, it had grown even more fierce. Designing was in her blood and she needed to do it.

Alice had made the three gowns she'd brought today for her niece's and her friends' formal. With the formal season approaching, it would be a fantastic opportunity to get her designs out there. She had some amazing plans for a teenage line she wanted to feature in the shop.

Alice turned on the coffee machine and began measuring out the ground coffee—French, of course, the only coffee Antoinette would drink—and warmed the milk to the exact temperature. Not too hot, heaven forbid, or the milk would scald the coffee, yet hot enough that the coffee wasn't able to be tossed down too quickly. Not that her boss would ever lower herself to *tossing down* anything.

Alice glanced again at the clock and twisted her fingers together as she paced. *Stay calm.*

She heard the key turn in the door and took a deep breath before plastering a wide smile on her face. 'Morning,' she said, handing over the coffee.

Antoinette Bonnaire could have just stepped from the pages of a French fashion magazine. At sixty years old, she still had the hourglass figure of Marilyn Monroe and the smooth face of a twenty-year-old, thanks to her frequent trips to a specialist plastic surgeon in Sydney and the occasional Botox top-up. As she sashayed towards the counter wearing her signature Christian Louboutin stilettos her jet-black hair, cut in an immaculate bob, shone like the paintwork on her Renault convertible.

'Morning, chérie,' she said, removing her designer sunglasses to reveal dark, heavily made-up eyes.

Alice squinted as a flash of sunlight caught her boss's diamond-bejewelled hand, momentarily blinding her. 'Ah, Antoinette, I was wondering if you could look at something for me,' she said before she chickened out completely.

'What is it, Alice?' Antoinette asked with the tiny hint of impatience that always seemed to linger in her voice.

Swallowing to relieve a suddenly dry throat, Alice walked across to the garment bag she'd brought in and unzipped it carefully, taking out the first dress and hanging it on the stock rack. The blood-red satin gleamed under the overhead lighting. She removed the two remaining dresses before her courage failed her. The second gown was a floaty design in a gold chiffon and the third, another satin gown, this one in sage, with a strapless sweetheart neckline and pleated skirt.

'I've been making my niece's formal gown and I realised this is something I really want to do. I want to sell my designs and I'd really like to do that here.'

'You made these for clients?' Antoinette asked, her gaze fixed on the three dresses hanging before her.

'Yes. Well, not exactly, just my niece and her friends.'

'So you've started selling gowns in competition to me?'

Oh. Crap. Of all the reactions she'd imagined the woman having, this was an angle she hadn't foreseen—anger.

'Only to friends of the family,' Alice said, striving for a calm, reasonable tone.

'But you want to go into business?'

'Yes,' she said, and heard the doubt beginning to creep in. 'But with you,' she tacked on.

'I told you before, I only sell recognised labels. I provide a boutique experience—garments most people would only find in a big city or overseas—I don't stock homemade dresses,' Antoinette snapped, her furious gaze pinning Alice. 'And I do not appreciate my staff going behind my back, stealing my clientele. After all I've done for you—this is how you repay me?'

'I haven't stolen your clientele,' Alice protested. 'Those girls couldn't afford to buy a dress here in the first place. Which is why I see an opportunity to provide a range of affordable yet beautiful gowns. Not everyone can afford a Camilla and Marc or a Carla Zampatti gown. You'd have the market on it.'

'Then they shop elsewhere,' Antoinette said simply, turning away from the dresses. 'I think you need to think long and hard about your choices. If you continue to sell dresses privately then you will not be working for me. I will not have an employee stealing my business. Do you understand me, Alice?'

Alice felt hot blotches of colour burning her cheeks as a wave of humiliation and disappointment swelled within her. She was twenty-four years old and she worked in a dress shop. When was it time to chase her own dreams?

'Alice!'

Her eyes snapped back to the angry woman before her. Alice bit back her frustration to force out, 'Yes. I understand.' She needed this job.

'Good, now let's get to work,' Antoinette said, turning on her impossibly high heels and regrettably *not* falling and twisting an ankle.

Chapter 4

'I told you that woman was a snake,' Gran said, shaking her head. 'Find another job. I don't know why you've stayed there this long.'

'Because I love the shop, Gran. If I can't design, then at least I'm working around clothing all day. And I don't mind the alterations.'

'It's an insult to your talent to be out the back hemming trousers and selling snobby women from out of town fancy clothing that isn't half as good as the dresses you make,' Gran said with a disdainful sniff.

'This is Gunnindi, Gran. Unless I want to get a job in the mine, there's not a whole lot of other places to choose from.'

She *was* lucky to have her job. It wasn't often you got a chance to work in an industry you actually loved when you lived in a small country town. If she really wanted to design, she'd need to move, and that wasn't likely to happen now, with an upcoming wedding and a house loan, so she just had to suck it up and get on with it.

'What about the Old Mill?' Gran asked. 'Years ago we talked about doing something with that place, remember? And only last year you were throwing around ideas about reopening the mill and breathing some life back into it.'

'That was just talk,' Alice said, but she felt a small hitch in her breathing. She *had* talked about the Old Mill—a local landmark, albeit a rather neglected, forgotten one—but she didn't actually have any idea how she'd go about doing anything with it. There'd been a spark of an idea when they'd studied fabrics and manufacturing during her course some time back. Once, a long time ago, milling wool had been a huge industry in Gunnindi and she'd thought how sad it was that it was now barely even remembered. Imagine reopening an industry like that again, the jobs it would create. She'd had images of Gunnindi wool taking the fashion industry by storm and putting the town on the international stage. Of course, that was all well and good to imagine, but the money needed to undertake the sheer extent of a project like that was too crazy to even contemplate.

'You could always start your own shop. That'd teach the uppity old cow,' Gran said.

'I'm not sure Gunnindi is big enough for two boutiques.'

'Why not? People already come from all over the place to visit Madam Kafoops' place,' Gran said. 'Why wouldn't they stop in and look at another shop while they were here? I bet she'd sit up and take notice if that happened.'

Alice gave a small twist of her lips as she momentarily envisioned the revenge before dismissing it. 'It would be nice, but we've got enough debt at the moment. I can't invest in a business venture I'm not sure about and risk losing all that money.'

'I suppose,' Gran said with a small sigh. 'Thinking of your future is a very admirable thing to do . . . I just hope it's the future *you* want, as well as the one Finn wants.'

'Of course it is. I've always wanted our own home.'

'Yes, but do you really want it here? In Gunnindi? You know that your talent is never going to reach its full potential stuck out in the sticks. You should be travelling the world and working overseas with those fancy-shmancy fashion designers you're always talking about. You've got all your qualifications and they're just going to waste.'

Alice shook her head irritably. 'They haven't gone to waste. I can always use what I learned.'

'Yes but you won that spot in the fashion week show last year and had all those job offers that you turned down. It's just such a shame.'

'It was *one* job offer.'

'With that big-name fashion designer—that hunky-looking fella,' Gran said, waving a finger about as she tried to think of the name.

'Frankie Esquire,' Alice said, trying not to sigh sadly. Yes, she'd had a chance to follow her dream and she'd turned it down. But it wasn't a mistake, she told herself firmly—for probably the millionth time. What else could she have done? Finn had proposed that same night and she'd had to make a choice. She'd chosen Finn.

Despite what Gran implied, Alice knew what a big deal last year had been. She'd thrived during her course, her teachers challenging her and pushing her further than she'd ever imagined herself going, and she'd finished in the top seven across the entire state, earning the chance to showcase her work in front of an international audience of retailers, buyers, celebrities and the press. It was a dream come true, even if it was kind of lost on the rest of her family. They knew it was something important since she was flown to Sydney and put up in a swanky hotel for a week, but none of her family and friends was really interested in fashion the way Alice was, so the magnitude of the event was somewhat lost on them. After all, she really wasn't considering leaving Gunnindi, so there wasn't much point in getting too carried away.

Finn was a farmer, just like his father and brother and grandparents and half of her own family. How on earth would an international fashion career work when her life was here? And yet, none of that had really registered once she was in Sydney and people were talking to her as though she were someone. Not to mention the fact she could talk fashion and design all she wanted and no one's eyes glazed over—not even once! She'd been among people just like her and it had been nothing short of magical. For the first time, a tiny bit of doubt had stirred inside her. *Could* she move overseas to work? Maybe for just a year or two? Surely Finn wouldn't mind if she tried it for a little while?

The thoughts had kept her awake all that week and she'd started to plan how she could make it work. Then Finn had knocked on her hotel door to surprise her with a proposal.

'I can't imagine life without you, Al,' he'd said, seemingly out of the blue.

'I'm not going anywhere,' she reassured him, but there was something hovering beneath his usually placid expression that she couldn't quite identify.

'When I turned up here tonight, I saw you talking to that group of people,' he said quietly. 'I haven't seen you look like that before.'

'Like what?'

'Lighter, glowing. Happy.'

'I'm always happy,' she protested doubtfully.

Finn shook his head slightly. 'Not like this. This was different. For a moment I felt, I don't know . . . afraid. That you'd leave me for all this,' he said, gesturing around the expensive room.

'I'd never leave you,' she said.

A long silence followed.

'I mean, if an opportunity came up, though,' she started bravely, 'would it be so bad if I wanted to take it . . . just for a little while?'

She felt him go very still. 'And what? We'd live apart?'

'Not forever, but what if it was just a year or so?'

'It wouldn't work,' he said with barely any hesitation.

'Why wouldn't it?'

'Because you can't be in a relationship with someone if they aren't with you.'

'That's not true. Lots of people do it. Fly-in fly-out couples do it all the time.'

'And how many people we know have survived that?'

Alice had to admit a number of school friends who'd lived that lifestyle had now split up, but still—'I'm sure we'd be strong enough to withstand a temporary separation if we had to.'

'What would be the point? A marriage is two people living under the same roof—just like our parents. I thought that's what you always wanted?' He pulled away to look down at her with a small frown etched on his handsome face.

'It is,' she said quickly. *It was.* Of course it was. For as long as she could remember, marrying Finn had been her dream. Nothing had ever seemed more perfect, only she hadn't really counted on falling in love with design as much as she had over the last few years and after this week and everything that had happened, she'd begun toying with the original dream, adding on a few extensions. Finn's words had put an end to that. What would be the point? She tried to picture a life without Finn in it and couldn't. For the longest time they'd been a couple and the thought of anything damaging that bond . . . it was too painful to contemplate.

The conversation had put everything else into perspective. Her life was back home in Gunnindi.

Gran had been the only one Alice had told about the job offer. They'd been sitting outside her parents' house after the surprise engagement party she'd walked into on her return from the Sydney trip. Gran had seemed sad as she'd listened, but she hadn't said Alice had made the wrong choice. Although, she hadn't necessarily said she'd made the right choice either, for that matter. She'd just smiled and nodded and patted Alice's hand. Which was why her attitude now, a year on, was a bit of a surprise.

'Have you thought any more about what you're going to do, Gran?' Alice asked, changing the subject.

'About what?'

'About Grandad and . . . everything?' Alice replied.

'I haven't changed my mind, if that's what you're asking. And yes, actually, I have been thinking about things.'

'And?'

'And I'll need to borrow your car tomorrow, if you don't mind. I've got an appointment in Burrandock.'

'Oh. Sure. Do you want me to go with you? Is it a doctor's appointment?'

'No. No, nothing like that. Just looking at some options.'

Options didn't sound exactly promising for her and Grandad getting back to normal. Still, as Gran said, she was a grown woman and not a child and they all needed to remember that.

'You know, it was that conversation we had last year that started me thinking about all this,' Gran said as they peeled vegetables at the sink for dinner.

'What conversation?' Alice asked.

'The one we had when you told me you'd turned down that job offer. My first reaction was to tell you to get back down to the city and tell them you'd changed your mind, then I suddenly realised—who was I to talk? When had I become an expert on taking chances and following dreams? I'd never once done anything that pushed me out of my comfort zone and here I am, eighty years old and nothing to show for it.'

'Gran, that's not true. Look at the family you created! And all the work you do for the community? That's not nothing.'

'When people walk through the cemetery years from now, what are they going to say about me? Oh, what a nice old lady, she baked for lots of stalls and raised money for local charities—big whoop!' Gran said sarcastically. 'I want to be known for something, Alice. For something I did. For *me*. I want my grandchildren to be able to look up to me and think how brave their gran was.'

'Gran, you're still here.'

'Which means I still have time. And I don't intend to waste any of it.'

'You don't have to prove anything to us. We love and admire you just the way you are.'

'What do you admire, Alice?' Meryl asked, tilting her head as she waited for an answer.

Alice was caught off guard at the directness of the question. 'You're the glue that holds this family together,' she said and smiled confidently—yes, that was a good point.

'And? That's it?'

Alice's smile faltered slightly. 'No, that's just one thing. You're loving and kind—generous . . . everyone loves you.' She forged ahead despite her gran's unwavering gaze. 'Those are important things.'

'Yes, they are,' Gran agreed. 'But they aren't going to make it to a headstone, are they? "Here lies Meryl Croydon",' she said, projecting the words into the air. '"Everyone loved her." *Boring*.'

Alice couldn't help the small chuckle that escaped. 'Oh, Gran, anyone who knows you knows you're anything but boring. What *would* you like on your headstone?'

'"Here lies Meryl Croydon—a woman who knew how to live",' she said after thinking on it for a while.

Alice grinned, but a lingering niggle made her bite the inside of her lip. 'Gran, you're not . . . sick or anything, are you? I mean all this stuff about chasing dreams and running out of time . . . is there something behind it all?'

'No, darling,' Gran assured her with a direct look that instantly put Alice's mind at ease. 'I'm the picture of health. I've just woken up from a very long sleep and I'm ready to tackle the next phase of my life.'

Alice wondered how many phases there were and tried to remember the last phase she'd started. She was alarmed when she couldn't. Did that mean it was time to look at her own life the same way Gran had? It was an unsettling thought, not because it sounded ridiculous, but because it actually held some appeal.

Chapter 5

Alice called out a hello as she opened the front door and headed down the hallway of her grandparents' home. 'Grandad, it's Alice.'

'In the kitchen,' he shouted back, and Alice stopped in surprise as she spotted him filling the jug. 'Figured you'd want a cuppa.'

'Ah, sure. You go and sit down and I'll make it.'

'I'll do it,' he said without relinquishing the jug.

Up until today she hadn't even realised her grandad knew what the jug was! She'd never seen him make a cup of coffee before—the kitchen was always Gran's domain. 'Okay. Mum sent over some groceries. Do you want me to put them away for you?'

'That was nice of her, but she didn't have to. I went to the grocery store yesterday. Did you know they've renovated the place?'

About two years ago, she thought.

'Couldn't find a flamin' thing—everything's all this open-planned nonsense,' he grumbled. 'Don't know why they didn't just leave everything the way it was. That's the trouble with the world today. No one's happy unless they're changing everything. Out with the old—in with the new.' He took two mugs from the cupboard above his head. 'Doesn't matter if the old thing still works or not—you've gotta replace it with something shiny and new.'

Alice couldn't be sure, but she had an idea maybe they weren't talking about supermarket renovations anymore. She made some comforting noises as she unpacked the groceries, noticing the fridge was filled with an odd assortment of chocolate custards, three flavours of soft drink and a variety of soft cheeses. When she went to the pantry, she found potato chips, cans of beef stew, baked beans and Pop-Tarts, which she was positive her gran had never bought in her entire life. It seemed Grandad had quite enjoyed shopping.

They took their coffee out to the back verandah and sat down at the table.

'Your gran's having an affair,' Grandad blurted and Alice choked on her coffee, coughing and spluttering.

'What?' Alice asked as she wiped her watering eyes.

'It all makes sense now. All this flamin' hoo-ha about leaving. For the last few months, she's been disappearing through the day and getting all flustered and cranky when I ask her about it . . . I just thought she was goin' through some kind of women's problem or something, but now I reckon it all makes sense.'

'Grandad, I'm sure she's *not* having an affair.'

'Oh, yeah? It's Wednesday. You got any idea where she is?' he demanded.

'Not exactly, I've been at work,' she started, then remembered Gran had borrowed her car earlier that morning for an appointment before dropping it back at the shop.

'Twice a week she meets up with him.'

'With who?'

'I don't know—whoever this bloke is she's been seeing.'

'You don't know that she's meeting a man, though,' Alice said, still trying to get her head around it all.

'You think it could be a . . . woman?' he asked, his eyes widening.

'What? No!'

'You hear of these things happening,' Wes said, shaking his head. 'I'd never live it down at the club house if my wife left me for another woman.'

'Grandad, I really don't think—'

'It's those new female doctors in town who've gone and put all these ideas in her head, I bet ya,' he said.

For over a year, Gunnindi had gone without a GP after Doctor Munroe retired. Then two new doctors arrived, looking for a tree change, and reopened his surgery. It was the best news the town had had in ages. All that was mentioned before their arrival was that the doctors were a married couple and it soon became quite the talk about town when it was discovered the couple were both women.

Alice had heard some of the grumblings and tried to ignore them—she, like most others in Gunnindi, was just grateful she didn't have to make the forty-minute drive to Burrandock to see a doctor. When she finally got an appointment with Linda, she'd been more than impressed with the doctor's thoroughness, sending Alice for blood tests and making sure all her regular tests were up to date.

'I don't see how Gran's doctor could have had anything to do with what's been going on.'

'I wouldn't put it past them—all these big changes they've been making to her medication. Old Doc Munroe had her on the same pills for years and she never had a problem.'

'I'm sure Linda knows what she's doing. Besides, Gran's seemed better than ever lately.' Maybe it *was* something to do with her medication—or maybe, as Gran had said earlier, she'd just realised she wanted to make some changes.

'Yeah, well, something's going on. You mark my words. A woman just doesn't up and leave a marriage of sixty years for no reason.'

Alice clamped her lips together tightly and bit back a snappy reply. She understood some of Gran's frustration—clearly Grandad had dismissed any possibility that he played a part in the whole situation. He simply refused to see that he *had* been taking Gran for granted all these years and *that* was the main reason for the drastic action she was now taking. It felt strangely familiar. Alice stilled for a moment as the thought whispered in her ear. Was this where she and Finn could end up? She shook off the notion. Finn was busy and stressed a lot of the time—it wasn't the same as taking her for granted. They were still very much in love. Alice pushed away the distracting thought and took another sip of her coffee as she studied the man across from her, thoughtfully. It was hard to see her grandad as an everyday, normal *person*. But he was and he had faults like everyone else. Maybe this was the shake-up he needed—they all needed—in order to stop taking Gran for granted.

Later that evening, her grandad's comments replayed in her mind. What *was* Gran doing in Burrandock?

She sighed as she tipped her head on the headrest to watch Finn lightly snoring beside her as they watched TV and realised she'd be having to explain the whole episode to him tomorrow when they sat down to watch it again. Sometimes she wondered why he insisted on watching a series together when he barely managed to keep his eyes open longer than the opening credits. She usually used this time to sew, only she'd finished her wedding dress and the rest of the bridal party's gowns so there was nothing else to work on.

The wedding was only four months away. Suddenly it seemed very close.

She and Finn had been together since Year 9. He'd been the typical shy country boy. Apparently he'd had a crush on her since Year 7 but had never worked up the courage to say anything until then. 'There's no rush' had pretty much become their motto over the years—which is why it probably took almost eight years to get engaged.

Finn's parents owned a large cropping property where he worked alongside his father and brother. When they'd decided to move in together, Alice had flat-out refused to move out to

Whyningham—the only time she'd ever really put her foot down about anything—and for a little while their easy-going relationship looked shaky.

'I just don't get it, Al,' Finn had said, not for the first time.

'I'm not moving into your parents' house. I want our own place. If I wanted to live with parents, I'd just stay where I am with my own.'

'But why would we rent somewhere when we can live for free at Whyningham?'

Because as much as she liked Leslie Walcott, there was no way Alice was going to live under the same roof as the woman and listen to her subtle negativity twenty-four seven. Leslie was the kind of person who seemed to enjoy a good debate—over everything. It didn't even matter if you were agreeing with her, she'd still find a way to turn the conversation into a mini argument: 'The sky is such a pretty shade of blue today, Leslie.'

'I'd say it was more periwinkle.'

Okay, Leslie.

It was only a little issue but still, Alice knew she wouldn't be able to handle living under the same roof as her future mother-in-law.

The wedding planning was causing enough headaches. Every time Alice made a decision on something, Leslie managed to add her passive-aggressive spin onto it and create doubt in her mind. 'Oh . . . so *that's* the colour you're going with for the centrepieces? It's very . . . different, isn't it?' Or her absolute favourite phrase, 'If that's what you like, dear.

But I'm not sure I would have been brave enough to try and pull that off.'

Naturally the whole buying a house in town idea had been an open invitation for even more subtle rebukes, but Alice had stood her ground. Finn's older brother, Matt, and his wife lived in a second house on Whyningham with the plan that, one day down the track, they would move into the main house, freeing up the cottage for Finn and Alice. However, that day depended on their father, Brian, retiring from farming and he and Leslie moving to Scotts Head on the Mid North Coast where they also had a house. The Walcotts had bought the modest two-storey brick house after a holiday there almost twenty years ago and it was now worth a small fortune. If it were up to Leslie, she'd already be in the house overlooking the beach and arguing with tourists about what colour the water looked today. Brian, however, was not so keen and planned on working for as long as he could.

Alice's mind was made up, but Finn couldn't seem to grasp the idea that they would need to have their own life and Alice felt like the bad guy for needing to point it out.

'We need to buy our own house, Finn. So we have some kind of security.'

'I just don't understand why we'd buy a house *in town*.'

'Because if something happens to the farm, we'd at least have our house.'

'Nothing's going to happen to the farm. Why the hell would you even be thinking about all this?'

'Because one of us has to. And you're right, hopefully nothing will ever happen to Whyningham, but look at the

Fergusons last year,' she said gently. 'Their property had been in the family for generations and the bank ended up taking it. Things happen, Finn.'

'That won't happen to us.'

Alice wasn't so sure. The property arrangement out at Whyningham was an issue she didn't fully understand, but it largely depended on the brothers working together and jointly owning the place once their parents passed away. Even after Brian retired, Finn and Matt wouldn't actually own anything, they'd simply be managing the property. This was perfectly fine as long as everyone continued to get on and no natural or financial disasters took place, but Alice wasn't as confident as Finn. She'd seen it happen to people they'd grown up with and others in the district, divorces causing families to have to sell off pieces of property and divide up inheritances in order to distribute assets and the like and ruin the hard work of generations. She didn't want any of that to happen, but the world was rapidly changing and there were no guarantees in life.

'Look at it as an investment,' she'd finally told him. 'Once you're running Whyningham, we can sell the house in town and use the money for our retirement. Your parents have the house at Scotts Head.' Somehow—fortunately—this point was the thing that made buying their own house okay, and they'd opened a savings account for the deposit the next day.

It was also the one thing that now trapped her in her current job at Chic Chateau. She couldn't afford to leave. Alice was practical, if nothing else.

She thought about Antoinette's threat about sewing privately and felt a rare moment of rebellion rise inside her. She sure as hell wasn't going to stop sewing. She'd just have to do it for family and friends—luckily she had a very large family.

Chapter 6

The tin sign with 'Whyningham' written across it had been nailed to the front fence for decades. Its paint was fading and the edges of the tin had rusted away, which gave it a rustic, country look. Home decor shops sold things that looked like that for a small fortune but there was nothing intentionally trendy or pretentious about Whyningham.

It wasn't a bad season at the moment, but it wasn't a particularly good one, either—they'd had a bit of rain now and again and there was water in the dams, but not as much as most farmers out here would have liked. Alice had been watching Finn and his family work and worry and stress their way through each season for close to a decade now, so she knew the struggles of farming life. There'd been good seasons along the way—some even great, when Brian had walked around with a smile on his weathered face a monumental occasion since she could count on one hand the number of times she'd witnessed his smile. Yet, lately, the number of not-so-great seasons seemed to always be tipping the scales.

She followed the long dirt driveway through the seemingly endless paddocks of cotton and wheat before the grove of huge old gum trees that surrounded the main house came into sight. The weatherboard house was big—more sprawling than imposing, thanks to the extra rooms each generation had tacked on—with a wide verandah that wrapped around the front and one side, all topped with a sloping tin roof. She drove past the house and parked in front of one of the three massive sheds a little further down the dirt track.

Alice slid her sunglasses onto the top of her head as she stepped inside the shed holding the box she'd picked up in town. Her eyes took a moment to adjust after the bright sunshine outside, and then she spotted Finn and Matt working on a large tractor.

'Hi,' she called and watched as Finn looked up, his face breaking into a wide grin that still had the ability to send the odd butterfly through her stomach. It was the little things like these moments when, for a fleeting second, all the big problems seemed almost insignificant and her world was perfect.

'Did you get the part?'

And then it was gone again. Of course. The *part*. The *food*. The *paperwork* . . . those were the only occasions she managed to get his full attention, brief as it may be.

She'd known what she was getting into when she realised she'd fallen in love with a farmer. Finn wasn't the guy who was going to make grand gestures or bring her flowers— except that one time when he proposed, which had only come about because her sisters had told him he couldn't propose without flowers. He didn't get mushy or watch romantic movies with her, they didn't have a favourite love song or call each other cute names. She'd known that going into this whole thing, but sometimes she wished he'd just—she silently sighed impatiently—she didn't even *know* what she wished he'd do, just *something* . . . Anything, really, to show that he loved her.

She knew he did, in his own way, and it wasn't like his family did anything different in their relationships. She'd never seen his parents hug or hold hands, and his older brother and his wife—come to think of it, they probably weren't the best examples to compare Finn to as all they seemed to do was argue. She supposed Finn really didn't have any role models in the romance department. And yet, occasionally, she wished he'd just *see her*. Make *her* feel like she was as important as the next crop going in or the next harvest or the next sheep or cattle sale.

Unless she suddenly sprouted some kind of exotic species of wheat or barley from her head or miraculously changed into a cow overnight, Finn apparently didn't have time to actually see *her*.

Stop complaining, she told herself irritably. She had lots of good things, like a fiancé who loved her. And here he came, his arms outstretched . . .

To take the box she carried under her arm, before turning away.

Right.

'Ah, hello?' she said, a tad more snappish than she'd intended. 'Thanks, Alice, for dropping everything to bring this part out. Oh, you're most welcome, Finn, it wasn't like I had anything else to do.'

Finn turned back to look at her. His brow creased slightly, before her words seemed to dawn on him. 'Oh. Yeah. Sorry. Thanks. We're just in a hurry to get this back in action—if that weather event they're predicting decides to hit before we get this fixed, we're stuffed.'

And just like that, the wind of righteousness was snuffed from her sails. Of course there were bigger issues at play here than her precious feelings. His livelihood depended on this—breakdowns were yet another obstacle in a constant battle to succeed. It seemed they were always fighting not only the elements but the unforeseen mechanical issues as well. More delays meant more money they had to find and more chance that they'd miss their window of opportunity to ensure the crop reached its full potential. *Not everything is about you, Alice.*

'Okay, I'll see you at home later, then.'

'I might just crash here at Mum and Dad's so I can get an early start again tomorrow,' he said, kissing her cheek before returning to where his brother was still working.

With a defeated sigh, Alice turned and walked back to her car. *The life of a farmer's wife,* she thought. *You'd better get used to it.*

Alice smiled as the shop door opened then swore silently under her breath. 'Good morning, Beatrice,' she said, closing the inventory book and sliding it under the counter. 'Can I help you with anything?'

'Oh, hello dear,' Beatrice said as she approached, looking the picture of concern. 'Tell me, is it true? What I've been hearing about Meryl and Wes?'

Alice clenched her teeth behind her smile and tried for a coolly neutral expression. 'I don't know. What have you been hearing?'

'That Meryl's left him.'

'I don't think you should believe everything you hear, Beatrice.'

'It comes from a most reliable source, dear.'

She could only imagine. The rumour mill would be going off the dial with this piece of juicy gossip.

'Lilith saw Wes grocery shopping the other day,' she said.

'So?' Alice replied, then wished she'd just kept her mouth shut. She really didn't want to encourage this woman any further.

'So? Wes has never done the grocery shopping. Naturally, Lilith was concerned, thinking dear Meryl might be ill or something, and when she asked, he said he didn't know where she was. Well, you can only imagine how strange *that* sounded, but he left before Lilith could find out what he meant and then Jencie said she heard from the Fletchers next door to your grandfather that they'd seen Meryl walking up the street with a suitcase!'

'Gran's helping with my wedding preparations,' Alice said, trying to think of something to keep from giving this woman some skerrick of information she could use elsewhere.

'Why would she pack a suitcase for that?'

'The suitcase had my wedding dress in it. She was just delivering it to me. See? No big secret.' She shrugged.

'Then why did Wes say he didn't know where she was?'

'Because he didn't know that day. Gran forgot to mention it to him. Can I help you find something, Beatrice? Did you have an event coming up you needed a new dress for?'

The woman gave an uncertain shake of her head and Alice quickly continued to forestall any further opportunity to continue asking questions about her grandparents.

'If not, I really need to get back to work.' She smiled before turning away from the counter to greet a small group of women who'd entered. *These rumours are going to be a problem*, she thought irritably. *Everyone will be wanting the lowdown on the Croydon scandal. Well, Gran, looks like your infamy has begun.*

Chapter 7

Friday night dinner at Alice's parents' place was pretty much a tradition: once a month everyone congregated for a family catch-up—even Granny Dot, who was Gran's mother and lived in the local retirement village. Tonight's gathering almost hadn't happened due to the current civil unrest, but Grandad had refused to stay at home, claiming it was just as much his family as Gran's, so Gran was more or less stuck pretending everything was fine so as not to upset her elderly mother.

Grandad took full advantage of Gran's request to keep everything amicable in front of her mother and seemed to be enjoying himself at Gran's expense—once even slapping her on the backside as she walked past him. Alice and her siblings swapped alarmed glances, fearing for Grandad's life the minute Granny Dot left the room.

It was always a rowdy affair with so many people—Alice didn't know how her mother managed it. There was plenty of food and somehow they all seemed to fit around the table, although the kids' table was now almost bigger than the grown-ups' one.

Her siblings and their spouses were all in attendance. Toby, who drove trucks at the mine, and his wife Cicily, who was a teacher at the local high school, had been married just over nine years and had two children. Daisy, who worked at the nursing home part time, and her husband, Merrick, had been married the longest at eighteen years, and they worked their own property a few kilometres out of town along with their six kids. Verity worked at the mine in a communications role and her husband, Rick, worked at the post office. They were the newest couple in the family, racking up their three-year anniversary and one baby, while Verity's twin brother Charlie, who worked in management at the mines, had been married to his wife, Steph, for five years and already had three children.

Alice glanced at Finn as they sat in the crowded living room before dinner and smiled when he caught her looking at him. Most men would have probably found a way out of coming along tonight, but Finn hadn't even batted an eyelid when she'd reminded him. He'd always fit into her family. She'd been watching him as he chatted easily with Merrick and the other men, talking footy and cricket. He looked tired. He'd been putting in long hours and they'd hardly had any time alone to actually talk. Having an unexpected guest in their spare room hadn't helped, either—although, in fairness, Finn had hardly been home this week so he probably hadn't even really noticed. But she missed their time together.

He held her look for a little while longer and Alice felt a tingle of awareness. They'd been together so long that most people simply saw them as a couple—she wasn't really just Alice, she was always attached to Finn. She loved that feeling of belonging to someone—to being part of a pair. She was fairly sure no one could really remember a time when she *wasn't* with Finn. And she was going to marry this man in a few months' time.

She felt a blush creep up her neck as he sent her a wink before he turned to listen to something Toby was saying.

'Ah, young love. Ain't it grand,' Charlie chuckled beside her.

She groaned.

'Grab a plate, kids,' her mother called, and a swarm of children appeared from seemingly nowhere. Organised chaos was the term best used to describe serving time at her parents' place. Arms reached for the stack of plates and, with some pushing and shoving, they attacked the vast array of dishes set out on the kitchen bench. The younger ones waited for their parents to sort their plates before serving their own meals.

Granny Dot sat at the head of the table like the regal matriarch she was and watched the circus unfolding around her with a contented smile on her face. Gran brought her meal across.

'Thank you, dear,' Granny Dot said, eyeing her daughter curiously. 'Aren't you getting Wesley's dinner?'

Conversation paused as all eyes swivelled to the head of the table.

'Yes, Meryl, you always put a plate together for me,' Grandad said, sitting back in his chair with a smug look on his face.

Alice saw Gran's eyes narrow slightly before she put on a bright smile.

'Of course. I almost forgot,' she said, picking up a dinner plate.

'I can get it, Gran,' Daisy offered.

'It's fine, dear. I can do it.' Gran eyed the dishes, then slapped a huge serving of curried sausages and rice on the plate and carried it back to her husband. She placed it on the table in front of him with exaggerated politeness. 'There you go.'

'I don't eat curry. It's too spicy for me,' Wes complained.

'I distinctly remember you saying when we got here that it smelled delicious and you couldn't wait to try it. I'm sure it won't be too spicy.'

'It's kind of got some heat to it,' Toby hesitantly said, but withered under the hard look Meryl sent him.

'You'll be fine, Wes. Eat it,' she instructed.

'I think Tabitha's getting her first tooth,' Verity blurted, giving everyone somewhere else to direct their attention.

'She's only six weeks old,' Daisy said, arching an eyebrow at her younger sister.

'The midwife at the baby clinic said she was very advanced for her age.'

'Yeah, sis, but she's not freaking *werewolf* kind of advanced,' Charlie scoffed.

'Did you seriously just call your niece a werewolf?' Verity snapped.

'If she's growing teeth at six weeks she'd have to be.'

'Mum!'

'Charles Albert Croydon, that's enough.'

53

'Uh-oh. The middle name came out—you're in the shit now,' Toby tsked from across the table.

'And that's enough from you too, Toby Arthur,' Kathy snapped, drawing sniggers from the rest of the siblings and spouses around the table.

The remainder of the meal was sprinkled with awkward conversation and Jim throwing around useless facts about everything from whale migration to the collective noun for hippos in a valiant attempt to distract from the occasional mutter and grumbling from their grandad as their gran gave him insincere encouragement to 'Just eat it, dear.'

When dinner was done, there was an unprecedented flood of volunteers to do clean-up as an excuse to leave the table, and Alice found herself left to make small talk with Granny Dot and Grandad.

'Not long now until the wedding is it, Alice?' Granny Dot said as they sat down in the living room.

Her granny was a local icon. Alice had never met her great-granddad—Granny had been widowed thirty years ago but always involved in the community and her various charities. The other day she'd said with a twinkle in her eye, 'The last time I did anything fun around here was the senior citizens' day trip to the gin distillery. Old ladies can't handle their drink,' she scoffed. 'I showed some of those young whippersnappers.'

Alice had bitten back a grin as she realised the whippersnappers Granny was talking about were probably in their late eighties.

Alice marvelled at Granny's zest for life. She'd always been going on cruises or bus tours somewhere or other when

Alice was growing up and would bring back small gifts from her adventures. The old green school suitcase of toys in the hall cupboard, now played with by her nieces and nephews, contained dolls from Spain and Fiji from trips her great-gran had taken.

'Four months,' Alice replied, smiling. 'Do you have a dress picked out to wear yet?'

'I'll wear the pink one you made me,' Granny said with a nod.

'I can make you a new one if you like. Just let me know what colour.'

'I don't need any more clothes; I have a wardrobe full. I don't go too many places anymore. Not like I used to.' For a moment Alice caught the slightest waver of Granny Dot's smile, before it was back in place once more. The others began to trickle in from the kitchen. 'But enough of that. I'm looking forward to this shindig. You're a lucky man to be getting my great-granddaughter,' she said to Finn. 'I hope you remember that.'

Finn nodded soberly. 'Every day, Granny Dot.'

'He's a fine, strapping lad,' Dot said, nodding her approval as she looked Finn up and down like a buyer inspecting a racehorse at the sales. 'Good in bed?' she asked, sending a sharp look across at Alice, whose mouth dropped open at the question. Granny Dot didn't give her any time to answer, sending her a knowing smile as she continued, 'You got to make sure you pick one who knows what they're doing in the bedroom department—trust me, you don't want to get stuck with a disappointment. Marriage is a long time to endure a dud. Isn't that right, Meryl?' she added, eyeing her daughter and son-in-law across the room pointedly.

There was a splutter of coughs and wheezes followed by a very undignified protest from Wes.

'Gran!' Kathy hissed at her husband's grandmother, mortified.

'Oh, calm down, Kath. I don't imagine you've got too much to worry about. Our Jim is the spitting image of my Harold, so you should be doing all right,' she said with a mischievous wink that only caused more smothered laughter and horrified gasps throughout the room.

'Gran,' Jim said, in a resigned tone.

'Your time will come, dear. When you get to be as old as I am, you get to say what you're thinking. After all, there has to be at least one perk to outliving everyone you know and making it to over a hundred.'

Her great-grandmother hardly looked like you'd expect a hundred—well, to be exact, a hundred-and-two-year-old—to look. In fact, Granny Dot and Gran were often mistaken for sisters. Granny wasn't in a wheelchair or tucked up under a lap rug in the corner, she was still living in her own self-contained apartment in the retirement village. It was only recently that she'd finally accepted the help of a cleaner and someone to deliver her meals. She went to bingo and played bridge once a week and enjoyed her glass of port each evening. It was almost humiliating to realise your great-grandmother had a far more interesting and active social life than you did.

She did, however, need to come with a warning label.

Granny Dot spoke her mind. All the time. If you wanted a comforting hug and gentle words you went to Gran. If you wanted to hear the blunt truth, you went to Granny Dot. And braced yourself. To be honest, you didn't even have to go *to her*, she'd usually tell you a few home truths whether you asked for them or not.

'You're looking old, Wes,' she announced now, just to prove the point. 'Have you been to the doctor lately?'

'Not these ones,' he grumbled.

'Why? What's wrong with them? I had a visit from one of them the other day. Bit on the skinny side but seemed efficient enough.'

'I'd rather stick with the one I got over in Burrandock.'

'A person could be dead by the time they drove all that way to a doctor.'

'We could only be so lucky,' Grandad muttered under his breath, drawing a series of rebuking frowns from those close enough to hear.

There was no love lost between Wes and his mother-in-law. Although, after all this time, Alice suspected it had grown into a mutual wary respect. They both seemed to enjoy the constant bickering they exchanged on the rare occasions they were both in the same room together.

'So it's true then? You've left him?' Granny Dot asked shrewdly, taking everyone by surprise.

'What?' Gran asked.

'I wanted to drag it out and see how long you two could keep up the charade, but it got boring.'

'How did you find out?' Gran asked stiffly.

'This is Gunnindi,' Dot said matter-of-factly. 'You think gossip's bad in town, just wait till you get to a retirement village. You two are the only thing anyone's talking about.'

'Surely not everyone,' Gran protested, glancing around the rest of the family. 'Have you all been hearing it?'

'You know how it is,' Alice said with a faint shrug. 'It'll all blow over soon enough.'

'People seriously need more to do in their lives than gossip about everyone else,' Gran snapped.

'Maybe if you weren't gallivanting about the countryside you'd be aware of all the talk in town,' Grandad said. 'But you've made your point, so put a stop to all this nonsense and come home.'

'The fact you still consider my feelings and my dreams nonsense is exactly why I'm *not* coming home. Honestly, Wes, for such a generous man in the community you can be an incredibly selfish husband at home. I won't be staying for dessert, thank you, Kathy. Come on, Mum, time to go.'

'Gran, we can drop Granny Dot back home if you like,' Alice offered.

'It's quite all right, dear, I'd rather be home watching my stories anyway,' Granny Dot said. 'Goodnight, everyone.'

'Night, Granny,' the family chorused out of time and somewhat despondently.

'Let's go out for a drink,' Granny was saying as they walked out the front door. 'I bet we can still get a couple of likely lads to buy us a drink or two.' She chortled and Alice caught her grandad's brow furrowing deeper.

'She's only kidding, Grandad,' she said quickly.

'Wouldn't put it past the old battle axe.'

'Come on, Dad,' her father said wearily, 'let's sit out the back with a beer.'

'Does anyone else think our family's weird?' Charlie asked.

'I've always thought it,' Finn volunteered.

'Why the hell didn't you run when you had the chance, then?' Charlie asked, and grunted when Alice elbowed him.

'This last week has been a pain in the arse, to be honest,' Rick said, leaning back. 'All the oldies I deliver to are askin' me in for coffee so they can pump me for info on Gran and Grandad. It's taking me three times as long to deliver the damn mail.'

'Try working in the nursing home,' Daisy groaned. 'Those coffee shop ladies are masters at extracting information. I've had to drink the crappy staff room instant coffee just to avoid being interrogated. I'd kill for a real coffee,' she said, sounding wistful.

'Let's just hope that they sort it out soon, then,' Verity said, burping baby Tabitha after her feed.

'What if they don't?' Cicily asked.

No one wanted to answer that question. It was almost impossible to imagine life without the two people who had always been the solid foundation of their family.

As Alice got ready for bed that night, she glanced across at Finn, softly snoring against his pillow. She knew he worked hard and was most likely exhausted, but she'd been really hoping that tonight they'd . . . Well, it was a moot point now. Alice slid into bed and turned off the bedside light.

She found herself trying to count back to see how long ago it was that they'd last had sex. Clearly a while, if it hadn't jumped out at her immediately. They were still young—twenty-four wasn't ancient—and yet so much of their lives felt like they were already an old married couple. Maybe it was because they'd been inseparable for so many years. They'd established a routine and life just naturally fell into its rhythm.

Alice had never questioned if there was anyone else out there for her—she'd known almost from the beginning that Finn Walcott was who she was supposed to be with. But lately it felt as though they were ships passing in the night—sometimes barely even passing, as the season got busier and his workload increased. And there was this tiny nagging . . . *something* inside of her that made her feel restless late at night when she had too much time to think. Like an itch she couldn't quite reach.

Closing her eyes, Alice snuggled her back into Finn's warmth and smiled as he lifted an arm and draped it across her—maybe there would be some kind of action happening after all. Then she heard his sleepy, 'Night.'

'Night,' she whispered, but her only reply was the sound of his soft snoring next to her ear.

Chapter 8

Alice opened her eyes and blinked a few times, trying to work out what day it was, almost convincing herself it was Sunday, until she rolled her head sideways and looked at the digital clock on the bedside table. As her sleep fog cleared she remembered it wasn't Sunday and it was 7.45 am. She had half an hour to get ready for work and be at the shop. 'Crap!' How had she slept through her alarm? She never overslept in the morning. She tossed the covers off in a frantic scramble to get to the shower, but her foot got caught in the sheets and she ended up sprawled across the bedroom floor. With a strangled, almost silent, scream, she gathered her scattered senses and pushed herself up from the floor, brushing back her bedhead hairdo as she stormed into the bathroom. Today was going to be a doozy. She could just feel it.

Dressed, hair and make-up kind of done-ish, she rushed to the kitchen to make a coffee in her travel mug. But as she fluttered about, an alarm sort of noise kept distracting her. She sent a swift glance around the room and couldn't spot anything, then another look at the clock had her swiftly spooning in coffee granules and sugar, as the jug decided, today of all days, to take a thousand years to boil.

'Keys, mobile,' she muttered, gathering her belongings and shoving them into her handbag, double-checking the constant ding-dong wasn't coming from her phone, then frowning as the sound continued. Alice put her bag on the bench and searched for the noise, lifting a stack of magazines Gran had been reading the day before and finding nothing, before scanning the remaining countertop space. As a last resort, she pulled the microwave out of its nook under the countertop to feel around the back of it. Her hand found a rectangle object that she pulled out to discover was a phone in a blingy pink case. Gran's phone.

She gave the gap in the countertop above the nook a frustrated glance. Only a few weeks ago, when she'd pulled out the microwave to clean behind it, she'd discovered an assortment of things she'd thought they'd lost, including the very expensive lipstick she'd bought and only used once before it mysteriously vanished. She made a note to get Finn to look at covering it up. The incessant noise continued and she opened the case to find an alarm flashing across the screen. Alice swiped her finger across the dismiss icon and blessed silence once again filled the kitchen. She went to close the case but a conversation on the screen caught her attention.

She didn't mean to look at it, but she'd automatically started reading the text because it was just . . . there.

Gran: Thank you, Phil. Today was just amazing.
Phil: Glad you enjoyed it.
Gran: You made an old lady very happy!
Phil: You put people half your age to shame. Looking forward to Wednesday.

Alice made a small sound in her throat, surprised and confused. Who the hell was Phil? And *how* had he been making her gran happy?

But there was no time to work it out now because she was already running late.

The jug clicked off and she closed the phone, leaving it on the bench where Gran would find it when she got up, then finished making her coffee.

Alice opened the back door to her parents' house and was immediately swarmed by her nephews, who greeted her and clung to her legs, giggling and shouting as she lumbered into the kitchen, dragging them behind her. In a family as large as theirs, you had to find a time to squeeze in a bit of one-on-one time—or as close to it as possible—and it had become Alice's tradition to pop by after work at least once a week for a quick visit with her parents.

'Kids, let Aunty Alice sit down. Go find Poppy and tell him his cuppa's ready,' her mother said. 'So, how's it going over at your place with Gran?' Kathy asked once they were left in relative quiet, except for the children's program singing merrily to itself in the background. Sometimes it was easy to get lost in such a big family but her mother always seemed to find time to make sure she touched base with all her children and grandchildren. She babysat two of Charlie and Steph's kids throughout the week and had Toby's and Daisy's younger kids before and after school.

'It's nice having her there,' Alice answered, toying with the handle of her mug. 'Finn's been working so much, I'm kind of glad of the company.'

'When the season's in full swing it's nonstop,' her mother agreed. 'Is everything okay with you two?' She picked up a tiny pair of shorts and a T-shirt from the laundry basket to fold.

'Of course. Why would you ask?'

'No reason,' she said with a small twist of her lips. 'You've been a bit quiet lately.'

'Just busy with the wedding stuff and work.'

'I know you were disappointed with Antoinette not taking your dresses. It doesn't make much sense, but that woman has always been a bit odd. Who knows what she's thinking? Still, once you're married, you and Finn will probably want to settle down and start your family, so maybe it's a good thing. Once you start having babies you'd be too busy to keep sewing clothes for the shop.'

Alice knew her mother was trying to be helpful but, for some reason, the comment just annoyed her. Yes, starting a family was something she and Finn had talked about, but they wanted to do it once they were settled and had themselves set up. She didn't want to be like most of her other siblings, who started having kids young.

Sometimes she thought her family forgot she was ten years younger than the twins, who had been the youngest for so long. She was what her mother called a happy surprise—her siblings were less polite about it and used to tease her by saying she was the 'oh shit, not again' baby their parents had by accident. While a late baby may be spoiled rotten in any other family, Alice had been thrown into the deep end, learning to cope with the established pecking order of siblings and dealing with all the teasing, name-calling and arguing that came with it.

But there was no point bringing that up now so she changed the subject. 'Do we know any Phils around town?'

'Phils?' her mum repeated thoughtfully. 'Well, there's Philip Conway, but I think he moved to the Gold Coast . . . Oh, and there's Philip Johns, you know the one, he and his brother live out on the back road to Burrandock with that huge front yard full of old cars and scrap. You can barely see the house now. Why?'

'No reason, just overheard someone mention the name the other day.' Neither of those Phils seemed a likely contender for Gran's text.

A cry went up from the backyard and indignant yells of 'It's mine' and 'You had it for ages', followed by a series of grunts and 'ows' and Jim's deep voice booming across the lawn, 'Break it up!'

'Oh dear, those two have been at each other all day,' her mother said with a sigh as they watched Jim marching two disgruntled four-year-olds to the back door. 'School in the new year can't come fast enough,' she added, wiping her hands on a tea towel before going to the door.

'I think some time to cool down in front of the telly with *Bonanza* might be the go.'

'Noooooooo, not *Bonanza*, Pop. Please. We promise we won't fight anymore.'

Alice bit back a smile. The old western had been her father's childhood favourite TV show and he'd recently discovered the entire series was now being streamed so he could—and often did—watch it all day if he wanted to. He saw it as a treat for the kids to sit down and watch it with him. The grandkids, however, saw it more as punishment. *Poor Dad.*

While her mum fussed around making the kids something to eat, her dad tossed his hat on the bench and passed Alice a pottery coffee mug that she had dropped over a few days earlier. 'Good as new,' he said and took a seat next to her.

Her father had a big shed in the backyard and spent most of his time out there building things or fixing a long list of broken items the family dropped off from time to time. If Jim couldn't fix it, it was unfixable.

'I knew you'd be able to save it. I really didn't want to throw this one out.' Alice kissed his stubbly cheek and went back to admiring the newly glued mug.

'How's Gran doing?' he asked.

'She's fine. I think she's enjoying some time to herself.'

'Well, she can't stay with you forever. She's going to have to sit down and talk to Dad eventually.'

'I'm sure they'll sort it out.'

'You saw how that went the other night,' he said.

'Don't you and Mum sometimes want to just have a bit of time apart now and again?'

'What for?' he replied, eyeing her oddly.

'You've been married for almost forty years. That's a long time to be with someone every single day. Gran and Grandad have been together for sixty . . . I just think it's probably normal that they might be discovering it's nice to do their own things separately for a while.'

Other than the times Gran was in hospital having babies, her grandparents hadn't spent more than a few nights apart in their whole sixty-year marriage. It was something that made Alice stop and really think. Sixty *years*.

'It's not normal,' he said stubbornly. 'They're both into their eighties. They should be enjoying their life, not carrying on like a pair of flamin' . . . Millennials,' he said, searching for a description.

'That's a tad harsh,' Alice muttered.

'You know what I mean,' he said, waving off her raised-eyebrow rebuke. 'Their generation don't get divorced or walk out when the going gets tough. It's just . . . not done. It's ridiculous.'

'I know it seems hard to imagine them leading separate lives when all we've known them as is a couple, but maybe they've been locked into this generational mindset for too long and they're just realising it.'

'Rubbish.'

'They came from a society where marriage was forever because that was pretty much your only option. All well and good in theory, but real life sometimes doesn't work that way. People grow apart.'

'Not by the time they reach eighty,' her dad insisted.

Alice shrugged. 'Who knows? I'm sure it'll all work out, but for now, Gran clearly needs some time alone and I don't think it's doing Grandad any harm, either. Maybe he's been taking her for granted a little too much and this will open his eyes a bit?'

Her father gave an unconvinced grunt and Alice stood up and put an arm around his shoulder. 'I've got to get home. See ya, Mum,' she called, waving as her mother played referee to Alice's two nephews.

'Bye, love,' Kathy called.

Who was Alice to try to figure out her grandparents' marital issues anyway? She wasn't even married yet. Still, she did believe there were older generations who were effectively trapped in marriages simply because they didn't know how to get out—or had decided it simply wasn't worth the hassle to bother trying this late in life. They may rail about how younger generations couldn't stick out a marriage that was supposed to be forever, but Alice was willing to bet that had they had the options available now, they wouldn't have stayed in marriages that were unhappy.

Another reason she was glad to be born when she had been. At least she had the ability to decide her own future and make her own decisions.

Chapter 9

Alice was buttering her toast and spreading Vegemite lightly across the top when Gran came into the kitchen the next morning.

'Morning,' Alice said, kissing her cheek. 'You're up and about early today.'

'Yes, I've got a few things on.'

'Oh? Like what?' she asked, taking a bite of her toast as she poured hot water into her coffee cup.

'You should sit down and eat. You'll get indigestion,' Gran cautioned.

'I don't have time.'

'You need to start making time. You need a proper breakfast.'

'What are *you* having for breakfast?' Alice asked pointedly.

'I don't eat breakfast,' Meryl said stiffly. 'Do as I say, not as I do,' she added, narrowing her eyes at her granddaughter.

'Yes, Gran,' Alice said obediently, but grinned when she received a smack on the backside as Meryl passed to make her tea.

Looking for a place to put her cup down, Alice moved her grandmother's handbag and a post-it note slid out. Picking it up to put back, she noticed *12:15* and the day's date scrawled across it—with five exclamation marks. She frowned. One exclamation mark was enough to signify something monumental, but *five*? What could possibly be happening at twelve-fifteen that was so exciting?

'So, what did you say you were up to today?' Alice asked, taking her cup and moving to the table. Gran had her car, and her independence, back and Alice had barely seen her.

'Oh, nothing really. Just doing a few errands and such.'

That didn't sound like it warranted five exclamation points. Alice became even more suspicious. What on earth was Gran up to? She still couldn't believe the whole bit-on-the-side thing as her grandad had claimed, not because she couldn't imagine her gran still having a sex life—okay, *maybe* she was having a slight issue thinking about her gran and the word sex in the same sentence—but she assumed if Gran *had* found someone else, she was more likely to have simply come out and told Grandad. After all, she'd had no qualms announcing to everyone she'd walked out on him. She would most likely have enjoyed the added shock value of having met someone else on top of it all.

'Okay then, have a good day. I'll see you tonight.'

'Yes. You, too.'

Alice narrowed her eyes. Gran hadn't tacked on her usual 'darling' and was acting fidgety and very un-Gran-like. She was clearly distracted and that was not like Gran at all.

❖

All morning Alice had been watching the clock. It was an unusually quiet day and time felt like it was dragging.

'Have you taken out the bins yet?' Antoinette asked as she glanced up from the counter, where she'd been flipping through the pages of the latest catalogues.

'Not yet,' Alice said as the tinkle of the doorbell announced customers.

'Then perhaps you should?' her employer asked in a tone that somehow managed to be both condescending and annoyed at the same time.

Despite the fact that they'd been empty when she'd checked them earlier, Alice turned away from the two women who'd entered the store to collect the bins.

'*After* you've served our customers,' Antoinette rebuked, loud enough for the women to overhear.

This was how it had been between them ever since the run-in over the formal dresses. It was as though Antoinette was determined to put Alice in her place, remind her that she was a hired shop assistant and nothing more. The attitude was growing extremely tiresome. As hard as she tried to accept her boss's decision, Alice couldn't let go of the disappointment that remained, especially when she worked right beside the woman every single day. In the past, Alice had managed to move on from Antoinette's dismissive attitude towards her designing but this time it felt different. Alice knew her designs deserved to be in the shop. It didn't make sense for Antoinette to dismiss them the way she had.

At twelve, she'd made a decision. Grabbing her bag, she left the store for her lunch break and headed for her car. It had looked like rain earlier so she'd decided not to risk walking, and now she was glad she had driven. The note she'd found in Gran's bag kept flashing through her brain. *Twelve-fifteen.* It was driving her crazy thinking up countless scenarios. She really shouldn't be this obsessed with her gran's behaviour—and maybe normally she wouldn't be—but she needed something to take her mind off how angry and hurt she still was. Maybe that's what was driving her to follow through on this crazy idea to stalk her gran—although anything to escape the shop and her prissy boss for a while would be a relief.

Alice parked up the street from her house, where she could see Gran's car out the front. She hadn't really thought this through too well, she had to admit. Her plan had gaping holes in it. For a start, she only had her lunch hour to complete the mission and she wasn't sure exactly where Gran was going or how early she'd have to leave home. But she had clearly fluked it because, barely a minute later, Gran came out and got into her car.

'Where are you going, Gran?' Alice muttered as she followed the pale yellow sedan out of town. Images of following cars in movies played through her head. It seemed a lot easier to tail a car in New York City traffic than it was on a quiet country road. She hung back as far as she could but hoped she wouldn't miss seeing Gran turn off somewhere—although *where* she could turn off out here would be the question.

Alice needn't have worried. They passed the airport and after another five hundred–odd metres, Gran's indicator went on and she turned into a service road and went through a security gate to park beside two other cars.

Alice parked outside the high fence and watched as Gran walked towards a large shed just as a man came out, sending Meryl a wave. Immediately, Gran's face lit up.

Alice turned her attention back to the man, who wore a baseball cap over grey hair. He had a thick moustache and was greeting her gran with a warm hug. He looked only a few years older than Alice's father. Could Gran really be having an affair after all? Alice wasn't sure if she was impressed or horrified by the discovery.

Her phone rang, and her surveillance was interrupted as she dug through her purse to find it. Finn's name flashed across the screen. Looking up, she realised she'd lost sight of Gran and the man.

'Damn it.'

'Pardon?' Finn asked.

'Oh, no, nothing. What's up?'

'You still at work? I thought you might be on lunch.'

'Yeah, I am. Sorry. I was just . . . It doesn't matter. What's up?'

'I had to come into town to pick up another part so I came home for lunch. I thought maybe we could mess around a bit since I fell asleep last night. But you're not here.'

Of all the days she didn't follow her usual routine. 'Oh. Bugger,' she said, and glanced at her watch. If she left now she'd make it before she had to go back to work. 'Look, I'll be home in fifteen minutes.' A midday mess-around with her fiancé sounded a lot more fun than sitting in a car spying on Gran.

'Where are you?' She heard the frown in his tone.

'I just had to drop off some stuff . . . at the post office. I'll be home soon,' she said, and ended the call, feeling icky that she'd lied. She wasn't sure why she didn't tell Finn where she really was. Maybe because he'd think she was crazy. She *was* acting a little strange, sitting here on a stake-out like she was some kind of private investigator. But still . . . they'd never had to lie to each other before and this seemed like a stupid thing to start lying about now.

By the time she made it home, she had a little under half an hour. She was going to make this happen.

Finn was seated at the kitchen bench. She sauntered across the room, took the sandwich out of his hand and dropped it on the plate before sliding onto his lap and wrapping her arms around his neck. She ignored his startled 'Hey!', kissing him deeply and running her hands down his chest to his shirt hem, which she tugged up over his head.

'Jesus, Al, steady on.'

'There's no time,' she said, pulling away from him just enough to unbutton her dress.

'Just wait a sec—' He caught her hands and stood up. 'Can we at least go to the bedroom?'

Alice bit back an impatient huff, but soon forgot what she was huffing about when Finn started kissing her again as he walked her backwards up the hallway. Maybe it was just all the stress she'd been under lately making her a bit crazy. This was what she needed—some alone time with Finn.

As they reached the bedroom door, he gently pushed against her, his lips moving to her neck as she ran her hands up his bare chest and lightly dragged her fingernails across his warm skin. Moments later she felt the bed at the back of her legs as he pushed her dress over her shoulders and let it drop to the floor, sliding his hands tantalisingly down her body.

Even if they had all day to explore each other, she still couldn't have taken things slowly. Her body felt as though it were on fire as a rush of need surged through her, making her catch her breath as she arched against him. They quickly removed the remainder of their clothing, before joining once more in a frenzy of heated kisses. Hands touched everywhere— running over smooth muscle and coarse hair, stroking and rubbing—their bodies moulding, fitting together perfectly like two pieces of a jigsaw, before sinking down onto the bed.

Alice could hear nothing but the rush of blood pounding through her body and the mix of their harsh breathing and muffled groans as they found a rhythm that rose ever upwards, the swell like a wave rising from the ocean and soaring in that moment just prior to it cresting, before tumbling down on itself as it breaks in a great rush and roar of release.

Alice closed her eyes as she felt the last throb of pleasure ease into satisfaction, waiting for her breath to steady once more. Underneath her palm she could feel Finn's chest rising and falling steadily and she smiled as his deep chuckle vibrated beneath her ear.

'Wow. Maybe I should start coming home for lunch more often,' he said.

'Maybe you should.'

'Pretty sure Dad and Matt would have a few choice words to say about disappearing every day for an hour or so, though.'

'Maybe you just need to break more stuff so you can come into town with a reasonable excuse.'

He sighed. 'We don't need any more help breaking stuff. Everything's bloody falling apart just when we need it.'

Alice gave a disgruntled groan as he eased her off his chest and rolled over to sit on the edge of the bed.

She reached for him. 'Let's just both call in sick for the rest of the day and stay in bed.'

Finn gave a sceptical snort as he leaned down and retrieved his clothing. 'Yeah. Right.'

'Why can't we do that sometime?'

'What?' he asked, looking back at her over his shoulder. 'Stay in bed all day?'

'Or just take a day off and spend it together . . . or a week, even.'

'We're taking a week for the honeymoon,' he reminded her. 'And that was hard enough to squeeze out of the old man.'

'We're taking exactly five days. That's not even a full week.'

'It's the best we can hope for. There's too much on.'

'When is there not?' she snapped. They'd had to organise the wedding around so many seasons she'd almost given up on finding a date.

'I can't wait till this wedding's over,' he muttered as he pulled up his jeans.

'Seriously?' She sat up to glare at him.

'Geez, Al. Lately you've been crabby at everything and the only thing I can put it down to is all the wedding crap going on.'

'The wedding *crap*?' she repeated, anger suddenly simmering. 'Do you have any idea how much work has been involved in planning this *wedding crap*? Of course you don't,' she said, tapping her forehead with her palm, 'because nothing else exists for you outside of bloody Whyningham!'

'Here we go again,' he said, shaking his head, which only infuriated her more.

'If this wedding means so little to you, then why the hell did you ask me to marry you in the first place?'

'Because I thought that's what you wanted. Trust me—I was more than happy with the way things were.'

Alice stared at him, too shocked to even try to respond.

He sighed again as he ran a hand through hair that was at least six weeks overdue for a cut because he was too busy to find time to stop at the hairdressers. 'Look, I have to get back. We'll talk about this later.'

'What's there to talk about? You don't even want to get married.'

Finn groaned. 'Don't do this now.'

'Of course not. How rude of me to bring it up.'

'We've both got to go back to work—there's no time to talk about it,' he said, impatiently.

'You're right. Let's just forget it ever happened.' Alice went into the bathroom, snagging her own clothing from the floor as she went and closing the door behind her.

She heard Finn pulling on his boots before he gave a soft tap on the door. 'I have to go. I'll see you tonight.'

Alice didn't bother answering, remaining rigidly silent as she stared furiously at her reflection in the mirror until she heard his reluctant footsteps leaving the bedroom and the sound of an engine starting up in the driveway.

She dropped her head, closing her eyes tightly against the sting of tears that threatened. There was no time for crying. She was already late.

After reapplying her make-up, she gathered her messed-up hair at the nape of her neck, twisting it and securing it with a few bobby pins to create a simple French twist. One last look in the mirror and Alice rushed out the door and back to the shop.

She forced a smile to her face as she passed her rather unimpressed employer, who pointedly glanced down at her watch.

'Sorry. I had a slight personal issue,' she said stiltedly.

'See that it doesn't happen again,' Antoinette said, before turning to greet a customer.

Because it happens so often, Alice grumbled silently.

She should have just called to say she wasn't coming back.

Chapter 10

Things only got worse that night when Finn called to say he wasn't coming home.

'Okay,' Alice said, her heart sinking. She'd spent all afternoon going through a range of emotions: hurt, confusion, anger.

'Al.' She heard his frustrated plea on the other end of the line. 'I'm not avoiding you. I want to come home and sort through this . . . thing, but there's bad weather coming through and we just can't stop. If we don't get this wheat in—'

'Yeah, I know, it'll be a disaster.'

'It will!' he snapped.

'I know!' she said, raising her voice. 'All right? I get it.'

And she really did. She knew the farm was dependent on so many variables—that at any point all their hard work and the long hours and sacrifices they made could be gone in an instant, along with a year's income. She felt like a terrible person for being so upset when Finn had to work late or through the night—or couldn't go somewhere with her because there was round-the-clock harvesting or seeding to do. But it took a huge toll on their personal life too and she just wished that they could hire someone else to help take the load off their shoulders now and again. That was a whole other row they often had and she didn't need to bring it up again right now.

'It's fine. Do what you have to do,' she said.

'I . . . Al . . . ' She heard him swear softly and could imagine his clenched jaw and steely blue eyes and the little creases that would be there between his eyebrows like they always were whenever he got frustrated. 'I'm sorry, okay? I didn't mean any of it. It came out all wrong.'

In the background she heard his father yelling his name. She swallowed over fresh tears.

'Yeah, all right, I'm coming!' Finn yelled back irritably, before adding a hasty, 'I gotta go,' to her.

'Okay,' she managed, just before the line went dead.

'Sweetheart, I wanted to have the family get-together tomorrow, would you mind if we had it here?' Gran asked later that evening.

'Here?' Alice replied, startled by the request. Family gatherings were always had at either Gran's place or Alice's parents'. One, because they just always had been and two, because both places had been set up over the years to cater for large numbers of people at a table. And three, her place wasn't exactly big enough to hold their whole family at once.

'Oh, not a meal or anything, maybe just drinks and some finger food . . . we could all sit outside in the backyard.'

'Sure,' Alice said slowly, eyeing her gran curiously. 'But why? What's the occasion?'

'Oh, nothing important. I just think with everything that's been going on, we need to make sure we're still keeping in touch.'

'Is Grandad coming?' Alice asked cautiously.

'Of course. He's still part of the family. Nothing's changed there.'

'Okay.' Her interest piqued as she realised Gran was avoiding eye contact again. If this was just a casual get-together then Alice was Lady Gaga.

'You don't have to do a thing. I'll make all the arrangements. You just do whatever you were planning to do. It'll be all taken care of.'

She hadn't been planning anything more exciting than housework and washing—which was clearly going to be a good thing since her family were all coming over.

Thanks to the weather event arriving—the one that had had Finn and everyone else in the district working flat-out to get things done before its arrival—the gathering had to be moved into the shed, so Alice spent most of Saturday cleaning it out. Luckily it usually only housed their cars. The last time they'd used the shed as a venue had been for the shed-warming they'd hosted after it went up. Her family celebrated pretty much anything—even new sheds being erected.

By the end of the day the place looked rather festive—for a *non-festive* event. They set up a few tables for food and scattered whatever chairs she had around, and everyone had been told to bring along a fold-up chair. The only issue was that Alice hadn't been able to get hold of Finn to let him know what was happening and suspected he was going to be stuck working anyway. The only good thing about the fact they hadn't seen each other was that at least they couldn't argue. She didn't feel like arguing anyway. She didn't feel like . . . anything, really. It occurred to her that maybe that could be the beginning of a brand-new issue, but quickly pushed it away. She'd deal with the whole thing later—if Finn ever decided to come home again.

That afternoon, as cars began to arrive, her quiet little home was filled with conversation and laughter. Alice smiled at how nice it was to see the place so full of life. They'd been making dashes from the house to the shed in between showers of rain and she was waiting for a break in the weather to bring out the last of the hot food when Finn appeared, running up the driveway, his T-shirt and jeans dirty from work.

'What's all this?' he asked.

'Gran wanted to have everyone over.'

'Why here?'

Alice shrugged. 'I don't know. I guess she wanted somewhere neutral.'

'Don't you think this thing's gone on long enough? How long is she planning on staying, anyway?'

It wasn't like him to get snippy like this—especially about Gran, whom he adored as much as she did.

'As long as she needs to,' Alice said firmly. 'I don't know why it would bother you? You've barely been home the entire time she's been here.'

'Wow. Not even five minutes since I walked through the door and it's started.'

'Why are you acting like this?'

'Like I'm pissed off that I come home, bone-arse tired and wanting to sleep, only to find you've organised a party without telling me? Gee, I don't know why I'd be annoyed, Al.'

'I tried to call you—multiple times since yesterday, if you bothered to check your phone or, heaven forbid, return a call.'

'I was a little bit busy,' he said.

'I'm sorry I'm not sitting at home twiddling my thumbs waiting like some well-behaved fifties housewife to ask your permission to have my family over!' she said, raising her voice just as the music on the stereo ended and conversation stopped.

Crap.

Her family were eyeing them with varying degrees of curiosity, so Alice plastered a smile on her face.

'You look like you could use one of these,' her father said jovially, handing a beer to Finn and breaking the awkward silence.

'Finn, I'm sorry, I should have checked with you before organising tonight's get-together,' Gran said, placing a hand on his arm.

'No, Gran,' Alice said, still angry that Finn had practically ignored her ever since their argument and then had the nerve to pick a fight in front of her family. 'You don't have to apologise for anything. This happens to be my house as much as his and I shouldn't have to ask permission to have you all over whenever I damn well please.'

'Maybe we all need a drink and a cool-off, hey?' Jim cut in smoothly.

'A man has a right to come home to his castle at night and expect that he can relax,' Grandad said, sending Finn a decisive nod.

'His castle?' Verity echoed, giving her grandad a raised eyebrow.

'Yes, his castle,' Wes said firmly.

'How very outdated of you, Grandad.'

'Outdated or not, there seems to be a little too much disregard for the sanctity of marriage around here, lately. The world's gone crazy.'

'Oh, stop it—you're just sore because, for the first time in your life, you have to cook and clean for yourself,' Gran said.

'I'm not talkin' about that. I'm saying if you mess with the order of things, then society just falls to pieces.'

A ripple of murmurs ran through the shed and Alice saw her gran stiffen indignantly.

'Mess with *your* order, you mean.'

'Look, why don't we—' her father started but was cut off by Wes.

'It's not my order, it's the way it is. We're supposed to be enjoying our retirement.'

'As long as it doesn't interfere with golf.'

'What's that supposed to mean?'

'It means that *you're* enjoying *your* retirement and have been for the last fifteen years, doing exactly what *you* want to do—playing golf every damn day.'

'I like golf,' he said, sounding a little hurt that his wife didn't seem to share his passion.

'What about what I've wanted to do? Travel, see the world . . . do something other than the same old routine, day in and day out, till we die from boredom?'

'Why would we want to fly to the other side of the world when we have everything we need right here? Besides, we've gone to places. We went to Melbourne last year.'

'For a golf tournament. We didn't even leave the resort!'

'I said you could go off and explore.'

'And, like a fool, I didn't. Which is why I decided I wasn't going to miss out on anything again. I want to *do* things.'

'Like have an affair, I suppose,' Grandad sneered.

'What?' Alice's father and mother said together, staring at Gran, horrified.

Meryl frowned at her husband. 'What are you talking about?'

'You think I don't know about it? That I haven't been aware of the secret phone calls and so-called *appointments*?'

Gran narrowed her gaze but didn't deny it and Alice felt her heart stop momentarily.

'Mum?' Alice's father asked the question no one else in the room dared. 'Is that true?'

'Of course it's not true,' Meryl said, then turned to her husband once more. 'You silly old coot—naturally you'd jump to the most ridiculous conclusion. Why the hell would I want to leave one man just to go to another?'

'Then what have you been doing?'

'Well, since you've asked,' Gran said, straightening her shoulders and turning to face the rest of the family, 'there was a reason I wanted you all here. I'm celebrating.'

'Celebrating what exactly?' Alice's father asked. He looked as though his mother was about to announce she'd decided to join a cult or maybe start a career as a stripper or some other totally bizarre thing to shock them all with.

'Today I passed my final exam and officially notched up the last of my flying hours. I am now a qualified pilot.'

Total silence echoed through the shed.

'A pilot?' Alice's mother ventured. 'As in flying a plane pilot?'

'Yes,' Gran said with a wide smile. 'I have a pilot licence.'

'Holy cow,' Toby muttered.

'Gran, that's awesome,' Charlie said, stepping forward to hug his grandmother. The action snapped everyone else from their stupor and Meryl was flooded with celebratory hugs and congratulations.

'Just wait a minute,' Wes said, raising his voice over the commotion. 'What are you saying? All this time you've been sneaking around . . . learning to *fly*?'

'Would you have preferred I'd been sneaking around having an affair?' Gran asked. 'I have to say I'm flattered you think I could pull something like that off, Wesley.'

'Why on earth would you want to take flying lessons at your age?'

Alice felt the air chill.

'You know what your problem is, Wes?' Meryl finally replied. 'You enjoy complaining about being old. You and all your cronies down at the club house, drinking your beer after driving around in your stupid golf carts, complaining about your knees and your backs . . . that's all you do. Complain and moan about being old. You know what I decided? You don't *have* to act your age. I might be eighty years old, but I'm not going to let that stop me living.'

'I think it's great, Gran,' Verity said.

'Congratulations, Mum,' Jim said, giving her a hug. 'But you know, most people who decide to celebrate turning eighty usually just try parachuting or something.'

'Why on earth would I want to do something silly like jump out of a perfectly good aircraft when I could fly it instead?'

Toby laughed, shaking his head. 'Gran, you are one in a million.'

'How insane is this?' Charlie added, standing beside Alice as they watched the family crowding around Gran. 'Did you have any idea she was doing this?'

'None,' Alice said, shaking her head. 'Poor Grandad. He looks completely floored.'

'Maybe Gran was right—maybe he just needed a bit of a shake-up. Hey, everything okay with you and Finn? Things sounded a bit heated there.'

'We're fine,' she said, shrugging his concern off with a blithe smile. 'It's been a really long few weeks. I think we're both just tired.'

Later, as she looked across the shed, she spotted Finn sitting with her brothers-in-law, drinking. He glanced up as though feeling her eyes on him and she smiled, but felt it slip when he didn't return it, dropping his gaze instead to the ground as he continued listening to the conversation.

Everything is fine, she told herself stubbornly as she went back inside to bring out more food. All they needed was a good sleep and everything would look better in the morning.

Chapter 11

The party wound down not long afterwards—the big announcement had been met with the shock and awe of a nuclear explosion, which Gran had obviously been counting on, and was followed by an awkward divide, with Grandad pouting in the corner, surrounded by a revolving roster of male relatives who felt obliged to drink and keep him company. It was official—her family had become a daytime soap opera.

'Why didn't you tell us you were taking flying lessons?' Alice asked Gran after everyone had left and they were clearing away in the kitchen.

'I don't know,' Gran said. 'Pride, I guess. Maybe I was scared of telling everyone in case I couldn't do it. If I failed, no one would have to know.'

'Gran,' Alice admonished gently, 'no one would be any less proud of you if you'd tried and failed. The fact you wanted to do something like that is just . . . amazing. We are all so proud of you.'

Gran smiled. 'Like I said, I decided to make a choice. The thing is, I don't *feel* eighty years old. I just don't. It shocks me when I think of my age—when I was young, eighty was so very old. The people I remember being that age when I was in my twenties, they *looked* old and tired, they were *supposed* to be old and tired back then. I guess that's the way society always saw them. I know I've been blessed with good health and I've had a wonderful life . . . there's a lot of people my age who aren't as fortunate as I am. But I just can't sit around and let the rest of my life pass doing nothing.' She searched Alice's eyes before adding, 'Your grandfather just seems resigned to acting like an old man. He's happy to be stuck in his rut. I want adventure and fun.'

Alice pondered her gran's words. 'I think tonight opened Grandad's eyes quite a lot. Maybe he'll think about what you've said.'

'Your grandad is a stubborn man. He likes his routine and doesn't accept change easily. The order of things, don't you know,' she said, mimicking her husband's gruff tone, 'you can't upset the order.'

They shared a sad smile before Alice said quietly, 'I guess the hardest thing to understand, for any of us, is how do you walk away from a marriage you've spent the last sixty years of your life in?'

She heard Gran's long sigh and felt bad for asking, but it was something that had been playing on her mind.

'I was angry when I called that first family meeting. Something just snapped inside of me. I'd spent the morning visiting with my dear friend Barb, whose family have just had to place her in the nursing home. You know Barb?' Gran asked, looking up at Alice, who nodded quickly. 'Such a terrible shame. She's had dementia now for a while and her family have been caring for her at home but it's suddenly gotten worse and there was no putting it off. I remember sitting with her most of the morning, watching her fade in and out, and I realised how lucky I've been. So many of the friends Wes and I have known all our lives have either passed away from terrible illnesses or moved into retirement places—it's very depressing to look around and realise there aren't as many of you left as there once was.'

Alice reached out and covered Gran's hand with her own.

'Anyway, I went home and your grandad was in a snit about dinner and I'd just had enough. Life is too precious to waste. At any age. Marriage is a wonderful thing and I've had some great years, along with some not-so-great ones, but we stuck it out because that's just what you did. For the most part, it was a good marriage. But in the end, marriage is about two people and a partnership, and if one of those people is unhappy and the other one doesn't believe they need to make any kind of compromise or find a way to help the other person in any way they can, then that's what I believe you young ones call a "toxic relationship". Maybe I'm silly to want something different at my age, but I don't think it's unreasonable to also want some respect and to be happy.'

'Does that mean divorce?' Alice asked hesitantly.

Gran made a disgusted kind of noise under her breath. 'And give a hefty portion of our estate to a bunch of solicitors instead of our children? I don't think so. No,' she said, shaking her head, 'it won't come to that, but we will be living separate lives.'

This was the first time since all this stuff about Grandad flared up that Alice had heard her gran sound sad.

'Maybe it'll just take a little time for him to come around.'

'My sweet, time is a luxury we simply don't have. It's precious—once it's gone you can never get it back. I intend to continue living my life to the fullest. I can't drag the man along with me if he's happy to just amble his way through each day, stuck on repeat. That's his choice.'

Which was true, Alice supposed. She understood her gran's side of everything that had unfolded over the last few weeks, it was just hard to separate that from the fact that these were her grandparents and she still held them on the very high pedestal of her childhood, where grandparents were always so wise and constant. They were always . . . there. Together.

'You should go along to bed,' Gran said, taking the dish-cloth out of her hands.

'No. it's all right. It's almost done.'

'I apologised to Finn for springing tonight on him. I got a little carried away in all the excitement of keeping my big surprise.'

'He's okay. I think he was just tired.'

'I think you both have some things you need to sort out before you go to sleep tonight.'

Finn would already be asleep. Alice searched for something to delay having to lay wide awake next to him for the rest of the night. When she realised there was really nothing more that needed doing, she reluctantly kissed her gran goodnight and headed down the hallway.

Alice climbed into bed slowly after her shower and eased the blankets up over her shoulders. She could hear Finn's rhythmic breathing. Why did a bed always feel so much bigger when you were having an argument? Usually he'd roll over and wrap his arm around her. Tonight, though, he remained on the edge of his side of the bed and the distance between them felt like a million miles.

When she awoke the next morning, Finn was gone. Clearly last night's events had changed his mind about coming home to sort things out. She dragged his pillow across, burying her face against it and breathing in the smell of him. She loved him so much. That was the crux of the whole thing: so much of her life was tied up in Finn—and his in hers—and yet something, somewhere, had shifted. She just couldn't help feeling that whatever was going on between them was going to tear them apart if they didn't stop and deal with it. She knew Finn didn't think there was anything wrong—he simply couldn't understand why she was being so disagreeable. The truth was, she didn't fully understand it herself, she only knew something wasn't right. All these little things that she'd always dismissed or accepted were suddenly getting harder to continually ignore.

Were they turning into her grandparents by allowing the expectation that she would always be on hand to be their normal? Always available to run after Finn the way his mother ran after his father? Or to simply settle for being taken for granted with little to no thanks like her gran?

They had to deal with this now, no matter how pointless Finn found it. The smallest scratches left to fester could turn deadly. They had to talk about the little things now so when they were in their eighties they didn't end up becoming two strangers.

Chapter 12

To take her mind off the fact Finn had left without saying his usual good morning and stop the endless conversations she was having in her head, preparing for when he came home, Alice decided to start making the wedding centrepieces. However, an hour and a half into the exercise, having burned her finger on the hot glue gun twice and only having one of the twenty centrepieces completed, Alice was ready to throw the lace and dried flower wreaths across the room. 'This has to be the stupidest idea ever,' she muttered, then frowned as she heard a knock on the front door.

Alice swore under her breath as a second knock came, louder this time. She wiped her hands on her overalls and hurried up the hallway. *So help me God, if this is someone wanting to talk about the Almighty, I will seriously lose my shi—*

She opened the door and came face to face with someone she'd never in a billion years have imagined.

'Alice Croydon,' the man said in a somewhat dry tone as he slid his sunglasses from his face onto the top of his bald head.

'Holy crap,' Alice heard herself breathe as she gaped like a trout.

'Can't say I'm used to being referred to as anything along the lines of holy,' the man murmured. 'Frankie will do. I'd even answer to "my lord", if you're really inclined to go down that track, but I draw the line at God.'

Alice literally could not have spoken a word if her life had depended upon it. She had to be hallucinating. Why the hell would world-famous designer Frankie Esquire be standing on her doorstep in Gunnindi on a Sunday? Not that any other day of the week would be any easier to accept—but a Sunday? Nothing exciting ever happened on a Sunday.

'Not that I don't enjoy standing out in the sweltering heat with the flies, but would it be too much trouble to perhaps step inside for a moment?'

Frankie's request had all the subtlety of a bucket of water being thrown over her head, instantly shaking her from her stupor.

'Of course. Please, come in,' she said in a rush, waving her hand like a hostess on a game show, before side-stepping the man awkwardly as they jostled for space in the narrow hallway. *Shit.* 'Sorry,' she murmured, ducking her head and closing her eyes in embarrassment as she found herself pressed up against the rather surprisingly solid body beneath a button-up shirt that would have more than likely cost the same as a few months of mortgage repayments. God, he smelled good. She hated to think how much his aftershave would have cost. Although if it was one of his own fragrances, probably nothing.

She wasn't dressed for a visit with a freaking celebrity designer! Why, oh why, did she choose today of all days to wear her patchwork denim overalls? She had however taken time to put on make-up earlier, which she was now eternally grateful for. And she supposed it had been lucky she'd decided this morning to revive her inner feminist with a fortifying forties-inspired head scarf and side braid. She tried to smooth some loose tendrils back as inconspicuously as possible.

Alice hurried down the hallway to lead the way to the kitchen, then fought off a moment of panic as she remembered its current state of disarray and stopped abruptly, causing him to slam into her. There was a soft humph before hands grabbed hold of her upper arms to steady her. Dear God, could this get any more freaking humiliating?

'I'm so sorry, I just . . . Maybe we should go into the lounge room,' she stammered, doing a small waltz to circle back to the lounge room door.

'Miss Croydon, I realise my visit is probably a little unexpected,' Frankie said.

A little? Opening my front door to find the Loch Ness bloody monster would have been slightly less of a surprise, to be quite honest.

'I won't beat about the bush,' he continued, his dark eyes holding hers intently. 'I'm here to see the dress.'

Alice blinked. 'What dress?'

'The wedding dress.'

'Why?' she heard herself blurt then regretted it as she saw his eyebrow lift slightly.

'I'd like to see if it can in any way be as impressive as it was in the photo I was sent.'

'What photo?'

Frankie pulled out a folded paper from his back pocket and handed it to her. 'You didn't send a photo to my office?'

Alice stared at the typed letter with a photo of her wedding dress attached and blinked. 'I'm sorry, no . . . I didn't send your office this. I'm not sure what's going on.'

'Do you have a wedding dress here? That you made?' he asked, pointedly.

'I have *my* wedding dress here that I made.'

'Then may I have a look at it?' he asked, beginning to sound slightly impatient and Alice immediately agreed. The last thing she wanted was to irritate a man she idolised.

'It's through here,' she said, retracing their steps down the hall to open her sewing room door. *Dear God . . . he wanted to see her wedding dress. Frankie freaking Esquire was interested in her design!*

She held her breath as he stepped around her and stopped in front of the mannequin.

For a long moment he simply looked at it, his head tilted slightly, before he slowly walked around it, reaching out to touch a sleeve, then leaning down to peer at an embroidered flower and inspect the train.

'I remember your design from last year's fashion week. I offered you an internship,' he said, his gaze still on the dress before him.

'Yes, you did,' Alice said, clearing her throat.

'You turned it down,' he said now, lifting his eyes to hold her startled glance. 'Why?'

'I . . .' She rubbed her lips together. 'Ah . . . wasn't in a position to take it at the time.'

'And now?'

'I'm getting married in four months.'

'I don't see how a marital status will affect your ability to work for me?'

'My fiancé's life is out here . . . we can't move.'

For a moment Frankie continued to stare at her thoughtfully. 'Does your fiancé realise how talented you are?'

Shut. The. Front. Door. Frankie Esquire thought *she* was talented? Last year she'd only met Frankie briefly, and even then she'd been a star-struck idiot and barely managed to string two words together in front of him. His job offer had come via her teachers and a representative after the awards long after the man himself had jetted out of the country, no doubt to attend some other important fashion event. To hear Frankie actually *say* she was talented, in person rendered her speechless.

Alice swallowed painfully over a lump in her throat. 'Fashion isn't really his thing,' she said, trying to figure out how one should reply to someone they were so awestruck by when they gave such an unexpected compliment.

'Then maybe someone needs to explain to him that you seem to have a talent in design—which still needs to be developed a little,' he hastened to add, 'but a talent nonetheless and it would be a shocking waste to not allow it to reach its full potential.'

Alice opened her mouth to protest because she really should when someone was basically telling her that she'd made a mistake turning them down once. But for the life of her, she couldn't find the words.

'Do you have any more designs?'

Alice gathered her senses enough to nod, before crossing the room to her design table and withdrawing a large art diary, which she nervously opened for him. 'I also have these,' she said, opening the wardrobe door and pulling out one of the formal dresses.

'This is a first for me, Alice Croydon,' he said after examining the dresses and then focusing on the drawings as he turned the pages slowly. 'I have never before travelled to the backwaters of nowhere in order to offer someone a job—for a second time. In fact, I don't believe I've *ever* offered anyone a second chance at a job before, considering the number of young, enthusiastic designers there are in the world who are begging for the opportunity to work for me.'

Had anyone else said something like this they would have sounded like a bit of a wanker, but somehow Frankie managed to state it as a simple fact.

'I knew there was something about those designs of yours last year—they were a burst of sunshine on a cold winter's day,' he said, shaking his head slightly. 'You have a freshness, an innocence, almost, that I haven't seen for a long time in fashion. I want you on my team. I believe that together we can do great things. I can take your career all the way to the top.'

'But I . . . I'm getting married. I can't just pack up and leave.'

A silence settled between them as her words hung in the air.

'You have a big decision to make, then, don't you,' Frankie said gently. 'Don't make it now,' he said when she went to speak. 'This is important, Alice. Far too important to answer right now. Last year you clearly weren't ready, but I suspect, from the quality of these designs, that deep down over these last twelve months you've been craving something more. Your designs are screaming for that leap of faith you've been too scared to take. You owe it to yourself to take that chance—you owe it to your *gift*. And make no mistake, Alice, what you have is a gift. Anyone can sew—anyone can be a seamstress, they just follow a pattern—but you have a God-given talent. You *create*. You're not a dressmaker. You are an artist.'

Alice felt an overwhelming rush of emotion at the man's words and a single tear slid down her cheek. She quickly brushed it away.

'I'm in Sydney until the end of the week. Then I'm leaving for London.' He handed her a business card. 'If you decide to take my offer, you'll be joining me in the UK as soon as you can arrange to fly out. I'll need to hear from you by Friday,' he said, giving her wedding dress one last look and heading towards the door.

Alice moved to follow him but he turned to face her. 'Think hard on the offer, Alice. It won't come around another time.'

He walked down the front path towards a dark car where a man waited patiently beside the back door, and Alice remained at her front door, watching the car drive down the street and disappear around the corner. His departure left a strange emptiness inside her. There was no way Frankie Esquire had just been here inside her house. Maybe she'd wake up in the morning and realise this had all been some weird dream.

She placed Frankie's card on the drafting board then stared at the dress, letting out a long sigh.

Just when she'd thought she'd made her decision and was walking towards her future, another crossroads had been plonked down in front of her, blocking her path. One way pointed to Finn and their wedding and the other to London. How was she supposed to keep making this decision when each time it felt as though her heart was being shredded? She wanted them both. Desperately. But she knew that she could only choose one. Last time she chose Finn because she thought she couldn't imagine a life without him and he'd wanted to get married.

She still couldn't imagine a life without him. She'd never wanted a life without him. But something had changed and his comments about the wedding had hit a nerve. She'd given up an opportunity to work with Frankie Esquire once, never imagining she'd ever have another chance and yet here it was. Once she would have been adamant nothing could ever break them up, but now she wasn't as sure. With things the way they were between her and Finn—the distance, the arguments— the thought of bringing up Frankie's offer with him made her very uneasy.

Chapter 13

Alice took a cup of coffee out to the backyard and jumped as she opened the screen door to find Finn sitting on the back steps.

'How long have you been home?' she asked, closing the door behind her and taking a seat beside him. She hadn't heard his ute pull up.

'A while. Who was that?' he asked, nodding his head towards the front of the house.

'He's that designer I told you about from fashion week last year.'

'He offered you a job last year?'

Alice glanced at him, realising he'd obviously overheard part of their conversation, and gave a reluctant nod.

'Why didn't you tell me about it?'

She shrugged, staring down into the caramel-coloured depths of her coffee. 'Because it wasn't an issue. I didn't take it.'

'Sounds like it *was* an issue.'

'Not really,' she said, shaking her head. 'You'd asked me to marry you.'

'Why didn't you mention a job offer?'

'I didn't see the point. Besides, you said afterwards that living separate lives wouldn't work. I would have had to live in Sydney.'

'And this job is in London,' he said in a tone she couldn't quite read. It almost sounded like an accusation.

'Apparently. But it doesn't matter. It's not like I'm going to take it.'

'But you're thinking about it?'

'No . . . I mean, he only just offered it to me now . . . But no, I'm not going to take it. How can I? The wedding's in four months.'

'But you *want* to?'

Alice sincerely meant to deny the idea; after all, it was ridiculous. However, for some unexplainable reason, she found herself hesitating.

'You do,' he said, staring at her now.

'No. I don't,' she protested quickly. 'It's just caught me off guard.'

'Why would he even come out here?'

'I don't know,' she said, shaking her head, still in shock about the whole visit. 'He wanted to look at the wedding dress.'

'Come on, Al, a guy like him wouldn't just happen to be in the neighbourhood. You obviously contacted him about it.'

'I didn't. He was sent a photo but not by me.' Now that she had a bit of space, though, she suspected Gran may have had something to do with it—this was the kind of thing she'd do. 'I answered the door and he was just . . . there.'

'Yeah. Because that happens every day,' he scoffed lightly. 'I don't understand why you wouldn't just tell me what was going on.'

'Because there's nothing to tell!' Alice snapped. 'I didn't contact him. I don't know why he came out here.'

'To offer you a job, apparently,' he shot back. 'Overseas.'

The mention of it had the same effect as pulling a bath plug: it slowly drained her of any remaining fight.

For a long moment they simply looked at each other.

'You're *seriously* considering it, aren't you?' he finally asked, his mouth a tight line and voice tinged in disbelief.

'I—' She stopped. Even in her confused and jumbled state she heard the taut silence that followed her hesitation before Finn abruptly swore and stood up.

'Finn, wait. He said to think about it, but—'

He paused before turning to face her. 'Let me know what you decide.'

She stared at his retreating back. 'Finn!'

'I'm staying out at Whyningham tonight. You need time to think about what you want.'

Alice felt frustration turn to an icy fear. She listened to his ute roar off up the road, her heart sinking as she lowered herself onto a chair at the kitchen table to stare through the screen door, willing Finn to return.

❖

She wasn't sure how long she'd been sitting there when the sound of the front door opening drew her attention and Gran appeared, carrying a shopping bag. She put it on the kitchen bench before noticing Alice seated at the table.

'Darling? Are you all right? What's happened?' she asked, coming across to open her arms as Alice stood up and started to cry. 'Oh, sweetheart,' Gran crooned. 'Is it Finn? Have you two had an argument? I passed him a few minutes ago on the way out of town.'

Alice managed a nod, before stepping out of her gran's embrace and crossing to grab a tissue from the bench.

'I'm sure it'll all blow over once he's had time to cool down.'

'I don't think this will blow over, Gran.'

'What is it? What's happened?'

'I had a visit today from Frankie Esquire.'

Gran drew back slightly in surprise. 'That designer chap? The famous one?'

'Yep.'

'He came here? To the house?'

'Yep.'

'Goodness. What did he want?'

'Gran, how would he have gotten a photo of my wedding dress?' Alice asked, holding her grandmother's gaze firmly.

'I didn't send it to him, if that's what you're implying,' Meryl said, sounding a little stilted.

'Why do I get the feeling you know something about it, though?'

'I think the bigger question should be, what did he think about the dress? What happened? I can't imagine he wasn't bowled over by it, not if he came all the way out here to see it in person.'

'He offered me a job,' Alice said.

'A job?' Gran stared at her, expectantly. When she didn't elaborate, Meryl gave an impatient huff. 'And what did you say?'

'Nothing.'

'The man offered you a job and you said . . . nothing?'

'He said he didn't want an answer until I thought it through.'

'And? Have you?'

'Finn was here and heard it all,' Alice said, lowering her eyes as she felt the sting of tears starting again. She could still see the hurt on his face. God, she was an idiot. What was she doing? Why hadn't she been able to reassure him then and there? Nothing had felt safe since that stupid fight over the wedding. Doubts had begun to creep in and everything she once took for granted suddenly didn't feel as secure as it once had. She should have insisted they talk about their fight—made him talk about it if need be—instead she'd been too busy with everything else going on and ignored it.

'Oh dear,' Gran said sadly, sitting down at the table. 'That would explain why he didn't even wave when I saw him. He did look rather distracted.'

'He thinks I contacted Frankie and wanted him to come out and see the dress. He thinks I wanted the offer.'

'And do you?' Gran asked quietly.

'I can't,' she said, feeling helpless.

She felt Gran's eyes on her but couldn't bring herself to look up. She knew what she'd find there—silent prompting. That was what Meryl did in a situation like this. She just sat quietly and made you listen to what your heart was saying. But this time Alice's heart wasn't making any sense.

'I love him, Gran. I've loved him for as long as I can remember.' They were supposed to be forever. Even though things had felt different lately, how did she walk away from that?

'I know you do, darling,' she said softly.

'So how can I still want something like this so badly if I love him?'

'Would it be impossible to find a way to have both? Sydney isn't on the other side of the world. It could work.'

'Sydney isn't, but London is,' Alice said dully.

'London?' Gran echoed, sitting back in her chair abruptly.

'If I take this job, Frankie wants me in London.'

'Oh, my,' Gran whispered, sounding stunned. 'I assumed it was the same job as before.'

'Apparently not.'

'But this is wonderful,' she said, shaking her head a little in astonishment. 'London? Alice . . . think of the opportunity he's offering you.'

'I know it's an incredible opportunity . . . I just—'

'Sweetheart, you need to think about *you* and what it is *you* want.'

'I want both.'

'Then have both,' Gran said simply.

Alice closed her eyes briefly before opening them to hold her gran's hopeful gaze. 'I can't ask Finn to wait until I'm ready to come back and get married. He doesn't believe in long-distance relationships. What if it's not just a year or two?'

'Then maybe you just play it by ear and see what happens?'

'That's not fair on him, to ask him to live in limbo.'

'If it's meant to be, it'll be,' Gran said softly.

'I don't think that's true, Gran. I have a chance to marry him now and be happy. If I take this job, I'm turning my back on that. I can't expect fate to just put our relationship on hold indefinitely.'

'Then maybe it's fate telling you that it's not meant to be after all?'

It just didn't make sense. If she loved Finn so much, why was taking the job even an option? It should be an irrefutable no. But it wasn't—and hadn't been, ever since she'd turned the first offer down. Now she knew this unfulfilled void inside her wasn't ever going away. The frustration she'd been dealing with, the urge to create that constantly ached day and night, that unfulfilled *need* she had to push away and ignore, wasn't ever going to subside and she knew she couldn't continue to live like that. There was something missing—a particular joy she just couldn't find in anything else despite the fact she had so much happiness. She just wasn't . . . complete.

Deep down she knew what she had to do and it killed her. How could making the right choice cause so much heartache?

Chapter 14

Alice walked along the dirt driveway, heading for the shed. She'd stopped at the house and been met by a stern-faced Leslie, who'd informed her of Finn's whereabouts. 'I don't know what's going on between you two,' she'd added, 'but you better sort it out quick smart. That son of mine's been walking around like a bear with a sore head.'

Alice paused in the shed's doorway to take a steadying breath. Finn was standing at a workbench. As he glanced over his shoulder, she saw his jaw tighten and her stomach dropped. In all the years they'd been together, their relationship had never felt as strained as it had recently. Everything was changing.

'What did you decide?' he asked.

It seemed they weren't going to drag out the pleasantries.

'I just need a year or two,' she said, standing by his side and holding his steely-eyed gaze.

He gave a disbelieving snort. 'Oh, is that all?'

'Finn, we were together for eight years before you proposed,' she said, clamping her lips together tightly before letting out a small breath. 'I'm just asking to postpone the wedding for another year or so.'

'We were *together* for eight years. You weren't overseas doing God only knows what.'

'I'd be working,' she said. 'Is that what this is all about? You don't trust me?'

'It's not you I don't trust.'

'It sure sounds like it.'

'You'll be on the other side of the goddamn world, Alice!' he stressed. 'You think there won't be men there wanting to take you out?'

'Finn, I'm not going there for the night life, for goodness' sake. I'm engaged. To you. This is about a job—learning to be a designer.'

'I was there at that fashion show, remember?' he replied, shaking his head. 'Don't think I didn't see how that all worked. The night life comes with the territory. The dining out and drinking, meetings and afterparties. You can't tell me you won't be going along to any of those while you're gone?'

'I can't believe you'd even think that just because I might go to those things I'd somehow forget that I was engaged. You have that little faith in me?'

'It's not that, it's just . . . the way it would be.'

'No, Finn. It isn't. Believe it or not, I actually take our relationship seriously. I would never jeopardise what we have for some fling . . . or whatever,' she snapped. She didn't even know how to go about having a fling. She'd only ever had one man in her life and he was standing across from her now. 'I get that being so far away isn't ideal for a relationship. But I *know* us. You're the one who's always said there was no rush—that we were already living the dream. Nothing will change that. I don't *want* to live overseas, that's just how this has worked out—maybe if I'd taken that internship in Sydney last year, everything would have been different, but I didn't. And now the job involves being further away, but only for a little while. Just until I gain the experience I need and then I can come home and use it wherever I want. It won't be forever.'

'Use it how, Al?' he demanded. 'That's what I don't get. Why do you need to do this if you're just coming back here to—what? Go back to working in a dress shop?'

'I don't want to work in a dress shop,' she told him, striving to remain calm. 'I want to design. I want to make my own clothing line. I don't know how I'm going to use what I learn, all I know is I will. I want to do more than just sell clothes someone else designed.'

His unreadable expression sent a cold chill to her heart.

She tried again. 'Designing to me is just like your dream of changing Whyningham when you get to run it. Moving over to cattle and sheep from cropping, starting your own stud. That's what this is to me.'

'Except my dream involves you—us . . . it's our future. Yours, you'll be doing on your own.'

Alice felt her throat close up as she stared at him, helpless. She didn't know what else she could say to get through to him, to make him understand how important this had become to her. How could she expect him to really understand when, in all honesty, she hadn't realised herself just how powerful her need to do it was until recently.

'You said the other day you were happy with the way things were before we got engaged. This would be just like that. I mean, how many more years were you planning on waiting before you asked me to get married anyway? Two? Three? *Ever?*'

His expression did change then, fading into something that looked more like frustration.

'I didn't mean what I said the other day. It wasn't that I didn't *want* to get married, it was just something we hadn't gotten around to doing.'

Oh, that made it seem so much better. Their wedding was like the side gate he'd been meaning to fix but just hadn't found the time.

'I just can't see it working out.' He took his hat off and rubbed a hand across his head. 'Not when you're halfway around the bloody planet.'

'So where does that leave us?'

He shrugged. 'I guess it leaves us wherever you decide.'

'So, if I take this job, you're saying . . . what? That we're *over?*' she asked incredulously.

'What am I supposed to do, Alice? Sit here and wait for you to *maybe* come home in a year or two and still want to settle down and get married? You seriously think that after living in London you'll want to come back to this place and be a farmer's wife?' He gave a harsh chuckle. 'Come on, Al. I might be a country hick, but I'm not stupid.'

'I said I'll come back and I will. I love you, Finn.'

He slapped his hat against the side of his leg before slamming it back on his head. 'If you loved me, I'd be enough,' he said roughly, and turned away. But not before she saw the glisten of tears in his eyes, which tore her heart in two.

'Finn,' she said, reaching for his arm. 'Please, don't make me choose.' She heard her voice crack as hot tears ran down her face.

'You already have. You made your choice a year ago, you just don't want to admit it,' he said softly, before taking his arm from her hold and walking away.

Alice returned to her car and drove home, struggling to see the road through the torrent of tears. She pulled to the side of the road and rested her head on the steering wheel, unable to continue driving as sobs racked her body.

When she managed to get herself under control, the sun had started to set, its fiery red and orange rays streaking across the sky. Inside, she felt empty—hollow, like the burnt-out tree stump she'd pulled up next to. She wiped the remaining tears from her cheeks and searched for a tissue in her handbag, her fingers finding the elaborate, gold-edged business card she'd dropped in there. She pulled it out to stare at it.

With a long sigh, she took out her phone and dialled the number on the bottom of the card.

As she listened to the call connecting, she had a moment of panic, her thumb hovering over the end call button before a brisk voice answered and she suddenly felt like a rabbit caught in a set of headlights.

'I'd like to speak to Frankie, please,' she told the receptionist. 'It's Alice Croydon.' She'd expected to be interrogated, if not turned away completely, but was surprised when neither happened.

'One moment, please, Miss Croydon, while I put you through. We've been expecting your call.'

And just like that, Alice realised the universe had been patiently marking time until she finally decided to stop fighting the inevitable.

Part Two

Chapter 15

Alice sat at the window of her small bedroom and watched the rain. She'd been in London a little over six weeks and could count on one hand the number of days she'd woken up to a full day of sun. Not that she'd had time to sit outside and enjoy any of them, she'd been too busy working.

Her days were full of running errands around the city—picking up supplies, signing for deliveries, fetching lunches and going on endless coffee runs. She helped out in the pattern room, cutting material and doing whatever menial tasks anyone gave her, and in between she worked on mood boards and read over fashion trend prediction reports, helping piece together new fabrics and colours for future clothing lines. The people she worked around were fascinating and talented, and being in the office each day made her feel that finally she was where she was meant to be.

But she was a designer and she wanted to *design*.

Alice glanced across at the table covered in prototype pattern pieces and fabric and she thought about her beautiful sewing room back home. Her apartment here was tiny, and cramped, but she made it work. She was experimenting with an idea to use wool, but in a different way. Usually wool was used for heavy winter overcoats and woollen jumpers, but Alice wanted to show how it could be adapted to use in the hotter seasons as well. It wasn't going to be an easy sell, but she knew if she could just get the pattern she was working on right, she could change people's minds.

She quite liked her little one-room flat in Queensborough Terrace only five minutes from Hyde Park. It had everything she needed—a bed, kitchenette and bathroom—and had been recently renovated. She was getting used to the fact there was no outside area or garden she could relax in, but then again, she worked almost constantly and really didn't have time to lie about in a garden anyway. Plus, if she did get time, she had plenty of places she could go nearby. She still had to pinch herself that she lived within a stone's throw of so many iconic places like Notting Hill, Mayfair and Piccadilly Circus—it was like a Monopoly game come to life. She was often awestruck by the history everywhere she looked—cathedrals and terrace buildings that were so much older than any buildings back home. She couldn't believe how everyone else seemed to just take all this for granted, and she had to restrain herself from snapping photos every five minutes like a tourist.

She'd been trying to keep herself busy since arriving in London—too busy to think of everything she missed—and it usually worked. She spoke to her family every day, either by phone or social media, but this was a big change from seeing them in person. It was only at night, once she was tucked up in her little apartment, that her thoughts would shift to Finn. A few times she'd reached for the phone to call him, but, after the short, painful conversation they'd exchanged after she'd arrived, she hadn't tried again. She'd hoped he'd want to know she'd landed safely, but his abrupt yes and no answers and lack of any of his usual warmth had hurt deeply.

Today, though, she had an unexpected day off work and, without the distraction, her mood had taken a nosedive and the homesickness she'd managed to keep at bay suddenly broke its banks and flooded her.

With an effort, Alice shook off the doldrums that had settled inside her and decided to go and explore Hyde Park and Kensington Gardens. She took the stairs and let herself out onto the street. She attempted to smile at a few people passing by but no one really made eye contact. It was a strange feeling, to walk among people and not smile or exchange a good morning or how are you. Back in Gunnindi she'd have learned the medical history of at least three people by now.

Tall, shady trees lined the street, and the sea of umbrellas ahead of her bobbed like coloured jellyfish as people hurried to their destinations. She passed a young couple tucked snugly under one umbrella with their arms around each other and smiled sadly. She held on to the belief that somehow, once she got back home, she and Finn would sort it all out. After all, you couldn't simply turn off your feelings for someone you'd been in love with for the last nine years, could you?

Alice walked slightly behind Julian and Freda, the head designers in Frankie's formal and wedding attire department, the click-clack of her heels echoing double time as she hurried to try and keep up with their fast-paced gait. Today she was tagging along to sit in on a meeting to look at some new season fabrics. Most of the meetings were held at Frankie's offices but today she was looking forward to something new. Her admiration grew daily for the people Frankie had chosen to work for him—both Julian and Freda were exceptional designers and the things she'd learned working under them had already been invaluable.

The meeting was at a manufacturer's showroom and Alice found herself overwhelmed at the multitude of different rolls of fabric on display. She itched to roam about, free to touch the beautiful material and let her imagination run wild with what she'd create with each piece. She felt an urge to pinch herself. She was here. In London. Working!

A tall male with a man bun and wearing corduroy jeans and a button-up shirt appeared, trailed by a harried-looking assistant dressed in a pencil skirt and white blouse, busily taking notes as he spoke at her over his shoulder.

'Victor, it's good to see you,' Julian said, taking the other man's hand in his, before Victor reached for Freda and kissed her on both cheeks.

'And who do we have here?' Victor asked, eyeing Alice up and down curiously.

'This is Alice Croydon,' Freda said with a light hand on Alice's arm.

'Ah, Frankie's new protégé,' Victor said, and he nodded, his eyes narrowing. 'I've heard all about you.'

'You have?' Alice blurted, shocked that her employer would have mentioned her in any kind of conversation, let alone to an industry colleague.

'Oh yes. He sees big things in you, young lady. Big things indeed.' He bobbed his head briskly and Alice was for a moment too distracted by the bun wobbling about on the top of his head for his words to fully sink in. Next minute, they were being shown to a large worktable where their new designs had been laid out with a display of fabric swatches.

Alice took out her notepad, glancing over at the assistant across from her, who was furiously scribbling down page after page of illegible writing. *Is she actually making a transcript of our conversation?* Alice briefly wondered. *Should I also be writing down absolutely everything being said?* Alice switched her attention back to the main conversation and soon forgot about what else was going on around her.

Julian eyed the fabric swatches critically, tilting his head slightly as he studied the texture and measured the weight in his hands. Then he took out his iPad to bring up certain specifications and discussed his selections with Freda, either dismissing or accepting the various fabrics as they made their way through the designs.

When they came to the final piece, Alice jumped guiltily when she realised Julian had asked her a question. He'd caught her out busily designing a wedding gown in her head as she lovingly stroked a swatch of beautifully embroidered lace adorned with dainty glass beads and Swarovski crystals. 'Sorry?' she stammered, her face hot. Four sets of eyes were on her, waiting for an answer to something she'd completely missed hearing.

'You have an eye for expensive fabrics, I see,' Victor mused, breaking the awkward moment as he nodded down at the fabric she hastily returned to the table. 'That's good news for me!'

'Not so much for Frankie who has to pay for it though,' Julian added, a twinkle in his eye. 'Alice, I was wondering what your thoughts were between the jacquard and taffeta. Which would you go with?'

Alice considered the two fabrics before her. 'I think the jacquard,' Alice finally decided after careful consideration.

'Why that one?' Freda asked, and Alice realised this was some kind of test. For a moment she panicked and felt sweat prickle along her hairline, but she forced herself to calm down. She knew fabrics—it was her passion, she just had to rein in her nerves and allow her intuition to speak.

'The design is extremely simple, yet elegant,' Alice said slowly as she pointed at the sketch on the table, 'so you could get away with using a material that's got a lot of texture and detail. It's not going to take away from anything in the design,' she explained, risking a glance at the others and taking some comfort in the fact they were nodding and not looking at her like she was an idiot. 'But if cost wasn't a factor,' Alice continued, walking across to another fabric that had caught her eye earlier, 'I'd go for something like this grey, metal-embroidered Chantilly lace over a silk satin sheath.'

'Yes, well, the bane of a designer's existence is budget, and at around eight hundred pounds per metre, that is not going to work for this particular collection,' Freda said with a tolerant smile before turning back to the table. 'I agree. The jacquard.'

Alice fought the urge to do a happy dance on the spot but savoured the small bubble of pride that momentarily burst to life inside her chest as the designers settled on the fabrics—feeling as though she'd somehow contributed something important to the meeting, even if she really hadn't. After the meeting, Julian and Freda had another appointment to attend to, so Alice headed back to the office, stopping outside the majestic cathedral they'd passed earlier, taking a selfie and posting it to her Instagram. She'd been exploring the city as often as she could between work, eager to soak up the atmosphere, and she knew her family enjoyed the posts. She did too; their comments and likes made her feel as though they weren't as far away as they really were. She paused as she came to the post she'd put up the day before of Buckingham Palace, scrolling through the list of names who'd liked it and telling herself she wasn't looking for anyone in particular. Still, she felt a little disappointed that Finn's name wasn't there. *He's probably too busy to be checking Instagram anyway*, she thought, but deep down had known he wouldn't be liking any of her posts.

She headed back to the office and sat down at her desk to finish her research notes for the department meeting the next day. If she kept busy she didn't have as much time to miss Finn and feel sorry for herself.

After work that evening, Alice unlocked the front door of her apartment building and walked across the small lobby area to the wall of letterboxes to check her mail. She smiled as she shuffled through the small pile and noted Gran's familiar handwriting and one from Daisy, which, judging from the fatness of the envelope, would likely include some new drawings from her nieces. She blinked back happy tears at the thoughtfulness—small touches of home that somehow always arrived when she was feeling homesick. She paused at the last envelope, which had a formal address and an unfamiliar solicitor's name in the corner.

She shoved the rest of her mail in her bag as a trickle of dread tingled at the base of her neck. She ripped open the envelope.

As Alice read through the stilted solicitor's correspondence, she fought the urge to sink to the carpeted steps beside her, instead forcing herself to climb the staircase until she reached her floor and unlocked her door with numb fingers. Dropping her bag, she lowered herself onto the edge of her bed and tried to re-read the rapidly blurring words on the page she held with shaking hands.

Finn had instructed his solicitor to inform her that he wanted to sell the cottage on Matilda Street immediately.

Alice hadn't thought her heart could break any more than it already had—but she was wrong. She could feel the remaining shards falling inside her with a brittle crash. He hadn't even called to tell her himself—he'd had a stranger notify her by mail.

They'd briefly spoken about the house before she left, if you could call the stony-eyed silence broken by the occasional grunt and nod a conversation. Alice had asked that they continue paying the mortgage repayments separately for the next twelve months in exchange for Finn continuing to live there. Clearly this was no longer a suitable arrangement.

The thought of selling the house was another painful stab to her already-destroyed heart. She couldn't lose the cottage as well.

After a sleepless night, she found herself a solicitor and had him reply on her behalf. She'd take over the mortgage, buy out Finn's half of the loan. Money was going to be tight, but if she rented it out, then maybe she could afford it. There was no way she was going to sell the house.

Her parents would tell her to let it go, get some money back on it and use it to start over again, but the thought of not having her little house to return to someday simply hurt too much.

Alice stood back and bit the edge of her fingernail as Julian studied the design idea she'd placed on his desk. He'd walked past her desk and asked to see what she was working on, surprising her with his request.

'I know I'm not supposed to be designing yet . . . but I've finished all my work so I was just . . .'

'You are a designer—it's what you do. I'd be disappointed if you weren't working on a design in your free time. Now show me something. I want to see your work.'

Caught a little off guard, her mind went to the dress pinned to her dressmaking mannequin at home but then quickly dismissed the idea. She wasn't ready to present that just yet, so she had produced a sketch of a dress she'd been working on that she thought would be a good fit in the new season evening wear line instead.

'It's good,' he said, and elation blossomed in her for all of two seconds before he continued firmly, 'but not good enough.'

Not good enough? She'd been working on that design for days.

'I've seen it a thousand times before.'

Alice blinked. Sure, her design had what she liked to think of as universal appeal—it was simple, but it had elegance.

'I want to see something unique. Different. I want to see some of that talent Frankie obviously sees in you. This is not it,' Julian said flapping a hand at the sketch before him.

Heat moved up her neck as she lowered her eyes. She was *not* going to cry. Professionals. Did. Not. Cry. She told herself firmly. She should have been able to handle rejection after the years with Antoinette, but this was different. This was rejection from an award-winning designer and, worse yet—the guy who was reporting her progress back to her employer!

'You have an eye for fabric, I've seen that in your work. If you are going to be a great designer, you have to think outside the box—take chances. Your ideas must come from in here,'

Julian said, tapping his chest. 'Try again.' And he dropped the design back on her desk and walked away.

Alice slumped back in her chair and stared at the sketch despondently before scrunching it up and tossing it into the bin.

Chapter 16

'Alice!'

Alice lifted her head from the sketch she was drawing at her desk and gave a small, impatient sigh. She put down her pencil and picked up her notepad and pen, having learned from experience that, when summoned by Frankie, he could want her to do anything from taking notes like a secretary— which she wasn't—to making him a cup of coffee, like an assistant—which she also technically wasn't. But she did whatever was asked because she was just grateful to be here. She tried not to be disappointed that the job hadn't been anything like she'd expected—reminding herself of the amazing opportunity she had before her. Maybe she'd been naive, thinking she'd be somehow designing under Frankie's label or at least be involved in something exciting . . . Okay, so she *had* been naive. She knew she had to still prove herself and it wasn't like she *hadn't* been learning or gaining experience. If the only way to get what she wanted was to do whatever was asked of her, then that's just what she'd have to do.

She passed by Adel's desk on her way to Frankie's office and they exchanged a quick eyeroll and smile. She had met Adel on her very first day. Alice had been sweeping up the scraps of material in the cutting room and ended up outside, crying by the rubbish bins, positive she'd made a huge mistake coming here, when Adel appeared. At barely five feet tall, with bright pink hair that matched her miniskirt and wearing big black army boots, Adel reminded Alice of a grungy fairy. She had also been hiding behind the rubbish bins, but she'd been sneaking a cigarette. Alice knew that without Adel, those first few days would have been unbearable.

'You called?' she asked as she entered Frankie's office.

'Close the door,' he instructed without bothering to lift his eyes from the folder before him.

Alice waited behind the chair across from his desk, itching to go back and finish her sketch. She took in her boss's wide shoulders in the pale blue business shirt he wore. The sleeves had been rolled up and she briefly let her eyes roam the length of his nicely toned and tanned forearms. Everything about Frankie was so . . . masculine. In an industry where masculinity wasn't exactly prominent, he was a bit of an enigma. He reminded her of the business tycoons in one of Gran's romance novels—with a hint of Jason Statham, she thought now as she watched him reading through a document. If you didn't know who Frankie was, you'd never immediately guess he was in the fashion industry.

'Take a seat. I've been speaking with Julian about your progress.'

Alice held her breath. Butterflies began to flap about inside her stomach. Had Julian told Frankie about the design she'd shown him? Was she in trouble? Was this going to be another Antoinette moment where he threatened her with unemployment if she continued designing on her own? Oh God, please no, she silently prayed.

'He's spoken very highly of you. He mentioned you've shown a lot of potential working on a few of the latest designs with the team. That's high praise indeed from a man like Julian.'

Alice took a moment to let out a slow, silent, *very* relieved breath before organising her scattered wits. 'It's an honour to be working with him. He's an amazing teacher.'

'I'd like you to take on a more active role in the department—do the researching and costing, reviewing fabric samples and meeting with the pattern makers and sample sewers so you get a feel for the business side of the job as well.'

'It was mainly the designing I was hoping to get more hands-on experience with,' she said tentatively. The last thing she wanted to do was sound ungrateful, but the business side of the job was not something that particularly excited her.

'And you will. But there's more to being a designer than just designing. You need experience in all aspects of the job. Think you're up to it?' His tone suggested he wasn't going to change his mind.

'Yes. Absolutely—thank you,' she said.

He nodded and the brief meeting now seemed over. Alice tucked her hair behind her ear and turned away, but stopped when Frankie spoke again. 'Julian has a lot of faith in your ability and so do I. I know you're impatient to start designing something of your own but learning from the ground up is how you gain the experience you'll need to run your own label or company one day. You have to learn to walk before you run.'

Alice swallowed past her frustration. 'Thank you for the opportunity,' she said, hoping she managed to sound adequately grateful. She wasn't ungrateful—it was just that this whole experience wasn't exactly what she'd been imagining.

'I just want to work on my designs,' Alice moaned as she sat opposite Adel at the cafe outside the office building later, on their lunch break. 'Time's ticking away. I'll be going home before I've had the chance to do anything meaningful,' she said, stirring sugar into her coffee despondently.

'It really hasn't been that long. There's still plenty of time,' Adel said in her soothing Scottish lilt. 'And remember what Victor said—he'd heard *all about you*,' she emphasised, her brown eyes widening in awe. 'Frankie doesn't make a habit of talking up just anyone.'

'Yeah, but how do we really know that? I mean he might have just been making some passing comment about hiring some Australian trainee or something while they waited in line for their coffee one day,' Alice said with a frown.

'When have you ever seen Frankie stand in line for coffee? Or anything for that matter,' Adel pointed out. 'And I can guarantee, Victor wouldn't have heard anything about *me*, so no, I don't think he talks up just anyone.'

Alice desperately wanted to believe Adel was right, and she knew that taking on more responsibilities at work was a good thing—she was working under the guidance of great designers—but it wasn't directly under Frankie and she wasn't designing her own stuff.

Alice let out a frustrated growl, then closed her eyes. She hated feeling so negative. This was not like her. 'Okay.' Alice straightened her shoulders. 'I can do this,' she decided.

'You can do this!' Adel cheered, between bites of her sandwich.

She *had* to do this. She'd given up everything to move here and take this job. It had to be for something. She'd work her way up and work in all the other parts of the business and she'd keep designing in her spare time. She'd prove to Frankie she was ready. One day she'd have a design—her very own design in a Frankie Esquire catalogue and all this will have been worth it.

The next few weeks were hard—very hard. Previously Alice had been simply sitting in on various meetings and watching Julian or Freda take the leading role, but now, *she* was having the meetings with pattern makers and sample sewers. She'd never been in a position where she told other people what to do, certainly not working for Antoinette, and now suddenly she had to give instructions and direction. For the most part, everyone was supportive and helpful as she struggled to find her feet, except for one sample sewer who constantly tested her patience. At first Alice was timid and excessively contrite whenever she had to come back and ask for alterations on a sample—something that happened quite a bit when the pattern was still in its fine-tuning stage—and that one sample sewer—Marcella—terrified her. She would throw her hands around and mutter in French as she sent Alice dirty looks before grudgingly starting the sample all over again—and that was on a good day. Other days she'd flat-out refuse to take in the requested changes. It was intimidating, to say the least.

On one particular day, when Alice had to come back for a second alteration on the same day, she felt almost sick to the stomach. Marcella was going to lose it. Which is how Julian found her cowering in the doorway, trying to psych herself up to go inside and make the request.

'Ah, yes, Marcella,' Julian said, and he nodded with a slight wince. 'She can be . . . challenging,' he observed, giving her a small sympathetic smile.

'Maybe I could just make the changes myself,' Alice suggested.

'You could,' Julian agreed, and for a moment Alice felt her hopes rise.

'But that isn't your job and it would put the whole production behind. You don't have time for delays. Delays cost money. You just have to go in there and be firm. Marcella isn't all that scary once she knows she can't make you quake in your boots,' he said with a shrug. 'I'll let you in on a little secret—but if you ever tell anyone you heard it from me, I'll deny it,' he warned. 'Marcella could once make even Frankie himself tremble like a leaf.'

'Frankie?' Alice breathed, then looked at Julian dubiously. Surely he was making that up.

'I swear on my mother's grave,' he said, crossing himself quickly.

'So what happened?'

'He won her over of course—with his natural charm and good looks. No woman can resist Frankie Esquire.'

'That's not exactly helpful advice for me, though, is it?'

'No, I suppose not,' he acknowledged. 'You'll figure it out,' he said, patting her on the arm. 'But you better do it fast, we need that sample for the meeting later today.'

What would Gran do? she asked herself, biting the inside of her lip.

Instantly she heard Gran as though in her ear. *You're a Croydon. You get in there and you tell that woman who you are and what you expect!* Gritting her teeth, Alice pushed open the door and marched across the room to where Marcella sat behind a sewing machine, forced on by sheer bravado and a hefty dash of terror.

She wasn't even that scary to look at—if you didn't know any better, Alice thought dismally as she took in the small woman before her. Her dark hair, greying in streaks at the temples, was pulled back into a harsh bun at the back of her head as it bent over the sewing machine in front of her. It was only when she lifted her dark gypsy eyes that she somehow managed to reduce you to a quivering mess. She had the coldest stare and the loudest temper for such a tiny woman.

Alice summoned Gran, like some pagan talisman, and set the pattern down on the desk in front of her. 'I need these changes made immediately. Please,' she tacked on, suddenly feeling awkward, although she felt Gran would approve. *Even when you have to be forceful you can still be polite*, she thought.

That cold-eyed stare held Alice's unflinchingly. 'I already made changes.'

'Yes, but we need more.' Alice surged on, trying her best to hold a level tone in her voice.

'Why I making more changes? Why you not do it right the first time?' she threw back, disdain lacing her tone like venom.

'Because it's a design and sometimes designs need to be altered.' *Hence the term design*, Alice added mentally.

'Leave it. Maybe I'll get to it tomorrow, if I have time,' Marcella said, dismissing Alice rudely by turning away.

Seriously? Suddenly the woman's unacceptable level of insolence hit a nerve. 'No. You need to do it *right now*. Tomorrow is too late.' Alice braced herself as the woman slowly turned back around.

Oh shit.

It's okay, Alice told herself, *she isn't really a gypsy, she can't put a curse on me . . . she's just a normal person.* The woman's cold stare began to chill Alice's insides. *This is ridiculous*, she could almost hear Gran muttering.

Alice decided to change gears before the situation escalated even further. 'Look, I know it must be a pain in the neck to have to continue altering designs all day—but like it or not that's just part of the job. I have certain parts of my job I really don't like too.' *Like dealing with you*, she thought to herself. 'But we can't do our job without you doing yours, and, quite frankly, no one can do it better than you. So even though I know you're extremely busy and you have your own deadlines, I would really appreciate it if you could make the changes that we need to this sample.'

For a moment Marcella simply continued to stare at her, and Alice struggled to hold her nerve, but then she remembered she was a Croydon and she was not going to back down. She braced her shoulders and held the woman's stare.

'Fine. Leave it. I will make changes today,' Marcella snapped.

'Right. Thank you,' Alice said, then found herself lowering her head slightly before leaving the room. *What the hell was that about?*

She was still pondering her bizarre farewell when she bumped into Adel and Julian waiting outside the door in the hallway.

'Did you just *bow* to Marcella on your way out?' Adel asked, through a strangled giggle.

'No,' Alice snapped.

'I think you did,' she countered, and even Julian was grinning.

'Well done,' he said, as he slowly clapped his hands. 'Very impressive.'

'Thank you. I couldn't have done it without your pep talk,' Alice replied, rolling her eyes as she walked past them on her way to yet another meeting to present yet another costing on yet another line Freda had her working on and wondering if it was, in fact, too early to have a drink.

The office was like a different place early in the morning. Alice had taken to getting off the tube a few stops early and walking the last part of the journey each day, making sure she got in to work before everyone else in the design department. She used the extra space of the office to spread out and create—which was so much better than the minuscule area she tried to work in at home. It was peaceful at this time of the day—no phones ringing or people standing about chatting in the hallways. No one clapping hands impatiently and demanding action somewhere. Just peace and quiet.

Sometimes, however, she wasn't the only one who seemed to have the same idea and often she'd find Frankie already working at his desk as he was this morning. Alice gathered he was on some kind of video conference, as he sometimes did this at odd hours in order to meet with clients or manufacturers from different time zones across the world.

Her initial reaction whenever she was around him was a cross between a tongue-tied, clumsy weirdo and an awestruck fan. It was difficult to separate his celebrity status and tabloid antics that she'd read about over the years from the man she found herself watching in the office each day.

'Frankie works as hard as he parties,' Freda had told her once, not long after she started working there after Freda had caught her reading a magazine that had been on the staff room table and featured Frankie and a famous model posing at a glamorous afterparty of some kind. 'The press don't like to show you all the good stuff he does—the charity events and the hours he puts in at work. That doesn't sell magazines apparently.'

It wasn't the first time she'd noticed how loyal his employees were. Everyone in the building it seemed, from the cleaners to the design team, seemed to adore the man. She'd had mixed feelings about him at first. She had sat in on a number of meetings since she'd arrived and had witnessed Frankie in action. He didn't suffer fools lightly—he detested a lack of work ethic and disorganisation—and she saw him cut down an advertising executive with that sardonic wit and tongue of his when the man had failed to prepare a properly researched presentation. She'd heard him blast department heads for not following up supply chain issues and for going over budget, and once he'd even fired someone who'd been reported to him for watching Netflix on their computer during a meeting— admittedly that was poor form and the guy had been a bit of a dick around the office, but Frankie had not minced words that day and Alice was pretty sure she'd never seen a grown man scamper quite like that before. On the other hand, she also saw him praise people. He was never stingy on appreciation or reward where it was due either. He was gruff and surly on the outside, but he was fair. He demanded professionalism and hard work, but increasingly she came to see for herself that these weren't things he didn't ask of himself. Many a night he was one of the last to leave—still bent over a draft board or working through a mountain of never-ending paperwork.

When Alice finished setting up the room, making sure everything the design department needed was on hand, she scrolled through the list of meetings and tasks that would need to be done that day. Satisfied she was on top of it all, she headed into the small workroom attached to the main design office and got busy cutting out her pattern pieces on the length of woollen fabric that had arrived a few days earlier. Since she'd just spent a small fortune on the fabric, she wasn't going to risk making a mistake by cutting out on her ridiculously small table at home. Nope—this was a big deal and she needed to be able to spread out the fabric and see what she was doing.

She took her time and double-checked everything before she made the first, nervous snip, but soon she fell into a comfortable rhythm and was lost in the familiar sound of dressmaker's scissors slicing through fabric as clean and easy as a hot knife through butter. It really was the most magical sound. It brought back memories of Gran cutting out patterns with her big, heavy, metal shears as Alice had sat and watched. The satisfying crunch of heavy scissors slicing through material on a timber table. It was a sound like no other.

When she finished, Alice straightened and took a second to admire her handiwork before carefully stacking the cut pieces on top of each other and packing them away to take home. Tonight she'd start pinning them together, ready to sew.

After cleaning up the room and walking out, she glanced across to the office on the far side of the room and watched as Frankie, now seemingly finished with his Zoom call, appeared to be gathering himself in preparation for another as he stretched his arms out in front of him and rolled his shoulders to release some tension.

Alice walked across to the coffee machine in the kitchen and took down two cups, quickly making the coffee and popping two slices of bread into the toaster. She wasn't sure if Frankie ever lowered himself to eat carbs, but something about the way he looked so tired brought out a mothering instinct in her.

She tapped on the door lightly as he ended the call and waited for him to look up before carefully carrying the cup and plate over to his desk. 'I thought you might need a bit of sustenance,' she said, avoiding his eyes. She could never look directly into them—it was kind of like when adults warned her not to look directly at a solar eclipse when she was a kid . . . she'd never been game enough to test if she really would go blind or not.

She worried for a moment that she might have overstepped some kind of workplace boundary when she saw confusion then surprise flash across his face, but he covered it up quickly, rubbing a hand across his stubbled chin and leaning back in his chair. 'Should I be worried?'

'Sorry?' Alice replied.

He nodded his head towards the plate and cup. 'Are you about to ask for a raise or are you buttering me up to hear some bad news?'

A flutter of irritation crossed her face. 'Neither. You just looked like you were having a busy morning and might like something to eat.'

He gave a rueful twist of his lips. 'My apologies. As a matter of fact, it has been a big morning and thank you. This looks great.'

'No worries. I'll let you get back to it.'

'I've heard you're settling well into your new role,' he said, stopping her retreat.

'It's been an experience,' she agreed, trying to keep her expression as neutral as possible, but clearly failing when he flashed another of his quick smiles—the one that kind of made her tummy swoosh against her rib cage a little bit. She'd spent far more time than she felt comfortable about trying to assess that smile lately. It didn't technically fall into the smile category—it was more of a leer, but not as sleazy . . . it came off as a little dangerous and mysterious. If a smile could even do that.

'Experiences are what you came here for, weren't they?' he asked, leaning slightly forward and reaching for his cup without taking his eyes from hers.

'Designing experiences,' she corrected lightly, but mustered a vague smile in agreement.

'You get here early, quite often.'

It wasn't a question, more of a statement and she wasn't quite sure how to reply. 'I like to be organised, I guess.'

'Something we have in common.'

'I suppose you'd need to be to run this place,' she countered. It was a big job—sure, he had people helping him, but he had his fingers in so many pies that she wasn't sure how he managed to keep it all moving.

'True. But I wasn't always. I had to be once I started designing. Now it's like second nature. My designing and the training I learned under my mentor prepared me for all of this. That's why I'm pushing you now, Alice,' he said in that smooth, yet somehow gravelly tone of his. 'You have a huge future in front of you and I want you to be prepared.'

Alice shook her head minutely as his words sunk in. 'But I'm not expecting to run a massive corporation—all I want to be is a designer,' she told him and heard the helpless tone that had crept in. She didn't need all this experience. She just wanted to learn her craft under the best in the business and take all that knowledge home with her. What she did with it then would unfold once she was home. She hadn't properly thought that far ahead.

'You have talent, Alice. Real talent. I knew that the first time I saw your work. I wouldn't have wasted my time on someone if I didn't believe in them. What you lack is ambition and drive—and in this business, you need those two things in order to be a great designer. Mediocre won't cut it in the fashion industry. Only once you find that ambition and drive will you be ready to be a great designer.'

She had ambition. She was here wasn't she? She'd given up everything she knew and the love of her life to move to the other side of the damn world. If that wasn't ambition then she didn't know what was.

'You need to trust me, Alice. I'll take you where you want to go—most likely places you didn't even know you wanted to go to. You'll see,' he said, before picking up a slice of toast and biting into it with his perfectly white and incredibly straight teeth.

How did one respond to that? 'Thank you?' Maybe, but she had a feeling he didn't need her thanks and he wasn't planning on asking her permission or asking if she even wanted to be taken to wherever it was he saw her going. She'd signed up for the ride and now she realised she just had to hold on tight and go with it. Part of her was terrified while a tiny other part had become more than a little intrigued. Maybe that was her ambition slowly waking up.

Chapter 17

Alice worked harder than she'd ever worked before in her entire life, making herself invaluable to the design team and before she knew it, she realised she'd been in London almost six months.

'That's much better. Good!' Julian said one evening, his Italian accent adding extra oomph to his praise. Alice smiled. She'd felt her confidence growing with every passing day. After developing a slightly thicker skin and realising that Julian demanded a high standard of professionalism, she had come to value his opinion, as well as his criticism. The desire to gain respect and approval from the people she worked with drove her to work hard and, even though Julian pushed her to her very limits, she knew, as a designer, she couldn't have asked for a better mentor.

'Your hard work has been paying off, no?' Julian said, nodding.

'Thank you, Julian. Your idea made so much sense. You were right.'

'Of course!' He chuckled and gave an offhand shrug. 'But it was your idea of using wool to create this particular design that brings this piece to life. *That* was a touch of genius.'

She'd eventually worked up the courage to show Julian her wool design after talking herself out of it for the last few months and he'd encouraged her to bring in the sample.

Her love of fabric, and in particular wool, had only grown since working with Julian. Watching the design team rake through different fabrics and seeing them used with such skill and passion had reignited the idea she'd been harbouring—to work with wool. She'd had to try a number of different wool blends and fabrics before finding the perfect one, which turned out to be rarely sourced, and underutilised, Australian wool. Designers and fashion houses over here would drool over the quality and versatility of the fabric if it were marketed and presented in the right way. She'd been discussing the idea with Julian for a few weeks and she knew with this latest design she had finally managed to win his support. If she could just get Frankie on board, she knew they'd have a shot at figuring out how to make it work.

'We will see what Frankie has to say when he returns from Milan.'

'*If* he returns from Milan,' Alice said, remembering the front page of the magazine she'd glanced at the newsstand on her way in this morning. 'It sounds like one big party over there.' Frankie had been attending elite clubs and celebrity parties and was front and centre with a new woman at every function.

'Don't believe everything you read,' Julian warned with a shake of his head and they continued to work.

Frankie was already in the office when Alice arrived the following day, on the phone and working at the computer at the same time. Alice headed to her desk to prepare for the pre-production meeting.

She was setting up her iPad in the meeting room, preparing to take notes, when Julian entered wheeling a mannequin— wearing the design she'd been working on with him.

'Wool. This is something different for you, Jules,' Frankie said thoughtfully as he examined the bright floral summer dress with its scalloped waist, pleated skirt, square neckline and thin straps.

'It's not mine,' Julian said, nodding towards Alice calmly.

'You did this?' Frankie asked, not bothering to hide his surprise at the news.

'Ah.' Alice sent a bewildered glance to Adel, who stared at her with wide eyes and nodded quickly in encouragement. 'Yes. It's something I've been working on . . . in my own time.'

'I see,' Frankie said, his attention back on the dress. 'Why wool?' he demanded abruptly, leaning back in his chair and interlocking his fingers behind his head as his gaze zeroed in on her. 'Sell this to me.'

Alice swallowed nervously before clearing her throat and standing. 'I come from a town where wool was a major industry and part of our history. I'm fascinated by how versatile it is as a fibre and I wanted to reimagine the role of wool—showing it can be worn season to season and not just as a winter textile. This wool is lightweight and breathable, which is what you want in a fabric during the warmer months. It's extremely adaptable and in today's market it ticks all the boxes: it's renewable, natural and sustainable. I'd like to do a line of spring and summer wear covering casual, formal and work wear to show just how adaptable it is.'

'So you want to use Australian wool in particular for this?'

'Not just Australian wool—Gunnindi wool,' she said. Adding quickly, 'Eventually. I mean, it's a project I'd really like to see evolve someday, but for now, yes, I'd like to use Australian wool.' Ever since the idea had come to her of using wool for something other than a heavy winter jacket, she'd been thinking more and more about it. Maybe it was just because the thought of her hometown made her homesick and she was looking for some kind of connection, she wasn't sure. All she *was* sure about was that now she said it out loud she was positive it made her sound naive and silly.

For the longest moment, Frankie remained silent as his gaze shifted from her face back to the dress.

'Work the numbers and get me the research,' he finally said.

Alice was dumbfounded. 'Numbers? . . . on the dress or . . . the whole line idea?' she asked hesitantly.

'The line, Alice,' he said, barely glancing up from the folder in front of him before abruptly moving on to the next item on the agenda.

Alice wasn't sure what had just happened. Was he actually considering her designs? She looked at Adel again and Adel grinned and gave her the thumbs up excitedly. Holy crap. Maybe Frankie actually *was* thinking about it. Alice barely registered anything else that was discussed for the remainder of the meeting and was still in a state of shock as Adel hurried her from the meeting room and back to her office.

'This is awesome!' Adel squealed.

'It is?'

'He's considering it!'

'He didn't actually say that. Maybe that was just his boss way of saying "We'll see." Which every kid knows is parent for "Absolutely no way".'

'Frankie Esquire never says something he doesn't mean. If he hated it, he'd have happily told you so. Trust me.'

She was right. Alice had always been secretly glad she hadn't been the one on the receiving end of his sharp dismissals in meetings before. 'Okay. I'll get him the numbers,' she said, realising her voice hadn't sounded as confident as she'd hoped. The task was going to be huge—certainly the biggest research project she'd ever done.

'It's just like any other portfolio you've put together,' Adel said calmly.

'Except this one is huge.'

'So? It's the same principle. I'll give you a hand. It's going to be fine.'

❖

Alice, armed with a tourist map and a list of hidden historical sites she'd googled, had been using her Sunday to continue exploring the city she was so fortunate to be living in. She'd been to all the major tourist places like Big Ben and the Tower of London, but now she wanted to find some interesting places off the tourist track. There were so many surprises to discover simply walking through back streets and little alleyways in the city—like the Winchester Palace, a twelfth-century ruin hidden in Southwark by the London Bridge. The remains of the once enormous palace were now just a crumbled ruin with a few decaying walls of the great hall and an impressive stone arch with a rose window still standing among a sea of modern buildings. She loved that about London—there was such a confusing mix of ancient and modern buildings, historical and contemporary, melding into each other—it shouldn't work but somehow it did. How amazing to be surrounded by so much of the past as you went about your daily life.

Her phone rang, intruding on her thoughts as she stood alone at the railing where she'd been daydreaming about how this place would have once looked, and then felt her breath hitch slightly when she saw the name on the screen. Frankie Esquire. She wasn't sure if she was alarmed or excited.

'Hello?' She hoped her voice sounded cool and professional but feared it didn't.

'I've been going through your presentation for the wool campaign.'

Silence greeted his announcement. For the life of her she couldn't squeeze out a single sound.

'Alice? You still there?'

'Yes. I'm here.'

'I'm impressed.'

'You are?' *He was?* Her thoughts scrambled in a thousand different directions, so much so that she almost missed his next remark.

'I'm approving it,' he said, before adding, 'however, at this stage I only want the formal wear. The range you've put together is exceptional, but targeting business apparel as well as casual and formal isn't in line with the company vision. We need to focus on our evening and bridal wear for the time being. I've scheduled a meeting first thing tomorrow morning. I'd suggest getting a good night's sleep because you probably won't be sleeping much over the next few months,' he said, and Alice thought she detected a hint of amusement in his voice.

Alice was stunned, still trying to process what he was saying, but thankfully remembered to respond. 'I will. Thank you,' she managed before the call ended and she was left staring down into the gardens of the once great hall below.

She was going to have her designs featured in a Frankie Esquire line. A small squeal of excitement escaped, and she covered her mouth with her hand, quickly looking around, but there was no one close enough to have noticed. Her first instinct was to call her parents and Gran, but she realised they'd all be fast asleep. She resisted the urge to cross over to the closest couple and share her good news and instead scrolled through her phone to call Adel.

'You will never guess what!'

Frankie had been right about the sleep thing. There had been no break in the pace to get the designs out in time for the upcoming collection. Part of her was a little disappointed that her entire range wasn't being utilised, but she also knew that one of the biggest rules in the game was knowing your market, and Frankie had proven time and time again that he knew his market back to front and upside down. Her biggest learning curve had been the fact she wasn't involved in every step of the process as she always had been.

She'd spent countless hours doing everything from the designing to the mock-ups to the sewing and fitting . . . this had been her baby and she was finding it strange to hand it over to other people.

'Good morning, Marcella,' Alice said, forcing a brightness into her tone as she walked into the room. 'We need you to work your magic on these new adjustments.' She still got nervous approaching the cranky old woman, but now she had Marcella figured out. The best way to smooth over ruffled feathers was always praise and admiration—something everyone needed to hear, even Marcella. She knew learning how to deal with temperamental or difficult situations in the industry had been one of those teaching moments Frankie had thrown her into. *Well played, Mr Esquire*, she'd thought. *Well played.*

There had been so much to do. Once the outfits had been made, there were photoshoots to organise and Alice had spent hours helping with the catalogue shoot—dressing models, finding the perfect accessories and watching the entire process with a critical eye, ready to step in and make adjustments to hair or outfits when the need arose. There were also meetings to attend—lots and lots of meetings—and she was exhausted. But it had been worth every second of the anxiety and stress she'd endured when she opened that glossy catalogue and saw her designs staring back at her with a Frankie Esquire tag hanging off them.

Late that night, after the last of the promotional work had been signed off on and most of the department had gone home, Alice closed her eyes as she sat at her desk. Her colleagues were already working on the next big thing, the designing process marching inexorably onwards. This might be her big moment, but, in the grand scheme of things, it was just one small range and there were plenty more waiting in the wings to be made and showcased. The Esquire juggernaut rested for no one.

'Good job, Croydon.' The deep voice from nearby jolted Alice awake and back to the present.

Throughout the last few weeks, Frankie had been a floating presence—there but not there. Attending the bigger meetings and asking for updates, but not around long enough for any one-on-one time at all.

'Thanks.'

'I thought you looked like you might need a bit of sustenance,' he said, placing a plate of toast and a coffee on the table, giving her that little wolf-grin as he threw her words of a few months ago back at her.

'Should I be worried?'

When his eyebrow kinked up a little at her teasing, she instantly regretted the spontaneous remark. 'You know . . . you said . . .'

'I remember, and you looked like you wanted to throw the plate at my head for questioning what I know was just a thoughtful gesture.'

Well this is awkward. 'Actually, I'm starving. I think I skipped lunch. And possibly breakfast,' she added as she searched her tired memory and came up empty.

'Then I'll take you out to dinner,' he said decisively, and Alice's gaze flew to his in alarm.

'Oh, no,' she said quickly, and cringed inwardly a little at the harshness of it. 'I mean . . . it's fine, I'm not *actually* starving. I'm pretty sure I'll be asleep as soon as my head hits the pillow.' She was rambling on like an idiot but there was no way she was going to have dinner with Frankie Esquire. Was he crazy? He could never eat out in peace, and she had no desire to be snapped in a photo for those stupid magazines to gossip about. Images of supermodels flashed through her head and she almost choked on a strangled laugh as she tried to imagine herself seated at an expensive restaurant with the guy who dressed celebrities and the rich elite of the world.

For the briefest of moments she was positive she saw something like hurt move across his face, but she quickly dismissed the idea. He would have thousands of suitable supermodels and dining partners on speed dial to have dinner with.

'I'll let you get home then,' he said, turning to leave.

'Thank you,' she called after him, quickly. 'For pushing me,' she said when he looked back over his shoulder at her. 'I think I understand why you've been making me do everything . . . now.'

When he continued to hold her gaze she added in a rush, 'I'm sorry if I ever sounded ungrateful before. I'm not. I'm very grateful to you for believing in me.'

'You're welcome. But it was always for selfish reasons,' he said. For a moment he seemed to consider her curiously before he added, 'I always knew you'd be an asset to my bottom line.'

Right. Alice thought, wondering at the tiny slice of hurt that went through her. It was business. *Of course it was business, Dummy*, a small voice chastised her impatiently. *What else would it be?* Alice cleared her throat uncomfortably and managed a nod, watching as he turned away and kept walking.

After she arrived home and got out of the shower, Alice smiled at the framed photo on her wall of the model posing in the delicate pink formal dress. She'd posted home catalogues with her designs featured among the others. It felt good to share her success with the people she loved, only she still found herself wishing she would hear from Finn. Even if it was as shallow as a like on a post or a quick text—just something that said he hadn't completely erased her from his life, despite the fact she felt that he had. With the house now settled and in her name, logically she knew it was an ending, and yet a tiny piece of her heart still refused to completely give up hope that maybe one day . . .

She still missed him when she thought too long about it, so she usually tried not to, with varying levels of success that usually ended in her wallowing in a glass of wine and eating chocolate late into the night.

Chapter 18

Before Alice knew it, Christmas had arrived and for the first time ever she was away from her family for the holiday. She could have flown home, but she would have been able to stay only a handful of days before she'd have to have turned around and fly the gazillion hours back to the UK again. Not to mention the money. She couldn't justify paying that much on a brief visit home when she needed most of it for rent in London and the mortgage on her cottage. Despite the company finding her the flat and paying a portion of her rent as a condition of her rushed employment, London living expenses were eye-watering.

So she'd reluctantly gone along to the staff Christmas party in a swanky, inner-city hotel and had a drink or two to cheer herself up.

It was different meeting people you worked with outside the office environment. Maybe because in public, on neutral ground, the hierarchy of the office didn't seem to be that big of a divide. Each time she listened to someone mention how they were spending their Christmas break—heading home to family—she had to force a bright smile to her face and take another large gulp of her wine.

It would be fine. It was just a few days, then everyone would be back at work and life would go back to normal, she kept telling herself.

She'd been invited to go with Adel to her family in Scotland, but she felt as though Adel already had enough on her plate with her parents having recently undergone a messy divorce and needing to divide her time between the two sides. The last thing Adel needed was a sad hanger-on who was missing her own family.

Then Frankie walked in—fashionably late to his own party, naturally, with a tall, willowy blonde on his arm who looked very much like a supermodel Alice had recently spotted on the front of *Vogue*. It really wasn't fair that there could be people that attractive in the world, though she supposed it made sense that they would be drawn to each other to share in all that attractiveness and do whatever it was that rich, attractive people did all day. She waved over a young, fresh-faced waiter doing the rounds of the room and took a drink from him. Maybe after a few more drinks she'd feel a little less bitter and out of sorts.

Unfortunately, after drink number five failed to lift her spirits, Alice realised—too late—that she may have gone a little too far. But by then, she didn't actually care that she felt like crying at the drop of a hat and so she drank a few more.

❖

'Alice!'

Alice frowned, trying to shrug off the hand that insisted on shaking her shoulder as she opened her eyes. She found her boss squatting down beside her, looking concerned. 'What?' Her voice came out in a low croak.

'What happened? Did someone hurt you?'

'What? No . . . I don't think so,' she said, lifting a hand to her head. When she pulled it away, she saw blood. Why was there blood on her forehead? She leaned back and discovered she'd been sitting against a giant pot plant in the icy courtyard and a sudden, unexpected memory resurfaced of needing some fresh air and a rather undignified experience of vomiting in said pot plant. She must have collapsed against it afterwards and grazed her forehead on the way down.

Frankie must have also pieced together the situation because, by the time he spoke again, some of his tension seemed to have eased.

'Come on, Croydon, let's get you up.'

'No, just leave me,' she said, moaning, as everything began to spin.

'I'm afraid I can't do that. The staff want to go home and can't while you're still out here.'

Alice groaned as Frankie pulled her to her feet. She rested her head against his shoulder and waited for everything to stop spinning.

'Come on, Cinderella, let's get you home.'

'I can't go home,' she sobbed as they began to make their way inside. 'I'll miss Mum's rum balls and carols by candle-light in the park and Gran's pork crackle.'

'I'm sure we can find you some rum balls and I know someone who does a pretty decent pork crackle over here.'

'It won't be the same. There won't be the love,' she said helplessly, staring up at him. 'Where's the love?'

He gave a small chuckle and smiled down at her then walked her through the hotel lobby, sending a wave to someone behind the front desk, and helped her out into a waiting limousine.

'In you get, Croydon,' he said, gently setting her inside and climbing in beside her.

As the car pulled away, she leaned her head back against the seat and closed her eyes. The gentle rocking of the car lulled her back into sleep.

All too soon, she heard Frankie asking, 'Do you have your keys?' They had pulled up outside her building.

Alice patted her pockets until she triumphantly produced the key, then she walked to the front door and tried unsuccessfully to fit it into the lock. 'I think someone has changed my locks,' she muttered, then sighed impatiently as Frankie took the key from her and managed to make it fit the first time. They went up the stairs to her flat and he let them in.

'Wow,' he murmured as they walked inside. 'You decorated.'

'It's Christmas,' she said, eyeing him as though he were slow-witted, then focusing on her small tree with its tinsel and twinkling fairy lights beneath her only window. 'Don't you decorate your house?'

'No, not really. I'm hardly there.'

'Not even a Christmas tree?'

'No. There's not much point really.'

'That's sad.'

'Not *everyone* gets caught up in all the hype, you know. Do you have a face cloth?' he asked and followed the direction she pointed, her arm feeling extremely heavy as she lifted it.

'But it's Christmas. It's special. What about your family? Do they decorate for Christmas?'

He came back to her side holding a damp cloth and began cleaning the graze on her forehead. 'I don't have any family to speak of. And Christmas was never a particularly special time when I was growing up,' he said almost dismissively as he examined the injury. 'It's not too bad. Just a scratch.'

'How come?'

'What?' he asked, looking at her with confusion.

'How come Christmas wasn't special when you were a kid?'

'It just wasn't. There was never much money at the best of times. My old man drank pretty much anything left over and my mother wasn't around very often.'

'That must have been really lonely,' she said, feeling unbearably sad for the little boy he once was.

'You don't miss what you never had,' he said briskly, then cleared his throat as he saw that she was on the verge of tears once more. 'Seriously, it's not that bad. I'm fine, I can buy myself whatever I want, any time of the year. I don't have to wait for Santa.'

'It *is* that bad,' she said, shaking her head as she stared at him. 'It's horrible. No wonder you've been a cranky bastard lately.'

When he frowned, she waved off his stern look. 'It's understandable. If Christmas dredges up bad memories, I can see why you'd act like a bit of a dick to everyone. But it's okay. I get it now.' She sank onto the edge of the bed.

'Thanks,' he said drolly. 'Although I didn't realise I'd been a cranky bastard.'

'You've probably been too distracted . . . thinking about Christmas as a kid.'

'I haven't been—' He gave an impatient huff. 'Look, you need to get to bed.'

'You don't get to tell me what to do after hours.'

'Okay. My mistake. Don't go to bed.' He went to the kitchenette and filled a glass with water then carried it back to the bedside table. 'But you'll thank me later when you wake up and see this beside your bed in the morning. Where do you keep your painkillers?'

'I don't have a headache,' she protested as he walked into her bathroom and opened the cupboard, scanning its contents before taking out a small bottle of pills.

'You will in the morning,' he said, placing the bottle beside the water. 'Get some sleep, Croydon.'

Alice watched him with heavy eyes. Damn him . . . she *was* tired. She could barely keep her eyes open, so she gave up the fight and lay back.

After a moment she heard the door open. 'Sleep tight, Alice.' Then the door shut behind him and she surrendered to the welcoming darkness of sleep.

❖

What. The. Actual. Hell. Alice tried to work out how she'd somehow woken up in that part of the *Jumanji* movie where rhinos and elephants are stampeding through the house.

She opened her eyes to find no wild African animals, though inside her head she could hear the pounding of loud tribal drums.

The night flashed through her mind, bits and pieces coming back like a very bad dream.

Oh. God.

She rolled her head to the side and saw the water and painkillers and gingerly reached for them. She was never, ever drinking again. Everything hurt too much to think about, so she closed her eyes and went back to sleep.

When she woke again later, her head hurt a little less so she slowly rose from the bed. She had no idea what time it was, her eyes couldn't focus on the tiny numbers of her phone yet, so she gave up trying and had a shower instead.

Once she was showered and dressed in clothes that no longer had the faint smell of vomit lingering on them, she felt marginally better. She picked up her phone, stunned to realise it was almost six in the evening. A list of missed calls caught her attention, as did a text message. She closed her eyes in dismay when she saw Frankie's name.

He was texting her to tell her she was fired, she just knew it. She'd made a complete idiot of herself and probably embarrassed the company. She wanted to skim over the message but his name on the screen seemed to glare at her as though to say, *Don't you dare!* With a resigned sigh, she opened the message and braced herself for the worst.

Frankie: Just wanted to tell you I still had your flat key so I returned it. Wanted to check you were still alive. You were sleeping. Drink the water.

Alice's gaze flew around the room and there on the small table was her key. He'd been here while she was asleep? The glass of water had been refilled the second time she'd woken and she hadn't even thought anything of it.

She felt a moment of discomfort at the thought of him watching her while she slept . . . well, when she put it like *that* of course it sounded dodgy. He only said she'd been sleeping, that didn't mean he'd stood there watching her, and if she hadn't answered his phone calls and he'd just popped in to check she was alive and hadn't choked on vomit through the night, then it kind of felt . . . sweet.

A word that would *not* normally come to mind when thinking of Frankie Esquire.

Still, sweet or not, she was now mortified that her boss had seen her snoring like a drunken sailor. How on earth was she ever going to look him in the eye again at work? She let out a long groan. This was why they made all those awkward movies about getting drunk at Christmas work parties—so you didn't do it!

Before she could chicken out, she typed back, *Thank you, I've survived.* Then dumped her phone on the other side of the bed.

Then it rang and she froze, staring at it with a horrified expression. When she finally worked up the courage to pick up the phone and look at the screen, she let out a loud sigh and quickly answered.

'Verity! Hi.'

'I was just about to hang up, I thought you weren't going to answer.'

'Sorry, I was just . . . in the shower. How is everyone?'

As Alice settled in for a chat with her sister, she felt some of her earlier misery ebb away. She both loved and hated these calls from home. She loved hearing all the goss, but hated that when they said goodbye she missed everyone, all over again. She was pretty sure the entire family had made up some kind of roster to call, and she loved being able to pick who was calling just by what day and time it was. The calls had been an almost constant stream during the first month or so. Now, though, it wasn't as regimented and it was nice to get surprise calls just to catch up.

'Is something wrong, Al? You don't sound yourself,' Verity said.

'I went out last night to a Christmas party.'

'Oh. That's good. Meet anyone interesting?' Typical Verity, she always managed to ask that question on every phone call.

'No.'

'You know you really should try and get out a bit more. You've got this amazing opportunity—you're living in London,' she said, a note of envy lingering in her tone. 'Get out and have fun.'

'I don't need fun, I need to work. I didn't come over here to meet someone. I had a perfectly good someone back there,' Alice said a little more mournfully than she'd intended.

Her sister was quiet before saying softly, 'You know, I don't think you should be worrying about Finn.'

'What's that supposed to mean?' Alice asked hesitantly.

'Nothing . . . it's just that—' She paused, and Alice felt her stomach drop. 'Rick's seen him out a few times at the pub and he seems . . . like he's moved on. All I'm saying is, if you're holding back because you feel like you'd be betraying Finn—*don't*.'

'I see,' Alice managed, swallowing hard. 'Well, it's not because of Finn. I came here to work for a year and then I'm coming home. So there's no point looking for love when I'm not staying.'

'Okay,' Verity said, sounding as though she were forcing the cheeriness into her voice, 'you do you. Personally, I think you're crazy being single and carefree in London and not making the most of the experience.'

Alice cringed at the memory of the previous night. 'I tried the whole partying thing, but it doesn't agree with me,' she admitted.

'Are you hungover?' her sister asked slowly. 'Is that why you sound so seedy?' She chortled. 'Alice! I'm so proud of you.'

'Yeah, well, I'm not. It was horrible,' she said, and felt her lip tremble.

'Oh, come on, it can't have been that bad.'

'It was—Verity, I made a complete fool of myself.'

'Oh,' Verity soothed. 'Tell me what happened.'

'It was mortifying,' she said, closing her eyes tightly as she replayed various moments of the night again. 'I think I got up on stage and sang.'

'Oh, dear God. No,' her sister said with a small gasp.

'Thanks,' Alice retorted.

'As much as I love you, I have to say as a singer, you've always made a better seamstress.'

It was a sore point. Alice loved to sing—there was nothing better than turning up the radio and belting out a tune on a long car trip—but she'd been banned from doing it at any time other than when she was alone in her own car.

'Come on, if that's the worst of it, you're pretty safe. We've all done embarrassing things when we've had too much to drink.'

'My boss found me passed out, hugging an outdoor pot plant,' she said dully.

'Oh.'

'He had to bring me home and I was so drunk, I can't remember what I said to him.'

'Did anything happen?' Verity asked slowly.

'What do you mean?'

'You were alone with your boss, and you were drunk . . . did you two, you know . . . sleep together?'

'What! Are you serious? No. He's my boss, Verity.'

'Ah, sure . . . 'cause that's something that immediately makes the whole thing impossible.'

'Nothing like that happened. He was very chivalrous.'

'I thought you couldn't remember anything?'

'That, I remember.' Her sister went silent once more and Alice gave an impatient huff. 'Nothing happened.'

'Okay, I believe you. I'm sure everything will be fine. It's not like he hasn't partied too hard once or twice. He probably hasn't thought another thing about it. Just go into work tomorrow like nothing happened. It'll be fine. Everyone will be too distracted by Christmas to even remember what happened.'

God, she hoped her sister was right. She only had two more days to get through then everyone would be going away for their Christmas break—and she'd be wallowing in self-pity all over again.

No. Stop it, she told herself firmly. *Feeling sorry for yourself was how this all started.* She was going to embrace the Christmas spirit, damn it! And have the merriest bloody Christmas ever!

Alone.

Chapter 19

Alice got off the tube on Monday morning, recalling what Verity had said: nobody would remember, none of them were even there at the messy end, so her humiliation was safe from the general office population. She'd deal with Frankie later.

She walked with a determined stride through security, smiling at the guards and trying not to worry that they didn't look her in the eye as they usually did. *They're busy. It's almost Christmas and everyone's in a rush.*

She waited for the elevator and stepped inside, giving a small smile to the two women already in there, who blinked back at her before swapping a look and giggling.

Stay calm, they were probably just recalling a shared joke. It's all in your head.

As she stepped out into the office, Alice felt her heart drop. She was not imagining it. Something was definitely going on. People were staring at her.

Adel swooped in and hooked her arm through hers, detouring them out into the empty stairwell.

'What on earth is going on?' Alice demanded, unable to stop the fear quivering in her voice. She was only seconds away from hyperventilating.

'I tried to call you this morning,' Adel said.

'I had my phone on silent.'

'Perhaps not the best day for that,' Adel said with a sigh, studying Alice's panicked face in silence for a moment before thrusting her phone towards her. 'Here. You best look at this.'

Alice searched her friend's gaze warily, knowing that whatever she was about to see, wasn't going to be good. Hesitantly, she took the phone. A headline on an online newsfeed made her stomach churn alarmingly.

FRANKIE ESQUIRE, CAUGHT SLUMMING IT.

FRANKIE ESQUIRE EXPOSED.

FROM SUPERMODEL TO LADY OF THE NIGHT?

As she scrolled through, the headlines got worse. She gasped at the photo of Frankie holding her as they got into his car and another taken in the hotel lobby, where it looked like they were gazing into each other's eyes in an intimate embrace. The fact that she'd just stumbled in the ridiculous stilettos Adel had lent her and Frankie had only barely managed to catch her before she face-planted the carpet didn't seem to get a mention.

But then there were the images of Frankie with the blonde he'd arrived with, looking sleek and sexy, beside a photo of Alice, her hair dishevelled and dress rumpled, as she and Frankie walked from the courtyard into the lobby, looking for all the world as though they'd just had some very serious, very outdoor sex.

For all the world . . . Oh. Dear. God. Her parents were going to see this! She felt the colour drain from her face.

'It wasn't like that!' she cried. 'I was drunk. Frankie made sure I got home. Nothing happened.'

'I believe you,' Adel said, putting a hand on Alice's arm. 'Unfortunately, the paparazzi don't care about context.'

Tears welled up in Alice's eyes. This was worse than anything she'd been expecting.

The only good thing seemed to be that none of the papers knew who she was, mentioning her only as 'the mystery woman' or implying that she was some kind of hooker. But it would only be a matter of time before someone told them her name.

'I have to call my parents. I can't let them find out like this.'

'That might be a good idea. I'll wait inside. You don't have to go back in there alone.'

'Thank you, Adel.'

'We'll get through this. It'll all blow over in no time,' Adel said encouragingly, but Alice didn't care about that—she just needed to figure out how to get through the day.

She dialled her parents' number then hung up before they could answer. What was she going to say? *Hi Mum and Dad, don't be alarmed when you see photos of me on the internet looking like some strumpet my boss picked up off the street. I was just drunk.* She closed her eyes and rested her head against the cold wall of the stairwell. This sucked so bad.

Straightening, she scrolled through her contacts and called the only person she knew she could call.

'Gran. It's me,' Alice said, then her voice cracked and she broke into a sob. 'Gran, something awful has happened.'

'Alice? Darling, take a breath and calm down. Now tell me what's going on.'

Alice blurted out the whole sorry tale, hiccuping at the end, 'Everyone thinks I . . . that we . . . slept together. Gran, I don't know what to do.'

'Now you listen to me,' Gran said firmly. 'You're going to walk back into that office with your head held high and your shoulders back. You have nothing to be ashamed of. You know the truth; it doesn't matter what anyone else thinks.'

'They think I'm a hooker, Gran!'

'Well, are you?'

'Of course not,' she said, momentarily stunned by the question.

'Right. Then they don't know anything, do they? Anyone who knows you will know that this is all just a bunch of—' Gran seemed to flounder as she tried to find a word bad enough. 'Sensationalism,' she said, coldly. 'I dare anyone to look me up and ask my opinion about all this . . . I'll give them such a serve they'll need to put ice on their ears!'

Alice sniffed through a small chuckle. 'I don't know what to say to Mum and Dad.'

'Leave your parents to me. I'll explain everything. Now, you just get back to your day. Remember, you're a Croydon and you are amazing. I love you.'

'I love you too, Gran,' she said, and felt the burn of fresh tears. She wanted to go home and feel one of Gran's tight hugs.

'Off you go. Wipe those tears away and hold that head up high.'

'Okay,' she said, taking a deep breath and doing as she was told. She had this.

Alice pushed open the stairwell door and walked into the office, ready to take on the world just as a loud voice boomed, 'Croydon. My office. Now.'

Shit.

Alice closed her eyes briefly, summoning her inner Gran, but felt even less than inadequate as everyone stopped working to stare at her. Just great.

Gritting her teeth, she walked through the sea of speculation and into Frankie's office.

'Close the door,' he said.

'I'd rather leave it open if you don't mind . . . you know, in case someone thinks I'm about to have sex with you on your desk or something,' she whispered harshly.

'Shut the bloody door, Croydon,' he all but growled and Alice bit back a mutinous sigh before following his instruction.

The room seemed unusually claustrophobic.

'I tried to call you this morning,' he said. 'I wanted to warn you to stay home.'

Note to self. Never put the stupid phone on silent again. 'Stay home? Why?'

'To avoid all this,' he said, nodding towards the office outside.

'And that wouldn't look suspicious at all. I haven't—we haven't,' she corrected, 'done anything wrong.'

'It doesn't matter. The tabloids have gotten hold of this and now we just have to ride out the storm.'

'Or,' she said, 'you could just tell them the truth.'

'They don't care about the truth,' he said bitterly. 'They'd only turn it around and make a bigger story about it. Trust me—I've been through all this before. Besides, I've got my PR team working on this.'

'So you're just going to—what? Let them say things that aren't true? You're not even going to try and defend your-self . . . or *me*?'

'They're not interested in you—you're not the story here. I am.'

'I kind of feel like I'm part of the story.'

'Trust me, this is all just an attempt to stir up some gossip about Gigi and myself. It's got nothing to do with you.'

'Who the hell is Gigi?'

'Apparently my current significant other, who I cheated on with you.'

'"Apparently"? The woman you were with at the party?'

'Yes. The woman I've only dated a handful of times over the last few months. The woman who's conveniently about to launch a new line of perfume and lingerie,' he said dryly. 'This whole scandal will do wonders for her sales.'

'Are you saying she was behind this?'

'Who knows? It's certainly good timing for her . . . And she was a little upset with me that night.'

'Why?'

'All you need to do is go home and lie low until this blows over.'

'But I didn't do anything wrong! Why am I being suspended?'

'You're not being suspended,' he said, rubbing the bridge of his nose with his fingers. For the first time since coming into Frankie's office, Alice noticed how drawn and tired he looked. 'I'm doing you a favour. I'm trying to look out for your interests. Trust me. They won't bother you if they can't find you. So go home and stay there.'

'This is unbelievable,' Alice fumed, standing up and storming to the door. 'I'm being sent to my room for my own good like I'm a *child*.'

'You're acting like one,' he snapped.

'You'd know!' she threw back at him angrily, before opening the door and walking out, not even caring that she sounded like a disgruntled six-year-old.

She kept her eyes straight ahead as she left the office and strode to the elevator, where she jabbed the down button. As the doors slid open in the foyer and she went to walk out, a uniformed man in a driver's cap stepped in front of her and gave a small bow.

'Miss if you'd follow me, Mr Esquire has asked me to drive you home,' he said in that impeccable English accent she found endearing. Usually. Not so much today.

'Thank you, but I'm fine,' she said with a tight smile.

'Mr Esquire was quite adamant,' he said, then nodded his silver-haired head towards the front doors of the building, where a mob of reporters had begun to congregate.

Damn it.

'Fine,' Alice reluctantly agreed, deciding that in this case discretion may actually be the better part of valour. She followed the driver through a door leading to a narrow hallway that came out at the loading docks at the rear of the building.

Inside the car, Alice sat back and fumed. This was ridiculous. She felt as though she was being hunted down like some criminal, forced to dodge reporters and *lie low*. Like this was some really bad TV cop show.

Her phone rang and she groaned as Frankie's name came up on the screen. 'What now? I'm in the bloody car you sent.'

'Change of plans. You can't go home.'

'What?'

'The reporters found your name. They're camped out in front of your flat. I've instructed René to drive you to a safe place.'

She remained silent and he let out a long breath. 'I'm sorry this is happening, Alice. I really am. This is my fault and I'm trying to fix it. Just let me do what needs to be done, okay?'

'But I don't have any clothes,' she said, suddenly overcome by fatigue, all the fight leaving her as the implications of the morning finally sank in.

'I'll send someone over to collect a few things and deliver them to you. Leave your key with René.' He paused and when he spoke again Alice heard the weariness in his voice. 'Everything will be all right.'

The call disconnected and Alice stared at her phone, mutely. Why hadn't she just stayed at home that night? None of this would be happening if she hadn't decided to cave in to peer pressure from Adel and go to that stupid party. Idiot.

Chapter 20

She watched the city pass by as they weaved their way through traffic and headed out into the countryside. Where the hell was this place? She suddenly questioned the wisdom of allowing Frankie to handle everything. Just as she was getting ready to call triple nine and report a kidnapping, the car turned into a narrow laneway and pulled up in front of a neatly manicured hedge.

'Here you go, Miss. I believe Mr Esquire mentioned leaving me your house key?'

'Oh. Yeah. Here you go,' she said, handing him a key then getting out. They'd arrived at a little house, which actually wasn't all that little, tucked in behind a cottage garden on the other side of a moss-covered stone wall.

'The door's unlocked and Mr Esquire said to make yourself at home. I believe he has arranged to have something for you to eat set out.'

'He's thought of everything.'

'He does like things to be just so,' René agreed with a smile.

'Thank you, for the lift,' she said, fluttering a hand by her side nervously. Or whatever his job had been. He seemed to be waiting for her to move, so she turned towards the house and walked up the cobblestone path.

Inside, Alice looked around the tastefully decorated house curiously. It didn't look anything like the man who owned it. The furniture seemed new but comfy and the colour scheme was lighter and calmer than the slate greys and blood-red shades in his apartment, which she'd seen featured in glossy magazines that displayed spreads of Frankie lounging about in modern, stylish surrounds, with expensive artwork on the walls behind him and luxury furniture, the kind that looked far too uncomfortable for any sane person to actually use.

She made her way to the rear of the house, which opened onto a large walled garden with rolling fields beyond. As promised, there was a note on the table informing her that a plate of sandwiches and fresh fruit had been placed in the fridge and that freshly brewed coffee was on the counter. Alice felt her stomach grumble and realised she'd skipped breakfast and had eaten very little the day before due to sleeping off her hangover.

She took the sandwiches and fruit to the small table by the window and sat down to eat. It was cold, the grey skies hanging low, and she wondered if maybe it would snow soon. She'd been warned that sometimes they didn't get snow right on Christmas as all the Hallmark Christmas cards liked to suggest, but she wasn't going to give up on the idea completely. Surely when it was this cold it *had* to snow? If anything could take the sting out of spending Christmas alone, it would be snow.

Her phone dinged and she spent the rest of the day answering texts and trying to reassure her family that she was fine. So far no one had contacted them for a comment, and she prayed they wouldn't—for their own safety. When someone went after one Croydon they took on the whole family.

It was late afternoon when Alice heard a car pull up. She crossed to the window to see Frankie walking up the front path. A cold gust of air followed him through the door.

'I hope you've found everything you need,' he said, taking off his coat and placing an overnight bag on the floor. 'I had Adel pack you a few things. Hopefully you won't need them for long.'

'Is it still crazy out there?' she asked, wrapping her arms around herself.

'Yep. I've had people looking into this debacle all day and it appears it may have been a publicity stunt after all.'

'So Gigi was behind it?'

'Or her publicity team. Word has it that she's given an interview to a major newspaper, so I expect we'll be hearing about that tomorrow.'

'What on earth did she stand to gain?'

Frankie shrugged. 'Publicity, with a side of malice.'

When Alice frowned, he gave a small shake of his head. 'She wasn't happy about going home early from the function the other night. It seems she had big plans to make an appearance at a private party I was supposed to take her to, where she was planning to reveal her new perfume line. I guess she decided I owed her.'

'You seriously need to start looking at the kind of friends you make,' Alice said, then realised that, prior to today, she would have been horrified at herself for speaking so bluntly to her boss. However, after being caught up in his crazy ex-girlfriend's diabolical plans of world domination, she figured she had the right to be a little snippety.

'I'm starting to agree with you there,' he murmured with a brief, bitter smile. 'I *am* sorry that you were dragged into this though.'

'It's not your fault,' she eventually said. 'And I am grateful for everything you've done today. In case I've come across a little . . .'

'Ungracious. Stubborn,' he supplied helpfully.

'Well, fair suck of the sav,' she said, 'this was the last thing I expected to walk into today. I think I deserve to be a little put out by it all.'

'Fair suck of the sav?' he repeated, then laughed. 'I haven't heard that in years.'

She felt her lips twitch a little in response to the way his face lit up when he smiled—a real, honest-to-God smile. 'My grandad says that all the time.'

'Mine too.' He grinned and wiped the corner of his eye with one large finger. 'Sometimes the past creeps up on me, you know. I've spent so long creating a new me that now and again something happens and there I am again, a scrawny kid playing out on the street, without a care in the world. Catches me unawares.'

'Surely you don't have to erase all your past just to be you?'

'I do,' he said, sounding sad. 'Otherwise, it leaves room for the bad things to come through.'

Now knowing a little bit of what his childhood had been like, she understood his need as an adult to recreate his entire self. Part of her wanted to continue talking about it—but the moment stretched on too long and the opportunity was lost.

'This place doesn't really seem like you,' she said eventually, as he took a seat on the comfy sofa.

'You think?' he asked, blunting the sarcasm with a smile.

'This *isn't* your house?'

'My assistant booked this place. She figured no one would think of looking for me here.'

'So you're staying here too?'

'We'll be having a meeting with Siobhan from my PR firm soon to figure out the best strategy to handle the fallout, so it makes sense we're both in the same place. It does have five bedrooms. I can promise I'll stay at the other end of the house if you're worried.'

'I'm not . . . Of course I'm not worried,' she said, suddenly feeling stupid. She was the one gate crashing, after all.

'I like your new look,' he said, abruptly changing the subject.

Alice sent him a confused glance.

'Your hair,' he said, and Alice lightly touched one of the wavy strands. Her wardrobe had also taken on a more stylish look to fit in with the people she dealt with on a daily basis. She'd always paid close attention to dressing for the boutique when she worked there; Antoinette had been strict about presentation and taught her that she should not outshine the clothing they were selling but portray a tidy, flawless look. Here, she'd realised, she could be herself. Maybe it'd been an act of rebellion, but recently she'd spent an obscene amount of money undergoing a hairstyle makeover. Her long, brownie-red locks had been turned into glossy copper waves with highlights in a delicious tone of iced pumpkin spice. Her hairdresser gave her a new, sexier side part and Alice loved the way her hair now fell in a gentle asymmetrical style that framed her face. 'Thanks. I thought it was time for a bit of a change.'

'It suits you.'

A van pulled up outside and Alice immediately forgot about the conversation and sent him a wary glance.

'I've ordered a catering service to stop by and handle dinner.'

'I thought you were trying to keep a low profile? Won't a catering service draw unwanted attention?'

'Not for the places around here,' he said without any kind of concern. 'How about we go for a walk and let them set up?'

Getting out in the fresh air sounded like exactly what she needed. As they stepped outside the back door and the cold air hit her face, she felt some of the day's stress blow away. They followed a walking track that wound its way along a little brook and the edge of a wood that hid the house from the road.

'I can't get over how green and beautiful everything is over here,' she said.

'It is, I guess, compared to where you're from,' he said. 'Have you lived out there all your life?'

'Yep. Born and bred in Gunnindi.'

'You miss it,' he said, and she wondered at the way he'd said it more as a statement than a question.

'Yeah, I do. I know it isn't pretty like this place, but there's still beauty in those wide-open spaces. And it's not always as dry and brown as it was when you saw it,' she said. 'When we get rain, everything turns green and comes to life. Maybe not this green. But it's my family I miss the most. I've never really been away from them all for this long before.'

'What about your fiancé?' he asked after a pause as they navigated a fallen log.

'We broke up.'

'I'm sorry to hear that.'

'I doubt that,' she said bluntly, then regretted it. It wasn't fair to place the blame for her break-up solely at Frankie's feet and yet it was true that, had he not come along that day, she'd have been married by now. A small part of her *did* blame him, wrongly or rightly; it was just how she felt sometimes.

'What's that supposed to mean?'

There's no point in backtracking now. 'You knew I was supposed to be getting married when you came to look at my wedding dress and made me this job offer. If you were really sorry, you wouldn't have offered me the job.'

'That's not true. I offered you the job because you have talent that was going to waste out there. I didn't intend to ruin your relationship. I'm not even sure why it did. He could have come over with you. Surely there could have been a way of working it out?'

'He's a farmer. His life is back in Gunnindi,' she said.

'But you miss him.'

'Yeah. I do. We were together for nine years. Love doesn't just turn off like a light switch.'

'And yet he let you walk away?'

'I tried to tell him it wouldn't change anything, but he didn't agree. I guess everything will be different once I go back,' she said, more to herself than to Frankie.

'So you plan on going home.'

'This job was for a one-year contract.'

'To start with. The sky is the limit if you work hard and want it badly enough. I'm not putting any time frame on it, if that's what you're worried about.'

'It's not. I wanted the experience and a chance to learn under the best in the business,' she said. 'After that, I'm happy to go home and see what happens.'

He stopped abruptly and she turned, surprised to find him staring at her with a hard-to-read expression on his face. 'You seriously believe you'll get this thing out of your system after a year and be content to return home to be some farmer's housewife?'

His tightly controlled anger made her cautious. 'I have a few plans I'd like to explore, and I don't know what will happen once I go back,' she replied, trying to force some confidence into her words. 'But the original plan was to only be here a year.'

'So, everything you learn over here, every opportunity I give you, it's all going to just get thrown away once your internship is up?'

'I didn't say that.'

'Why should I even waste my time on you then?'

'Because you said you'd give me a year,' she said, straightening her shoulders.

'That's when I assumed you'd continue to use your skills.'

'Who says I won't? I don't have to be in the UK to make something of myself.'

'Of course you do,' he said dismissively.

'*You* didn't,' she said, placing her hands on her hips.

'I admit I made my start in Australia, but that's nothing to what I managed to create over here. If you want to be the best in the business, this is where you have to be.'

'I don't want to be the best. I want to design and create. I don't need to build an empire. I'm not interested in all that other stuff.'

'"All that other stuff" is what happens once you create your own label. It comes with the territory.'

'That's not who I am.'

'It can be,' he said, holding her gaze. 'I don't think you realise your full potential.'

'Then I guess that's what you're here for. Nothing you teach me will go to waste,' she promised. 'I have plans of my own. They're just not as big as yours.'

'What plans?' he asked in an abrupt tone that sounded more like a challenge than a question.

'I still want to release a full collection made from wool—I want to source Gunnindi wool.' She hesitated slightly before adding almost tentatively, 'Maybe process it all locally as well.' The idea had been brewing quietly. During her research for the wool collection, she'd been thinking about it a lot.

'That's a pretty ambitious plan.'

'It is.'

'Do you really think you can do that without the backing of a company like mine?'

God she hated that self-assured attitude of his. Even when he was right—*especially* when he was right. 'Probably not as easily, but I've been researching the idea and there have been a lot of small communities who've managed to get bigger projects than this up and running in the past. Anyway,' she added, straightening her shoulders again and tilting her head slightly to hold his gaze, 'you turned down my collection.'

'I turned down the lines that didn't reflect my consumer base. I didn't say it was something I wouldn't look at further down the track.'

'You didn't exactly say you would, either.' She'd have remembered something like that.

'I like the idea of promoting Australian-grown and -produced wool. However, I'd like to take it further than just Gunnindi wool,' he said.

'What do you mean?'

'I'd like to invest in a number of different communities to get quality products and industries up and running. I'm a big supporter of Australian produce. I think the idea of yours holds a lot of merit, but you'd need a partner with the kind of industry contacts to get the product on the world stage.'

'That's you, I take it?'

'I'm just pointing out the realities of your situation. If you think heading home with a year of experience under your belt is all you'll need to get a project like the one you're talking about up and running, then I think you're going to be sadly disappointed. You have a big future ahead of you, Alice, but I fear if you go back too soon your talents will be wasted.'

'Then I guess I'll have to work harder to prove you wrong,' she said quietly as they headed back to the house, slightly subdued. Stay more than a year? How would she do that? She already missed her family more than she thought possible. The idea of not returning home just seemed so . . . not her.

By the time they reached the house, the van was gone. Alice let out a small gasp of surprise.

In the front window stood a fully decorated tree, complete with twinkling lights.

She let out a delighted laugh, clasping her hands together excitedly and turning to Frankie.

'I take it you approve?' he asked, as they stepped inside.

'It's beautiful.'

'It was the least I could do since I was taking you out of your place for Christmas. I figured you'd like a tree, at least.'

'You didn't have to do this.'

'I wanted to. And you're right, maybe I needed a bit of Christmas spirit too.'

The meal was divine, and they ate at the dining room table, which had been set like something out of a five-star restaurant. Even Alice, a complete wine-tasting novice, knew the wine had probably cost more than an average person's monthly income.

'I would have been happy with toasted sandwiches,' she said, sitting on the lounge after, feeling full and relaxed.

'Now you tell me,' Frankie said with a lazy smile. He seemed like a different person from the man she saw in charge at the office each day.

'I can't believe it's Christmas Eve tomorrow,' Alice said with a small sigh, her thoughts turning to her family and what she'd be missing.

'What would you be doing if you were back in Gunnindi?' he asked, and she looked at him in surprise. Could the man also read her thoughts? God, she hoped not. She'd been admiring the way his shirt fitted his torso earlier when he'd come down to dinner.

'I'd be at my parents' place,' she said. 'The whole street sets out fold-up chairs in their front yards and hands out lollies to all the passing cars as they drive around looking at Christmas lights.' She'd always looked forward to Christmas Eve, it was such a fun night. A hollow pain burned inside her chest and, to her horror, tears stung her eyes. She swiped her eyes and blinked rapidly. 'Sorry. It caught me a little off guard.'

'You've had a lot going on. I'm sorry you got caught up in all this, Alice.' His voice wasn't the usual clipped version he used around the office, this one was softer and somehow deeper. Alice looked up at him and her breath caught at the expression in his slightly hooded eyes.

'I shouldn't have been drinking that night.'

'It was a party.'

'I was feeling sorry for myself,' she corrected with a small wince.

'I'm sorry you miss your family. And I'm sorry I can't make that any easier for you.'

'You have actually,' she said a small smile tugging at her lips. 'You usually keep me working so hard I barely have time to miss them.'

'Clearly I shouldn't have allowed you a night off then,' he said and that lazy smile he so rarely showed had her pulse doing a stupid little two-step.

It was while she was trying to figure out *how* he managed to have this effect on her that she realised they'd both been studying each other quietly. The silence was suddenly as taut as a stretched rubber band quivering under the pressure of being strained so tightly.

'There's something about you, Alice Croydon,' he said in almost a murmur as he searched her face as though trying to find an answer to a question he wasn't quite sure of.

His fingers lightly touched her cheek and she saw his eyes darken. She'd always been fascinated by his eyes but had never really had the chance to examine them up close. They were what would generally be called hazel, but were a light green colour like bright moss around the edges with a darker, chocolate brown ring around the centre. Up close, that brown seemed to darken even more.

'You have the prettiest eyes,' she said, meaning to only say it to herself but realising too late she'd said it out loud when the corners of his eyes crinkled and she heard his soft chuckle. The warmth of his breath touched her skin. Her eyes fluttered shut as she tilted her head back slightly, the hum of the wine they'd shared earlier still running through her veins, dulling her common sense but heightening her emotions. She wondered what it would feel like to be kissed by Frankie, moments before his mouth touched hers, only to feel . . . nothing.

Her eyes popped open. Frankie had pulled away and was getting to his feet.

Alice swallowed her disappointment then frowned. She hadn't been looking forward to being kissed by her boss. That would have been . . . wrong. And very, very bad.

'Goodnight Alice,' he said, as she tucked her hair behind her ear and smoothed down her top.

'Goodnight,' she said, before hurrying to her room and closing the door. What was that? Had she really just been moments away from kissing her boss, until he'd had the good sense to stop before it actually happened? How were they supposed to act tomorrow in the harsh light of day?

Christmas Eve dawned even colder. Alice forced herself out of her room. Any awkward encounters were temporarily forgotten as she found Frankie on the phone in the kitchen, tearing shreds off someone. She skidded to a halt just inside the door and was about to beat a hasty retreat when he looked up and saw her. Too late to make her escape, she tiptoed instead to the coffee pot and made herself a strong coffee. Something told her she was going to need it.

She cringed at the parting farewell that had Frankie suggesting something she was fairly sure was anatomically impossible and gingerly held the coffee pot up as a peace offering.

'Yes,' he said. 'Please,' he tacked on almost bitterly.

'Dare I ask?'

'Probably best not to,' he said, still sounding furious, so instead she handed him the coffee, glancing at the newspaper on the table as she did so.

SUPERMODEL CLAIMS SEXUAL HARASSMENT AGAINST FASHION GURU, FRANKIE ESQUIRE.

'What?' Alice exploded, picking up the newspaper and peering at it. 'You have to be kidding me.'

'I wish I was,' Frankie said, sitting at the table, folding his arms in front of him and staring into his coffee.

'It's not saying she's actually pressing any charges . . . so— what? She's allowed to just say stuff like this about someone? This was her big bombshell interview?'

'Yep.'

All thoughts of the night before vanished. 'Surely *now* you're going to do something? Right?'

'I've got my legal team on it.'

'She *cannot* get away with this crap,' Alice said, outraged on Frankie's behalf.

When he didn't make any comment she looked up and found him watching her thoughtfully. 'What?' she asked self-consciously.

'You didn't ask if they were true, the claims she's making in the interview,' he said.

'Of course they're not. As if you'd need to even do any of the things she says in this piece of . . . gobbledygook.' She almost spat the word.

'I'm not even sure if that's actually a compliment or not.'

'It's the *truth*,' she clarified. 'I mean, clearly you're *a man*, and that goes a long way in explaining why you'd want to date someone like Gigi in the first place—I mean, she's beautiful and obviously very ambitious,' she pointed out as his eyebrows raised slightly. 'But she needed *you* more than you need her. You could have any supermodel in the world—and by all accounts, you have,' she added dryly, '—so it makes no sense that you'd try and blackmail her then force her, a barely up-and-coming superstar, to endorse your clothing line when you could have any A-list celebrity on the whole planet to do it . . . probably as a favour.'

'Thanks . . . I think.'

'Besides, she's already proven she's a lying, conniving little—'

His phone rang, cutting off further commentary. He sent her an amused glance as he answered, which soon turned serious as he settled in for another round of angry exchanges.

Alice headed outside to give him some privacy, shrugging into her warm coat as she shut the door behind her. She walked down to the seat tucked away in the garden and sat to go through her messages and return a missed call from Daisy, who she'd been playing phone tag with for the last few days.

'Hey, sis, how are you holding up?' her older sister asked when she answered.

'Yeah, I'm okay. I think my part in the whole drama has fizzled out, thank goodness. Poor Frankie is still copping it though. She's a nasty piece of work, this Gigi woman.'

'Listen, Al . . . there's something I wanted to talk to you about.'

'What is it?' she asked, already sensing this was going to be one more thing she didn't need at the moment.

'It's about Finn.'

'Is he okay? Has something happened?' Her mind was already running through a variety of scenarios—everything from a tractor rollover to a car accident.

'No, no, it's nothing like that, he's fine . . . It's just that, well, he's kinda . . . married.'

'Kinda *married*?' Alice asked weakly.

'No, definitely married.'

Finn was married? Alice put a palm to her forehead to ease the sudden pounding that had started as she tried to process the news. Surely she had to be hearing this all wrong?

'I don't understand. Who to? When did it happen?'

'Apparently he's been seeing Shelly Turnbull for a while now. Then last week he went away for a few days and came back . . . married.'

'Verity mentioned he'd been going to the pub a bit lately. I thought he was just blowing off steam and hanging out with his mates.'

'I think Verity was trying to lead in to telling you about what was going on. She probably didn't expect him to run off and marry her this quick. We only found out yesterday.' Alice could picture her sister screwing her face up in a sympathetic expression and knew this must have been a hard call to make.

'Thank you for telling me,' Alice managed. She was not going to cry. She and Finn weren't together, he didn't owe her anything . . . Only, deep down, she believed he really did. How could he just throw away all that history to marry someone he'd known five minutes?

'I'm so sorry to tell you after everything else you've been through, but I was just worried you might see it on Facebook or something before we had a chance to warn you.'

'No. it's fine . . . really. I'm glad you told me.' In all honesty, Alice wished she didn't know. She just wanted to bury her head in the sand and pretend everything was all right and nothing had changed. But everything *had* changed.

The future she'd been dreaming about after everything she'd sacrificed was never going to eventuate.

Finn was gone.

And now she had no idea where she was headed.

'Why do I feel like this is some kind of déjà vu,' Frankie drawled as he came out to find her drinking from a bottle of wine she'd found in the fridge.

'It's okay, you don't need to play my knight in shining armour this time. I can get myself to bed,' she told him, taking another swig.

'You don't think it's a bit early for wine?'

'Nope.'

'Want to tell me why you feel the need to be drinking wine before ten am?'

'Nope.'

'Okay,' he said slowly, taking a seat beside her on the bench and settling back.

'I don't need babysitting.'

'I'm just sitting on a bench minding my own business.'

'Don't you have some crisis or other to go sort out?'

'I'm fairly sure I've dealt with enough of those for one morning.'

'God, it's freezing out here,' Alice said as a cold blast blew across the yard. 'You don't even have a jacket on. Go inside.'

'Not until you tell me what's going on.'

'You'll die of hypothermia or something,' she said, then muttered, 'and I'll be on the front page of the newspaper, *again*, being blamed for your death.'

'Then tell me what's wrong.'

'I just rang my sister, who informed me that my fiancé— ex-fiancé,' she amended grudgingly—'has just gotten married. Merry bloody Christmas, Alice.' She toasted herself with the bottle of wine before taking a long sip.

'That sucks,' he said.

'It does actually.' She sniffed, wiping at her eyes angrily. 'I have no idea what I'm going to do now.'

'Why do you have to *do* anything? You just keep on working and doing what you came here to do. Nothing has changed.'

'Everything has changed,' she wailed, turning to face him. 'All he had to do was wait one lousy year. Now he's gone and I have nothing to go back for. This wasn't my plan!'

'I'm sorry to break it to you, princess, but life has a way of screwing up even the best-laid plans and if it's taken this long for you to get burned by it, then you've done pretty well.'

'You're no help!' she snapped, getting to her feet and swaying slightly. She leaned down in front of him, her thumb and forefinger held apart a tiny fraction. 'Is it too much to ask for just a tiny bit of sympathy?'

'Sympathy won't change anything,' he said. 'The only way to make things better is to take charge of your own destiny and work for it.'

Alice took a step back as he stood up, the heady scent of his expensive cologne filling her senses.

'Your fiancé did you a favour. He cleared the path for you to do what you were put here to do. So make it count.'

For a long moment, Alice felt trapped in Frankie's gaze, held in place by some invisible force, until he took a step away and the spell was broken, leaving Alice to stare after him as he trudged back to the house and she was left alone with the wind nipping at her nose, chilling the trail of tears that ran down her face.

❖

'Merry Christmas,' Alice said, putting on a brave face as the video panned around and captured her family, gathered around the table at her parents' house. It was Christmas morning in the UK and Christmas evening back home, where her family had been waiting for her to wake up so they could call her.

She waved at her nieces and nephews. 'Look at all those gorgeous faces. Gosh, I miss you guys.'

'We miss you, Aunty Alice,' Teagan, Toby and Cicily's daughter, said, and that was followed by a chorus of more *we miss you*s that was almost her undoing. She found out what they all got for Christmas and was taken for a walk by Max, Charlie's two-year-old, when he took off with the phone, causing an impromptu game of chaseys as they tried to get the phone back before he disconnected the call.

By the time she'd spoken to everyone, it was time to go, so they could finish their Christmas dinner.

When she hung up, Alice felt drained from keeping a smile on her face despite the fact her heart felt battered, bruised and broken all over again. She should just stay in bed—go back to sleep and wait the whole day out. But it was Christmas. With a drawn-out sigh, Alice got up and headed for the kitchen to make coffee.

The day before had been a disaster. Although she hadn't finished the bottle of wine, she'd drunk enough and cried enough to make her sleepy and had napped for a solid three hours, waking in the afternoon to find a note from Frankie informing her he'd gone to a meeting and wasn't sure when he'd be back. Her mind fleetingly went to that near kiss and she wondered if maybe that had something to do with the fact he'd left without saying goodbye in person. Then she abruptly dismissed the idea. A man like Frankie Esquire wouldn't flee into the night over something as simple as a kiss—and he certainly wouldn't have lost any sleep over it. His departure was more likely to do with the most recent drama in the Gigi saga. She decided to put the whole kiss thing out of her mind for her own sanity.

In the living room, she stopped and admired the beautifully decorated Christmas tree with its twinkling little lights and shiny baubles, feeling a tiny flicker of something happy unfurling inside her. Beneath the tree, there was something that hadn't been there the previous day—presents. Or to be more exact, the presents that had been under her tree in her flat.

She dragged the first brightly coloured package towards her and smiled as she unwrapped it, discovering a bounty of items she'd been craving ever since leaving Australia, including chocolate, Tim Tams, Vegemite and a huge tin of Milo.

Another package revealed her siblings had all put in and sent a gorgeous charm bracelet with all her nieces' and nephews' names made into tiny charms. The gift brought on a fresh wave of homesickness, and she clasped the bracelet tightly to her chest as she blinked back tears.

There was another present, one she hadn't seen before, no bigger than the palm of her hand. She hesitated before picking it up. Her name was written on the card. *To Alice, from Santa.* She smiled a little, recognising Frankie's handwriting.

Carefully, she tugged at the ribbon and opened the wrapping paper to find a jewellery box. As she opened the lid, her breath caught at the sight of the delicate gold chain with a small, incredibly intricate ship's wheel attached. There was another handwritten note inside: *Be your own captain. Steer your own ship. The waters ahead are uncharted, waiting to be discovered.*

Alice stared at the beautiful chain for a few moments, touched by the sentiment. Her boss was one of a kind, there was no doubt about it. His message was clear: her plans had changed and she was now living without a map. What she decided to do about it was up to her.

Chapter 21

'Boss man wants to see you,' Adel said on her way past Alice's desk. 'He's been on the war path most of the day.'

'Oh, joy.' It had been a while since Alice had been called into Frankie's office. She'd hardly seen him since the Gigi fiasco and Christmas, and even then it was usually only in a meeting or around the office. She'd be lying if she said she wasn't a bit confused by his sudden turnabout. She'd thought they'd become friends, or at least a version of that, after their time in the cottage, but once they were back in the office, he'd retreated. She knew, of course, he'd had a lot to deal with and the tabloids had continued to circle and torment him with Gigi's bombshell interview, but still, she couldn't help but wonder how he could give her such a thoughtful gift one day and then treat her like just some employee the next.

You are *his employee*, she reminded herself blandly. Which was true, and yet . . . No. There was no point going round in circles about it all. She didn't have the time or the energy to try and figure out a complicated man and whatever his issues may be.

She knocked on the door and stepped inside when he called for her to come in.

'You wanted to see me?'

When Frankie looked up he seemed weary, as though he'd forgotten he'd been the one to call her in. 'Sorry. I was distracted,' he said and the softer tone caught Alice by surprise.

'You look tired,' she said, almost automatically.

He seemed surprised by her observation, staring at her silently for a moment before giving a short, bitter laugh and rubbing a hand across his face. 'Is that your Alice way of politely saying I look like shit?'

'No, of course not. You look great . . . as always,' Alice blurted, then wished she could take back the stupid words but found herself continuing to babble. 'You always look good . . . I mean, you know . . . in a fashionable way, of course . . . not in a—I mean, I wasn't implying . . . that I took notice of you or anything . . . you know in a pervy kind of way or anything.' *Shut the hell up!*

'Alice,' Frankie said, sitting back in his chair as she dug herself into a hole. 'I was joking. It's okay. And yes, as you so rightly pointed out, I am tired. But that's not why I called you in here.' He leaned forward and reached for an envelope on his desk. 'I wanted to give this to you. Make yourself available.'

She eyed the gold engraved lettering on the front of the envelope and gaped as the esteemed award's logo caught her eye. 'Oh my God,' she whispered. 'The Belagottis?' She glanced up and saw a small smile on his lips. The Belagottis were only *the* most prestigious event on the fashion world's calendar. She trembled slightly as she opened the envelope and pulled out an invitation.

'I want you to design something to wear.'

Alice blinked. 'I don't understand.'

'You're coming along and I want you to design something for you to wear.'

'Me? Why?'

'You don't want to go to the Belagottis?' he asked and lifted an eyebrow.

'Of course I do,' she breathed, her heart beating erratically just at the thought. 'But I don't understand *why*.'

'Because your debut evening wear pieces have been selling exceptionally well and I think it's time to take you to the next level. If you want to design, you need to know your market. Think of yourself as a walking, talking advertisement for the company. If we manage to catch someone's eye with your design then all the better.'

'But why would you want me to wear it? Wouldn't it be better to get a professional model to wear it instead of me?'

'No. I want people to see how this would look on anyone,' he said, jotting down some notes and yelling for his assistant.

'Oh.' It made sense, she supposed. Then the implications of all he'd just said sank in. No pressure, just design something everyone will want to buy . . . sure. And in less than three months.

'I'm not sure there'll be enough time . . .' she said.

'Then you best not waste any more of it standing here, had you?' he suggested with another of his cool glances.

Alice left his office and walked back to her desk almost in a daze.

'So?' Adel asked in a harsh whisper as she stood by the filing cabinet and pretended to file something. 'What happened?'

'He wants me to design a dress for the Belagottis,' she murmured, still in shock.

'Holy. Shit.'

Alice stared at her friend. Frankie wanted *her* to design a dress for the biggest fashion awards night on the entire planet. Holy shit, indeed.

The office was quiet at this time of the night and Alice usually enjoyed the solitude, but tonight all she shared the space with was frustration. The garbage bin beside her desk was already overflowing with discarded balls of paper, accompanied each time with an increasingly descriptive vocabulary regarding her lack of talent and Frankie's stupid ideas. Was he deliberately setting her up to fail? He wanted her—practically a novice— to create a dress for a major global awards night in only ten weeks? Sure, she'd created her wool collection from scratch, but she'd been working in a team, this was something he wanted her to throw together on her own. *You wanted to be in the big league*, a little voice reminded her, which was true so, with a weary sigh, she bowed her head and tried to regroup.

'I didn't think I'd ever see that look on you, Alice Croydon,' a voice said from the doorway, making her yelp.

Damn. The last person she wanted to see right now, when she was feeling like such a terrible failure.

'What look would that be?' she asked.

'Like you're about to give up.'

Her shoulders straightened at the words. Had she been? Hearing it spoken out loud sounded a lot more confronting than thinking it had.

'It's okay to ask for help, you know,' he said, slouching in the doorway in a way only Frankie Esquire could make look sexy.

'A little more time to prepare would have been helpful,' she muttered, unsettled by the fact she could find him attractive despite feeling so inadequate.

'We don't always get the luxury of time in this industry. Besides, preforming under pressure can sometimes bring out the unexpected,' he said, withdrawing his hands from his trouser pockets to fold them almost lazily across his chest.

'Is that why you sprung this on me?' she asked, surprised.

'Let's just say, I wouldn't have asked you to do it if I didn't think you *could*.'

Alice held his gaze, feeling a tiny bud of optimism begin to unfurl inside of her.

'Take some time out tomorrow and focus your thoughts. When you come back, you'll be ready,' he said, leaving her still without any kind of design or concept, but with the tiniest bit of hope.

Know your market. The phrase wasn't a new one, but when Frankie had said it as part of his *very* limited brief, she knew it was a vital one. The Belagottis were for the rich and famous. Any gown designed for something like that would have to be elaborate. Alice mentally flipped through her portfolio of evening gowns for something she could use but knew none of them would do for an event like this one. She'd have to start from scratch and come up with something show stopping.

An image of her wedding dress and the elaborate beading and detail that had gone into her dream dress flashed before her eyes as she got ready for bed. She hesitated before dismissing the idea. A wedding dress was slightly over the top, but then again, it had been that dress that had caught Frankie's eye and prompted him to make the trip out to see it in person. She felt a little tingly as she thought about seeing her beautiful dress on the red carpet, centre stage for the whole fashion world to see, then gave a small scoff at the notion. If only she could use the dress for some other purpose. It seemed a shame it had never had its day in the spotlight. While the pain that had once attached itself to any thought about her cancelled wedding had gone, there was still a melancholy kind of regret for a path not taken. *If only wedding dresses could have more than one day in the sun*, she thought wistfully before finally drifting off to sleep. She dreamed of butterflies and white dresses floating beneath a brilliant blue sky.

Bright and early the next day, Alice sat bolt upright in bed, brushing back her bedhead hair and frantically searching for a piece of paper and something to draw with. She knew what her design was going to be. It had come to her through a night of weird, abstract dreams—her past interweaving her present, throwing together a concoction of images and ideas, until her excited brain could take no more and she'd awoken.

Alice sat on a park bench, sketch pad open on her lap as she stared thoughtfully at the huge old trees that graced the grounds of Hyde Park. She'd taken Frankie's advice and skipped the office in order to find some inspiration for her new design. She'd spent the majority of the early hours of the morning getting her idea down on paper and that part had come together beautifully, however she still needed to find the inspiration that would bring the idea to life. That's when her rush of enthusiasm had come to a grinding halt.

She'd needed to get out of the four walls that had begun to feel as though they were closing in on her and, after spending a day walking and trying to clear her head of all the noise and doubts that had suddenly returned, she'd finally found her inspiration.

The air was crisp—at least it would have been if it didn't feel like it was freezing her lungs with each breath—but it made her feel revitalised, and once that tiny spark of inspiration had taken hold, it soon built into a roaring fire inside her, keeping her warm with its unrelenting enthusiasm.

Her pencil flew across the page as she deftly sketched the textured trunk of a sweet chestnut tree, its spiralling fissures wrapping around the grand old trunk. She glanced at the earlier sketch she'd made of the tall London plane tree with its straight trunk and rounded crown of leaves and scrawled a thousand notes about colour and texture and hues. Her vision for the dress was gradually taking shape. As she flipped through the pages, she returned to the earlier drawings she'd made at Kensington Palace and in particular the ones of the sunken garden, so formal and structured, yet elegant and regal. She'd sat and soaked in the quiet tranquillity of the Diana, Princess of Wales memorial fountain, mesmerised by the flow of water, wanting to capture the different moods it created as it cascaded and bubbled its way along the path before settling, calm and still, in the pool at the bottom. There was an energy and a peacefulness in the process, and she itched to try and replicate that in her design.

The sketches would most likely make no sense to anyone other than a designer or artist—they were conceptual, instinctive and completely chaotic to look at—but they had unleashed a creative urge inside Alice that had her eager to rush back to her drafting board and get started.

With her face numb and her fingers cold, she packed away her pad and pencils and put her gloves back on. It was time to go home and defrost.

Chapter 22

Alice let out a long, slow breath and counted to five before knocking on the office door. For the last few days she'd sketched and coloured and recreated her original design, putting together colour boards, sourcing her fabrics and preparing to present Frankie with her completed concept. She'd worked late into the night, sometimes even getting up only a few hours after she'd gone to bed because she just couldn't sleep. She had tweaked and perfected everything multiple times. She'd existed on takeaway and sandwiches and copious amounts of caffeine, but she'd finished. All she needed now was Frankie's approval, and she was terrified. What if he hated it? What if he said go back and start again?

No, she couldn't think like that. This was the dress that was going to get people talking.

'Finally,' Frankie said, glancing up and putting down the pen he'd been using. 'I've been wondering when I'd see something from you.' He tilted his head as he examined her. 'You look like shit, Croydon. Have you slept recently?'

'Not much,' she admitted. It was always a joy when your boss told you how horrible you looked.

'Sleep's for the weak, anyway.' He nodded at her cheerfully. Far more cheerfully than she'd recalled seeing him recently. 'So, show me what you've got,' he said.

She placed a large presentation folder in front of him. 'You wanted something that will get people talking,' she said, fighting back her nerves and concentrating on the drawings and sample swatches. 'I think this could be it. I've combined my love of formal wear and wedding dress design and come up with a dress that can be both.'

'Both?' Frankie repeated doubtfully.

'I know the brief was only for a gown, but then I started thinking this could be so much more. I'm suggesting a wedding dress that can convert into formal wear and then cocktail wear. A three-for-one kind of thing. Brides have always had the dilemma of what to do with their wedding dress after the wedding. Why put it away in a box for decades, to save it for a future daughter who probably won't even want to wear it? Why spend all that time finding the perfect wedding gown only to wear it for a day? It's a waste. It's actually a crime that such a beautiful garment that took so long to create gets worn for a handful of hours then shoved away in a storage box.'

When Frankie didn't immediately dismiss the idea, she became braver and warmed to her theme.

'My design takes shape as a wedding gown, but then has panels that can be removed—sleeves, trains, skirts—and, depending on the design, can create three completely different looking dresses. The bride can look picture perfect at the church in her flowing gown with an eight-foot train, then arrive at the reception minus the train and bulky skirt in a slimmer fitting dress that would serve as an evening gown for any other function in the future. Then she can remove *that* skirt and be out on the dance floor in a cocktail-length dress.' She placed the various stages of the dress's evolution in front of him as she spoke, her nerves gone as her excitement rose.

She'd found her inspiration that day in the park—the tall, graceful trees with their rounded leafy crowns, which, when the leaves fell, left an elegant and classy silhouette. The silky material would flow and cascade like the water of the fountain, then turn into something fun and energetic like the splash of beautiful flowers that complemented the formality of the Sunken Garden at Kensington Palace.

'As you can see from this design, the beautiful bell-shaped sleeves of the wedding dress can be removed and the bodice turns into a sleeveless evening gown. Or, it can convert into a halter neck, as in this design.'

Alice straightened as Frankie flipped through the folder and studied the images before him. As the silence lengthened, she felt her nerves returning. *Oh God, oh God, oh God . . . he hates it.*

'Which of these designs would you be wearing?' he asked, sliding the folder towards her.

'I . . . ah.' She swallowed nervously, before flipping through the pages. 'I thought maybe this one,' she said, stopping at a shimmering halter-neck evening gown in latte tones that peeped through cut-outs in the original wedding gown of ivory. 'The evening gown version.'

Frankie nodded slowly. 'I like it,' he finally said, lifting his gaze to meet her relieved one. 'But,' he said, causing her elation to balance rather unsteadily on an imaginary precipice, 'I want you to wear the full version.'

Alice eyed him, somewhat confused. 'You want me to wear a wedding dress to the Belagottis?'

'I do,' he said, holding her startled stare.

Right. A wedding gown at an awards night. No big deal.

'I asked for something people would take notice of—you delivered. A wedding gown will get people's attention immediately. As the evening continues, you can reveal the other layers. It's actually genius,' he said quietly, his fingers steepled beneath his chin.

Well, genius might be going a little far, but she *was* chuffed that he liked her idea. Then she remembered something else that had been playing on her mind ever since he'd told her his big idea for her to wear her design to the awards night.

'What if they recognise me . . . the press?' she asked, feeling quite a lot like she was being dragged along behind a runaway horse.

'Maybe we turn the tables on them—use what happened in the tabloids as publicity. They'll assume it was all staged as a publicity stunt of our own,' he said. 'I'm going to assign Julian to assist and he'll be able to pull a few others off projects to help out. This is no longer one outfit—we're treating this like a collection and we're going to have to move fast to get it done. I'm making this project top priority as of now.'

'Can I have Adel on the team?' Alice asked, seeing that he was rapidly losing interest in her presence as the list of things that would need doing grew.

'Take whoever you want,' he said, before snapping out some new orders to his harried assistant, who'd silently entered the room. Then he turned his attention back to Alice. 'Get this made up. I want to see a prototype ASAP.'

'Okay,' Alice agreed, feeling slightly light-headed. This was really happening. 'Thank you.'

Frankie gave a sharp nod as he reached for the phone and Alice gathered up her presentation folder and all but scampered from his office.

Outside, Adel was waiting, looking hopeful. 'Well?'

'He liked it!' Alice said, keeping her voice low, mindful that they were still in the office.

'I knew he would! Well done, you! We have to go out and celebrate.'

'I can't. I need to get this down to production and oversee the design. I think it's going to be a long few days.'

'You need to eat. I'll bring dinner back to the office tonight and we can celebrate while we work?'

'You don't have to do that,' Alice said, but was genuinely touched by the gesture.

'Of course I do. We're a team here, remember? And we can't let your first major achievement go by without celebrating it. I simply will not allow it,' she said firmly.

'Thanks, Adel.'

'Croydon! Production!' Frankie bellowed from his office doorway.

'On my way,' she called back, sending an apologetic glance at Adel before hurrying towards the elevator. Inside, she let out a long breath and found herself smiling, before breaking out in a giggle. Frankie liked her design. She could do this!

Chapter 23

She couldn't do this!

The last two weeks had been utter mayhem as Alice and her team poured themselves into the creation she was wearing as she sat in the back of a stretch limousine, wondering what the hell she was doing here. Outside the car she saw the milling photographers and media that lined the red carpet and gaped in alarm. *Is that Rihanna? Holy crap.*

'Just breathe,' Frankie's amused voice said beside her and Alice dragged her gaze from the celebrity-studded crowd to him.

'I can't go out there.'

'Yes, you can,' he said.

'I don't belong here. I'm just a girl from Gunnindi, Frankie, I signed up for design experience, not to be the model. There are honest-to-God professional *supermodels* out there!' she squeaked. Sure, she'd met a few celebrity models during her time at Esquire, but not these ones—the ones she'd grown up seeing in magazines and on TV. These were icons of the fashion industry.

'Croydon. Calm down and focus. Look at me,' he commanded, and she turned back to him reluctantly. 'No one thinks they belong here at first—do you think I did? A skinny kid from the outskirts of Melbourne? Everyone out there has a story of who they were before they made it. And every single person did what you're going to do. They pulled their shit together and they got out of the car. The rest is history.'

'They're going to recognise me from the whole Gigi thing,' she whispered, her fingers clenching tighter to the seat. Although that fiasco had quickly taken a back seat to the bigger, juicier scandal that Gigi had been orchestrating the whole time, so it was possible no one *would* recognise her.

'We're ready for this. I've got our PR people all over it. They'll handle any potential crisis that could possibly come up. All you need to think about is this,' he said, gesturing to the dress. But that only brought on a fresh wave of panic.

'I'm in a wedding dress, Frankie!' she cried dolefully. Everyone was going to be staring at her. She wasn't a size-zero model. She didn't even work out! What the hell was Frankie thinking?

'You designed it.'

'Yes, but we were only supposed to be showing the evening gown part.'

'I like the shock value,' he told her. 'I'll be right there beside you. I'm not feeding you to the wolves.'

'Promise?' she asked, hearing the desperation in her voice but beyond caring.

His eyes softened slightly and his cocky grin lost some of its sexy, I'm-Frankie-bloody-Esquire swankiness. 'I promise. I won't let you out of my sight.'

The car crept forward and their driver let them know it was their turn to get out.

Frankie opened his door. 'You look beautiful,' he said, before adjusting the light veil over her face and climbing out.

His words seemed to echo inside the car for those few moments she was left alone, but were swept away in a rush of loud voices throwing questions around and the flash of cameras going off when Frankie opened her door.

She heard a collective gasp as she stepped from the car and gathered her train over one arm, grateful that she had the veil to hide behind.

'Frankie! Frankie! Over here!' one photographer yelled.

'Frankie! Over here?' another called.

'Is this for real? Are you doing a surprise wedding at the Belagottis?' someone else shouted.

With her arm tucked securely in Frankie's, Alice felt marginally safer, but she feared her expression was that of a terrified church mouse facing a hungry cat. They stopped in front of the sponsor banner for the official media photos and Frankie smiled, at least as much as Frankie Esquire ever smiled for publicity photos, before he signalled he was ready to answer questions.

'Tonight, we've chosen the Belagottis to reveal our latest wedding collection,' he announced. 'Allow me to introduce

Ms Alice Croydon, the talent behind the design.' He nodded towards two assistants lurking in the wings, who stepped forward to carefully lift Alice's veil and straighten her dress. Alice hadn't even noticed them.

The immediate flash of cameras disorientated her and she blinked and tried to focus on the swarm of people gathered behind a roped-off section of the red carpet.

'This latest collection features wedding dresses that convert into three distinct outfits designed to go from chapel to reception to dance floor and on to the nightclub for the afterparty,' Frankie announced.

Although Alice did her best to smile and look like she was completely comfortable standing in a wedding dress in front of a pack of international media and celebrities, inside she was hyperventilating. So she concentrated on the spot just above her hip where Frankie's hand rested reassuringly, feeling the warmth seeping through the fabric onto her skin.

She was so distracted by his touch that she was surprised when she found herself walking inside the venue. The first part of the torture was over.

'I think that went down okay,' he murmured as the two assistants hastily lifted her train and another scampered along behind tossing confetti.

'Seriously?' Alice replied, feeling ridiculous.

Frankie looked down at her with a lopsided grin, and for a moment Alice forgot to breathe.

'If we're going to make an entrance, then it may as well be memorable. Now, smile for the cameras.'

Alice managed to drag her attention back to the task at hand and summoned a smile at the fake wedding guests, who parted for them to walk through.

Once inside the grand old building, the confetti-throwing ceased and an usher came forward to show them to their table. Alice and her assistants retired to a private dressing room to dissemble the wedding gown while a photographer took photos for the promotional package. When Alice emerged, she wore the sleek under gown of shimmery latte. The halter neck exposed her shoulders and skimmed her torso and hips to fall to the ground in an elegant cascade of satin. She posed outside the room for the media before joining Frankie at the table. More photos were taken.

Alice tried her best not to allow her jaw to drop when she realised who else was at their table as Frankie pulled a seat out for her.

'Alice, let me introduce you to George, Amal, Naomi and Kylie,' Frankie said.

Sure, Alice thought faintly. *An A-list Hollywood actor, a human rights barrister, a supermodel and the queen of pop music, just a typical Monday evening . . .*

'I am loving this whole concept,' Kylie said, leaning closer after the introductions were made.

'Oh, thank you,' Alice replied, feeling breathless all of a sudden. 'I'm sorry, this is all really new to me . . .'

The singer's expression softened and her smile widened. 'It's okay. It's a lot to take in at first, isn't it? I'm really keen to see what else you've designed.'

'I'm hoping Frankie will be just as keen,' Alice said. 'Tonight was a kind of baptism by fire. I guess we'll have to wait and see if anyone likes the designs.'

'I don't think you'll have anything to worry about there,' Kylie said, patting her hand reassuringly before offering Alice a drink. 'I don't think I've ever seen Frankie bring along a date to this before,' she said, as they sipped their champagne.

'Oh no, it's not a date. This is purely a promotional thing. It's just business.'

'I wouldn't be too sure about that if I were you.'

Alice followed the other woman's gaze and found Frankie watching her as he listened to the conversations around him.

She quickly looked away and gave a weak laugh, before shaking her head. She hoped she wasn't blushing. 'It's not like that. I'm just here to work.'

Kylie grinned. 'I say live for the moment and enjoy it while you can.'

Alice gave an awkward smile as they clinked glasses, remembering to take it easy on the alcohol. She still had another dress change to make and tottering around on these damn heels would not be made any easier if she were tipsy.

'Everything okay?' Frankie asked quietly.

'Yep. All good.'

'You seem a little . . . distracted.'

'I think it's more gobsmacked,' she said. 'I feel like I'm in a dream. It doesn't seem real. Everywhere I look there's someone famous.'

'Something you'll soon get used to,' he said, offering her another wine.

She declined with a shake of her head. 'I think I'd prefer to just design.'

Frankie laughed. 'Wouldn't we all. However, this is part of the job, Croydon. You have to sell. People want to know the face behind the fashion. They want to know who dresses them. It's all about the brand.'

Alice couldn't imagine doing this kind of thing often. She felt like an intruder—a fake—and it was only having Frankie by her side that held her here. There was no way all this was going to be part of *her* job. At least, not the job she thought she was here to do. This wasn't what she wanted from her career. This was something else. She was here to design and work behind the scenes—to learn her craft. Frankie could keep his fame and fortune.

After the meal, Alice excused herself to complete the final reveal.

Removing the halter straps and attaching the thinner spaghetti ones, she stepped out of the satin skirt and unbuttoned the pleats tucked away at the waist of the dress to release the shorter underskirt: a white sequined miniskirt.

Her table mates, once she returned, were full of encouraging compliments and Alice was happy to allow Frankie to do all the talking.

'Alice, it's amazing,' another of the guests said, admiring the new outfit. 'It's like a magician's dress. How does a whole other skirt come out from under that slinky one without looking bulky?'

Alice glanced over at Frankie, who gestured with a sweep of his hand to indicate she should take the question. 'It's all in the folding and pleats,' she said. 'Everything tucks away under the waistband and is secured with buttons. The choice of fabric is important too. You need something that will sit flat and not add any bulk.' That part of the design process was one of her favourites—choosing or discarding fabric until she found the perfect fit for the design. As much as she loved working with wool, for this project, it wouldn't have worked as effectively. But that was part of the challenge—problem solving. She loved the challenge of using different fabric and there were so many different types of fabric to work with.

'It's very clever.'

'Thank you.'

'I think you're on to a winner here, Frankie,' another man said.

'You just keep your beady eyes off it, Marcus,' Frankie said in a light enough tone, although Alice saw his eyes narrowing in a warning of sorts. Nothing was ever really exclusive in the fashion world. All Frankie's competitors would be waiting to read the reviews tomorrow morning and, if they were favourable, there'd be versions of Alice's dress from all the other fashion houses within weeks. However, Frankie had already had the line in production and it would be coming out ahead of anything his competitors could rush through.

Of course, if the reviews were bad . . . well, that was too terrible to even contemplate, so Alice pushed the idea from her mind.

❖

Alice had to pinch herself numerous times as she looked around the room of the swanky hotel afterparty with wall-to-wall celebrities drinking, laughing and doing what celebrities did best at these functions—be in the spotlight. She was sure she spent most of the time with her mouth hanging open as she trailed behind Frankie like an obedient puppy, smiling at the people he introduced her to and trying to make interesting conversation, but they talked about people she didn't know and things she really didn't understand.

This was not her world. Sure, it was exciting and an experience, but she couldn't ever really see herself working a room with the same ease and coolness that Frankie did. Admittedly, he had been doing it almost twenty years, but still . . . it was a lot to take in when you weren't used to it.

In the wee hours of the morning, when the strobing lights and heat of too many bodies in the one room became too much to bear, Alice caught Frankie's eye to say goodnight.

She immediately protested when Frankie said he'd come with her. 'Please don't. Stay. I'm just a lightweight and can't party quite as hard as you.' She smiled.

'I've been hoping you'd give me an excuse to leave for the last three hours,' he told her.

It took another half an hour to actually leave the ballroom when practically everyone stopped him to say goodnight, but finally they were inside an elevator to go up to their hotel rooms. The quiet almost hurt her ears after the noise of the last few hours. Her feet ached and she was dreaming of a hot shower and that comfy-looking bed she'd eyed earlier as she'd gotten dressed, but she was also still on a bit of a high from the whole night. It had truly been an extraordinary experience.

'Did you have a good time?' Frankie asked.

'I had the best night. Thank you, Frankie . . . for everything. I know you took an incredible chance on me. I just hope my design doesn't let you down.'

'You looked stunning,' he said. 'Whatever the reviewers say, in my books, your design was a knockout. I couldn't be prouder of you.'

Alice swallowed the lump of emotion his words brought up. His respect and approval meant a lot to her.

The elevator door slid open and they walked out into a silent corridor, coming to a stop outside her room. As Alice dug through her purse for her key, she could almost feel that hot water running over her tired body and she itched to slide in between those crisp white sheets and sleep till midday.

'Goodnight, Frankie. Thank you,' she said with a soft smile as she pushed the door open. 'Tonight was magical.'

He took her hand, lifted it to his lips and kissed it gently, sending her heart rate into a gallop and making her knees go a little bit wobbly, then turned away and headed down the hallway to his own room.

It took a few moments for Alice to pull herself together. Just when she thought they'd managed to return to a professional relationship, he went and got all Christmas Frankie on her again—the one who was thoughtful and kind and made her laugh . . . and maybe even swoon just a little bit.

She took her time in the shower, letting out a long sigh as her tired muscles cried out in relief and all the stress washed away. With her hair wrapped in a towel and her body swathed in the fancy hotel's enormous white robe, she headed to bed.

Then a soft knock sounded at her door.

Hesitant at the late-night interruption, she looked through the security peep hole, stepping back in surprise before slowly opening the door.

Frankie leaned against the door jamb casually, holding up his phone in one hand. 'The reviews are in,' he said, lifting an eyebrow in a conspiratorial manner.

Alice felt her eyes widen. 'What did they say?'

'I don't know . . . I thought maybe you'd like to find out together, since it was your baby and all?'

What if they hated it? What if everyone thought she was a laughing stock? Oh my God, she'd be finding out right beside her boss! 'Sure,' she said, forcing a smile she hoped looked enthusiastic.

'You look like you're about to be marched to the gallows,' he commented before following her inside.

Alice cleared the sofa quickly, turning in a small circle as she searched for a place to dump her clothing, settling on a table in the corner. When she turned back, Frankie was seated and had the web page up on the screen. Taking a shaky breath, she held it for a moment before slowly releasing it as she sank onto the sofa beside him. *Please be positive, please be positive*, she begged silently as he scrolled down until he found the reviews section on the newspapers page and started to read aloud.

'Frankie Esquire made an entrance and a half at the Belagottis tonight, arriving with a bride! But, alas, it was all to showcase his latest protégé, Alice Croydon, and the new line she and Esquire Design are about to release. The clever and stunning three-in-one dress is a show stopper and, dare we say—a game changer? Taking the bride from the church to the dance floor with just a flick of the wrist and a twist of a button. If this was a taste of what we can expect from the line due to hit this season, then it's safe to say we're hungry for more.'

Alice stopped biting the corner of her lip and looked at Frankie hopefully. 'That means they liked it, right?'

He grinned. 'That means they loved it.'

'Thank goodness,' she said in a shaky whisper.

'Congratulations, Alice Croydon. You've officially made it to the big league.'

Holy. Crap.

Alice tore her gaze from his and returned it to the screen. There was a photo of her and Frankie standing on the red carpet. It was surreal to think that it had been taken barely a handful of hours earlier.

She'd done it. The thought echoed inside her head, sparking an unexpected sting behind her eyes.

'Thank you, Frankie. For believing in me. If it wasn't for you, I wouldn't be here.'

'Thank *you* for trusting me with your talent.'

For a long while they continued to hold each other's gaze, until Frankie slowly reached out and wiped a stray tear with the edge of his thumb. His touch set off a tremble inside her and she felt her heart skip momentarily.

His lips were warm and soft, gently caressing her own with a masterful touch that sent an instant wave of longing through her. It had seemed like a lifetime since she'd been kissed—felt wanted by someone—and her body ached for the touch of his as he tugged her closer and the kiss deepened.

It should have felt wrong. He was her boss. But instead, it felt . . . right. Tonight, he was just a man who wanted her, and she was a woman who needed to feel wanted.

He eased the robe from her shoulders and she shivered in anticipation as his hooded gaze roamed across her bare skin.

Chapter 24

As early morning light began to filter in through the window, Alice lay awake, quietly contemplating everything that had happened in the last twenty-four hours. None of it seemed to make any sense. She'd taken this job to further her education, to learn her craft and fulfil her passion for design, but now that it seemed she was going to get everything she wanted, she was beginning to realise maybe her dream had been a little naive. Sure, the design part was everything she'd ever dared imagine and more, but in her dream world, it had only been her career she'd been thinking about. There hadn't been any distractions and there sure as hell hadn't been any sleeping with her boss involved.

A tingle went through her at the thought of Frankie, whose heavy arm was draped across her hip. Oh, Lord, the things they'd done last night. Heat began to burn its way up her neck and into her cheeks as a few choice clips of the evening not so helpfully flashed before her eyes. Who was that woman last night?

You wanted this life, a little voice reminded her. But had she? Really? Had she known that all of this would come along with the dream, would she still have taken the job? *Of course not*, another voice piped up, *you would have stayed where you were—comfortable and happily unexceptional.*

Could she go back to unexceptional? She wasn't sure that word sat comfortably with her and yet she knew, after last night, her old life had felt rather ... well, not as magical as the evening before, her designs in the spotlight, standing in a room full of people she'd never in a million years have met if she'd stayed in Gunnindi.

She could feel herself changing, almost like her old skin was being peeled away and someone new was emerging. There was pain in shedding her old self, but there was also something empowering about it too. She felt stronger somehow.

'Have you decided yet?' Frankie's deep voice was a molten-chocolate cascade, sending a warm puddle of longing through her.

'Decided what?' she finally managed to ask.

'If you're going to try and sneak out of bed and run away, or stay and face this thing between us?'

'The first option seems to be out, since you're awake,' she said. She wished she *had* tried to sneak out while he was still asleep instead of lying there pointlessly contemplating.

'So, I guess that leaves option two,' he said, a touch of amusement infusing the words.

However, there was nothing funny about the anxiety brewing inside her and she fought a moment of panic at facing the future that had been changed forever after last night.

With a long sigh, Alice rolled over and swallowed nervously as she fixed her gaze on Frankie's smooth chest, unable to look him in the eye.

'Why are you so nervous?' he asked.

At this she did look up, staring at him as though he'd lost his mind completely. 'Oh, I don't know, maybe because I've just woken up naked beside my boss,' she scoffed, irritably. 'That mightn't be a big deal for you, but it certainly is for me.'

'I can't say I've ever slept with any of my bosses before,' he said thoughtfully, 'but in all fairness, it was only because I didn't swing that way. I've had a number of offers, though, over the years.'

This surprised her, then she realised he'd made an excellent point; she was clearly not from this world at all if the thought had shocked her. God, she was still such a small-town Debbie Do-Right.

'I don't do this with anyone,' she said, intent to get her point across.

'So I noticed. Why is that?' he asked.

'Because I'm not here for . . . that,' she said, swallowing hard again and lowering her gaze once more.

'You aren't engaged anymore, though?'

'No,' she admitted, 'but that's not the point.'

'What is then?'

'I'm here to work.'

'Your dedication is admirable—it's something that I've always admired about you, Alice,' he said and smoothed back a strand of her hair. 'But you're not really living, are you?'

'Of course I am.'

'Are you happy?'

'I have a job I love and I'm living in London—which is something I'd never even imagined I'd be doing.'

'But are you *happy*?' he pressed.

'Of course I am.'

She saw his lips give a slight twist as he continued to run a finger down the side of her face. 'You can do a lot of things, Alice, but you can't lie to save your life.'

'I'm not lying.'

'Only to yourself,' he agreed. 'You're only allowing yourself to live a half-life through your work. That's not living to your fullest.'

She didn't like that he had somehow seen through her like that. She wasn't even sure how he did it—why would he even care? He was just her employer. What business was it of his if she were living life to the fullest or not?

'Will this change things?' she asked hesitantly. 'What happened between us?'

'Do you want it to change things?'

'No,' she said cautiously. 'But I don't understand it.'

'Surely it's not that much of a surprise? I know you picked up on the chemistry between us over Christmas.'

'I thought I did . . . and then you acted like nothing happened.'

'I was trying to protect you. It wouldn't have done your reputation any good to be connected to that whole mess. The more distance I put between us, the more chance of letting all the gossip die down. And it worked.'

It *had* worked. She had been sure that whole debacle was going to follow her around forever but it was as though everyone had forgotten about it. She suspected there'd been a warning around the office about releasing information to the press, and most people would rather keep their job than risk unemployment over whatever had gone on between their boss and a coworker. Alice had taken Gran's advice and simply held her head high—or as high as she was game to hold it. She preferred stay out of the firing line, which had also seemed to work.

'But that wasn't the only reason I was keeping my distance,' he continued and the slightly reluctant tone she heard in his voice piqued her interest, despite herself. 'You've been a thorn in my side ever since I first laid eyes on you. Your talent caught my attention back at fashion week, but then you turned down my job offer,' he said, still sounding perplexed. 'Maybe it was pride, but I often found myself thinking about that and it still stung. I couldn't believe someone with your talent would throw away an opportunity like that. I was waiting to see if you'd taken a better offer somewhere—I was sure that's why you'd turned me down—but then when I didn't hear anything . . .' He paused. 'Then a photo turned up of a wedding dress and I saw your name.'

To this day she still wasn't sure how Gran had managed to pull that off. Of course she'd denied it when Alice had confronted her, only she didn't actually say she *hadn't* been involved, just that she didn't send the photo. She must bring it up with her again one day. Nothing her gran did surprised her anymore.

'I was in Sydney and suddenly I found myself heading to the middle of nowhere. Once I'd seen you again, I knew there was no way I was going to let you turn down an offer a second time.'

This news surprised her. 'I almost did.'

'I'm glad you didn't,' he said, his expression was serious. 'I appreciate what you've given up in order to be here. I respected that dedication. I've tried to keep a professional distance between us, Alice.'

'Which is why this was a mistake,' Alice said, as dread began to seep its way through her.

'This doesn't change anything.'

'It won't,' she agreed and eased away from him. 'Because it's not going to happen again.'

'It doesn't have to be like that.'

'Of course it does. How will anyone take me seriously if they know we've been sleeping together?'

'Your talent will speak for itself.'

'And you think I'm the naive one?'

'Your designs got rave reviews.'

'That doesn't mean people aren't going to think I only got a chance to show them off because of you.'

'You did only get a chance to show them off because of me,' he said simply, and Alice felt her face drop. 'Because I'm the one who saw your talent and took a chance on you. That's it. It hasn't got anything to do with the fact we've slept together.'

'That's not going to stop people thinking it, though.'

'So what?'

'This is why it was a mistake,' she said, scooting to the edge of the bed and leaning down to pick up the fluffy robe from the floor. 'You don't have to care what people think. But I do.'

'Only if you allow yourself to. You're not in Gunnindi anymore, Alice. Small-town gossip doesn't have to hold you back from living your life.'

'This place isn't any different from Gunnindi,' she said, shaking her head. 'People make up their minds here just the same as they do back there. I can't afford to risk everything I've given up and worked so hard for, for . . . this.'

'I'll try not to take that personally,' he muttered, leaning on one elbow as he watched her tie the sash of her robe with a little more force than was warranted.

'I don't want this decision to get in the way of our working relationship. If you think it will . . . I need to know so I can look for another job.'

'Alice, you're overthinking this way too much.'

'Will this be an issue for you, Frankie?' she repeated firmly, refusing to back down from his irritated expression.

'Of course not. I'm a professional,' he said stiffly.

'Okay then. I'm going to take a shower,' she said.

She forced herself to walk to the bathroom, where she sank against the door with a deflated sigh. This was worse than waking up with a hangover. She wondered what the equivalent was after a night spent having amazing sex. Regret, she supposed, but without the nausea and throbbing headache.

When she came out later, dressed and feeling a little more in control of her senses, she found the bed empty and the room quiet. Part of her was relieved—a large part, actually—but she couldn't ignore the other part that felt disappointed. *I've done the right thing*, she told herself firmly. There was a reason office relationships were always so dangerous. You had to be able to work together and have your coworkers' respect. Frankie didn't need to worry about the latter—he'd already proven himself and his talent. Alice, on the other hand, was yet to really prove anything. Sure, last night seemed to be a success, but she needed to prove she wasn't a one-hit wonder—she needed to establish herself before she could even think of being involved with a man like Frankie—*especially* a man like Frankie. She just hoped he was a man of his word and wouldn't hold a grudge.

Chapter 25

When Alice walked into the office the next day, she knew she'd made the right decision. There was a festive cheer in the air and there were interviews and meetings and a whole string of publicity requests to be seized upon.

'So how was it?' Adel demanded as the two women stepped inside Alice's office and shut the door on all the noise. 'The afterparty? I'm absolutely dying with jealousy, you know. Was it as amazing as I'm imagining it?'

Alice grinned at the puppy dog look her friend was giving her and gave a blow-by-blow account of every famous person she saw and who she spoke with, leaving out any mention of Frankie or the sparks that had flown between them throughout the night.

'You're so lucky,' Adel sighed.

'I wish you could have been there too. You and everyone else. I feel like I've been singled out when really it was a team effort.'

'You deserve all the attention and more—this was your creation.'

'I don't think I can do this, Adel,' Alice said.

'Of course you can! Frankie wouldn't have placed all this confidence in you if he didn't think you had what it takes. And he was right.'

As though Adel had somehow conjured him out of nowhere, Alice saw the man himself enter the office outside, instantly swarmed by more congratulations and handshakes. Almost as though he'd sensed her presence, his eyes turned to Alice through the office window and, for the slightest moment, their gazes held. Alice felt her stomach flip a little and bit her lip as memories created a PowerPoint presentation of their night together.

'What?' Adel asked, dragging Alice's attention back to her friend.

'What?'

'What was that?' Adel elaborated, pointedly glancing from Alice to Frankie and back again with narrowed eyes.

'I don't know what you're talking about,' Alice said sitting behind her desk.

'Something happened.'

Oh for the love of—'Nothing happened,' Alice said, and cursed silently as she felt her cheeks begin to warm.

'You are a terrible liar, Alice Croydon. Did I ever mention that my granny had second sight and that I also seem to have the uncanny ability to sense things?'

'No, you've never mentioned that. And I hate to disappoint you, but whatever you're sensing right now is way off.'

'Oh my God,' Adel gasped, making Alice look up sharply. 'You slept with him.'

How the hell could she have possibly known that?

Adel's eyes widened and she let out a small giggle. 'You did, didn't you?'

'Would you shut up,' Alice whispered harshly.

'I knew it!'

'It was an accident. A one-off. It's not a thing.'

'Accidentally fell into bed,' Adel scoffed. 'Aye, I hate when that happens.' She rolled her eyes and laughed.

'Please don't tell anyone, Adel,' Alice said, feeling desperate. Everything she'd been afraid of happening might very well come true if word got out.

Adel looked almost hurt. 'Of course I won't tell anyone.'

'I know,' Alice said, shaking her head irritably, 'I'm sorry, I know you wouldn't. It's just been . . . a lot.'

'I can imagine.' Adel softened her voice and sat on the desk beside Alice. 'You don't have to tell me anything.'

'Thanks for understanding,' Alice said, managing a grateful smile at her friend.

'Just . . .' She sent Alice a concerned look before a cheeky grin broke free. 'Tell me how good he was in bed.'

Alice fought a surprised chuckle as she crumpled up a wad of fabric samples and threw it at Adel. 'Go and do some work.'

'Fine. Be like that,' Adel said, sauntering to the doorway. 'But I bet he was good.' She sent Alice a saucy wink and laughed as she left the office.

Alice gave a disgruntled huff, closing her eyes briefly as yet another memory surfaced before she quickly shut it down and forced herself to concentrate on the day ahead. It was going to be bedlam and she better be ready to face it.

She'd been worried about how Frankie would act when they saw each other again, but her fears were alleviated when he behaved as he'd always done in the office—as though the night before hadn't even happened. Which is exactly what she wanted . . . *Of course it's what I wanted*, she repeated to herself firmly.

She was grateful for his presence later that day, though, when she found herself in an endless round of interviews.

'Are you doing okay?' Frankie asked quietly once the stylists and photographer had retired to the other side of the room to discuss lighting.

'Fine,' Alice said brightly.

'I mean about the other—'

'I said I was fine,' she said quickly, sending a fearful glance towards the others in the room. 'I don't want to talk about it.'

'As you wish.' He nodded abruptly, and Alice felt a small pang of regret that she'd spoken so harshly.

For the most part, the interviewers focused on the clothing and the design—the ones who were working for the bigger magazines at least—but then there were the newspapers and the tabloids, which, by Frankie's orders, had been severely limited to a select few. These went straight for the bigger story.

'Miss Croydon, firstly, congratulations on the huge success of this new line. It's quite an achievement for a relative unknown designer,' the slim male reporter gushed.

His enthusiasm caught her off guard and she felt a smile etch itself across her face before his next words caused it to abruptly disappear.

'Is there any truth in the rumours though that you and Frankie have been involved, romantically, ever since the story broke about Gigi and the assault accusations?'

Frankie cut the man off. 'Right. You're done.'

'I still have ten minutes,' the man protested.

'I gave strict instructions as to what questions we'd be answering today. You can deal with your boss when you tell him you blew your paper's only chance to get a formal interview.'

'We were only after confirmation or a quote anyway. The story's already written,' the reporter said smugly.

'Don't worry,' Frankie said, noticing Alice's terrified expression following the man's retreat. 'I'll get the paper slapped with a lawsuit if they even think about releasing anything we haven't agreed to.'

'But that didn't stop them last time,' she pointed out.

'This time we're ready. I've had the PR department working on media releases and damage control—anything they try to bring up will be either taken down or overshadowed by the stories we've released ourselves. We won't be caught on the hop this time.'

'I knew they'd make the connection eventually,' she groaned.

'Alice.' Frankie's stern voice cut through the dread that was threatening to drown her. 'Trust me, okay? I won't let them ruin this for you. I promise.'

And just like that, all the stress went away. While she was trying to figure out what kind of black magic trickery that was, she realised the next interviewer had come in and prepared to smile and answer questions once more. There was no time to dwell on whatever had just happened.

As the weeks went on, her life grew more and more chaotic. The company were doing a wedding special event and Julian had been giving Alice more freedom to design, often asking her to take the lead in presenting her ideas at the design team meetings.

With her convertible wedding dress ensemble thrusting her into the fashion spotlight practically overnight, her role as an intern had now been well and truly dwarfed by the attention she'd been receiving. While the initial interviews and frenzy around the Belagottis had died down, there'd still been a steady trickle of requests from bloggers and magazines who wanted to feature Alice on their channels. She spent at least an hour or two of her day in front of the computer, either replying to emails or doing video calls and podcast interviews but she knew at some point very soon her position in Frankie's company would need to be addressed, she'd just not really had the time to chase it up formally. If she were being completely honest, she was also a little afraid. The initial time frame of working for a year or so was no longer an issue, not since Finn had pulled the rug out from under her at Christmas, but she still wasn't sure what she wanted to do about it. She didn't have to worry about being able to afford to stay on in the

UK. Financially, she'd never been in a better position. She'd received a substantial pay rise after the Belagottis, which had made her utter a very surprised curse on a crowded tube one evening when she'd logged on to her bank account to check her balance. Human resources had assured her that it wasn't a mistake, and that her pay had been reviewed and adjusted accordingly. She knew who she had to thank for that, however, she hadn't seen him to get the chance.

Since the initial interviews, Frankie had withdrawn from any direct contact with Alice. Everything went through her design team and there'd been no more summonses to his office. She wasn't sure what she should do—they hadn't been alone again since that morning and she supposed it was for the best. However, despite the fact he was keeping his promise that what happened between them wouldn't get in the way of their working life, it kind of had. Alice had settled into a new routine of being distracted by her boss's schedule—her mood dependent on whether she managed to catch sight of him that day or not.

Then, late one night when she'd stayed back to finish working on a design, she'd looked up to find Frankie leaning against the door jamb of his office, watching her. It was so unexpected to find themselves alone that she was momentarily dumbfounded.

'I thought you left earlier,' she managed to say.

'I came back. You were clearly deep in concentration.'

'I . . . yes, I was having trouble working out how to get this bodice to sit right . . .'

'Did you figure it out?' he asked, and Alice found herself remembering the sound of his deep voice close to her ear, whispering things that still managed to make her catch her breath.

'I did,' she said.

'I've been impressed with your quality of work. Julian tells me you've been putting together some extraordinary pieces for the wedding special coming up.'

'I've really enjoyed it.'

'That's good.'

Alice tried to drag her gaze from his but found that she couldn't.

'You've been avoiding me,' she finally said, surprising herself with the impulsive courage she found.

'That's what you wanted.'

'No, it wasn't,' she said, shaking her head. 'I wanted us to be able to work together. Like we did before.'

'You can't have it both ways, Alice,' he said, and his voice lowered as his hazel eyes darkened.

Alice lifted her chin. 'You said it wouldn't affect our working relationship.'

'It hasn't.'

'You barely look at me during meetings and you never address me directly.'

'Which, correct me if I'm wrong, is exactly what you wanted. Impartial and professional.'

'You used to at least like me before,' she muttered.

'We wouldn't want anyone thinking your promotion was influenced by any personal emotion, though, would we?' he replied coolly.

'What promotion?' she asked slowly. She hadn't heard of any promotion.

'Your own wedding collection.' He said it so casually that, for a moment, it didn't actually register.

'My what?'

'The prototypes you made for the wedding special feature were good. Very good, in fact. So good that we've decided to offer you your own label.'

Alice stared at him, speechless. Her own label? This was . . . this didn't happen in real life. Maybe she was dreaming the whole thing and would wake up and find herself back in her own bed in Gunnindi. Then another thought occurred to her and some of the numbness wore off: Maybe this *was* too good to be true.

'I don't understand why you'd do that.'

'Before you jump to conclusions, I didn't make the decision. It was Julian's idea.'

She'd been working closely with the talented designer for months and respected his judgement immensely. The knowledge that he'd recommended her for something like this was more than flattering, and yet, it just felt *too* good to be true. 'Why would you take a risk with an unknown on a label?'

'You're not an unknown. In case you haven't been paying attention at meetings lately, the Belagottis wedding dress collection has taken off. Julian rightly pointed out that your latest designs are spectacular and we'd be crazy not to offer you a deal before someone else came along and stole you away with a better offer.'

Alice was still in shock, but the last thing he said pierced the fog. 'You seriously think I'd up and leave if someone offered me something like that?'

Frankie shrugged nonchalantly. 'It wouldn't be unusual, and I'm surprised it hasn't happened yet. Fashion is a cut-throat business. I'm not willing to take that chance. Hence the offer.'

'Then you really don't know me at all, do you?' she snapped, feeling ridiculously hurt. 'You don't need to make me an offer like that just to stop me leaving.' She stood to pack away her workspace, feeling his gaze on her back as she moved.

'So, you're angry that I offered you your own label?' he asked slowly.

'No. I'm not angry.'

'Then what's the problem?'

'It's just'—she gave an irritated click of her tongue—'I don't know,' she said, throwing her arms in the air.

'What the hell do you want from me, Alice?' he asked, taking two steps into the office to stand in front of her. 'Nothing I do is right. I've stayed away from you. I've let you work in peace . . . Christ, I offer you your own label and I'm still somehow managing to piss you off. What do I have to do?'

'Nothing. You don't have to do anything. I didn't ask for my own label and I didn't want you to stay away from me.'

'There is no in between,' he said, stepping closer. 'I can't be around you and pretend I'm not thinking about that night and how good we were together. I stayed away so you could concentrate on your career, but it's killing me, Alice, to sit in that damn office and watch you and not be able to touch you.'

His words hit her in the chest with the force of a physical blow. She had been feeling exactly the same way. What were they doing? This was madness.

She closed the remaining gap between them and tilted her head. The kiss was explosive—not gentle, and certainly not tentative. It was a kiss that released all the torment of nights lying awake, consumed by memories and need, and long days forced to keep their distance and ignore the simmering heat that boiled just below the surface.

She heard the crash of stationery hitting the floor and felt the hard desk beneath her. Everything she'd warned herself against doing was suddenly forgotten. She didn't care. All that mattered was this.

Chapter 26

'Your own label?' Gran almost shouted through the phone. Alice had called when she knew everyone would be at her parents' place to make the announcement. Now she couldn't stop the tears that had begun to flow.

'We're all so proud of you!' Gran continued, taking the phone off her daughter-in-law to peer into it earnestly. 'I knew you could do it!'

There was a chorus of congratulations and some good-natured sibling teasing as the phone did its rounds of the table and a wave of homesickness rushed through Alice that was almost crippling. 'I haven't formally accepted yet,' she said.

The phone was ripped once more from Charlie's hand and Gran's stern face appeared on the screen. 'What do you mean you haven't accepted? Why on earth not?'

'Well, it would mean signing a contract and staying over here longer.'

'So?'

'So?' Alice repeated faintly. So much for her family declaring how much they missed her and wanted her to come home! 'I miss everyone. I wasn't planning on staying here long term.'

'Meryl, give me the phone back,' Alice heard her mother say and Gran's face was quickly replaced by her mother's ear.

'Mum, it's a video call, remember?'

Her mother appeared on screen. 'Darling, we miss you terribly, but Gran's right. You've worked too hard to turn down an opportunity like this. We can save up and visit and you can always come home and see everyone, but I think you should take advantage of this offer while you're still young.'

'Yeah, Mum's right,' Verity added, sticking her head over their mother's shoulder. 'Do not turn down this job. You'd be crazy.'

'Besides,' Toby added, taking the phone, 'we need free accommodation if we ever get over there.'

'Give that here,' Gran said, glaring at her grandson. 'Listen to me, Alice Croydon. You live your life and enjoy every single moment while you can. We'll all be here when you decide it's time to come home, but first you have a job to do, so you stay and you follow that dream as far as it takes you, do you hear me?'

'I hear you, Gran,' Alice said, sniffling, but she wiped her eyes and drew in a deep breath. Okay. She could do this. They were right. She would be crazy to turn down an offer like this—it was more than she'd ever imagined. She'd come to London hoping to gain some valuable experience and somehow ended up with more than she'd ever dared dream of. After everything she'd given up to get here, she knew she couldn't just walk away now, otherwise it would have all been for nothing. She had to make it count.

The wedding special event was finally approaching and the announcement of Alice's collection was going to be made during the show. She was a mass of nerves whenever she thought about it and the publicity that would inevitably follow, but this time around she didn't feel as intimidated. It was still a lot, but this was her collection and she knew all these pieces—she'd lived and breathed them. Of course she still worried about people thinking Frankie was giving her preferential treatment, but her confidence in her own talent had grown considerably since taking on more of the responsibilities and role of fashion designer. For the first time she was allowing herself to believe in her talent as much as Frankie did.

Alice and Frankie had reached an ultimatum of sorts with their relationship—at work they were professional, but she could count on one hand the number of nights she'd actually spent in her little flat over the last two months, spending each night with Frankie and stealing every spare moment in their crazy schedule to be together. So far, if anyone had their suspicions about them, no one had brought them up, but Alice was fairly sure there were rumours. The thought should have caused her considerable anguish, but she realised it didn't. Not really.

Two days before the wedding show, Alice opened the door of her suite in the hotel and almost collapsed in shock as she came face to face with her family.

'Surprise!' her mother sang as Alice stood in the doorway, too stunned to do more than stare.

'Well, don't just stand there, darling, give me a hug!' Gran said, stepping forward to pull Alice into a tight embrace.

Tears flowed as soon as she caught the first whiff of her gran's moisturiser and talcum powder, the same brands she'd been using since Alice was a child.

'What are you all doing here?' she asked after she'd greeted each of them with long hugs.

'We're here to celebrate your first fashion show, silly,' Kathy said, as they moved inside the luxurious room. Her family cast appreciative glances around.

'This is rather fancy,' Gran noted with a decisive nod.

'But it's such an expensive trip—you shouldn't have worried about going to all this trouble.'

'Didn't cost us a cent,' her father informed her as he picked up a statue of a naked woman pouring an urn and examined it doubtfully.

'What do you mean?' Alice asked, turning a confused glance onto her mother.

'That lovely Frankie sent us the tickets and an invitation.'

'Frankie brought you over?'

'Wasn't that kind of him? He said it's what he does for all his new designers on their first big show.'

Alice stared at her parents and grandmother and blinked as she tried to digest this new information.

'It wasn't easy keeping it from you,' Kathy continued.

'I only spoke to you yesterday,' she said, still unsure this was actually happening.

'Yes, that was tricky. We were in the airport waiting for our transfer . . . I was sure you'd hear the announcements on the loud speaker and it would give us away.'

Alice shook her head and laughed, feeling tears well up once more. 'I can't believe you're here.'

'Oh, darling, we've missed you so much,' her mum said, wiping her own happy tears as she held her daughter.

'How long are you here for?'

'Two weeks, can you believe it?' Gran replied, her eyes lighting up. 'We've got so much to see, and no time to waste. I've made a list,' she said, reaching into her pocket to pull out a creased sheet of paper.

'I've got to work for the next few days—it's going to be crazy in the lead-up to the show,' Alice said, suddenly devastated that she wouldn't be able to immediately spend time with them.

'Oh, we know. Frankie explained it all. That's fine, we can entertain ourselves. We're going to do some sightseeing and Frankie's already booked us on some lovely tours. Then you'll have your leave and we can go off exploring to our hearts' content.' Her mum smiled.

Her leave? This was the first time she'd heard anything about having time off. Clearly she underestimated Frankie's ability to plan a surprise and keep a secret. He hadn't even given a hint of anything going on before he left for his business trip to India to meet with some buyers. She swallowed a lump of emotion at how thoughtful he'd been to do all this for her. He'd known how much she'd missed her family and what a huge deal this show was, but she'd never in a million years imagined he'd go to all this trouble for her.

A knock announced room service and when Alice opened the door, she found a friendly waiter with a huge trolley of afternoon tea treats and hot coffee.

'I could sure get used to this,' her father said, as he took a seat on one of the two sofas that faced each other with a coffee table in between.

'You better not,' her mother said drolly, sitting next to her husband. 'When we get back home it's plain old instant coffee and a SAO biscuit if you're lucky.'

'But this *is* nice,' Gran said, reaching for a delicate lemon tart on the tiered cake stand before them.

'So you'll all stay here?' Alice asked. Now that she had her parents and Gran here she didn't want to let them out of her sight for a minute.

'Oh no, we've got our own rooms just down the hall—all paid for. You'll need your space without us being on top of you,' Kathy said.

'I wouldn't mind.'

'We won't be here very often. We have a full itinerary, starting tomorrow,' Gran reminded them.

'How is everyone? Is Grandad, okay?' Alice asked hesitantly, unsure how to bring up the fact he was absent.

'He's fine,' Jim said, 'he had that knee replacement not long ago, though, and didn't think sitting on a plane for that long would do it much good.'

'Oh. Yeah, of course,' Alice agreed quickly. 'It's a long flight.'

'He sends his love,' Gran said cheerfully. It was strange to think now how normal her grandparents' living arrangements seemed when only a year or so earlier they were all worried about how things would turn out. Gran seemed happier than ever. She had comfortably settled into Alice's old house and joined the local aviation club, often going away on trips. Grandad's life had barely changed—he simply got even more time to spend playing golf, so everything appeared to have worked out for the best.

Two hours later and having caught up on almost everything important, her family started to wane and decided to head off to their rooms.

'We'll have a nap and then we'll see you tonight at the restaurant.'

'Ah . . . okay,' Alice said. 'Which restaurant?'

'The one Frankie booked . . . he didn't tell you about dinner?'

'No . . . it seems he's missed telling me a few things lately.'

'Oh, well, maybe give him a call, he said he'd be sending a car. It all feels very *Pretty Woman*–like, doesn't it?' Gran said with a glint in her eye.

'Private cars, expensive motel rooms . . . the bloke must be worth a fortune. Hope he's paying you right,' her father muttered.

'I'm sure he is,' Alice said, having to still pinch herself each time she looked at her bank account. 'More than fairly.'

As she closed the door behind them, she let out a long sigh and reached for her phone.

'Hello,' Frankie said. 'Was wondering when I'd hear from you.'

The rush of rebukes about how much he'd spent and all the trouble he'd gone to, not to mention the secret keeping he'd done, melted away and she wasn't sure what to say. It was too much. He was too much—but in an utterly wonderful way.

'Alice?' he prompted when the line remained silent.

'Thank you,' she said quietly, unable to disguise the crack in her voice.

'It was my pleasure.'

'They're actually here. I can't believe you did that.'

'Happy?' he asked and she could almost picture the sultry look he'd be wearing.

'Very. I don't know how I can ever thank you.'

'I can think of a few ways, if you're really stuck for ideas,' he drawled.

'I have no doubt. Although it'll have to wait—apparently we're going out to dinner tonight?'

'I've booked a table at Mario's. I'll have to meet you there, I'm heading straight from the airport. I've missed you.'

Alice smiled. He'd only left the morning before. 'I've missed you too.'

'I've got to go. I'll see you tonight.'

Alice disconnected the call and smiled, closing her eyes. She wasn't sure life could possibly get any more amazing. Sometimes she felt guilty that she was so happy. It almost seemed like a dream, but at the same time, she was fairly sure she wouldn't feel this exhausted if it was all some figment of her imagination.

She had just over three hours to finish the paperwork she'd brought to the hotel and make the calls on her list. She wanted to make sure she had nothing left to do later tonight. That time was going to be spent showing Frankie how much his thoughtful gift really meant to her.

Chapter 27

Later that evening, when their limousine glided to a halt in front of the iconic restaurant, Alice felt her heart catch a little as a familiar tall shadow came forward and opened the door.

Alice took the hand Frankie offered and stepped out, determined not to make a fool of herself and cry again. The warmth of his skin sent a shot of desire to the centre of her being. No man should ever be as devastatingly handsome as this one was—he wore his good looks with all the subtlety of a sledgehammer. It was almost too much for a mere mortal. Tonight he was dressed in one of his signature form-fitting suits made from the most luxurious of materials. Frankie Esquire was a walking advertisement for his sexy, suave, James Bondesque lines. This was why Esquire was a red carpet must-have for celebrities all over the world.

As her father alighted from the car, followed by her mother and her gran, Frankie greeted each with a handshake and smile.

'Thank you so much for the beautiful room,' Kathy was saying as she beamed up at Frankie, who cradled her hand between both of his.

'It's my pleasure. I hope everything's to your liking?'

'It's far too extravagant for us. We'd have been happy in a motel room half as fancy.'

'I wanted to make sure your visit was memorable.'

'I reckon we'll be remembering this for a long while,' Jim said, clasping Frankie's hand firmly and giving it a shake. 'Jim Croydon. Nice to meet ya.'

'Good to meet you, too. I'm glad you were all able to make it on such short notice.'

'The missus always keeps the passports up to date. We've been waiting for an opportunity to do some travelling, just didn't think it would be for a while yet with all the grandkids at home.'

'What's happening with the babysitting?' Alice asked, remembering her parents usually had at least two of her siblings' children before and after school.

'It's all sorted. In fact, this trip has made us realise we're not as indispensable as we thought. We might actually plan a few more holidays here and there once we're home,' her father said.

'And I believe I have you to thank for sending me the photo that brought me out to Gunnindi?' Frankie said to Gran.

'I took the photo,' she admitted with a nod, 'but I had nothing to do with sending it to you, young man.'

'Gran,' Alice said, rolling her eyes, 'it's okay to admit it.' After all this time she still had no idea why Gran would be so reluctant to acknowledge her part in what had happened.

'If I'd done it, I would. But I didn't. It's not my story to tell.'

'Then whose is it?' Alice asked, exasperated.

'Like I said, it's not my place to say. But you'll work it out one day.'

Alice turned her curious gaze onto her parents, who both shook their heads. 'It wasn't us,' her mother said.

'For goodness' sake,' Alice muttered.

'I think it's time we go inside, before they give our table away,' Frankie cut in smoothly, guiding the small party towards the door. Gran smiled serenely and allowed Frankie to take her arm and escort her inside.

Alice's irritation evaporated the minute they were settled in their seats. She watched her parents and Gran look around, wide-eyed, as they spotted the celebrities seated at other tables. She was by no means immune to any of this either, but she was enjoying her family experiencing it and caught Frankie's eye to share a smile. Her heart felt as though it would explode inside her chest with love for his thoughtfulness. She would never have imagined being able to give her parents the experiences Frankie was giving them.

It took a moment to process that idea and when she did, she felt a tingle run through her veins and into her fingertips. It was love. Without a doubt, she knew she was in love with Frankie Esquire.

'Are you all right?' he asked, leaning closer to her briefly.

'I'm fine,' she answered, feeling those tingles in her extremities once more. 'I couldn't be better.'

Whatever he saw on her face must have reassured him, because his eyes softened and he gave her one of his lethal half-smiles.

Frankie was the perfect conversationalist, asking questions, listening intently and even sharing more than a few funny anecdotes about his time working with celebrities. He managed to wrap her mother and grandmother around his little finger and, even more surprising, seemed to have gained her father's approval, if Jim's hearty laughter was any indication.

After they'd finished dessert and turned down coffee, the group rose from the table and headed back to the waiting limo. As Alice made to follow the others into the car, Frankie took her hand and held her back.

'If you don't mind, I've got a second car to take us back.'

Alice glanced at her parents, but found them smiling as they waved her off.

'Don't worry about us. We'll be hitting the hay as soon as we get back to the room. We'll see you tomorrow,' Gran said, closing the door.

Well, fine, Alice thought, slightly put out.

Inside their car, Frankie sat in silence. Alice glanced over at him more than a few times, uncertainly, as the car drove through the quiet streets back to his apartment.

'Is everything all right?' she ventured.

'Of course,' he said with a swift smile, then looked almost relieved when they pulled up outside the building.

Inside the elevator, he tugged her close and, for the first time that evening, kissed her. They came up for air when the muted ding to announce the floor sounded and they reluctantly pulled apart.

His apartment was nothing short of stunning. Each time she came here she felt as though she were walking into an art gallery, there were so many beautiful works hanging on the walls. Even the furniture looked like art.

The views from the balcony were just as breathtaking. Alice was surprised by the bottle of champagne and glasses set out on the table, but didn't have time to think on it as Frankie slipped his arms around her and kissed her again.

'I don't think I will ever get tired of doing that,' she murmured drowsily when he lifted his head a little while later.

'That's good to hear,' he said and Alice opened her eyes to find him watching her almost warily.

'What's wrong?'

'Alice, bringing your parents over here wasn't exactly a purely selfless act on my part,' he started, sounding unusually nervous. 'In fact, I did it for a reason . . . I mean, other than because I wanted you to have them here to celebrate your first show.' He paused then swore softly and stepped away from her. 'The thing is, I wanted to see them in person. To ask their permission for something.'

'Their permission?' Alice stared at him blankly. What on earth would a man like Frankie Esquire need her parents' permission for—

She went all tingly once more, only this time it felt a lot more like she was going to pass out.

'Alice, would you do me the honour of marrying me?' he asked before she had the chance to faint.

Marry him? They'd only just become a couple! Surely they didn't know each other well enough to get married? She'd been with Finn for eight years before he proposed. 'Yes,' she heard herself say.

What? Hang on—what?

The relief on his handsome face would have been almost comical if she hadn't been freaking out herself.

But her confusion disappeared when he kissed her again, making her forget everything else except how right this felt.

'Well? What did she say?' her father's voice boomed from the open glass door.

Alice spun around and found her family standing on the patio behind them.

'She said yes, of course, son! Do you think she'd be kissing him like that if she said no?' Gran admonished with a click of her tongue.

'Congratulations, darling,' her mother said, hugging Alice tight.

'I thought you went back to the hotel,' Alice stammered.

'You seriously think we could have slept without knowing what your answer was?' Gran asked.

'Thank God it wasn't no,' Jim said, slapping Frankie on the back with a chuckle. 'That would have been a bit awkward.'

'Hey, sis! Congrats!' Charlie said, walking into the apartment, followed by her other siblings and their spouses.

She turned her disbelieving gaze to Frankie and stared speechlessly, her eyes rapidly filling with tears once more.

'Surprise,' he said softly. 'You didn't think I was going to let an occasion as special as this one happen without the whole Croydon clan here to celebrate, did you?'

'I can't believe you did this,' she said, slipping into his arms to hold him tightly. 'It's too much.'

'It's never too much. Not for you,' he said as she pulled back to smile up at him.

Alice couldn't help the laugh that escaped as she stared at the sea of faces around them. She had the man of her dreams and a career most people could only wish for. Life didn't get any more perfect than this and here it was, hers for the taking.

Part Three

Chapter 28

The endless ribbon of grey bitumen stretched out before her, flanked by wide-open paddocks of brown and the shimmering heat haze dancing in the distance. It was hard to believe this time last year she was rugged up in winter clothing as carollers sang on street corners and snow blanketed the streets.

Alice swore as the shadow on the edge of the road stood up and bounded straight across the road in front of her car. She gritted her teeth and squinted, bracing for impact, and was grateful when none came. In the rear-view mirror she caught the indignant way the large kangaroo stood and stared after her, and she gave a hollow chuckle.

She hadn't missed dodging kangaroos over the last few years; it wasn't something she had to consider that often in London. An image of busy streets with red double-decker buses and taxis zooming by flashed through her mind. The city was about as far as you could get from the narrow country road she was driving along now.

She cringed as a rock flew up and hit the underside of her new Range Rover Sport. She knew her father and brothers would laugh themselves silly at her latest purchase. Their idea of a Range Rover was the boxy old four-wheel drive her grandparents had once owned, not the luxurious cross between a sports car and an SUV she was currently driving. But she loved her new car and maybe she was just a little too excited to see her brothers drool over it . . . okay, she was *very* excited. The last time they'd visited her, shortly after she'd arrived back in Sydney, they'd given her a hard time about her practical little second-hand hatchback. 'Sis, you're worth a fortune and you drive a shitbox like this?' Charlie had exclaimed, shaking his head at the car parked under her apartment.

'I don't actually need a car very often, so I just picked this one up to run around in.' It had seemed logical at the time.

It was only when she'd run out of excuses to return home to Gunnindi that she'd had a sudden urge to splash out on a new car. Most of it was just to show off to her brothers, but there was another tiny voice that she tried to ignore that wondered if perhaps there were also a few other people around town she wanted to impress. She really didn't want to be *that* person who flaunted their success, and up until now she hadn't been. She'd been too busy working and designing and creating her own business to give much thought to enjoying the fruits of her labour except for the bare essentials—although they were pretty nice bare essentials, she had to admit.

Now, though, it was time to wind down a bit—as much as she could with her own label and fashion house, that was. She'd made the return to Australia six months ago and it was the start of a new chapter—one she was determined to enjoy at a slower pace. There'd been too many signs lately that life could change in a heartbeat and make you reassess everything you'd thought you had control over—like time.

She'd missed her family. Over her years in London she'd only returned to Gunnindi twice and they'd been flying visits—one for her grandad's funeral, three years after she left home, and once for Christmas about five years ago. She'd been back to Australia a number of times for the fashion week and various events, but her family usually met her in Sydney, and once a year her parents and Gran had come to the UK to stay with her. But it wasn't the same as living in the same hemisphere.

Ten years was a long time to be away and a lot of things had changed since she was that small-town girl who only dreamed of a simple life in Gunnindi. She wasn't the girl who'd left town, certain she'd be back to pick up her old life, anymore. But her old life had up and married Shelly Turnbull. And Alice had married Frankie.

The society pages had loved them—they were dubbed the fashion world's Ryan Reynolds and Blake Lively and her life had been a fairy tale come true.

But as in all fairy tales, there always came the dark moment when everything falls apart, and that moment had come eighteen months ago, when Frankie was killed in a plane crash.

She pushed away the hollow feeling inside. It always caught her by surprise. Just when she thought she'd managed to move a few steps ahead, the grief dragged her back again. Her chest ached—a dull pain now, but it was still there when she thought of him.

Through her polaroid sunglasses, the sky took on an impossible blue that stretched out forever. She'd missed all this space with nothing but the odd tractor or windmill to break the vastness of the landscape, till eventually one little remote farm house became two and then a few more appeared, then eventually the road signs advertising motels and pubs emerged.

The Welcome to Gunnindi sign had been revamped, now sporting a pretty flower bed and modern timber sculpture. Alice smiled at the familiar landmarks she drove past: the netball courts she played on as a kid; the primary school and swimming pool. Christmas decorations adorned the light posts and there were happy-looking Santas and reindeer in shop windows. She'd missed Christmas in summertime. Her smile turned melancholy as she passed the high school and memories of Finn instantly came to mind.

That didn't take long. She'd thought she'd have a little longer before he invaded her peace of mind. Once the floodgate opened, though, the memories came thick and fast: the park where they used to hang out after school and the tree they spent many an hour making out under. She could almost smell the scent of Brut, the only fragrance Finn had ever worn.

She passed the houses of friends and the showground, where she recalled the annual show and all the excitement that used to come with it: the rides and the fairy floss; toffee apples and ring events. Alice felt a stab of longing for those days when she had been plain old Alice Croydon and everything had seemed so simple. For a moment, she wished she could turn back the clock and stay there.

She'd never gotten used to the world of the paparazzi or celebrities, despite the fact she'd lived in it for most of the last decade. She'd eventually learned to deal with it, but nothing had prepared her for the feeding frenzy that followed Frankie's death. She'd been followed around and mobbed by paparazzi during the worst time of her life—the media circling like vultures, desperate for the photos of a weeping widow as they searched for any juicy gossip that might have slipped out. They'd been disappointed when nothing surfaced, but it didn't stop them following her to the funeral home or hiding behind bushes to snap a photo of her greeting people who came to visit—red-eyed and without make-up—to splash across the front pages of trashy tabloids.

Alice's whole world had turned upside down overnight. She'd lost her business partner, her best friend and her lover in one fell swoop, and she soon realised there was an enormous burden on her shoulders, as she was left with the responsibility of running Frankie's vast fashion empire. Alice went from fashion designer to boardroom businesswoman, thrown into the deep end, suddenly having to make decisions about a multitude of dilemmas. She'd been left with little time to grieve. It had taken almost twelve months to sort out the legalities and figure out how best to continue Frankie's businesses without him at the helm.

Alice had never had the drive for business the way Frankie had—that side of things just hadn't interested her. But she hadn't been able to turn her back on the legacy Frankie had created either, so she'd given up her own designing in order to find the best way forward for Frankie's businesses. For the second time, her passion and creativity had taken a backseat.

Julian and Adel had become her closest friends over the years and had been there with her, holding her up during the excruciating days after the accident, but as for all Frankie's celebrity friends, they'd disappeared and Alice had realised just how shallow a lot of their world had really been. She missed her family. She missed home. London wasn't home without Frankie.

One positive to have come out of all of the heartache was having her siblings' support. Charlie, in particular, was a godsend. She had financial advisers and accountants, business advisers and consultants coming out of her ears, but the only one who had helped make any of it understandable was her brother. They'd spent hours on phone or video calls, going over her options. More than once, Charlie had reminded her he wasn't the business tycoon her husband had been and wasn't sure he'd be much help, but he knew enough to explain in layman terms what all the so-called professionals had been dumping on her.

In the end, she had sold off the bulk of the businesses and decided to concentrate only on the things she had any hope of trying to understand, like the fashion labels. She'd then moved everything back to Australia to establish a new label under her own name.

She hadn't been back to Gunnindi since her relocation from London—she'd been busy setting up her new head office—but Christmas was around the corner and this year she was going to focus more on family and less on work.

She caught her breath as she rolled to a stop outside her little cottage. The string of Christmas lights on the front fence and the neat row of plastic milk bottles with tiny electric tea light candles inside a cut-out window made her chuckle. The milk bottles were her mum's idea, and most houses on the street had them.

In the lead-up to Christmas, Kathy went into a frenzy of baking, decorating and planning. It started with the lighting of the Christmas lights, on the first of December, when the entire street had a party, going from house to house to turn on their lights. Alice hadn't made it home in time for it this year, but the street looked amazing as usual. Except for one house in the middle. Old Mr Townsend was a bit of a grump at the best of times, but he really came into his own during the festive season. It annoyed her mother no end, and Alice suspected that was exactly why Mr Townsend did it. Kathy, though, never one to give in, determinedly placed plastic milk bottles on the footpath in front of his house and lit the candles inside them every night between the first of December and the twenty-sixth.

Of course, Mr Townsend had blustered and ranted about having the candles in front of his house, but seeing as they were on the footpath, there was really nothing he could do. So her mother had her small victory, which took away some of her irritation that the street hadn't achieved the one hundred per cent decorating rate she would be so proud of.

Alice's cottage hadn't changed at all, and an avalanche of memories unexpectedly crashed through her. Over the years, Gran had lived in it, as well as other family and friends, but it was currently empty after the last tenants had moved out a little over a fortnight ago. Alice knew she had to make a decision on this trip about whether to sell it or hold on to it.

She'd thought maybe once she came out and saw it again she'd realise she'd simply been holding on to an idealistic memory of the past—that once she was here, she'd see it was only a little old house and all those feelings she had for it had just been blown up as part of her homesickness.

She was wrong.

Her attachment *had* come from all the memories, but now that she was here, she knew her mind had actually played them *down*, not *up*, and an overwhelming sense of homecoming flooded her senses, which resulted in an unexpected sting of tears.

Her phone ringing had Alice quickly wiping her eyes as she answered the call.

'Hey, Mum.'

'Where are you? Are you almost here?'

'Put the jug on, I'll be there in five,' she said.

'Jim, quick, switch on the jug!' Alice heard her mother call to her father.

With a determined breath in, Alice forced away the unexpected emotion, put her car into gear and drove away from the house.

Chapter 29

As she turned into her parents' driveway and caught sight of the house she grew up in, her smile stretched wide. It was decorated with Christmas lights and a small lean-to manger and plyboard cut-outs of Mary, Joseph, the wise men and assorted animals. Her father had painstakingly made the Nativity scene one year when Alice had been in primary school. It was a family heirloom that had all five siblings fighting over who would inherit it—or rather, who *didn't* want to inherit it. From a distance the scene looked amazing, but close up, it was the stuff of nightmares. While her father was an outstanding carpenter, he was severely challenged in the artistic department. The faces he'd attempted to paint on Mary and Joseph were truly horrific and one of the wise men had a Freddy Krueger vibe that had given Alice many a night of bad dreams growing up. Still, it was part of the Croydon

Christmas tradition and it always gave Alice a warm, fuzzy feeling to see the house in full festive spirit.

Alice had barely had time to turn off the engine before the front door was thrown open and her parents appeared on the verandah. With hugs and kisses duly dispatched, Alice left her father with the keys to explore the Range Rover while she and her mother headed inside to have a cuppa.

'It's good to have you home again,' Kathy said as she took down coffee cups. 'You look better than when we saw you last time. You've got a bit more colour about you.'

Her parents had met her at the airport when she'd arrived from London and been alarmed at how pale and thin she'd become. 'It just doesn't get that sunny in London very often,' she'd tried to explain. Alice had been mindful that she needed to rectify that issue before this visit and had been taking regular walks and doing some outdoorsy stuff and clearly it had made a difference, if her mother's lack of concerned lecturing was any indication.

'Where's Gran?' Alice asked, looking around.

'She's at Zumba, she'll be home any minute,' her mum said, glancing at the clock on the wall.

Of course she was. Gran hadn't slowed down at all. Meryl was now ninety and doing even more than she did a decade ago, it seemed. She'd only given up her beloved flying a couple of years ago when her eyesight let her down and she'd failed her annual test.

A decade? Had it really been that long? In some ways it felt like it but in others it was almost as though Alice had only just left. She was still sad she hadn't been able to get home for

Granny Dot's funeral. She'd made a hundred and three, and had still been smiling and singing until the very end. At the time, Alice had been sick with a flu that had put her in bed for close to two weeks, making travel impossible.

'Speak of the devil.' Her mother chuckled as she reached for a fourth cup as a horn gave a merry toot outside. 'That'll be Estelle dropping Gran back now.'

Alice stood up to greet her gran as she came inside. She seemed frailer as Alice wrapped her arms around her, but her hug was tight—sending Alice back to when she was a little girl in her gran's fierce embrace.

'I've missed you,' Gran said, stepping back to look at her. 'You look better,' she added with a note of approval.

'I've missed you too, Gran.' Alice smiled fondly at the sight before her—Gran dressed in bright pink activewear and joggers. The woman was an unstoppable force of nature. There was no way she looked ninety.

'Here we go, a nice cuppa after a long drive,' her mum said, placing a tray on the table with coffee and freshly made scones, still hot from the oven.

The back door opened and Alice's father came inside, dropping her car keys on the bench and shaking his head. 'It goes like a shower of shit,' he said approvingly.

'Jim. Really,' her mother tsked, frowning at her husband as he washed his hands at the sink before returning to the table.

Alice grinned at him. 'You thinking about getting one then, Dad?'

'Not bloody likely. No, thanks, I'm happy with the old Nissan. She might not be fancy, but she does the job.'

Alice wondered if she was being subtly reprimanded for wasting her money on something so expensive, but her father was already reaching for a scone.

'Everyone's coming for dinner tonight,' her mum said. 'It feels like Christmas already.'

It kind of did. Alice had never been home this early for Christmas. Last time she only came back a day or so before the big day and then had to leave again, but this time . . .

She had nothing to hurry home for now. She'd closed down the business for a Christmas break, and there was only an empty apartment waiting for her back in Sydney. For the first time in years, she was looking forward to surrounding herself with family and food and happy memories.

Chapter 30

Alice wandered out of her room later that afternoon and spotted Gran sitting on the swing seat in the garden.

'Here she is.' Gran smiled and shuffled over so Alice could sit down beside her. 'Did you have a rest?'

'I can't sleep through the day,' Alice said, her mouth twisting in a self-deprecating smile.

'Me either. Plenty of time to sleep when I'm dead,' she said cheerfully.

'Gran,' Alice said with a small frown. 'Don't talk like that.'

'Well, it's the truth, I've got too much to do before then.'

'You really are amazing, you know that?' She nudged her gran's shoulder lightly.

'I've got an amazing life,' Gran corrected. 'Just like you have.'

They looked out across Jim's manicured back lawn and Kathy's lovingly tended veggie patch, enjoying the quiet.

'I'm so proud of everything you've achieved,' Gran said, taking her hand.

A rush of love surged through Alice as she felt the soft coolness of her gran's wrinkled hand. 'I'm not sure I would ever have been brave enough to do it if you hadn't been the role model you were.'

'You followed your dreams. Just like I did.'

'Did it make you happy, Gran?' she asked. 'Following your dreams? With Grandad and everything.'

For a few moments, Gran didn't answer. 'It came at a cost— as does any change,' she admitted. 'Your grandad and I had been growing apart for a long time, so long that by the time I'd decided to speak up, our marriage had just become a habit. I still loved him,' she said with a sad smile, 'but we ended up wanting different things, which caused a lot of friction. Still it worked out in the end. Our family was always the most important thing in our lives, so nothing changed there. We just spent the last years of his life more as friends. I know a lot of people our age who had a relationship far worse than that.

'And what about you?' Gran asked as the swing rocked gently back and forth. 'How are you doing? Really.'

Alice managed a brief smile at the tone of her gran's voice. It was the same one she used when she had to get to the bottom of an argument or fight between Alice and her siblings when they'd been younger. The one that they all knew you didn't try and fib your way out of.

'It's been tough,' Alice admitted. 'But since I've moved back, it's gotten a little easier.'

Gran patted her hand gently. 'It'll take time. It can't have been easy. Frankie was a good man.'

Alice swallowed past the tightening of her throat and nodded. He *had* been a good man. He'd been her whole world. Every aspect of her life had been wrapped up in Frankie— professionally, privately—and it had been impossible to see where she ended and he began. After his death, part of her had been shocked by just how much of her life had revolved around him. It hadn't been intentional, it was just the way it was. They may not have spent every waking hour together in the office, but the business was always around them. Then at home, they simply enjoyed their downtime with no one knocking on office doors or phones ringing with an urgent crisis that demanded attention. Once he was gone, though, she realised the enormous gap he'd left in her life. Over the last eighteen months she'd felt like a toddler learning to walk and talk—learning to live on her own.

Those first few weeks after the accident had been a blur of grief. She'd had so many decisions to make: the funeral arrangements; the press; the business. Everything needed her attention despite the fact her heart was broken and she felt like a zombie as she tried to contemplate the fact her husband was dead. But, in a way, it was the business that had stopped her hiding from the world under the bed covers. There were staff who needed their jobs, bills that needed paying, obligations she couldn't simply ignore. And so she'd masked her grief and gotten on with it. But without Frankie England no longer felt like home.

'I'm glad you made the decision to come home.'

'Me too. I don't think I could have let go of the past if I'd stayed. Everything was connected to Frankie.' Sometimes Alice felt as though it had been a betrayal of sorts to leave the UK and return home, but she'd known she had to do it. While she stayed in the home Frankie had owned and ran the business he'd created, she'd never truly felt ready to move on.

Once she'd made the decision to leave, a weight lifted from her shoulders. She still grieved, but it wasn't the kind of dysfunctional grief that had her hugging her husband's pillow each night and curling up with one of his T-shirts so she could pretend he was still with her, as she'd done in those first hollow months after his death. Now she could think of him and not crumple in pain. She could smile at the memories and not feel guilty for being happy on occasion. She was no longer angry at the world. She was, however, restless. It was understandable, she supposed, so much of her life had been turned upside down, but lately something had been niggling at her—a need for something she couldn't quite put her finger on. A change. It didn't make any sense—she'd already made huge changes and yet there was still this . . . *feeling*.

'We're all incredibly proud of you, darling,' Gran said, squeezing Alice's hand gently. 'You've come so far. But I can't help thinking that there's still so much you've yet to do.'

'World domination, Gran?' Alice quirked her lips dryly.

Gran smiled. 'Who knows?'

'I think I've done everything I set out to do.'

Gran shook her head adamantly. 'There's a reason you came back,' she said, holding Alice's eye. 'You've got more to do.'

And here I was thinking I'd just come home for Christmas to relax for a while.

❖

The next morning, Alice dropped her mother off at the hospital where she volunteered in the cafe once a month. She helped carry the containers of treats Kathy had baked the night before and greeted a few of the ladies who worked with her mother, catching up on gossip and local news. Alice had been shocked to learn that so many of the hospital services had been lost and that the town could lose what remained if the population continued to dwindle.

'I had no idea things were this bad,' she said, as she helped set up for the day.

'It's not just happening here,' one of the women said with a weary kind of acceptance that Alice found sad. 'Places all over are facing the same problems. The more remote you are, the less you're heard in the city by the people making the decisions.'

When Alice was done, she kissed her mother's cheek and promised to be back later that afternoon to pick her up. Instead of heading directly back to the house, Alice decided to explore the town.

The river situated on the edge of town might not be the most attractive river—its murky colour didn't look overly inviting—but she and her siblings and friends had spent countless hours swimming in it as kids. It held fond memories of hot summer days, freedom and happiness. To this day, the smell of sunscreen still sent her right back to those times.

She closed her eyes and could almost feel the cool water on her skin as it beaded after a swim, eating hot chips as they sat on towels under the shade of the huge eucalyptus trees, music blaring from a CD player. *Wow, way to date yourself,* she thought with a snort. Her new car didn't even *have* a CD player. Apparently, they were *so* last decade.

As she turned towards town, she came to a stop outside the old wool mill gates. As kids they'd once broken in on a dare and convinced themselves the place was haunted. To be fair, it *looked* haunted. When she'd snooped around inside all those years ago, it had saddened Alice to find the place had been abandoned. All the old machinery that had been used for almost fifty years to turn the local wool into balls of fine, dyed yarn and ship it around the world had been left where it stood to time and the elements. As had the art of wool spinning—lost to a modern age in factories far away.

The building itself was heritage listed, hidden behind an ugly security fence and strangled by weeds and vegetation. It didn't seem right. With a reluctant sigh, she pulled back onto the road, but something bothered her, making her glance in the rear-view mirror as she drove away. Thoughts of a long-ago conversation she'd once had with Frankie about investing in Gunnindi wool production came back to her. They never had got around to releasing that collection of business wear, summer casual wear and formal attire made of one hundred per cent pure wool. Her focus had been on her wedding collection—that's where she'd made her name and created her following. And Frankie had been right, it was hard to deviate from her core clientele. Changing your business focus was a big risk, but that was back when she was working alongside Frankie and the Esquire empire. She was no longer tied to all the restrictions—real or imagined—of a celebrity label.

She wasn't sure what to make of the sudden spike in her pulse rate after recalling her old idea. She'd once had such a passion for putting Gunnindi wool on the world stage, back when she'd still been a wide-eyed novice and nothing had seemed impossible. Was it just this melancholic trip down memory lane making her all nostalgic? Or something more?

The main street still looked the same, just older and more tired looking. Last time she'd been home the place had been bustling. Now she was sad to see a number of empty shops with faded For Rent signs in the windows that suggested they'd been on the market for some time.

When the local mine closed down a few years earlier it had forced a number of people, including some of her own family and friends, to try and find another job, but most had had to relocate. It was a fickle industry, mining. It moved into a district and the whole economy boomed, then the company shut the doors and small towns paid the price, losing businesses and families when the work and money dried up.

Toby and Charlie had been two examples of the fallout—both had had well paid, secure jobs until the mine shut down. Toby had started his own trucking company and seemed to be doing well, while Charlie had found employment with the local council. Although he'd been lucky to find a job in town, Alice knew the cut in pay had taken a bit of adjusting to. One thing mining jobs did was pay well.

It wasn't like the situation was anything new, though—the gold rush era had done the same thing, creating boom towns with fifty pubs and thousands of people that were abandoned and left for nature to reclaim once there was no more gold to be found.

Still, it was sad to see Gunnindi looking so . . . empty.

There was one place that didn't seem to be suffering the recent downturn in town, though. As she parked outside the little store, with its familiar black and white striped awning and old bicycle with a basket of bright flowers out the front, she felt a fond smile fill her face. Chic Chateau was still as elegantly out of place in the small town as ever, and yet so integral to the landscape.

She pushed open the front door and instantly Alice was taken back in time—almost as though the last ten years hadn't happened. It still smelled the same, and yet another flood of feelings came rushing back: Finn, moving into their house, family get-togethers, opening and closing the shop—the memories flashed through her mind like a kaleidoscope with dizzying speed and her chest squeezed with an almost forgotten pain.

She pushed it away as she spotted Antoinette, busy with two customers on the other side of the room, and wandered over to a nearby rack to idly flick through the garments.

Nothing seemed to have changed. The clothes were different, but they still hung on the same racks and the displays were all just as chic and stylish as ever. A familiar logo caught her eye on another rack and she walked towards it. *Esquire.* The bold, yet eye-catching logo was instantly recognisable all over the world. A smile pulled at her lips and she swallowed hard over a lump in her throat. Grief was a funny thing, the way it liked to creep up on you and pounce. She blinked quickly as her fingers touched the delicate silk dress. Maybe it was seeing Frankie's name here, among all her other memories, that had somehow managed to catch her off guard; maybe it was just because she missed him.

'I was wondering if you'd ever drop by.' The familiar softly accented voice also brought a smile and Alice turned.

'Hello, Antoinette.' She looked older—still perfectly made-up and smooth skinned, but older. It seemed, even with all the surgery and Botox, you couldn't hold ageing off completely.

'Hello, chérie,' Antoinette said, a fond smile touching her lips. 'You're looking well.' She took a moment to run her gaze across Alice's face. 'I'm so sorry for your loss. It must have been a terrible shock.'

'Yes, it was,' Alice said, still not comfortable with condolences. There'd been so many when it first happened, too many. She never really knew what to say, other than thank you. And yet that seemed so . . . insignificant.

'He was a brilliant designer—the fashion industry has lost one of its brightest stars.'

'Yes. It has,' Alice agreed, turning her attention to the store, quickly. 'The shop is looking as beautiful as ever.'

'Thank you. Not much has changed,' Antoinette said. 'I imagine you're used to far more glamorous showrooms.'

KARLY LANE

Her comment surprised Alice as she tried to decipher the woman's tone, which seemed light, but didn't match the guarded look she wore. 'I can still appreciate a lovely window display—even if it *is* in Gunnindi and not Paris or London.'

The smile Antoinette gave bordered on a wince. She straightened a coat hanger on a display rack. 'I must say you've come quite a long way from the shy little shop assistant who worked here.'

'It's funny where life leads you.'

'It is.'

'Or who had a hand in making things happen,' Alice added, holding the older woman's gaze firmly.

'I'm sorry?' Antoinette asked.

'I often thought about the day Frankie arrived on my doorstep, completely out of the blue, to look at that wedding dress. Gran admitted she took the photo, but she never would say who sent it to him.'

Antoinette lifted a sculptured eyebrow and held her look silently.

'I thought, who would have the connections to get something in front of Frankie Esquire? It was pretty obvious you'd be the only person able to pull something like that off. My only question is, why? Why would you have done something like that, but refuse to ever sell my designs?' Alice had never been able to make any sense of Antoinette's actions.

'Why do you think?' Antoinette asked, lightly resting one arm along the top of the nearest rack.

'Trust me, I've searched my brain for years,' Alice said. 'You never once showed any interest in my designs.'

'That's not true, you know.' Antoinette shook her head. 'I was astounded by your designs. They were too good for you to be wasting them on a place like this.'

Alice frowned as she stared at her old employer. 'But you barely even looked at them.'

'I looked. I saw so much potential in you, Alice. But you were completely oblivious to your talent.' She threw a manicured hand in the air theatrically. 'All you thought about was getting married and having babies with that boy you were with. If I'd agreed to let you sell those dresses in my shop, you would never have gone on to do what you have. You would have been content to sew your little garments and hang them in my store.'

That's exactly what Alice had wanted to do back then. Would that have been so bad? But then the truth of Antoinette's words sank in. She wouldn't have met Frankie again and he wouldn't have offered her a job . . . her life in London would never have happened.

'Chérie,' Antoinette said softly, 'I know I was hard on you—perhaps too hard sometimes—but I was so *frustrated* by you . . . maybe even a little jealous.'

'Jealous?' Alice repeated, eyeing her former boss oddly. This woman had been the epitome of style and grace—a confident, beautiful businesswoman who seemed to be the most together person Alice had ever met.

'When I was a teenager, I ran away from home. I couldn't wait to go out into the world and travel and explore—do amazing things. I, like you, loved fashion. I dreamed of being a designer—I worked whatever jobs I could find in the city and

I saved like no tomorrow, until I had enough money to fly to Paris.' Antoinette's eyes lit up the moment she mentioned the beautiful city, and the transformation was quite astounding. She looked twenty years younger.

'I applied for every job I could find, with every fashion house there was, but none would take me on,' she said, shaking her head. 'I thought I had talent—and maybe I did—but it wasn't any more special than the talent of a thousand other people who were chasing their dreams in Paris. The realisation crushed me and all my dreams simply died. I ran out of money and was forced to come home with my tail between my legs.'

'That must have been heartbreaking.'

'It was,' Antoinette agreed, 'but my dream wasn't where I thought it was. It wasn't until I came home that I realised where my passion truly lay and that was in the clothing itself—not designing it but selling it. Sharing it with people and helping women find the right clothing to make them look and feel special. *That* is my gift. My calling.'

And it was. That was the secret behind Chic Chateau's success. People came here because it was an experience and because Antoinette knew her stuff. This little store in the middle of nowhere would simply not work with anyone else at the helm.

'That is why I was frustrated with you. You had talent—*real* talent—and you were wasting it out here. When you turned down that internship after the fashion show with Frankie Esquire, of *all* people,' she added with a note of incredulity, 'I couldn't believe it. I'd thought winning that fashion week spot would be when you finally *did* something with your life, but you came back!

'Your grandmother came into the shop one day while you were out, just after I refused to sell those dresses you brought in. She was so angry,' Antoinette said, and chuckled. 'I thought she was going to start throwing things. She demanded to know why I wouldn't sell your dresses and told me how talented you were, and I agreed. I explained to her that I had not given up hope that one day you would come to your senses and realise your talent. Your grandmother agreed with me, and we got talking. She asked me if I knew how to get in touch with Frankie and I said I could try through a buyer friend of mine. She took the photo of your wedding dress and I sent it away.'

'I don't know what to say,' Alice finally admitted.

'You don't have to say anything. Everything worked out the way it was supposed to.'

Had it? Maybe on some level, but it was hard to understand why Frankie had been taken from her. Was that also meant to be? They hadn't had anywhere near long enough together. She wasn't ready to be a widow.

'I'm so proud of how far you've come, Alice,' Antoinette said, breaking into Alice's dull pain.

'Thank you. I might not have understood at the time, but without you stepping in, I would never have led the life I have so far.'

Antoinette shook her head slowly. The once jet-black hair was a little less dark nowadays, there were a few fine streaks of silver, but it was still worn in a meticulous, elegant bob.

'It was all you, my dear. Without your talent you would never have gone as far as you have.'

Alice thought about that conversation for a long time after she left the boutique. If all those little pieces of the plan hadn't fallen into place, if Frankie had never come out here to find her, what would her life have looked like now?

She would have married Finn and worn her beautiful dress, which had been lovingly packed away in a chest at her parents' house once the wedding had been called off. She hadn't thought about that dress in years, she realised. Funny, because it had marked the start of her new life, just not in the way she'd expected.

Without that dress, Frankie would never have come looking for her. Fate—it sure was a strange beast.

Chapter 31

'Look what your father found,' her mum said as Alice came into the kitchen searching for coffee the next morning.

Alice regarded the small cardboard box sitting on the table warily. From past experience, that box could contain anything from a fruit bat to a blue tongue lizard. Her dad was always finding things and bringing them home.

'What is it?' she asked without moving any closer.

'A bird. We just googled it. We think it's a quail.'

That sounded harmless enough. Alice switched the jug on and walked across to peer inside the box. 'Oh, it's bigger than I was expecting,' she said, jumping a little and closing the lid quickly as the scratchy sound of claws seeking traction on the floor of the box sounded. 'Where did you find it?'

'In the garden at the men's shed,' her father said. He'd joined the organisation a few years earlier and spent a couple of days a week hanging out with other local men his age, building stuff. The shed had given him purpose again after his retirement. 'No idea where it came from—there's nothing around out that way.'

It was true, the men's shed was located in an industrial estate and didn't seem like the kind of place a quail would be found.

'What are you going to do with it?' Alice asked, taking down a mug.

'Dunno,' her father said, thoughtfully. 'Thinkin' about keepin' it.'

'Really?' Alice asked.

'I heard they're good eating.'

'Oh, yes,' her mother added. 'They're quite a delicacy. *Very* fancy.'

Alice had often seen quail on the menu in restaurants over the years, but never tried it. 'So, you're going to *eat* it?'

'Maybe? Although it wouldn't be much of a meal . . . just one,' her father said.

'Well, regardless, you can't just have one bird. It'll need company,' her mum said.

'You'll have to build an aviary or something to keep them in,' Alice pointed out. They'd had a cat and a dog when she was younger, but once they both passed, they'd never gotten any more pets. Her parents probably always had their hands full with kids and grandkids. Although this was sounding more like a paddock-to-plate venture than a pet situation.

'I reckon I could build something.' Jim nodded. 'Yeah,' he decided. 'I'll do that.' He stood up and headed for the back door.

'Where are you going?' Kathy called.

'Down to the shed to make up some plans,' he said, pulling on his work boots.

'What about the bird? What are we supposed to do with it?' But he'd already gone.

Her mother shook her head as she ran water in the sink to wash up the few dishes from breakfast. 'Honestly, he's getting worse as he gets older. What are we going to do with a bunch of birds?'

'It might be relaxing.'

'We don't even know what to feed it. What do they eat?'

'Don't look at me. I have no idea,' Alice said.

'I've got to get ready for the CWA Christmas luncheon— would you be a darling and pop down to the feed store and ask Vernon? Who knows how long it's been since the poor thing's eaten.'

'Sure,' Alice said, sipping her coffee. She had no plans today anyway.

'Goodness knows where we're going to put it until your father builds this aviary of his. He didn't think of that did he? We'll keep it, he says. Might be fun, he says,' her mother muttered as she left the kitchen.

The Feed Shed was the local rural store, situated on the outskirts of town and owned by Vernon Croydon, one of her father's cousins. It supplied most of the local farming community with everything they needed for every conceivable form of livestock and farming need. She pushed open her door and walked across the parking lot towards the massive grey shed.

Despite the fact she'd dressed in jeans and a T-shirt and pulled her copper-toned hair back in a ponytail, she still felt conspicuously overdressed. But she suspected most of the staring she felt was to do with being recognised, not really because of how she was dressed. It felt strange for all that to follow her back to Gunnindi. Here she'd always felt like plain old Alice.

She slipped her sunglasses onto the top of her head and looked around as the familiar smells of fertiliser, pet food and hay instantly took her back in time. Once, she'd been a frequent customer here—dropping in to pick up couriered parcels for Finn and his family, bringing out a bag of feed or any number of other urgent 'before you come out, can you grab something from the feed store' calls. A lifetime ago now, she thought as she looked around for Vernon.

He was serving a customer at the far end of the shed and she decided to idly wander the aisles while she waited. She stopped in front of a wall filled with an assortment of rubber bands and long-handled implements that looked slightly off-putting.

'Thinking about castrating someone?'

Alice turned and froze. She knew the voice but she'd reacted so quickly, she hadn't given herself time to form a polite mask before facing him. Now she feared her face might actually be locked in some kind of gaping, fish-out-of-water type expression. 'Finn.' She'd been mentally preparing to see him again, she just hadn't expected it to be today . . . like this.

'Hi,' she said, shaking off the lingering fog of shock.

'Thought it was you,' he said, 'but then I wasn't sure . . . it's not exactly the first place in town I'd think of finding you.'

His voice sounded strange to her ears, yet so familiar. It was like having déjà vu.

'No, I . . .' she began, struggling to grab hold of her senses so she could function like a grown adult. 'Mum asked me to come down and ask Vernon . . . something.' She waved a dismissive hand nervously. 'But, wow, it's good to see you. It's been . . . ages.'

Finn gave a slightly amused grunt. 'Probably close to ten years, I reckon.'

'That's crazy.' It sounded like a lot. It *was* a lot, but it still only felt like yesterday that everything ended and she'd left for London.

'Yeah. We're, like, officially old now.' He grinned slightly.

'Well, *older*,' she amended, echoing his smile. A small silence settled between them. 'So how have you been?' she asked, feeling awkward making small talk like a stranger with the man she'd once been about to marry.

'Can't complain,' he said with an offhand casualness. She noticed for the first time that he'd changed, maybe not his looks so much, but there was a maturity to him now. It was hard to think that they'd been teenagers when they first met. She'd always felt so ready, so adult. But she'd been a mere babe in the woods.

'Mum and Dad have moved to the coast,' he continued.

'I heard.' Alice nodded. 'So, you and Matt are running Whyningham at last?'

'Nah, Matt's running it now. I've got my own place.'

'Really?'

'Yeah, bought the old Murphy place a couple of years back.' Alice watched as he lowered his gaze and reached out to fiddle with a price tag on a shelf. 'Things weren't going great for a while there, between Matt and me. We clashed a lot over decisions and had a couple of rough years when the market dropped off a bit . . . It got me thinking about what you used to say about having a backup plan. Once Dad retired, I knew Matt and I would probably kill each other trying to run the place together, so I branched out on my own.'

'Wow,' Alice said, wondering if she sounded as surprised as she felt. She'd clearly missed hearing about this little piece of information.

'Yeah. It was a pretty big step.'

'So what do you run? Sheep and cattle?' That had always been his dream—branching away from cropping to livestock.

'I've been slowly building up the livestock side of things, but the Murphys' place was set up for cropping, so it just made sense to continue with that for a while. It's been tough, but this year is looking great—haven't seen bumper crops like this in the district in years.'

'That's really great.'

Finn gave a nod, and once again silence fell. 'I'm sorry about . . . your husband,' he said, seeming to stumble over the last word. 'I was sorry to hear about it.'

'Thanks,' she said quietly.

'Merrick said you've moved back to Sydney.'

'Yeah, it was time.'

'After ten years,' he said, looking up to hold her gaze.

The implication of his tone was not lost on her. She knew him too well even after all this time. A year turned into ten. It would have only been one if he hadn't decided to go and get married.

'How's Shelly?' she asked, striving for a light casualness she was far from feeling.

A shuttered expression came down over his face. 'We're not together anymore,' he said in a clipped tone that had a tinge of something that sounded a little defensive.

When the hell had that happened, she wondered, and why hadn't anyone thought to mention it to her? Then again, maybe telling everyone she didn't want to hear about Finn after they'd broken up had something to do with it. Not that it was any of her business, she supposed, but still . . .

'Apparently the novelty of being a broke farmer's wife wore off.' His tone belied the bitterness of the words, but she suspected it was only a front for the sake of being civil. Clearly the break-up had hurt him deeply.

'I'm really sorry to hear that,' she said, genuinely meaning it. She'd hoped he'd found someone who'd made him happy. At least that way their own break-up would have been worth it.

'That's life, I guess,' he said. 'Anyway, I should probably get going.'

There was a small pause and Alice was about to say goodbye when he tacked on, 'How long are you back for?'

''Till New Year's Day.'

He nodded. 'Nice. Your mum and dad will love having you home again.'

'I love being home,' she countered. 'I've missed it.'

'You haven't missed much. Nothin' really changes out here.'

'That's what I've missed the most,' she said with a slight smile.

'Look who it is!' a booming voice interrupted, making Alice jump slightly. 'The most famous thing to come out of Gunnindi.'

Alice tried to hold back a cringe as she sensed a few people lifting their heads. 'Hi Vernon.'

'It's like a reunion,' Vernon continued, grinning like the Cheshire cat. 'The two of you in here, again.'

'Yep, it's been a while,' Alice agreed, wondering if Finn was feeling as uncomfortable as she was.

'What can I do for you?' Vernon asked. 'Or are you here together?'

'No, we're not together,' she assured him, then cleared her throat. 'Mum sent me down to ask you what to feed a quail.'

He looked at her doubtfully. 'Since when were your parents into breeding birds?'

'They aren't. Dad found one and brought it home.'

'Quail, huh? Not much bloody use as a pet, but pretty good eating,' he said. 'Your old man must have too much time on his hands or something if he's taking up bird collecting.'

'Maybe. They don't have as many babysitting duties as they used to.'

'Must be time for some more grandkids, then.' Vernon winked and Alice gave a half-smile, deliberately not looking at Finn. 'Righto then. You want a twenty-kilo bag?'

'Does it come in anything smaller? There's only one bird.'

'He's gonna need more than one. They don't do too well on their own,' Vernon warned.

Alice frowned. 'Do you know where we can get some more?'

She saw him scratch his chin thoughtfully. 'Old Mrs Marshall used to be into quail, but I think she went into a home not too long ago,' he said. 'Leave it with me. I'll have an ask about and see if I can track someone down. Anyway, follow me and we'll see what feed we have down the back.'

Alice glanced at Finn and smiled an apology. 'I'd better go. It was good to see you again.'

'Yeah, no worries. You too.' He nodded, sticking his thumbs through the belt loops of his jeans. 'See you around.'

As she hurried after Vernon, Alice wondered about Finn's parting words. *Would* she see him around? It'd taken ten years to run into him the first time. Chances were she wouldn't; she doubted either of them would go out of their way to visit. There was too much history between them for a casual drop by. The thought left her feeling oddly sad.

Chapter 32

Alice arrived home to an empty house. Her father had gone down to the men's shed to start on his aviary and her mum was still at the Christmas party.

Alice hadn't slept much the night before and found herself battling to keep her eyes open as she tried to watch TV. Giving up, she switched it off and laid down on the lounge, deciding to shut her eyes for a few minutes. The gentle hum of the fridge in the kitchen soon lulled her into that peaceful place just before drifting into sleep.

A sudden, shrill scream cut through the silence and Alice bolted upright on the lounge, her heart pounding inside her chest. What the hell was that? She froze, poised to stand as she tried to figure out if she'd dreamed the sound. Barely a second later, another scream had her leaping to her feet and searching the room.

She crept into the kitchen and grabbed a rolling pin from the utensil jar on the bench, then listened, waiting to see if it came again.

It had been an inhuman sound—a screeching, ear-splitting noise—and when it came a third time, Alice spun around, lifting the rolling pin in readiness to defend herself against God only knew what, only to realise it had come from . . . the box on the table.

It was the quail! How on earth did such a horrendous sound come out of something so small? She picked up the box.

'What on earth was that?' Gran's said close beside her, making Alice jump and let out a squeak, the box falling from her hands as she spun around.

'No!' she cried, catching the darting movement of a brown-feathered creature as it shot across the floor and behind the TV cabinet. 'Oh, God, it's out,' she moaned.

'What's out? And what was that hideous noise?' Gran asked, still confused.

'Dad's quail.'

'Since when has your father had a quail?'

'Since this morning.'

'What's he going to do with a quail?'

'Apparently he's going to eat it.'

'One won't be much of a meal.'

Everyone has a view on quail, Alice thought as she pulled the cabinet away from the wall and tried to reach for the bird, with no success.

'Use a broom handle,' Gran suggested.

'I'm trying to catch it, not kill it, Gran.' Alice stretched her arm, wedging herself in behind the cabinet as far as she could and swearing under her breath as her fingertips just managed to brush soft feathers but were unable to get a hold on the small, yet surprisingly fat, body.

'Ow!' she yelped as she tried to lift her head and realised her hair had gotten caught on something. 'Gran, can you help untangle my hair?' she asked.

'Let me see,' Gran said, leaning over her.

'Hello?' A deep voice came from outside and Alice froze. Not twice in one day, surely?

'Oh, Finn. What a lovely surprise. Come on in,' Gran said, and Alice heard the back door squeak as it opened.

'Gran! No!' *Oh, God, no, don't let him in while I'm stuck, bum up, wedged behind the furniture!*

Alice tried to wriggle out backwards, knowing that her face would be an attractive shade of beetroot red from the blood rushing to her head. Gripping her hair, she gave a final tug and it came free from wherever it had been caught. She hastily straightened and attempted to smooth back the hair that had escaped her ponytail, turning to face an amused Finn.

'Oh, hi,' she said, casually wiping the sweat from her forehead as inconspicuously as she could.

'Hey,' he said, eyeing her curiously.

'It's lucky you came over,' Gran was saying. 'We need longer arms.'

'To do what?' he asked, hesitantly.

'To reach the quail.' Alice indicated the piece of heavy furniture. 'It escaped. Behind there.'

'Oh. Righto.' He nodded, then attempted to switch places with Alice.

'Sorry,' she muttered. She watched as he leaned down and stretched one arm behind the cabinet before backing out and straightening up to produce the escapee, securely clutched in his large hand.

'He's a solid little fella,' Finn said.

'He can move pretty quick, so don't let go of him,' Alice warned, bringing the box over so Finn could place the bird back inside.

'Crisis averted!' Gran declared, bustling from the room to head down the hallway.

Alice turned her attention back to Finn and gave a nervous chuckle. 'That was pretty spectacular timing. Thanks for your help.'

'No worries. I overheard you talking to Vernon earlier about tracking down more quail. I got on to a mate who has some he wants to get rid of. They're out in the ute.'

'You brought over more?' she asked, her eyes widening in alarm.

'I found an old cage in the shed you can keep them in until your dad builds the proper one. Might be a bit safer than a box.'

'Oh. Thanks. You didn't have to go to all that trouble, though.'

'No trouble. My mate was only complaining the other day about how many quails he had—or his wife kept incubating,' he said. 'So it was kind of lucky that you were at the Feed Shed today and I overheard you.'

Another screech sounded from inside the box and Finn let out a sharp curse. 'Is that coming from the bird?'

'Yep,' Alice sighed.

'What the hell?'

'Right? It sounds possessed. Surely it can't be natural?'

'No idea. I've never heard them make a noise before,' Finn told her. 'Probably better to put it out in the cage though. I'll go and unload it.'

Alice followed him outside and watched as he lifted the cage from the back of his ute and carried it across the yard. He placed the cage inside her father's shed. She'd forgotten how strong Finn was. It had been quite some time since she'd watched a man do any kind of physical work. She'd become used to men in suits—office workers, not the dusty jeans, rolled-up sleeves, dirty hands type workers.

Alice stood back as he carried the larger box from the cabin of his ute across and transferred the birds into the cage, then handed him the box containing the original quail. She quickly lost it in among the new ones.

'Dad's going to get a surprise when he gets home,' Alice said, watching the frantic scurrying of the small birds in the cage.

'Hope he hasn't changed his mind,' Finn said. 'I think there's a no-return policy in place.'

'Awesome,' Alice said with a grimace. This had the potential to backfire big time.

'You might end up having to take them home to Sydney,' he added.

'Yeah, nah,' Alice said firmly. 'Pretty sure my apartment has a no-pets policy.'

'Maybe you'll have to move back into the cottage,' he said lightly, although there was a strange undercurrent of something tense beneath the words. 'You never got rid of it.'

'How do you know that?' she asked, throwing him a curious glance. She wasn't even aware that he knew she still owned it.

'I've never seen a for sale sign on it.'

'I still have it.'

'Why? Why would you hold on to a house out here in the middle of nowhere for all this time?'

The intense way he held her gaze as he waited for her answer sent a rush of mixed emotions through her.

Why indeed? It wasn't the first time the question had been asked.

'It's a good investment.' She slid her hands into the back pockets of her jeans and let her eyes wander around the shed once again.

'I can't imagine it's worth much compared to the rest of your portfolio,' he said with an edge of dryness. 'So why hang on to it?'

He was not going to let this go, she realised, feeling a little unsettled. 'I just never got around to selling it. Actually, it's one of the things on my list to sort out while I'm back.'

'So you *are* planning to sell it?'

Oh, for goodness' sake. Why was he harping on about the house? She didn't want to talk about it—especially with *him*.

'I haven't decided yet. Thanks for bringing all this over,' she said, changing the subject quickly. She didn't want to start feeling all these melancholy emotions that always arose whenever she thought too hard about the little house they used to own together. It was in the past.

'Finn, are you staying for a cuppa?' Gran called from the back door.

He glanced at Alice briefly, as though gauging her reaction, before he answered. 'Sure. Thanks, that would be great.' Then he slammed the back of the ute shut, dusted off his hands and followed Alice back inside.

It shouldn't bother her. So what that he was her ex-fiancé? He'd been part of her family since he was in high school and he still kept in touch with her brothers and brothers-in-law. Gunnindi was a small town—there was no avoiding anyone around here. And yet, it *did* bother her. Not in a bitter way— far from it. They'd broken up years ago. They were grown adults who'd gone on to lead their own lives and were simply old family friends now. Only they weren't. Not really. They shared a history. They'd almost married.

A tiny voice inside her head warned her that adding Finn Walcott to the equation right now was asking to reopen a very messy tin of worms.

And yet here she was, following him inside to share a nice cup of coffee and make small talk.

'How is it being back? I mean, from the UK?' Finn asked, reaching for a biscuit from the plate Gran set on the table between them.

'Busy.' Alice grinned, overruling the voice inside her head that warned her not to even *think* about taking a shortbread from the plate, before remembering her London socialising days were over and there wasn't any need to make sure she fit into evening wear and gowns to attend fashion shows and gala events. 'It's been a huge project to relocate the business.'

'Sounds like it. Bet it's been a bit of a culture shock coming back?'

'A little bit. The weather for one. It's not supposed to be summer when it's Christmas. That's taking a bit of getting used to. I've missed it.'

'I was only over there for a week and the sun didn't come out once the whole time we were there.'

'You came to the UK?' Alice asked. This was news.

'Yeah. A few years back. Went with a couple of the boys from here on a local charity cricket tour. We played some games and the Poms came over here and played a few.'

'You should have told me you were in town,' she heard herself say, then wished she'd kept silent when he glanced at her before dropping his gaze to reach for another biscuit.

'I didn't think you'd have time to hang out.'

'Of course I would have.' She saw his lips twist a little at her reply and frowned. 'I was always homesick—it never really went away. I would have loved to see you.'

'A reminder of home, hey?' he replied, lifting his eyes to hers again.

'A catch-up with an old friend,' Alice said carefully, trying to figure out what the unspoken message was. 'It would have been nice.'

Would it have been, though? How would she have handled a visit from Finn? She'd begged him to come and visit when she'd first moved, despite the fact they'd been broken up when she left. She'd even sent a late-night, drunken text begging him to come to London to see her. He hadn't replied.

She hadn't thought about that in years.

'I did see you on the front of a magazine while I was there, though. You were in a wedding dress at some fancy awards night,' he said.

The Belagottis? He was there then? What would have happened if he'd seen her? *Nothing would have happened*, she told herself firmly. She and Frankie hadn't really been together at the time, but Finn had been married. Maybe, a little voice nagged, instead of getting over Finn, seeing him would have made her miss him even more. She might never have gotten serious with Frankie. Would she have come home, her tail between her legs, and given up the opportunity to get to where she was now? Who knows? Fate, with all its twists and turns, could send a person crazy if you dwelled on it for too long.

'How are your parents?' Gran asked, putting an end to the conversation.

Alice was distracted as the two of them talked, not quite listening, and jumped a little guiltily when Finn stood up from the table to go.

'I guess we'll see you around, over the Christmas break,' Alice said, walking him to the back door.

'Probably not much. I'm running behind in the harvest. We've had bad weather and a few breakdowns, and it's put us behind schedule. Looks like we could be working right through Christmas.'

'That sucks,' she said, commiserating.

'Yeah. And there's a rain event everyone's been keeping an eye on that's supposed to be coming this way. We have to get harvest done before that hits or we'll lose it.'

A familiar sensation ran through her, one she hadn't felt in a long time: apprehension, worry and stress. She may not have been the one directly affected by all the trials and tribulations of the farming season in their past, but she'd shared them with Finn regardless. When he was dealing with stress, so was she—and there'd been a lot of it.

'I hope the rain holds off, then,' she offered, feeling inadequate when a tired smile flashed across his face.

'See ya, Al.'

'See ya,' she parroted, watching him walk down the side of the house.

'That was an interesting visit,' Gran said as she cleared the table. 'Nice of Finn to drop by.'

'Yeah. It was,' Alice muttered, placing the empty coffee mugs in the sink. 'He's a different man from the boy I used to know. He's been through a lot with his marriage break-up and what not. But I think he's come out the other side a better person.'

He *was* different. But she had no idea if he'd changed in any of the ways she'd once hoped he would. Would he still be so focused on the farm that nothing else mattered? His marriage had broken up and he'd said farming had been a cause. Admittedly, she didn't know Shelly—she'd been younger than Alice and Finn in school, so she really didn't know much about her. Not enough to judge her reasons for not making a marriage with Finn work. Anyway, it wasn't any of Alice's business. She and Finn had moved on. He was just someone Alice used to know and from now on, whenever they met, it would just be as old friends.

Chapter 33

Alice couldn't remember when she'd ever had so much free time on her hands. It seemed strange. And yet, she found herself enjoying the fact she had no schedule or alarms dictating her every waking hour. She checked in with her emails daily and occasionally found herself having to handle the odd issue, but with the business closed down for the Christmas break, there wasn't the usual volume of crisis management.

This was what she'd needed. For the last ten years, she'd been consumed by work and the business. Frankie had often talked about winding down, putting more people in place to run the small empire he'd built, but Alice knew he'd never truly been able to let go of the reins. In the end—after his death—she had saved her sanity by dividing up the company.

She hadn't won any friends, but then, she didn't need them, at least not that sort, not anymore. Her own label was a success in its own right, which gave her the freedom to do whatever she wanted.

And now she would have a life separate from the business.

She loved her life, and her career, but she loved her family more. She missed spending time with them. She missed her hometown and just being Alice from Gunnindi.

Alice dressed in a bright sun dress and slipped on a pair of tan flats before heading out. Verity had invited her over for the morning and she was looking forward to it being just the two of them together.

Her sister's house was a striking red brick Californian bungalow, popular in the years between the first and second world wars. Alice knocked on the dark green front door and, hearing Verity call out to come in, headed down the long hallway and out into the kitchen. Verity and Rick had renovated the modest house over the years as their family had grown and despite the modern appliances and details, it had retained its 1930s character and charm.

'You just missed Rick, he was going to hang around and say hi but he had to get to work.'

'How's the courier thing going?'

'It's going better than it was in the beginning. Everyone shops online now so Rick's busier than ever. Too busy, actually. He's hardly home.'

'Can he afford to hire an extra hand?' Alice asked, settling onto the bar stool across from her sister.

'No. Unfortunately we had quite a bit of debt hanging over our heads when we went into this venture and we paid way too much for the business.'

It hadn't been easy for Verity and Rick over the last couple of years. After losing his long-term job at the post office, Rick had started his own courier company, but it had taken a while to build up their clientele and reputation.

'What about your online shop? I saw the post you put up the other day for the knitted fairy village. It looks absolutely stunning, Ver,' Alice said, grinning as her older, usually assertive, sister ducked her head a little at the compliment. In every other aspect of her life, Verity was the most calmly confident person Alice knew. She understood where it came from. You could be a successful businessperson and not think anything of what people might think about you, but if you were creative that opened you up to a different set of emotions. Being creative, no matter in what field, made you vulnerable. You were showing the world a piece of you—something that came from inside. It was personal.

'Thanks,' Verity said, busying herself with tidying up. 'The shop's going okay, but there's a lot to be said for a reliable pay cheque. I do miss my old job that way.' Verity had worked as a communications adviser at the local mine for years until it closed down.

Alice had offered to help, but the Croydons were such a proud bunch and money was a sensitive issue. She knew if her sister had been in real trouble she'd have asked for help, but there were times when Alice wished her siblings and parents would allow her to do more.

'You know I'm more than happy to get you a job with the business any time you want. You've got a marketing degree and I have a marketing department,' Alice said, trying to keep her tone light.

'I know,' Verity sighed. 'But honestly? I'm just venting. I'm not even sure I want to go back to marketing after all this time. I actually do quite all right with my little shop and I like being my own boss.'

'Is this something you've been working on?' Alice asked, noticing a pile of neatly folded jumpers on the table. They looked soft and comfortable, making Alice immediately think of lazy, cold winter days curled up in front of a fire.

'Yes, I've just finished an order for a store in Burrandock that wanted to stock them.'

'That's awesome. They're gorgeous.'

'Thanks. I just wish I wasn't limited to the shades I can order online. I'm actually thinking of trying to make my own, so I can get unique, one-of-a-kind colours.'

'That sounds like a great idea. Have you looked into it?'

'Not seriously. I never seem to find the time, to be honest. There's so many orders I have to turn away. I can't keep up with them.'

'I guess that's a good problem to have?' Alice replied, tilting her head slightly as she studied her sister. 'I know I've mentioned it before, but I really would be keen on backing you if you wanted to turn your business into something bigger.'

Verity took a moment before she met Alice's eye. 'I know, but I honestly don't think I could make something like that work. Not if you're talking about making a line under your label or something. I don't want my collection to become mass produced.'

'It wouldn't have to be. We can do whatever you wanted. It would be yours.'

Verity shook her head and crinkled her nose. 'It's a generous offer, Alice. And I really appreciate it, honestly,' she said, sending Alice a warm smile, 'I just don't think I'm ready to do anything on that big a scale. I kind of like what I'm doing at the moment. I take on the work I know I can finish and there's no real stress involved.'

'I'm happy you're doing something you love.'

'What about you? Do you still love what you do? You've been doing it for a long time now.'

'I do,' Alice started.

'But?' Verity prodded gently.

Alice let out a long sigh. 'But I guess there're times I wish I could just go back to designing without all the business side of it hanging over my head,' she said. 'I know that sounds terrible. I have everything I could ever have wanted in a career and I'm sitting here whingeing about the responsibility that comes with it.' She shook her head.

'I think it sounds quite normal. The business side of things always takes away from the creative side. You've been doing a huge job, wading through all the legalities and business affairs you were left to deal with. And for someone who was never interested in business, that's a lot to handle. It's no wonder you're feeling burned out.'

'I was,' Alice agreed. 'Which is why I decided to scale it down and move home. I think I've finally realised that I need to step back from the management side of things and delegate a bit more. I'm thinking of asking Charlie to come on board.'

If she'd learned one thing after dealing with Frankie's top advisers, it was to find people who were loyal and trustworthy to work with her.

'You haven't asked him yet?'

'No,' Alice said, biting the corner of lip. 'Do you think he'd be interested?'

Her older sister shrugged. As Charlie's twin, if anyone knew his mind, it would be Verity. 'I know he's been pretty miserable in his current job for the last year or so. Maybe a change would do him good. Can't hurt to ask.'

'Sorry I'm late, Gran,' Alice said, kissing her grandmother's cheek before taking the chair opposite her in the Paragon cafe, one of her teenage haunts. The place hadn't changed a bit—its 1950s decor wasn't some trendy makeover, it was authentic, and brought back a slew of memories.

Gran flapped a hand in front of her. 'I only just arrived myself. Did you have a nice visit with Verity?'

'I did,' Alice said, reaching for the menu.

'You look happier. Time with the family is exactly what you've been needing.' Gran nodded decisively.

It was. She'd been home two weeks and couldn't remember when she'd felt this relaxed. She was feeling so much lighter, too, like the load she'd been carrying for so long was easing from her shoulders with each passing day. And it was nice to have some one-on-one time with her siblings. She'd spent a morning with Daisy and Merrick out on their farm and tomorrow she'd sit down with Charlie and Steph to bring up the job offer.

'Gran, I've been thinking about the old wool mill,' Alice said after they placed their orders. 'Do you remember when we spoke about it once? Do you know much about its history?'

Gran scrunched her face up as she concentrated on the question. 'I know it was one of the biggest employers in the district at one time. They used to barge all the local wool from the area up the river and process it on site.'

'See? This is the stuff that I love,' Alice sighed. 'Frankie and I were always interested in the source of our fabrics—where they came from, how they were manufactured. We both had a passion for Australian products and used to talk about one day getting more involved with maybe producing fabric locally. Lately I've been obsessed with this idea of getting back to using wholly Australian fibres. Gran, I think I really want to do something crazy . . . like bring the mill back into operation.' She stared at Meryl, stunned by what she'd just revealed. In truth, she hadn't even been sure exactly what her recent thoughts had been about, but saying them out loud, it suddenly all made complete sense.

'Is it crazy? Or just pioneering?' Gran asked, smiling at the waitress who'd delivered their drinks.

'I think it's crazy,' Alice said. 'But ever since I've been home, I've been having all these ideas. The building itself has always fascinated me. I'd love to bring it back to its former glory somehow. So many other places are bringing the history of their towns back to life and drawing in tourists.' She'd recently been reading about a town who'd turned their old butter factory into a specialty ice-cream factory and were now exporting their product far and wide. There were plenty of other examples, like old factories being converted into smaller boutique shops and museums. The options were endless if you just had a vision . . . and plenty of funding, she thought dryly.

'The Old Mill could be a working museum. It would make Gunnindi the only town of its kind with working vintage looms. We could do tours, and include a cafe and a gift shop selling products that we make on site . . . and I can feature Gunnindi wool and cotton in its own collection and take it worldwide. We could totally do this.'

Gran's smile broadened the longer Alice spoke, until she chuckled and clapped her hands in delight. 'It sounds like you've been doing more than thinking about it. Count me in. Give me a job to do. I want to see this thing happen.'

Alice reached across the table and squeezed her grandmother's hand. She could always depend on Gran.

'Right. First stop after we eat lunch is a visit to Jacob Flanders,' Meryl said.

'I haven't heard that name in ages. Why are we visiting him?'

'Because he owns the building. We'll go and see if he wants to sell it!'

Alice blanched a little. Whoa. It was one thing to paint this inspirational image of all the possibilities, but being faced with making it happen? Was she seriously going to do this?

Deep down, she knew the answer was yes. She wasn't sure why or how, but somehow, over the last few weeks—ever since she'd stopped outside the Old Mill—the idea had been quietly brewing away, waiting for her to understand what she needed to do.

Alice barely noticed eating her meal once it arrived, her mind was racing with a million different thoughts. Soon, Gran had directed her to the aged care facility in town, where they tracked down the frail-looking owner of the mill, seated by a window reading a newspaper.

'Well, this is a nice surprise,' Jacob said as Gran greeted him and dragged a seat over to sit down. 'Meryl Croydon. I always wondered when you'd wake up and realise you were supposed to be my girl. So today must be my lucky day.' He chuckled.

''Fraid not, Jacob. I'm a modern independent woman, doin' it for myself,' Gran informed him and Alice bit back a grin.

'This has to be one of your granddaughters. She's the spitting image of you.'

'This is Alice, Jim and Kathy's girl.'

'Ah, the famous one.' Jacob nodded. 'I read an article not too long ago on you, young lady. Very impressive.'

'Oh. Thank you. I've been very lucky.'

'Luck doesn't have anything to do with it. You obviously have talent.'

Warmth filled Alice's chest at the compliment. She'd been praised before from people in the fashion industry whose opinions were important and had always felt somewhat embarrassed by it, but a compliment from this man—someone who wasn't standing to gain anything, other than maybe win over her gran—somehow meant a lot more.

'To what does this old man owe the pleasure of a visit from two beautiful ladies today?'

'Oh, stop it, you old charmer,' Gran tsked briskly, but Alice caught the sparkle in her eye. 'We're here on business. Do you still own the land the old wool mill is on?'

'I do.' Jacob said, nodding again, though now he squinted slightly.

'My granddaughter here is interested in getting the mill up and running again. Are you lookin' to sell it?'

For a long moment, Jacob seemed to consider Alice, pinning her with an intense gaze. 'Why would you want to do that?'

'I think the history surrounding the mill and the town would make a fantastic tourist attraction and I want to bring back a local wool and cotton connection to the area.'

'Be easier to knock the whole place down and start from scratch,' he mused, rubbing a hand over his scratchy chin.

Alice glanced at her gran before answering. 'Then we'd lose the history.'

'Be a bit of outlay involved. The building's been locked up since the late eighties.'

'I guess I'd have to have an architect and a building inspector look it over and see if it is salvageable,' she agreed.

'It'll be structurally okay. I've had it seen to over the years, the roof maintained and what not. You're not the first person to make an offer on the old girl, though.'

This news surprised her considering the state of neglect the front of the building and land was in. Why wouldn't he have jumped at the chance to off-load a huge, empty building? 'How come you haven't sold it, then?'

''Cause all of them wanted the land—not the building,' he said, settling back and folding his arms across his plaid shirt as he watched her shrewdly. 'None of them cared about the history of the place. They wanted to knock it down and build apartments or a shopping centre on it . . . a shopping centre!' he scoffed at Gran and shook his head. 'What would Gunnindi do with a shopping centre?'

Gran shared a bemused look with Jacob before he turned back to Alice. 'You're the first one who's wanted the place for its history.'

Alice held her breath. Did this mean he was considering her offer? She didn't dare look away.

'Tell me more about what you had in mind,' he said.

Alice quickly shared the ideas she'd come up with. 'In all honesty, Mr Flanders, I haven't even begun to price this thing out. I'm not even sure it's a viable project. All I know is seeing the mill sitting there the other day . . .' She paused, searching for the words she needed. 'I could just picture how it would look and what it would do for the town. We would be showcasing our farmers with their cotton and wool, and the cafe and gift shop could stock local produce and be a platform for displaying artists and crafts from around the district. We'd quite literally put Gunnindi on the map by selling our products all over the world. I want to give something back to my community—make a difference, no matter how small—and I think this could be the way.'

'She's got your fire, Meryl,' Jacob said. 'All right. Drop around to Bill Sanders at the real estate and he'll organise to get you inside the building when you're ready. Have a look and get back to me and we'll talk figures if you think it's worth going ahead with.'

Alice felt a smile begin to spread across her face. This was seriously happening.

Oh. My God! What have I done? she thought as they drove home.

Ever since she'd returned to Gunnindi, almost every conversation she'd had with someone had included mention of either the lack of jobs in town, the decline in population or facilities threatening to close. They needed something to keep people in town so the schools and services they had didn't shut. Teaming up with the local wool industry just made sense. She could introduce a whole new line of clothing and underwear to the UK using locally sourced and produced fibre. She could set up the manufacturing line from right here, creating, designing and printing the fabric then have the finished product sent down to her Sydney factory to be made up.

A thousand ideas swirled inside her head—there was so much to think about. After returning home, she searched frantically for a notepad and began jotting down a list of things she'd need to check out.

When she finished writing, she was surprised to discover she'd been at it for a solid two hours and the notepad held a million things she'd need to carefully go through and address, but she had the bare bones of an idea she was confident could be something special. She'd need to do a lot more research before she got her team involved—not that she could do anything for the next few weeks since everyone was on Christmas break, but that would give her time to polish her idea and have it ready to present as soon as they went back to business.

With most of the business side of things scribbled down, Alice's mind went once more to her designs. She grabbed her sketch pad and opened it to a blank page, realising it had been almost two years since she'd felt this kind of excitement for anything, let alone designing.

Her pencil flew across the page, which exploded to life with a stunning array of new ideas as she drew late into the night.

Chapter 34

The next few days were nothing short of insane. Gran made the announcement to Jim and Kathy, which then spread to Alice's siblings and a family gathering followed within the hour.

In her parents' living room, voices talked over the top of each other and questions were being thrown around, most of which Alice had no answers for.

She sighed. 'Look, I don't know how much it's going to cost. Not until we get a look at the inside.'

'Who are you going to get to run all this? Surely *you* can't take it on?' her mother asked, worry marring her face. 'Unless you're moving back?'

Alice shook her head. 'No—at least, not yet.' The idea of moving back to Gunnindi had been rattling around inside her head lately. Over the last few days she'd realised she needed to start making serious changes so she could get back to what she loved doing the most. Her heart was still in designing but being home had reminded her how much she loved the place she'd grown up in. Maybe one day she could see herself returning full time, but that would be a long way off; she had a business that ran out of Sydney and that was where she needed to be.

'As for who will run it, well . . . I mean, I want to support hiring locals, but I'm hoping that maybe we can make it a bit of a family affair? There'd be the cafe and gift shop that would need a manager who could hire staff. Then the mill itself—we'd need to find someone with experience to oversee the training of machine operators. We'd need maintenance staff and cleaners. Also, someone to design and create the giftware and apparel to complement the yarns. Someone who knows wool and how to use it . . . and also run the online store,' she said, looking at Verity. 'You could create that range of specialty colours you've been talking about to sell and add your own stock to the gift store and have complete control over how it's produced.'

'So, this boutique approach,' Toby began, 'you don't think it's a bit of a risk? I mean, your company buys stuff in bulk from factories all over the world and that's why these old mills went bust to begin with—once it became more economical to send production overseas, right?'

'Sure, it's a risk. All business is. But I've been seeing a steep rise in consumers wanting to buy local. During Covid, the world basically came to a grinding halt when everything we relied on from overseas was suddenly no longer available. It made a lot of people reconsider how we do business. Me included. I think now is the perfect time to be investing in home-grown products. We can buy straight from the producers and you can't get more local than that.'

Her parents nodded encouragingly.

'Look, I don't expect any of you to give up your lives to jump on board with this—you've all got your own jobs. I just wanted to put it out there. If anyone wants a job, it's there. But I know this is going to be a good thing for the town and, whatever happens, I'll be travelling back and forth to help set it up and run it alongside whoever goes in as manager.'

It would be a massive undertaking and one with lots of red tape and regulations to wade through, but as ideas were thrown around and the excitement grew, Alice realised this thing might actually become *a thing*. She had the contacts to draw on, so the biggest issue would be finding millers—but they'd be able to figure that out, she was sure, given time. The sheer age of the machinery would appeal to a number of enthusiasts who should be eager to get involved and train up a new generation of millers.

By the time everyone had left, Alice felt utterly drained.

'I remember you wearing that same look the day you got the offer to go to London,' Gran said, sitting on the lounge beside Alice.

Alice gave a small, unamused chuckle at the memory.

'You were terrified then too, if I recall.'

'For completely different reasons.'

'Not that different, not really. You didn't think you could do *that* either. But look at everything you've accomplished.'

Well, that's an unfair point, Alice thought irritably. 'This time it's not just me counting on it being a success. If it fails, it'll impact the whole town,' she said, feeling panicked once again. People would lose jobs.

'Or,' Gran said slowly, 'it may be the amazing triumph you've imagined it to be.'

She could always count on Gran to be the optimistic Pollyanna voice in an argument.

Meryl gave her a one-arm hug before getting slowly to her feet. 'Just let it be. Once you get some answers to all these questions, you'll be in a better position to make up your mind about it. There's nothing you can really do until then, so put it out of your head for now.'

Easier said than done, but she knew Gran was right. Getting her idea out there in front of her family had at least made it feel somewhat tangible.

A project of this size was probably the last thing she needed, but there was no denying its pull. The desire to bring this dream to fruition was something she felt down to her very soul, something that needed to be done. It just felt . . . right. And if there was one thing she'd learned to trust over the years, it was her intuition. If it felt right, it usually was.

Alice unlocked the front door of the cottage and stood at the threshold as her eyes adjusted to the darkness inside.

It still smells the same, she thought as she walked along the hallway and listened to the echo of her heels on the timber floor. It was the first time she'd been back inside since she'd returned to Gunnindi and the memories swarmed about her. The walls were still the same shade of pale, misty blue that leaned more towards grey, but it was looking a little drab. A change of colour was needed, she decided. The little kitchen with its pine cupboard doors was looking dated and more than a little unloved, and she imagined how great a stone benchtop would look with white doors and a black tiled splashback over the stove.

Her list of jobs grew and she mentally tallied up the cost. It was becoming quite a bit of outlay for a house she wasn't even sure what she was going to do with. If she sold it, she wouldn't be making much back. Only, somehow, between pulling up outside earlier and right now, she'd changed her mind about the whole selling it possibility.

She didn't want to.

She knew Frankie would be shaking his head at her, reminding her that it wasn't a very logical decision and, heaven knew, he always told her she needed to think with her head not her heart when it came to money or business. But deep down, she knew she wasn't a businesswoman so it stood to reason she did more decision making based on sentimentality than what was likely to be more profitable or sensible. She could almost feel his arms around her now as he smiled that tolerant, *I give up!* smile he'd eventually give her when he'd failed to change her mind about something.

'I still miss you,' she whispered softly and followed the gentle flutter of the lace curtain at the window as it moved in the warm breeze.

After a moment she straightened her shoulders and let out a decisive breath. She was going to keep the cottage and use it as her base whenever she came home. And there was no time like the present to start moving in.

❖

'But why?' her mother asked, eyeing her as though she'd just informed them that she was flying to the moon.

'Because with all this mill planning, I need some room to spread out, and I think it would be better to do it in my own place.'

'You can spread out here,' her mother said as Alice pointedly looked around at Gran's painting easels set up in the living room and Kathy's sewing nook in the corner of the sunroom at the back of the house.

'Mum, it's literally four doors up the street.'

'Yes, but . . . it's been nice having you here again.'

Alice hugged her mum and chuckled. 'I'm not going away. Besides, having the cottage will mean I have to come home more often to make use of it,' she said.

'I suppose so,' Kathy reluctantly agreed. 'I guess after living on your own for so long, you'd find us a bit overwhelming.'

Even though Alice loved her family, the constant stream of drop-ins did border on the ridiculous. There was always someone coming or going and she seriously didn't know how her parents did it. Even mealtimes were often a surprise until they actually sat down to eat—one was never sure who was actually going to be there. Her mother was a damn saint.

'Will you come and help me pick out some furniture?' Alice asked, softening the blow with a sure-fire way to get her mother excited—a shopping trip.

Chapter 35

Two days later, Alice knocked on Toby's front door and smiled as her brother opened it.

'G'day, sis, you're up and about early,' he noted, stepping aside so she could enter.

'Yeah, thanks to Dad's new pets. Noisy damn things.'

'Not sure you'd call them pets, per se. He plans on eating them.'

'Yeah. Right,' Alice scoffed. 'He was out there baby-talking to them when I left.'

'*Our* father?'

'Yep. Clucking over them like a proud mother hen. There's no way he's going to go through with eating those things.'

'Huh,' Toby said. 'Who would have thought? Anyway, what are you doing here?'

Alice held up a bag. 'Mum sent over some cooking.'

'Thank goodness. Hey, I heard you're moving back into the old cottage?'

'Yeah, I decided not to sell it yet. Thought it might make a good base for when I come home.'

'When you moving in?'

'Later today. I've got some furniture being delivered, then I'll do the painting once I'm in.'

'Yourself?' Her brother eyed her doubtfully.

'Yes,' she said, pushing his shoulder. 'I can hold a paint brush.'

'Yeah but . . . why, when you can afford to just hire someone else to do it for you?'

'Because it's practically Christmas and everyone is shut. But that's beside the point. I'm looking forward to doing some renovations. It'll be therapeutic.'

'Sure, it will. Tell me how therapeutic it is when your neck is sore and your arms are aching.'

They'd reached the kitchen and Alice took in the mayhem happening around her.

'Mum! I need my hair done,' Bella, Alice's niece, called, walking from the hallway holding up a brush and hairband.

'I can't find my shoes,' her nephew George called from his room, while Billy sat in the lounge room, happily pulling baby wipes from the container in his nappy bag. At the kitchen counter, Cicily was a one-woman production line, making sandwiches and wrapping and shoving them into lunch boxes. She glanced up and offered Alice a harried smile.

'Morning,' she said, her eyes lighting up as she spotted what Alice carried. 'Oh, thank goodness, that's dinner tonight, can you put it in the fridge for me? Kathy's a godsend.'

Alice gave a silent chuckle as she soaked in the chaos and felt a small pang. Often over the years, when she was surrounded by her siblings and their families, she'd found herself wondering if this would have been her life had she chosen differently. She thought back to her spotless apartment and her home back in London as she took in her brother's modest house, kids' toys scattered all over the lounge room floor, a dining table piled high with laundry waiting to be folded, and the fridge covered in kids' drawings, school permission notes and happy snaps of the family. This house was full of life. It had a soul. In comparison, her apartment in Sydney sat empty and silent—soulless and cold.

Alice was shaken from her musings when an argument broke out between the two youngest children over who got to feed the goldfish. She stepped in, almost automatically.

'Bella, can I do your hair today?' she asked.

'Thank you, Alice,' Cicily said, finishing up the lunches.

'Any more news on the mill front?' Toby asked.

'I've got an architect looking at it after Christmas. It's a bad time of year to try and get anyone to do anything.'

'Mum! My shoes are missing!' George called once more from the other end of the house.

'Daddy's coming to help look for them,' Cicily called back, sending her husband a meaningful glance. 'Sorry about this, Alice. Last week of school and we're all just over it.' She sighed. 'Anyway, how are you doing? Bet it's strange being back.'

Alice grinned. 'I'm really loving being home actually. It's nice to slow down a bit.'

'Enjoy it while you can. You know how this family gets around Christmas. It's going to get crazy, very soon.'

It was true. The Croydons did everything over the top, including Christmas Day, which started with a huge breakfast cook-up followed by a traditional baked dinner with *all* the trimmings and ending with everyone vowing they were not eating again until New Year's . . . which usually only lasted until *later* Christmas night, when leftovers were pulled from the fridge and once again raided.

She secured the hair band in the neat braid down the back of her niece's little head and gave her a hug. 'There you go. All done.'

'Thanks, Aunty Alice.'

'Wow, maybe we need to hire you to do hair every morning, Aunty Alice,' Cicily said. 'That's pretty fancy compared to what I can do.'

'I'd forgotten I knew how to do it,' Alice admitted, feeling a bit smug that it had turned out as good as it had.

'Teagan! Marcus! I'm not going to call you out for breakfast again. We're leaving in ten minutes!' Cicily yelled down the hallway. 'Seriously. Teenagers. They do my head in.'

Alice wasn't sure how her brother and sister-in-law managed to juggle the age gap between their children. It was almost like two separate families. The three younger children had come along much later than their two older ones, who were almost finished high school.

Toby came out of George's room, talking on his phone and looking grim. 'Yeah, okay, mate. Will do. See ya.'

'Did you find the shoes?' Cicily asked, packing the lunch boxes in a selection of backpacks lined up near the door.

'Yeah. All good,' Toby said, sounding distracted as he slid his phone back into his pocket and glanced up. 'That was Finn,' he said.

'Is everything okay?' Alice asked, concern creeping in as she took in the frown on her brother's face.

'Not really. His entire contracting crew just cancelled on him. They're flooded in up at Woolaroo. He was hoping I might have some info on another way for them to get out, but I've got trucks stuck all over the place too. The roads are blocked in every direction.'

'Oh no,' Cicily said. 'He was due to start today, wasn't he?'

'Yeah. This is really bad. He was already cutting it close when he booked them in—now they can't get here at all.'

'What will he do?' Alice asked.

'He's going to lose pretty much his whole crop. He's got a header of his own, but with this big rain event unfolding, he won't get much harvested before it hits. Once it does, if we get the flooding up north has got, there won't be anything left to save.'

'When are they expecting the rain?' Alice asked, feeling sick as she thought of the potential damage.

'It's due within the next three to five days. It's not lookin' good.'

She watched as her brother kissed his wife goodbye and sent her a wave before heading out the door, her mind still stuck on Finn's bad news.

Later, when Alice left her brother's house, she found herself driving out of town. She had no idea what she was going to do when she got to Finn's place but going there was the only thing she could think of doing. She needed to make sure he was okay. She could only imagine the heartbreak he would be going through as he watched his first bumper crop in years be ruined before his eyes—unable to save it before the rain came.

She found him walking around the big harvester, talking on the phone as he kicked at the tyres and scratched the stubble on his face irritably as he listened to whatever the person on the other end of the line was saying. He abruptly pulled the phone away from his ear and shoved it back in his pocket. He watched her walk towards him, but there was no fond welcome or smile.

'Hey,' she breathed. 'Toby told me about the contractors. Have you had any luck trying to get someone else?'

'Nope. There's no one available. Everyone's scrambling to get harvest finished before the rain hits. I should have known everything was about to go downhill fast. My chaser bin driver called me last night to tell me he broke his leg dirt bike riding. I couldn't even find anyone who can fill in for *him*. Then this all landed in my lap.'

'None of your neighbours can help out?'

He shook his head. 'They would if they could, but the whole district is in a panic.'

'You've got your harvester, though?'

'Yeah. But now I'm down a chaser driver.' He sighed, his voice heavy with defeat. 'There's no way I'm going to get through all this in time.'

'You're not giving up?' she asked.

'No, I'm not giving up; I'm just stating a fact. You just can't win against mother nature. Jesus, Al . . . Last year we barely had anything of any quality to harvest and this year it's been bumper crops everywhere—the best in years. I planted three times the amount I normally do and thought I had all my bases covered, then it bloody floods upstream!'

'So you'll get through as much as you can in the time you have.'

'Just nowhere near the amount I need to,' he muttered, taking his hat off before breathing a harsh curse and turning his face up to the overcast sky.

It wasn't fair. This life never was. Not for the first time, Alice tried to wrap her head around the concept of earning a living while having little to no control over the endless parade of possible threats: the weather; insects; machinery; no rain; too much rain; fire; flooding . . . It was an endless circle of uncertainty. Farming was not for the faint of heart. The life was hard, and when everything went right, it was great, but when everything fell apart—it was heartbreaking. She felt Finn's frustration rolling off him and a gaping helplessness began to claw inside her.

'What can I do to help?' Alice asked.

'Do you remember how to drive a chaser bin?' he asked. She could tell he was expecting her to turn him down, but at least he wasn't still talking about giving up.

'I'm pretty sure it'll all come back to me soon enough,' she said. It was a job she'd done many times over the years on his parents' property, driving the tractor that pulled a large bin behind it that collected the grain from the header as it harvested the crops.

'I wasn't serious,' he said, shaking his head.

'I was,' she told him firmly, holding his gaze steadily. 'Let me help.'

'You're a fashion designer.'

'So? Before that I used to help you out on your parents' place for years. From the looks of it, I don't think you have the luxury of turning down *any* offer of help. So let's stop wasting time—tell me where to start.'

For an agonising moment she thought he was going to brush off her offer again, but then he simply let out a hollow chuckle and slapped his hat against his thigh before cramming it back on his head.

'Okay then. Follow me,' he said, walking back to the machinery parked at the edge of the partially harvested paddock. 'You sure you want to do this?' he asked, standing in the open door of the tractor cabin.

'Absolutely. We've got to try, right?' she replied, mustering a smile.

'Yeah,' he said, if not exactly enthusiastically, then at least somewhat more positively than he'd been sounding earlier. As he gave her a brief rundown of the job, Alice tried to ignore the warmth of his arm, which rested close to her thigh where she sat in the driver's seat.

'Okay, let's see how far we get. I'll be on the radio, keep an ear out,' he reminded her, before jogging back to his header and climbing inside.

The job did come back to her with only a few false starts. Alice got the hang of driving the tractor and lining up her bin after a few unloads of the header, and she began to feel a lot more confident.

At the entrance to the paddock was a large field bin that the smaller chaser bins were emptied into. Later, semitrailers would collect the grain from the bins, so keeping those bins away from the paddocks saved the heavy trucks driving across the fields they were harvesting. Alice lost track of how many trips she did back and forth.

As they worked through the rest of the afternoon, Alice found herself smiling. It was just like old times. She fell into a steady rhythm, and it was like the last ten years had never happened. Like nothing had changed.

Later in the afternoon, as she finished her last run to unload the chaser bin, she noticed her brother's car pulling up.

'Hey.' Toby greeted her with a wave as he ambled over. 'Making any headway?'

Alice glanced across the dusty paddock and winced. 'Doesn't feel like it, but I guess slow and steady is better than nothing. It's just so frustrating. He needs help.'

'It's a major stuff-up all around. But it is what it is. You get home, I'll take over tonight. Merrick's still under the pump at his place or he'd be here to take over from Finn, but we can only do what we can do.'

'You're a good mate,' she said, giving him a hug.

'He'd do the same for me—for anyone, really.'

She knew Toby was right, but there had to be *something* more they could do.

On her way back to town, Alice pulled up on the side of the road and took out her phone. Without more help, they weren't going to get enough of the harvest in—despite her pep talk earlier, things were indeed dire and the thought of Finn losing everything he'd been working so hard for tore her up inside. Alice had been racking her brain all day to think of where else they could turn for help and suddenly she thought of one thing she could try. She still had a few contacts from school days and, although she wasn't sure she'd be able to do anything more than Finn and Toby had already done, she knew she wouldn't be able to rest until she tried.

'Merrick?' Alice said, after multiple phone calls and dodgy reception drop-outs, barely able to keep the excitement from her voice despite the frustration. 'I'm sending you a number. You need to talk to this guy and fill him in on all the details. I think I might have found a way to help Finn.'

Earlier in the day, Alice had put in place a contingency plan to have her mother meet the delivery truck with all her belongings at her old house, and as she pulled up outside, exhausted from her long day, she almost considered heading instead for her parents' house, but she was too tired to find the energy. At this point she really didn't care what state the house was in, she'd be happy to just find a place to lie down. But as she pushed open the door and walked inside, she sucked in a surprised breath, catching the delicious aroma of home cooking as she walked into the kitchen and found that her furniture had not only been delivered, but unpacked and arranged. She walked across to where a small kitchen table was set with one place setting and reached out to pick up the note which had been left on the placemat.

Dinner's in the oven. Enjoy your first night in your new/old home. Love Mum and Dad.

A surge of gratitude and love bubbled up inside her chest as she hugged the note to her and continued looking around—a small whimper of relief escaping when she poked her head in through the doorway of her bedroom to find her new bed, made up with linen her mother must have brought with her from home. *God, I love my mum. She thinks of everything.*

Hunger drove her back to the kitchen, where she devoured a plate of shepherd's pie before taking a quick shower and climbing into bed. Tomorrow was going to be another huge day and, hopefully, if everything worked out the way it was supposed to, they might *just* be able to save Finn's crop.

Chapter 36

The next morning, Alice climbed out of her car and headed across to the big shed. Finn walked out, wiping his hands on an old bit of rag, which he tossed onto a tall drum as he approached her.

'Did you get any sleep?' she asked, taking in his red-rimmed eyes.

'Nah. Just came in to grab something to eat and refuel before I get back out there again.' He looked up to the grey sky and gave a disheartened sigh. 'Not sure how long that'll hold off for.'

It was darker than the day before and there was a definite feeling of an impending storm on the rise.

'Glad you weren't scared off yesterday,' he said quietly.

'I'm back for more,' she said, then pressed her lips together. 'And I found some extra hands to help out,' she added, unable to keep her excitement under wraps a second longer.

'What?' he asked, his confused eyes searching her face briefly before looking over her shoulder towards the farm entrance. His expression changed to outright disbelief. 'Al? What's going on?' he asked as the sound of a loud engine rambled up the driveway behind them. Her brother-in-law, Merrick, sat inside a large header, followed by an assortment of other machinery.

'I brought reinforcements,' she said. 'Merrick managed to finish his harvest last night, so he's here to lend you a hand to get yours done.'

'Al,' Finn asked, 'how did you organise all this?'

'I didn't do much. Merrick organised everything.'

'Those other blokes are contractors,' he said, narrowing his eyes as he read the signage on the other vehicles, 'and not from around here.'

'They're *half* a contracting team,' she corrected. 'They were finishing up and on their way back to Woolaroo but couldn't get there because of the floods. So it's all worked out, but that doesn't matter right now.' Alice was unwilling to admit to Finn that it had taken a considerable amount of ringing around and calling in favours to get this team. He'd freak if he realised how much she'd had to offer these guys to come back for this job. 'That rain's on its way and you need help. So just forget about it.'

'Al, it's not that I don't appreciate all this . . . it's just that . . .' He rubbed his hands across his tired face and stared at the cavalry with a look that was a heartrending mix of disbelief, hope and bruised pride.

'It's okay. It's all sorted. Just get back in that header and go harvest your crop. We'll talk later,' she said.

He stared at her a moment or two before shaking himself out of his stunned stupor then heading across to meet the men and fill them in on where to go.

Alice went over to his tractor and sat inside the cabin, fighting back a rush of unexpected emotion. It felt good to do something to help. Finn was a proud man, and he would no doubt have plenty to say about all this later, but he wasn't stupid. Without these extra machines and the manpower to use them, he'd have no chance of beating the rain and his profit for the year would be lost. He still might not finish the harvest.

She let out a long breath and focused on the job at hand.

They worked like a well-oiled machine all through the day and night and late into the following day and, by some kind of miracle, the rain continued to hold off.

Alice was driving the tractor back from the field bin when a rumble of thunder sounded. She looked over, yet again, at the dark bank of cloud growing ominously on the horizon. For two days they'd all been watching it approach and circle, like some massive beast biding its time, and every hour their tension grew as they wondered when it would stop toying with them and pounce.

As the afternoon had stretched on the huge dark clouds had begun advancing and a wind had started to blow, making the leaves on the trees that bordered the paddock sway like drunken sailors in the distance.

Light levels had dimmed, headlights had gone on and Alice knew that this time it was going to hit—and soon. She could feel the storm's energy all around them. The air smelled of rain and frantic desperation as they tried to outrun it.

They were down to the last paddock now and she watched the impressive sight of the huge headers working their way in a staggered formation across the open, endless plains. Lightning streaked across the sky and thunder cracked in sharp accompaniment. The image took her breath away with its ruthless beauty. Despite the urgency, Alice was entranced by the magnificence of mother nature unfolding herself before them, so much so that she couldn't help but take her phone out and try to capture the moment. There wasn't any time to see if the photo turned out, though, as her radio crackled to life once more.

There was less than a quarter of the paddock to go when the clouds all but blacked out the sky above them, day turned to night and the heavens opened up.

They raced back to the field bin and dropped off the last of their loads, then the headers turned and made for home.

Within minutes there was a deluge, filling the freshly cut rows in the paddocks with water and creating a white veil over the property. Alice scrambled from the tractor and slammed the door shut, making a dash for the nearest shed, where she breathed in the heady aroma of rain and the earthy, clean smell of freshly harvested crops. Her shirt and jeans were soaked despite the short distance from the tractor to the shed and her hair was dripping water down her face. She ruffled her fingers through it in an attempt to shake out some of the dampness, but it didn't make much difference. There was very little of Alice Croydon, London fashion designer, in the drowned rat who stood dripping in her designer jeans and sweat-drenched T-shirt. She'd borrowed a pair of Daisy's work boots, since the brand-name slides she'd been wearing the previous day had been all but ruined when she'd unexpectedly ended up working.

The rain cascaded over the edges of the tin awning as she watched the men climb out of their machinery and jog across to the open shed where the esky was already being opened and beers handed out in celebration.

Her heart skidded to an unsteady halt as Finn stopped beside her, water streaming down the sides of his face, but she saw nothing other than his wide smile, which enticed a grin of her own.

'Done!' she said triumphantly.

'Done,' he agreed. 'I can't believe it held off just long enough to get most of that paddock out today.'

'You certainly have someone looking out for you.'

'Yeah. So it seems,' he said. 'I seriously don't even know where to start,' he said quietly. 'Thank you doesn't seem to really cut it.'

Alice smiled shyly. 'It's no big deal.'

As soon as she said it, she wanted to take it back. It *was* a big deal. She knew that. She just didn't want to make it a huge deal between *them*.

'It was the difference between saving this place and not. I'd say it was a big deal,' he said in a hollow voice.

'I just meant—'

'It wasn't a big deal for you,' he cut in briskly.

Alice opened her mouth to protest, but decided against it. 'I just wanted to help,' she said instead. 'I wasn't looking for thanks. Just enjoy the fact we got it mostly all in.'

'It's easier said than done to accept stuff like this . . .' His words drifted off before he shook his head. 'A man's got his pride, Alice.'

His words should have sparked anger, but one look at his face and the sadness etched there made her pause. 'I get that accepting help can sometimes feel like charity or something,' she conceded. She'd had her own battle with pride when Frankie had given her so much in the beginning of their relationship too. She understood that reflex to automatically reject any offer considered too generous. 'But this *wasn't* charity.'

'What was it then?'

'I don't know.' She shrugged. 'I saw someone I cared about struggling and I wanted to help.'

'I don't want to sound like an ungrateful jerk,' he said. 'I *do* appreciate everything you did, it's just . . . Christ, Alice, I've barely been able to keep my head above water for the last five years. Every damn day I've just managed to stay one step away from a foreclosure notice.' He stopped and her heart ached at the crack in his voice. 'I took this place on, certain I could handle anything that came my way. I had big plans, but this last drought cut me off at the knees. It took everything, my wife, my dreams . . . my confidence. All I had left was my pride, not that that was worth much. Then the last of that vanished when you came in to save my arse,' he said, hollowly.

'What was I supposed to do? Stand by and watch you lose everything because of a stupid rain event and a chance that your pride might get hurt if I tried to help?'

'Yes!' he said, before lowering his head in defeat and shaking it wearily. 'No. I don't know.'

'If you think for one minute that I could have turned my back on you, then you've obviously forgotten who I am,' she said sadly.

'Here you are some big, successful designer—who's achieved everything she wanted to do—and here I am . . . still struggling to stay on my feet. I feel like a failure, Al.'

Alice bit her lip as she watched the emotions pass across his face.

'I'm sorry,' she said softly when the silence became too heavy to bear a moment longer. 'I didn't mean to make you feel that way. You're not a failure. Not by any means.'

Finn gave a quiet growl and rubbed his hands briskly over his head before looking at her. 'You have nothing to feel sorry about,' he said, trying for a calmer tone. 'I'm the one who should be sorry.' He swore and turned away slightly, before taking a breath and facing her again. 'And you're wrong, Al. I do remember who you are,' he said, holding her gaze firmly. 'I tried for a long time to forget you, but I never really could.' He touched the side of her face, making her breath hitch. She was too scared to even breathe in case he stopped. 'Thank you for everything.'

Alice swallowed over a tightening throat but managed a small smile. 'You're welcome.'

She glanced down at her clothes and screwed her nose up at the dust which had turned to mud. Her stomach grumbled, reminding her that she hadn't eaten anything since the sandwich someone had tossed her earlier in the day. But she was too tired to eat. All she wanted to do was step into a hot shower and fall into bed.

A loud cheer went up inside the shed, drawing their attention, and she caught the tired smile on Finn's face as he turned back to face her.

'Sounds like the party's started. You coming in for a drink? You earned it.'

Something inside her chest fluttered as she took in the exhausted but warm smile he sent her. 'I think I'll just go home and sleep for at least a week, if it's okay with you,' she said.

His smile widened then wavered a little as they looked at each other. Somehow, they were standing closer than before. She caught a whiff of that familiar scent of Brut and a hint of sweat mixed with the clean smell of rain and was momentarily distracted. He looked like he wanted to try and change her mind, but then he closed his mouth and simply nodded.

'Thanks again for all your help.'

Alice managed a small smile before turning away and making a run for her car, feeling shaky. *Probably just hunger*, she told herself firmly as she drove down the driveway towards the road into town. *Anything else would be*—she clamped down on that train of thought. No. Opening that particular can of worms would be just plain crazy.

Chapter 37

Alice didn't see Finn for the next few days, not that she would have had time between painting the kitchen and living room in her little cottage and the Christmas preparations in full swing at her parents' house. Her mother was in her absolute glory as she'd finished up her volunteer commitments for the year and was now busy preparing for the family celebrations, baking and prepping for the feast that would start with Christmas Eve and run through until well after Boxing Day. Alice could already feel her waistline expanding.

It was the twenty-second of December and Christmas was everywhere Alice looked. She found a place to park quite a distance from the grocery store due to the number of cars in the main street and breathed in the warm, summer-rain smell, as the sun came out briefly to heat up the wet bitumen and create a rainbow at the end of the street. It had been raining nonstop since the day they'd finished harvest and the distant

347

rumble of thunder still echoed. It seemed as though there might be more rain to follow.

She heard her name and her heart gave a silly flutter as she watched Finn jog across the road towards her.

'Hey,' he said easily, and Alice gave herself a mental kick to snap out of her ogling. He wasn't even wearing anything especially ogle-worthy, just his standard denim jeans and rolled-up long-sleeved work shirt, although it was in her favourite shade of royal blue, which always made his eyes seem bluer. He still had the most annoyingly thick, dark lashes. Lashes she had to pay a small fortune for at a beautician to achieve herself.

'Hi,' she managed after blinking away the memory of the moment they'd shared after harvest.

'Are you busy?' he asked.

'I . . . ah . . . no, not really. I'm just heading to the grocery store to get Mum a few things.'

'Do you want to grab a coffee?' he asked, hunching his shoulders slightly as he hooked his thumbs into the front pockets of his jeans.

'Sure,' she said, after only a small hesitation.

'The pub has a cafe of sorts.' He nodded towards the Royal, one of three pubs in town, located in the middle of the main street.

Alice followed him across the road and smiled her thanks as he held the door open for her to walk in ahead of him. She gritted her teeth against the urge to turn her head and bury her nose in his neck as she passed close to his body and caught his alluring scent. *Knock. It. Off!*

After they'd ordered, Alice sat back in her seat and took in her surrounds. The pub hadn't changed much since she'd last been in here. It was still dimly lit and the distinctive smell of hops and yeast lingered in the air. In the background the rolling arpeggio of the poker machines mixed with the dulcet tones of Amber Lawrence coming from the juke box.

'I guess this rain's kept you busy in the shed fixing everything since harvest?' she asked.

'Yeah—same old routine. Cleaning the harvester up, maintenance, doing all the jobs I've been putting off. Sheep work.'

'How many head are you running?'

'I'm down to twenty-five hundred. I cut it back from about four thousand so I could dedicate more room to cropping this last season. Speaking of which,' Finn added, 'I've been hearing all the talk around town about the plans for the old wool mill. It's causing a bit of a stir.'

'In a good way, I hope?'

'Yeah, everyone seems excited. There's a few doubters—but, you know, there'll always be the ones who reckon they could do something better with it. I think it's a great idea.'

'You think the local farmers would be on board with it?'

'I reckon they would be. I'm assuming you'd be having a community meeting about it?'

'Eventually . . . if it goes ahead. I still need to make sure it's feasible. But, yes, I'd put together a package of what was in it for locals and hope that we got a lot of support.'

'I hope it works out. We need some life breathed back into this place.'

'My main focus is on the mill and marketing the fabric and designing,' she said, 'but the tourism side with a cafe and the museum and everything will play just as big a role for local employment opportunities and bringing people into town.' She felt the bubble of enthusiasm begin to rise once again as she filled him in on her plans. She couldn't help it—the project just filled her with so much excitement.

'You're practically glowing, and that's saying a lot, since it's pretty dark in here,' he said gently.

'Sorry, I know I go a bit overboard. You can't shut me up once I start.'

'I don't want to shut you up,' he said, holding her gaze. 'I like hearing you talk so passionately about it.'

Alice ducked her head slightly. 'It's something I really want to see work out here. I think it'll be good for the whole district.'

'I do, too. Count me in on anything you need help with.'

'Thanks.' She grinned at him. 'Going by the state of the mill, it's going to take a lot of help to get it back in shape.'

'How bad is it?'

'I won't have the official report until after Christmas, but the preliminary advice is that structurally, it seems pretty solid. And I don't want to change the design of it too much—I want to keep it as authentic as possible, since it's all about showcasing the heritage of the place. But it'll take a bit to update the storefront area and the cafe, and I've got big plans for the landscaping.' She'd been thinking about creating a park with picnic tables and a rustic feel using old cars and a dry creek bed with little bridges as garden ornaments to complement the mill. She could already picture it being the backdrop to her new fashion line's catalogue shoot. Although she may have been getting a little ahead of herself.

'Sounds like you'll have your hands full for a while, then. Does that mean you'll be staying longer in town now?'

Alice paused as their coffees were brought over by the young waitress. 'No, I'm still planning to head back after New Year's. The business needs to be my main focus right now.'

'Fair enough. I just thought maybe this mill was something you'd need to be based here for.'

'I'll be back and forward a bit, I'd imagine.'

'So no plans to move back permanently?'

'Not really. At least, not yet. I mean, the whole point of moving back from London was so I could focus more on my own designs and less on the business side of things, but it still seems to take up most of my time. I've been thinking of putting in someone to manage it all. I have advisers, but I really need someone I trust to take over all the stuff that does my head in,' she said, blowing out a breath and picking up her cup.

'I hear ya. Not that it's the same as what you're going through, but the amount of bookkeeping and paperwork involved in running the farm kinda took me by surprise too when I left Whyningham. Mum and Matt used to mainly handle all that stuff.' He toyed with the handle of his mug briefly. 'It was a steep learning curve.'

'Shelly wasn't interested in the administration side of it?' Alice asked.

'Nope. She made it clear from the start she didn't want anything to do with the property. Was probably something that should have raised a few red flags.'

Alice screwed up her nose. 'We live and learn.'

'We sure do.' Finn picked his mug up and took a hasty sip, before putting it down and clearing his throat. 'About all that,' he started, glancing at her before lowering his eyes once more. 'How things ended between us.'

Alice felt her stomach drop and she looked down at her coffee.

'Look, I want to apologise. I was a jerk back then. I should have supported you and your career the way you always supported mine, and I didn't. I took you for granted. It's something I've regretted for a long time.'

'We were both young,' she said, shaking her head as she gazed at him.

'Maybe. But that wasn't any excuse. It wasn't until a few years later that I started taking notice of how Dad treated Mum, and how Matt acted around Jen, and it hit me that I'd just accepted it. You know, I've never once heard my old man thank my mum? Not for the meals she cooks him every night, or the trips into town she makes for parts . . . nothing. And that's how I used to treat you. Maybe if I'd have woken up to myself sooner, I wouldn't have lost you.'

Alice hadn't been expecting this at all. The shock of it momentarily robbed her of words. 'I'm not sure how things would have turned out if I'd stayed,' she finally admitted. 'I left to follow my dream. I don't think either of us would have grown into the people we are today, though, if I hadn't.'

'Yeah, I guess. You wouldn't have become a celebrity, rubbin' shoulders with the rich and famous,' he said with a crooked grin.

'I didn't mean that bit,' she corrected gently. 'I mean, we wouldn't have had all the life lessons we've had. Loving people, losing people. Being forced to make decisions we might not have made otherwise. I think all of it—the good and the bad—was needed so we could appreciate everything else still to come.'

'Yeah, I guess that's true. It was a hell of a lesson though.' He chuckled sadly.

'Yeah.' It had been.

'Were you happy?' he asked after they took a moment to drink their coffee in silence. 'In your marriage, I mean.'

'Yeah. I was. I wasn't expecting to fall in love with Frankie. It wasn't the reason I took the job,' she added, watching his face carefully. 'I had no interest in anyone when I went over there. I just wanted to design and learn the craft. But at some point, once I realised you'd moved on, I figured there was nothing really for me back here and I began to look at the UK as my new future. Frankie and I just seemed to make sense.'

He nodded, but his expression remained tight.

'What about you? Your marriage must have been happy in the beginning?'

Finn studied the mug in his hand. 'After you left, I drowned my sorrows in too much alcohol and buried my feelings by partying way too hard.'

Alice frowned at this. The Finn she'd known had never been a party animal. They'd gone to bonfire nights and camping with friends, but he'd never been interested in drinking to wipe himself out, even when it was the usual thing to do. He'd been too busy working.

'Shelly was part of that scene. When she met me I was someone different. I guess I outgrew the phase and she wanted to stay in it. She didn't like farm life—had no interest in it, really. She hated it even more after a few bad seasons and finding out my parents controlled all the money from Whyningham. Apparently I was a lot less attractive when I was broke.'

'I'm sorry things didn't go better there.'

'It is what it is, I guess,' he said with a small grimace. 'I have to take a lot of the blame. I wasn't in a great place at the time and I shouldn't have gotten into a relationship with someone out of whatever the hell I was feeling back then. I'm not proud of myself. We did try and make it work for a while, but we were too different. I think she realised—way before I ever did—that I couldn't love her the way she deserved.'

Alice gave him a confused look. 'Why not?'

'Because I was still in love with you,' he said simply, knocking the air from her lungs so fast that she momentarily forgot how to breathe.

Finn cleared his throat and placed his mug aside. 'I guess I should let you get back to your shopping. Your mum's probably champin' at the bit.'

Alice swallowed quickly and grabbed hold of her scattered senses. 'Yeah. She's been cooking up a storm for the last few days.'

'I bet.'

'What are you doing for Christmas? Are your parents coming back?'

He glanced at her, looking a little uncertain, and Alice wondered why.

'Your parents invited me over for Christmas lunch. They didn't mention it?'

'Oh. No, they haven't yet. I'm sure it just slipped their minds,' she said, forcing a smile. More likely they decided not to mention it until the day.

'I don't have to come if you'd rather I didn't.'

'No. It's fine,' she said, shaking her head. 'Of course you have to come . . . don't be silly.'

'They invited me ages ago. They probably forgot about it.'

'They wouldn't have forgotten,' she assured him. 'I'm glad you'll be there.'

'You sure?'

'Of course.' She smiled. She wasn't sure why she was so surprised. Finn had spent quite a few Christmases with them over the years and her mother wouldn't have allowed him to spend the day alone once his parents left town and his marriage ended. Kathy was always watching out for lost souls to coddle. What *did* confuse Alice, though, was the delight she found filling her at the thought of seeing him there. She wanted to believe it was simply because, despite everything, she still cared about him as a friend. But she couldn't ignore the tiny, annoying voice that suggested maybe it was more than that.

While she searched the shelves in the grocery store for the items on her mother's list, Alice found herself pondering those strange feelings. Could it ever be more than friendship between her and Finn again? She knew deep down they weren't just old friends. She cared about him. They'd once been a team, practically inseparable for years. They'd shared a life. You didn't just go back to *friends* after that. Despite all the pain of their break-up, she felt no lingering resentment towards him. Once she'd been angry and had felt betrayed, but at some point she'd let go of all that and moved on.

She'd never given much thought to life after Frankie—life with someone else. She'd been consumed by grief and then buried under all the stress and drama of the business. The possibility of finding love again never even entered her head. But Finn was different. Finn wasn't just *someone else*. He wasn't a new love in her life. He was tied to her, even after all this time. Part of her, somehow.

She hadn't been prepared for these feelings to emerge, but now they'd begun to stir, she wasn't sure how to make them settle back down.

Chapter 38

In the Croydon household, Christmas Eve was almost as big a deal as Christmas Day. For most of the family, it was the celebration of the end of work and the beginning of holidays. All the favourites came out: the rum balls and reindeer biscuits; chocolate elves and eggnog. They picked at grazing boards and cheese platters, cob loaf and spring rolls and, after eating their weight in finger food, it was time to go out and look at all the other streets and their Christmas lights, then head home with sugar-hyped kids, excited for Santa to come. Their parents had no hope of getting them to sleep early.

At least that was the Christmas Eve Alice remembered. She'd feared that some of the older kids would be too grown up for all the Christmas stuff, and that somehow the magic would be dimmed, but she needn't have worried. The food and Christmas spirit remained, and she was relieved to find that there were enough little ones left who believed with wide-eyed innocence that the weatherman on the news had just received Santa's flight plan, which said he was on his way. Alice loved being back, surrounded by her family once more.

Christmas carols blared from her parents' stereo as Alice sat at the table helping Bella build her gingerbread house from the kit Kathy had spent hours putting together for the grandkids the day before. The older kids had all finished theirs and a row of brightly decorated, if somewhat shonkily leaning, gingerbread cottages were lined up on the kitchen bench to set. It had been bedlam in here half an hour ago with seven older, much rowdier kids reaching across each other and arguing over the lolly allocation. This was far more civil.

The kitchen door opened and Alice's heart did a little unexpected lurch as Finn walked into the room.

'Aunty Al,' Bella chided in a stern, five-year-old voice. 'You're making the roof fall down.'

'Sorry.' Alice dragged her gaze away from Finn, quickly straightening the lopsided roof while making sure the walls below didn't collapse. There was a lot to this gingerbread house–making business.

'Wow, this looks impressive,' Finn said, leaning down to inspect their creation.

'Thanks,' Bella said, giving him a wide grin. 'Aunty Alice helped me. We waited till the whores got out of the way.'

Finn lifted an eyebrow at Alice.

'*Hordes*,' Alice corrected. 'We waited until the rest of the kids had finished so we could take our time.'

'Yeah. Plus, Gran hid some of the lollies, so we get all of them,' Bella declared triumphantly.

'Sounds like you two had the whole thing planned out.'

Alice grinned. 'You learn a thing or two when you're the youngest in the family.'

'Can I help?' Finn asked, pulling out a chair beside her.

'Sure,' Bella said, passing him a bowl of Smarties. 'Just stick 'em on anywhere.'

Alice could feel the warmth of Finn's arm as it touched hers and she breathed in the smell of him as he leaned across to reach for the Smarties. *This is so stupid*, she chastised herself. She was acting like a teenager, her face warming and her insides all fluttery. It was embarrassing.

'I didn't know you were coming in tonight,' she said, at a loss for any kind of offhand conversation.

'I wasn't planning to, but Gran bumped into me down the street and told me I had to come.'

'You *can* say no to Gran, you know.'

'*No one* says no to Gran,' Finn said, looking up from his careful placement of a red Smartie on the wonky roof.

For a moment Alice found herself mesmerised by the picture before her—Finn, casually decorating a gingerbread house, following the somewhat bossy directions of the five-year-old site supervisor. Her gaze fell to his hands—callused and hardened from the elements, so big and out of place working with the small decorations. He looked more than comfortable seated at the dining table in her parents' house, as though there was no other place he'd rather be.

His eyes softened ever so slightly as he caught her watching him. She couldn't drag her eyes away from his and the moment stretched into something . . . more. She knew he felt it too by the way the curious light in his eyes melted into something deeper. Her pulse was racing and she felt a little light-headed at the sudden rush of unexpected emotion. It was obviously just some kind of leftover attraction from a long time ago, flaring up.

'Are you two helping or not?'

Bella's irritated tone snapped Alice from her stupor faster than a bucket of cold water being thrown over her.

'I think it's done? What do you reckon?' Alice asked, giving her niece an overly cheery smile.

'But there's still lollies left over,' Bella protested.

'You can eat them. But don't tell your mum,' Alice said.

Bella's eyes lit up. She put a handful of brightly coloured chocolate into her mouth before scrambling from the table with the rest of her loot.

'Dad and the boys are all outside in the shed, I think,' Alice told Finn as she gathered the empty bowls of icing.

'I know,' he said, helping to collect the things from the table and carry them across to the kitchen sink.

'I'm sure you didn't come over just to hang around in here and clean up.'

'Nope. I came here to see you,' he said bluntly, which made her look up at him quickly.

'Me?'

'I haven't been able to stop thinking about you,' he said, putting the containers he held into the sink before turning to face her. 'Everything you did for me with the contractors and driving the chaser bin—' he gave a small incredulous grunt, '—talking me down from one of my worst moments in recent history . . . You're all I've been thinking about, Alice. Ever since you came back.'

She couldn't seem to look away—or move, for that matter; she just stared at him, her heart racing as though she'd almost trodden on a snake.

'I know I'm just some country hick you used to know and there's no way you'd consider . . .' His words faded and she saw his shoulders slump slightly. 'Never mind,' he said, moving across the room to leave. 'Merry Christmas, Al,' he muttered, opened the back door and left.

Alice stared after him, shocked by the suddenness of his departure.

'Are you just going to stand there and watch him walk away?' Gran demanded, making Alice jump.

'Gran!'

'What? I was just walking past and I overheard. Go on, go and tell him.'

'Tell him what?'

'The boy still loves you. Any idiot can see that. And you still love him.' Her grandmother had a stubborn kind of certainty that Alice found annoying right now.

'I don't—' Alice began before Meryl raised an eyebrow, holding her eye with a steely stare.

'Careful now,' Gran cautioned. 'You know how I feel about fibbing.'

Oh, for goodness' sake! She was not a five-year-old. She was a grown woman and could deny her feelings whenever she damn well pleased . . . Bloody hell.

As much as she *wanted* to deny it though, Gran was right. As usual. Christ, that was annoying.

'He's leaving,' Gran said, turning away from the door, a disappointed look on her face.

'I can't do this right now,' Alice said. She wasn't even sure what *this* was. Finn had caught her off guard with his unexpected announcement. What was she supposed to do with that? One minute he's telling her he can't stop thinking about her and the next, he's walking away. She needed time to process what it meant.

'Maybe you're right,' Gran said slowly. 'Maybe it's wise to sleep on it.'

'Gran, I don't know what you think is going to happen between me and Finn,' Alice said, 'but it's not possible.'

'Why?'

'Because, for one thing, I live in Sydney and he has a farm here.'

'So?'

'So, it's not exactly practical.'

'People commute all the time.'

'That's one hell of a commute. Besides, we don't have a very good track record when it comes to long-distance relationships.'

'You want something bad enough, you'll find a way to make it work.'

'I don't even know if I *want* Finn—that's the whole point. I didn't come back here to get back with my ex-fiancé.'

'Haven't you learned by now that it doesn't *matter* what we plan,' Gran said, 'life makes its own decisions?'

'*I* make my own decisions, now,' Alice said, shaking her head.

'Of course you do, darling. You keep telling yourself that.' Meryl patted Alice's arm as she walked away.

'I do!' Alice called out to the doorway Gran had gone through. She swore she heard a chuckle float back. *I bloody well do.*

Alice tried to enjoy the rest of the evening but found herself distracted by Finn's words far more than she wanted to be. By the time the family had come back from the walk around town admiring the Christmas lights, Alice knew she would have to deal with it.

'Darling, you're not heading home already are you?' her mother asked, as Alice grabbed her handbag and keys from the table.

'I think I will . . . I'm a bit tired,' she hedged.

'Tell Finn we expect to see him tomorrow—or else,' Kathy said with a knowing smile that turned into a laugh as Alice muttered under her breath. How was it that everyone else knew what was going on between her and Finn and she was still trying to work it out?

The road stretched out before her, a narrow path surrounded by endless dark shadows lit only by her headlights. Alice wasn't sure what she was planning to say once she got to Finn's place, she wasn't even sure why she was driving all the way out here on Christmas Eve when she should have been tucked up in bed, but here she was.

She couldn't leave whatever it was they'd started back in her mother's kitchen unfinished. It needed to be settled. She was only doing this, she told herself firmly, so she'd be able to sleep tonight and not lay there tossing and turning. She knew if Gran were here, she'd hear that same knowing little scoff she'd heard a thousand times before.

As she pulled the car to a stop, Alice heard dogs barking. The outside security light switched on.

Swallowing her nerves, she headed across to the gate that led to the house. The front door opened and Finn stepped out onto the small verandah, still dressed in the clothes he'd been in earlier, minus his boots. He wore a carefully neutral face.

'Al? What's happened?'

'Nothing. I'm sorry I didn't call to say I was coming out . . .' What on earth made her think she had any right to turn up on his doorstep in the middle of the night?

As she hesitated, he nodded his head towards the screen door he held open and waited for her to walk past him.

'Coffee? Something stronger?' he asked as she stopped inside the living room doorway. She spotted a glass of amber liquid on the coffee table beside the chair where he'd obviously been sitting.

'Coffee would be good,' she said, feeling her bravado rapidly deserting her now she was here.

'Take a seat, I'll be right back,' he said, waving an arm towards the lounge and disappearing into the kitchen.

She hadn't been inside his house before. From the outside it was the quintessential farmhouse with a wraparound verandah and bull-nosed roof. Alice found herself admiring the original fittings, including the moulded ceiling and timber floors. She also noticed that the internal doors all looked to have their original round brass doorknobs and stained-glass windows above.

Despite the charm of the old house, the furniture was mismatched and there was very little in the way of personal touches. There was nothing of Finn's personality at all in the decor—except maybe for the few farm magazines scattered on the coffee table—but it was the other thing on the table that caught her attention. An open photo album. Alice moved closer as she studied the photos.

Finn, bare chested and wearing football shorts, holding up a yabby caught in the dam on his parents' property. Beside him, sitting on the bank, was her nineteen-year-old self, wearing denim shorts and a bikini top, face tilted to the sun. The photo next to that was of the two of them dressed up for their Year 12 formal and another caught them slow dancing later that same night. She swallowed hard at the look captured on her face—she had been completely and irrevocably head over heels in love.

'I—ah, was looking through the old album earlier . . . for something,' Finn muttered, giving her a start as he came into the room carrying two mugs.

'It was open,' she said, feeling inexplicably guilty for having been caught looking at something private, until she remembered these were her memories as well and she really didn't have anything to feel guilty about. She took the cup he offered with a smile of thanks. 'What were you looking for?' she asked.

'Oh. Nothing. It wasn't important,' he said, scooping the album up and closing it before placing it in a drawer of the large TV cabinet.

Alice followed his lead and settled herself beside him on the lounge, far enough away that she could still face him.

'I guess you're wondering what I'm doing here,' she said, after taking a sip of her coffee.

'I figure it's got something to do with what happened earlier tonight.'

Alice gnawed at the inside of her bottom lip, before deciding to just get it out in the open. 'I want to know what you were going to say before you stopped. You said there was no way I'd consider . . . what?'

Finn let out a frustrated sigh as he rested his forearms along his denim-covered thighs and cradled the coffee cup in his hands. 'It was stupid. I don't know why I even said all that.'

Alice pondered the tense set of his shoulders. 'I've been thinking about you, too, since I got back.' There. She'd said it. *Oh my God.* She'd *said* it.

She didn't look at him when she saw his head turn towards her, she was too scared he'd see the truth she was trying so hard to ignore, even now.

She still had feelings for him. *Still?* Surely that couldn't be the right word. *Still* would imply she'd never stopped loving him even when she'd loved Frankie, and that seemed as though she'd been unfaithful somehow. This feeling she had now didn't have that scary, leap-into-the-unknown kind of heady sensation of new love, it felt . . . familiar. And yet that wasn't right either . . .

A frustrated growl escaped her and Alice straightened in alarm. She hadn't meant that to slip out, but all this second guessing was driving her crazy.

'No,' she said, putting her cup down quickly and standing up. 'You're right . . . this is . . . I don't actually know what this is. I thought coming over would clear the air, but I don't think it will after all.'

'Al, wait,' Finn said, standing up and reaching for her hand as she turned away. 'Don't go. Stay. Please.'

Alice wanted to say no, wanted to leave, but one look at his face and the uncertainty she saw there, and she knew she couldn't do it. She stared down at their joined hands and a tingle began to weave its way up her arm. The last of her resolve melted.

'I don't know what I'm doing here,' she said softly.

'Yes, you do,' he said, stepping closer.

The touch of his lips sent a jolt of something hot and urgent through her. She'd been expecting something that felt familiar and safe, not this sudden rush of need that had suddenly been unleashed. There was nothing in this kiss that reminded her of the Finn she thought she remembered—this was different, so very different from anything she remembered.

Soon his kiss wasn't enough. They were hampered by too many layers of clothing. Alice impatiently tugged at the hem of his shirt as he tried to wriggle his way out of it. Within moments the layers were gone and there was nothing but body heat and the delicious friction of rough stubble against smooth skin as Finn walked them backwards to the lounge.

It'd been so long since she'd had anyone touch her like this. The thought should have sent her into a tailspin of guilt, but it didn't. She'd grieved—was still grieving in so many ways—but she knew life had to go on. That had started with her decision to sell off part of the company and move back home. This was just another step.

Everything healed in its own time.

There was so much about Finn that was familiar and yet now, as she ran her hands down his back, she realised everything was also different. His body had changed—as had hers, no doubt. He'd filled out and matured from the boy she remembered and even though he'd been a man when they'd parted, he'd still been so young compared to the man he was now. Older and wiser and still so incredibly . . . hot. She gave a small whimper as he lifted his head to trail kisses down the column of her neck.

'You're beautiful,' he whispered.

'I'm not nineteen anymore,' she said, remembering the photos he'd been looking at. A wave of self-consciousness washed over her.

'No, you're not. You're even more beautiful now than you were back then.'

'You never said stuff like this when we were together,' she said, seeing the sincerity behind his words and letting his hungry gaze sweep away her earlier discomfort.

'I was an idiot.'

'No you weren't,' she said with a small smile. 'We were just too young to really appreciate each other back then.'

'I appreciate you now,' he assured her with a cocky grin that *did* take her back in time and could apparently still make her weak at the knees.

'I'd appreciate it if you'd get back to what we were doing,' she said, then gasped as he did. She didn't want to think too hard about how he may have learned some of his new moves, but she was grateful he had.

Chapter 39

The only sounds Alice heard in the quiet room were the croaking of frogs and clicking of night-time insects. A slight breeze stirred the curtains at the open window and moved across her naked skin like a gentle caress.

'Do I want to know what you're thinking?' Finn asked, breaking the silence after their breathing had settled.

'How do you know I'm thinking anything?' she murmured drowsily.

'Because some things never change. I could always tell when you were overthinking something.'

'I wouldn't say I was overthinking anything . . . exactly.'

'Yeah. Right.' She heard the gentle smile in his voice and something warm inside her shifted at its familiarity.

After a few moments, Alice gave a small sigh. 'Okay, fine. Maybe I'm trying to work out what we're doing and where this might go.'

To his credit, Finn didn't laugh, but she sensed he had an amused glint in his eye.

'I wasn't expecting . . . this,' she said slowly.

'Neither was I,' he admitted. His hand stilled on her back. 'But I don't regret it. Do you?'

'No,' she assured him quickly. 'Not exactly. I mean, I just wasn't expecting to add any more . . .' Her voice trailed off uncertainly.

'Any more what?' he asked slowly.

'I don't know . . . whatever this is,' she said, lifting herself slightly to move off his chest.

He rolled onto his side to look at her. 'I know I was the one who blew it last time—big time,' he added solemnly, 'but I'm not that same person. If you're worried about things being the same way they used to be, they won't.'

'Honestly, I don't know what I'm thinking right now.' There was so much going through her mind that it threatened to overload her senses. Everything felt so right—so familiar and comfortable—like she was where she belonged again. And yet it was new. Finn wasn't the same man he'd been, just like she wasn't the same woman. They'd married other people. They'd left behind past dreams and made new ones. The young couple they'd been, so sure of their future—so positive they knew each other better than they'd known themselves, now seemed naive—like they'd been kids playing house.

She'd left here a young, unemployed retail assistant with little confidence and no idea where her dreams would take her, and returned a strong, successful businesswoman with her own company. For the first time in forever, she felt like Alice again—but maybe a new, improved version.

'We don't have to make any decisions about what this is or isn't if you don't want to,' Finn offered, watching her face carefully. 'We could just see where it goes?'

That was a sensible idea. One that filled her with instant relief. Yes, they could act like two rational people and see what happened. Crisis averted.

Alice began to relax and allowed herself to savour this new closeness between them. While she wasn't entirely comfortable in her nakedness, covered only by a thin sheet, she didn't feel the need to immediately jump up and get dressed either. It was nice having Finn's hand on her hip as they faced each other—seemingly content to soak in the newness of the situation and readjust to each other once more.

Finn cast a glance over her shoulder at the bedside table. 'Merry Christmas.'

'Crap. I should go,' Alice said.

'Stay.'

'And do the walk of shame into my parents' house as they're serving the eggnog and unwrapping presents?' she asked dryly, 'I don't think so.' She'd promised to be there bright and early.

'It's not like they'd be surprised.'

'Maybe not. But still, I'd rather not have to face an inquisition first thing in the morning.'

She rolled away and Finn lifted his hand from her, letting out a reluctant groan. He unashamedly watched her dress.

'You're still coming over tomorrow?' she asked in an attempt to divert the growing arousal his heavily lidded gaze was inspiring in her. She found the bulging of the bicep tucked under his head just a little too distracting.

'Of course. I've been hangin' out for the famous Croydon Christmas feast all year.'

'Oh? So it's the food you're looking forward to then?'

Faster than she'd thought possible, he slid across and snagged her hand, tugging her rather ungracefully back onto the bed. 'It's you I'm looking forward to devouring—the food's an added bonus.' He grinned.

His kisses were intoxicating—stronger than any shot she'd ever thrown back—but they had the same effect on her, as a slow burn spread from her toes right up to her head. Her clothes were once more removed, and she didn't even care that she was supposed to be leaving. It was like they were kids again—unable to get enough. It went on and on, as they unhurriedly explored each other, gently teasing one moment only to become caught up in a burning need for fulfilment the next.

The next morning, Alice woke, disorientated. Something heavy rested across her and the room she was in made her think for one crazy moment that she was dreaming, before everything fell into place. At some point last night, Finn had insisted they return to her place so they could join in with her family early in the morning.

They were in her *new* bed in their *old* bedroom. It was a modern twist on déjà vu.

'I still can't believe you've moved back in here.' Finn's deep voice reverberated against her back, making her jump a little.

'I didn't know you were awake,' she said, rolling over to face him and smiling as he tugged her a little tighter against him. 'It does feel a little bit strange.'

'I miss this place.' He sounded almost wistful. 'Brings back a lot of memories.'

'Yeah. It does.'

'Can't imagine it compares with the places you've been living since you left here though.'

It was true—she'd lived in a beautiful apartment in London and had a six-bedroom country manor home to spend weekends and holidays in, but neither held the memories and history of this modest little cottage with the uneven floor in the kitchen and the rusty gutters that needed replacing.

'Somehow I managed to sell both those places, but I've held on to this one.'

'I'm glad you kept it,' he said softly. 'I'm not proud of the way I tried to hurt you by trying to force you to sell it when you left.' He looked miserable as he held her gaze. 'I wasn't in a good place back then. Every time I drove past, it nearly tore my heart out to remember you.'

'That's all in the past, now. We came through it in the end,' she said, turning to touch his face. 'No more digging up all that old hurt, okay?'

'Sounds good to me.' He kissed her, managing to wipe the lingering threads of past pain away and replace them with something far more enjoyable.

Chapter 40

Christmas carols played over the speakers in the outdoor entertainment area where three long tables had been set up. The whole family was crammed around them, pulling crackers and reading out the lame jokes inside as they piled plates high with food. Alice felt her heart swell as she looked around the table. She'd never felt so lucky.

'Ah, Dad?' Toby said, staring down at his plate with a confused expression. 'I don't see any quail? Weren't they supposed to be on the menu?'

Alice bit back her grin and lowered her head as she heard her father's mumbled reply.

'There's no shame in admitting you've become attached to them, Jim,' Gran soothed from the end of the table.

'I'm not attached to the bloody noisy things, I'm just breeding up numbers. They're not big enough yet.'

'Uh-huh.' Charlie nodded, wearing a sceptical grin. 'Sure, Dad.'

Alice's gaze connected with Finn's and she felt that strange sensation of falling back in time. This could have been ten years ago, and yet they were different—both of them had learned to deal with loss and pain and had overcome it to find themselves back where they started. But would it be different this time? It would have to be, because Alice was still struggling to figure out how this would work. Part of her worried there wasn't going to be the happy ending everyone, including Finn, was hoping for.

'So, it's official?' Daisy asked later as they stood in the kitchen drying their mother's special crystal and china that didn't go into the dishwasher.

Alice sent her sister a frown. There was no point playing dumb—everyone somehow knew she and Finn had been together the night before. She supposed it wasn't too hard to guess, considering they hadn't been able to stop looking at each other since they'd arrived.

'I don't know,' Alice said now, hoping to avoid an inquisition, but realising she was really clutching at straws if she thought she could wiggle out of her sisters' and sisters-in-law's grip once they homed in on some juicy news.

'Finn looks like a devoted puppy,' Verity said, and Cicily chuckled as she reached for another glass.

'I think it's great,' Daisy said.

'What's great?' their mother asked, carrying in another stack of plates.

'Mum, go sit down. You cooked,' Alice said quickly.

'Finn and Alice,' Daisy said, ignoring Alice's frown.

'Oh, so it's official?' Kathy's face lit up.

'No!' Alice said, a little louder than she'd meant to, causing everyone to stare at her, wearing varying degrees of curiosity.

'Oh, for goodness' sake!' Alice snapped. 'I don't know what it is—but it was one night.' She threw a small wince across at her mother. 'Sorry, Mum.'

'So? It's not like he's some stranger you picked up at the pub,' Daisy scoffed. 'You know him.'

'I *knew* him. Ten years ago. And that's not the point.'

'So what is?' Verity asked, leaning against the counter.

'I have a business in Sydney to think about.'

'You always have a business to think about,' Verity said.

'What's that supposed to mean?'

'Just that business is all you seem to *ever* think about. You're thirty-four years old. When are you going to put *you* first for a change?'

'I put me first all the time.'

'No, you don't. Look, I loved Frankie too—he was an awesome guy—but his life was centred around his business empire and look where that got him? You put yourself second to Frankie and his work. You guys didn't have kids, you rarely came home to visit—your whole lives were centred around the business. You sold that off so you could start living again, remember?'

'It wasn't like that.'

'Verity,' their mother said with gentle warning.

'No, Mum. We've all kept our mouths shut for too long. It's time she heard it.'

'Heard what? What are you talking about?' Alice asked.

'We've been worried about you, Al,' Steph said, speaking up for the first time. 'We thought once you decided to move back home, you'd finally be able to concentrate on something other than work. Maybe meet someone *out of* the fashion industry and settle down.'

'Settle down? I was married for close to a decade,' Alice said, throwing her hands up.

'You were practically married to a business,' Verity said.

'I loved Frankie and our life. Just because I didn't want to pop out a million kids doesn't mean I didn't have a happy marriage.' Why were they ganging up on her like this? 'You know, there is a bigger life outside of Gunnindi,' she added and saw Verity flinch.

'Yes, we know, you went away and became a famous fashion designer—*we know*,' Verity snapped. 'And we all stayed here and led boring little lives.'

'I didn't say that,' Alice said, losing some of her indignation.

'You didn't have to. It was clear in the way you were happy enough to never come back and visit. Like you were ashamed of where you came from.'

Alice gaped at her sister and saw a few of the others lower their gazes as she looked around. 'What? That's not true. I'd never be ashamed of my family or where I grew up.'

'Let's not get into all this,' their mother said, looking sad. 'It's Christmas.'

'Mum? Is this how you feel too?'

She saw Kathy open her mouth to deny it before a look passed between her siblings and mother.

'We just really missed you over the last few years. Days like today were never quite the same when you were missing.'

The bottom of Alice's stomach fell away in dismay. It had been such a long trip to make and Frankie had always booked somewhere exciting for Christmas for the two of them. Her family had seemed to understand. Only now she realised they hadn't. They just hadn't wanted to make a big deal over it.

'I'm sorry. I didn't mean to make anyone feel like I didn't want to be here.'

'You're home now,' her mum said, reaching for her.

But was she? She'd been skimming through her emails yesterday and knew that she was going to be buried under so much paperwork by the time she went back that she'd barely be coming up for air any time soon. But this time it was *her* business. That made it different, surely? And yet, as she thought about it now, she realised she was still in the same situation she'd been trying to dig herself out of in London.

Things weren't going to change until she found someone to take over the business side of things. She needed to talk to Charlie. So far every time she'd planned on doing it something else had come up and she still hadn't gotten around to it.

'Come on, leave the rest of this,' her mum said briskly, pulling away from her daughter. 'We'll take coffee outside.'

In the backyard, Alice instantly felt Finn's gaze; she didn't have to look, she could sense its warmth as sure as if he were touching her. She didn't look at him, instead taking a seat beside her father. She leaned back, letting the voices of her family swirl around her.

So far she'd talked about all the changes she needed to make but she'd done little to action them. She didn't want the business to take over her life the way it had with Frankie. Although, to be fair, the business hadn't taken over Frankie's life—it *was* his life. And she'd allowed it to become hers.

Frankie had loved her—there was never any doubt about his feelings—but she'd also known having children wasn't going to be in the plan. Frankie had been happy with the way their life had unfolded. She had, too. There'd been no time for babies when they both had to travel so often, sometimes needing to throw together an overnight bag and leave on a flight with barely an hour's notice. That was no life for a family. And to be honest, she hadn't been willing to give up her career to be the one who stayed home and raised children—and she would have stayed at home, because she'd been raised that way, as had all her siblings and their families. There was no way she would have been able to have a baby and hand it over to a live-in nanny to raise.

Was she seriously wondering about having children? Now?

The thought stunned her. Surely not? She couldn't. She still had her business. She didn't even have a . . . Her gaze swung across to Finn and an image of a small, blond-haired boy sitting with him in a tractor flashed before her eyes. She inhaled sharply.

'You okay, love?' her father asked.

She offered a weak smile and nodded, grateful that her mother chose that moment to come out with a tray of coffee cups.

What was happening to her? None of this was making any sense—she hadn't even thought about children until now—at least, not seriously.

A claustrophobic sensation pressed in around her and she stood abruptly. 'I, ah, I think I'll head home for a lie down. I've got a headache,' she murmured as she passed her mother.

'Are you sure? You can take your old room here,' Kathy said, but Alice shook her head and winced. The headache was not simply a fib to get her out of there.

'I think I need a bit of quiet. I'll come back later this evening,' she said, kissing her mother's cheek before heading for the door without a backwards glance. She couldn't risk looking at Finn, she knew he'd be wondering what had happened and she fully anticipated him following her, but apparently he either thought better of it or her mother cautioned him to let her rest, because she left the house alone.

Alice hadn't expected to actually sleep once she laid down in her bed, but she must have because when she woke up, it was late afternoon and she felt the groggy, disorientated feeling of not knowing where she was.

She noticed her phone flashing on the bedside table and reached for it, letting out a slow breath as she caught Finn's name. He'd sent a text telling her to call him when she woke up and he'd come back into town. Alice thought about it but then forced herself to put the phone down. She did want to see him again but the conversation she'd had with her sisters, sisters-in-law and mother in the kitchen filtered through her mind and she was once more filled with a confusing cocktail of emotions.

How did one conversation suddenly change everything? Sure, she knew her business was still too big and time consuming— she'd been planning on making some changes—but after today it felt as though the blinders she'd been wearing had been ripped from her eyes. She'd been heading down the same path as Frankie, totally caught up in her business. She could see how she'd have to start turning down invitations to come home for the weekend . . . for Easter . . . for Mother's Day . . . next Christmas . . . because she'd be busy, drowning in business commitments. She felt torn. She wanted her business, but she didn't want it to become her life at the expense of her family.

Then there was the small dilemma of children. The image of the blond-haired boy had been burned into her mind. It was almost as though it had been some kind of glimpse into the future, it felt so real. But it couldn't be. She wasn't ready to deal with something like that yet.

Throwing back the bedspread, Alice gave an irritated growl and got to her feet. This had to be sorted. She scrolled through her contacts until she found the name she was after and hit call.

'Hi. It's me. Are you at home? I need to talk to you.'

The knock on her door wasn't totally unexpected. Neither was the jumble of nerves she fought as she opened the back door and found Finn standing on the doorstep later that night.

'I got worried when I didn't hear back from you. Are you okay?'

'Yeah. Sorry. I wasn't feeling too good. I should have called you,' she said, then faltered as he continued to stare at her. 'I had some things to sort out.'

'I take it those things didn't involve me.'

'Not directly, no. Business things.'

'Can I come in?'

'Of course,' she murmured, stepping back to let him inside. She'd spent the last few hours talking to her brother and sister-in-law, putting a plan to them and talking business, which had left her drained and reignited her earlier headache, but at least it was done. Now she just had to wait until she heard back from them. She wasn't sure which way it would go, if she were totally honest. There was a lot for her brother to process, which was probably why she'd found it near impossible to read him.

'You don't seem fine. I'm worried, Al. What happened today? One minute everything was great then the next you were gone.'

Alice swallowed the lump in her throat. 'Everything was moving too fast. I don't think I'm ready to make this into something.'

'I thought we agreed to just go slow and see what happens?'

'I just can't see it working.'

'Why?'

Alice let out an impatient huff, turning to lead the way into the living room. 'Because I suddenly realised I have a business to run and I don't think that will work in a relationship that's separated by six hundred and fifty kilometres.'

'It has to be something more than that. I know you, Alice. Something spooked you—and it's not the business.'

'Everyone kept asking were we back together, but it was one night. My family practically have us married off.'

Finn studied her silently before asking, 'Would that be the worst thing in the world?'

His question stole the breath from her lungs. 'It's too soon,' she said, shaking her head.

'I mean, not tomorrow, but one day . . .'

'Finn . . .'

'I know it was shit in the past, but last night proved we still have something—I know you felt it too. It was more than just two people with a past hooking up. Tell me I'm lying.'

She couldn't. There was no point denying it. 'That doesn't mean it's going to work out any better this time around.'

'Why not? I know you've got the business, but surely there's a way to work remotely. You would have done it like that before?' he said.

'Yes, occasionally, but—'

'So work out a way to make it happen again. You said yourself you loved being back here. And you've got the wool mill to get up and running. You've even done up the cottage. Everything you've done has been you planning on being here again. No matter what you say, I know deep down you don't want to be back in Sydney.'

'That doesn't mean I'm ready to give it all up yet,' she snapped. 'You don't get it—still! Yes, I've said that the business is taking up too much of my time and I'm trying to fix that, but it doesn't mean I would suddenly have nothing to do. I still want to design—I still want to contribute to the business and spend more time designing and doing the things I wanted to do in the first place.'

'Except get married . . . again.'

'I didn't expect any of this when I came back here, Finn.' She couldn't hold his gaze, there was too much hurt there.

'Neither did I,' he told her harshly. 'It nearly killed me getting over you the first time around. I can deal with the fact you'd live between places,' he said quietly.

'But for how long? You wouldn't wait last time.'

'How long are you going to throw that in my face?'

'I'm sorry, Finn. I don't mean to throw it in your face, but it was a big deal to me at the time. You broke my heart,' she said. 'So you have to understand why I might be a little hesitant to trust that everything would be different this time around.' Alice dropped her head and closed her eyes. She sighed before looking back up. 'I feel like it'll still be the thing that comes between us eventually.'

'Only if we let it,' he said softly.

'Are you really willing to take the risk?'

The hum of the refrigerator nearby sounded loud in the silence between them.

'What are we going to do then?' he asked, looking at her with an expression that ripped her heart in half.

'I don't know. Maybe we just need to take a step back and let things settle down a bit before we try and figure things out?'

'Sounds like you've already made a decision,' Finn said quietly.

Had she? All she knew was suddenly the walls felt as though they were pushing in on her and she was suffocating. She didn't want to make this decision again. It almost destroyed both of them last time—she wasn't sure she could face that again.

In the end, she didn't. She did what any mature, professional woman would do.

She ran.

Chapter 41

Alice stood beside her window and looked down at the traffic snaking its way along the street below, the odd bus horn blowing as pedestrians darted across the busy road. Everyone seemed to have somewhere to be and was in a hurry to get there. A small smile tugged at her lips as she thought how different this scene would be back in Gunnindi. No one *darted* anywhere. Everything was done at a slower pace—people stopped to chat and catch up with neighbours and friends in the street, cars double parked while they called out to someone about dropping by later, and no one blew a horn or yelled at someone to move out of the way.

She'd been back in Sydney for almost six weeks and it felt like Christmas had been a year ago.

A knock on her door brought her head away from the window and a genuine smile lit up her face as her brother poked his head inside her office. She still hadn't gotten used to him being here.

'I'm about to head off, is there anything else you need before I go?' Charlie asked.

'Nope. I think I've got it all under control.' The truth was, Charlie had it all under control. The years he'd spent in management in his previous job had made the switch to her company almost seamless. Of course, he'd had to learn a lot more about the fashion industry than he'd probably ever cared to, but Alice was impressed by how fast he'd picked up everything.

Charlie and Steph had decided to make the move to the city in order to give their kids more access to different opportunities and it seemed to have been a great decision. Alice had never seen them happier.

She'd officially bought the Old Mill three weeks ago and now was busy organising the fit-out and design as well as handling all the red tape that went along with restoring a heritage-listed building. Charlie coming on board couldn't have happened at a better time.

'See you tomorrow for lunch, then,' Charlie said with a wave.

That was another bonus of having a sibling in town—she was forced to get out of her apartment and there was always company, even if she hadn't been the best company herself lately.

She turned back to the window and noticed the grey clouds creeping across the sky.

When another knock came at her door, she expected Charlie.

'Would you just go home already!' she said, then froze as she stared at a face that did not belong to her brother.

'That came a little quicker than I'd anticipated,' Finn said, standing in the doorway, his hands shoved in his pockets, shoulders slightly hunched, the way he always stood when he was uncomfortable.

'Finn. What are you doing here?'

When he didn't immediately answer, she took the opportunity to drink him in. God she'd missed him.

He shook his head and took a hand out of his pocket to run it irritably across the back of his head. 'Stuffed if I know now. At the time it seemed like a good idea.'

'Why did you want to come at the time?' she asked slowly.

'To tell you something,' he said, sending a quick look around the office. He walked in a few more steps and studied the drawings she had on her drafting board. 'I never told you before, but Frankie was right—you do have a talent, you always did. I even knew it back then, I was just so wrapped up in the farm and my own stuff that I didn't think to tell you. But you do, Al. You're amazing.'

Alice blinked and felt her throat tighten as she bit the inside of her lip.

He touched a tuft of wool stuck on the page and looked up at her. 'Is this what you're working on for the mill?'

Surprised, she nodded. 'How did you know that?'

'Lucky guess. I noticed some work trucks there the other day. So, it's still going ahead?'

'Why wouldn't it be?'

'I thought maybe you'd changed your mind.'

'Nope. It's all full steam ahead, but at a council's pace.'

'So barely moving?'

'Very slowly,' she agreed with a soft smile and saw his face relax. For a minute she thought maybe he wasn't going to go back to the reason he was here, and forced herself to wait patiently, desperately trying to control the butterflies flipping about madly inside her.

'I tried to give you some space,' he finally said, coming to a stop an arm's length away from her. 'I figured there was a reason why you chose to run instead of staying. I even thought maybe you were right about this not standing a chance, but the thing is, I can't see how anything could actually *be* any worse than the last six weeks have been. I mean, I got used to you not being around before, but then I was mostly drunk, so I don't really remember much about it. After seeing you again, being with you—my head knew this was only early days, but the rest of me fell back in love with you like it'd never stopped.'

He lifted a hand and smoothed a whisp of hair back from her face before resting his hand against her cheek. 'I don't care if I have to make a million trips to the bloody city to see you when you have to be here to work—I'll do it. I'll support whatever you want to do, wherever you want to do it. Just don't shut me out, Al. Please?'

Alice heard a small sound escape—a cross between a groan and a sob—as she stepped into his arms and felt them close around her tightly. He was right, nothing had made sense once she came back here and yet, this was what she wanted to do, this was where her work was. But ever since she'd been back, she felt as though part of her was missing. Nothing felt right anymore.

'I'll do whatever I have to do to make it work,' he promised. 'We'll figure it out. I want you to have it all, Al. I want you to be happy.'

'I'm happy, now,' she told him, reaching up to kiss him. And she was. Gone was that emptiness she'd been carrying around inside her since she'd left Gunnindi because she finally realised it wasn't a *what* that had been missing, it was a *who*.

Epilogue

The smell of lanolin, citrus, lavender and that intoxicating new-fabric aroma wafted through the air as Alice soaked in the view before her. Around her was the comforting murmur of conversation from her family and friends as they gathered in small groups around the room.

It had taken six months longer than she'd anticipated and gone over budget by quite a significant amount—something Charlie, her business adviser and head of finance, had been having a slight meltdown about—but the wool mill was up and running and today was its grand opening.

The old building had undergone a facelift inside and out and walking through the front, barn-like doors felt almost like stepping into another place and time. Alice loved the rugged, rough-cut timber the original building had been built from, which gave the place a rustic, pioneer charm she could never have created in a newer building.

A few weeks earlier, she'd finished her new winter collection featuring Gunnindi-sourced wool and the photos from her catalogue shoot were being proudly displayed in the mill, gaining their share of admiring comments from the crowds as they wandered through to finally see what all the fuss had been about over the last eighteen months.

Verity stood behind the counter of the wool store in front of a dazzling array of beautiful custom-coloured wool. Their online shop had gone live a week ago and already the interest in the premium wool and their unique colours had exceeded all expectations. And it was only going to get bigger.

With the addition of a tourist information centre, which they'd managed to save after its old location on the outskirts of town had closed, they'd decided to expand and had created a camping area in the rear of the grounds to tap into the lucrative grey nomad market. What had started out as her dream to use and showcase Gunnindi wool, had continued to grow into something even bigger and more vital to the community and the town they called home. Alice was proud of how it had turned out—bigger and somewhat more expensive than she'd counted on, but worth every cent to see her dream become a reality.

Already she'd felt a change in their little community. A few new businesses had opened in some of the previously empty shopfronts and she suspected, with the gradual influx of travellers following their recent advertising campaign, there would be more to follow. There was optimism in the air—change definitely, but good change. For too long, Gunnindi had been forgotten, bypassed as too small and with nothing special enough to warrant any real tourism boom . . . until now.

'I like that look on your face,' Finn said quietly, coming to stand beside her.

'What look?' she asked, smiling up at him.

'Satisfaction. Contentment. You've worked hard to make this happen.'

'It took more than just me to get this thing on its feet,' she said, shaking her head. 'I couldn't have gotten this far without you and everyone else.' She leaned in to kiss him softly. 'In case I haven't said it recently, thank you.'

'I believe you thanked me earlier this morning,' he said, kinking an eyebrow suggestively.

'That was for something entirely different,' she said, rolling her eyes. 'But I mean it. Thank you for all your hard work and for putting up with me these last few crazy months. You've been amazing.'

Finn slipped his hands around her waist. 'Don't you know by now there's pretty much nothing I wouldn't do for you?'

Their relationship had only grown stronger since that Christmas when she'd returned to Gunnindi. Somehow, they'd managed to overcome all the hurdles life had thrown at them. Alice had worked hard to get her business running efficiently so she could focus her attention on the thing she loved doing the most—designing. Her creativity had come flooding back once all the business stress had been removed from around her neck, where it had been slowly drowning her. She was designing better than ever and felt more alive than she had in years.

Reconnecting with Finn had filled her with a different kind of contentment. They weren't the same people they'd been the first time around—taking each other for granted and too young and inexperienced to really understand what they'd each needed in order to grow into strong individuals: Finn had needed to get out from underneath his father and brother to find his own potential and she'd needed to move to London and follow her dreams. Now everything that had been working against them the first time around was gone and they were free to rediscover each other as two people who knew who they were.

'Nothing?' she asked, as a sudden wave of emotion washed over her.

'Anything you need, just ask,' he said, his gaze holding hers with an unexpected seriousness.

'Marry me?' she asked simply and saw the flicker of surprise cross his face momentarily.

'For real?'

Alice smiled. 'For real.'

'Are you sure? If you're worried that I'm not okay with all the commuting, you don't have to be.'

'It's not that,' she assured him. 'I've realised lately that I'm ready to move back. The business doesn't need me as much and I can design anywhere.' In fact, her designs had only gotten better since she'd started working from her little cottage. 'I'll still need to go back to the city now and again, but there's nothing I really need there. Everything I love is here,' she said. She traced her fingers along his strong jawline.

'In that case, hell, yeah, let's get married.' He grinned.

'Finally!' Gran cried behind them.

Alice turned to find Meryl staring at them with a bright smile.

'I thought you two would never get your act together.'

'We got there in the end,' Finn said, holding Alice's gaze with a look that made her heart give a painful kick against her chest.

'Yes, we did. I love you, Finn.'

'I've *always* loved you, Al. I never stopped and I never will.'

And right there in front of everyone, Finn kissed her—leaving no doubt whatsoever that she'd finally found her way home.

Acknowledgements

To everyone who answered the call for help with questions or some early reading, a huge thank you; Neil Westcott, Charlie Bartlett, Kaitlin, Lyn and my trusty Facebook friends who are always up for a bit of brainstorming.

A big thank you to my incredible team at Allen & Unwin who go above and beyond to get my books out to you as fast as I can write them.

If you loved *Time After Time*, read on for a sneak peek into Karly Lane's new book . . .

The One That Got Away

Alex Kelly's future is nearly sorted: she has a life she loves in London, a dream job, and plans to buy a cute cottage in the English countryside. There's just one last step: sell the family home in the small Australian seaside town of Rockne Heads. The place she spent almost two decades trying to forget.

Alex hopes to get in and out again as quickly as she can, however word that she's back in town instantly spreads . . . along with old gossip and dangerous grudges.

Sully McCoy has spent the last twenty years distancing himself from his father's reputation and has made a good life for himself and his daughter in Rockne Heads. But now Alex Kelly is back in town and somehow still turning his life upside down.

He thought he'd never see her again. And Alex is making it perfectly clear that she's not here to relive old memories— she's here to end them once and for all.

As old wounds reopen, Alex fears the secret she vowed to take to her grave will be exposed. And this time, she won't be able to run.

One

Alex Kelly drove over the last rise into town and caught her breath at the sight before her. The bluest of oceans, its shades blending in a wide arc framed by a strip of sand, row upon row of white caps curling as waves broke onto the shore in an endless, soothing rhythm as old as time. She hadn't been back in Rockne Heads—or Rocky, as locals referred to it—in years, but the view was always the same: beautiful.

A small stab of pain went through Alex as a bout of homesickness flooded her. *Home.* The word echoed in the silence of her car almost as though it had been spoken out loud. But Rockne Heads wasn't home—and hadn't been for a long time.

As she continued along the road, her gaze fell on a large handwritten sign stuck to someone's front fence: *No! to Ermon Nicholades!* Across the road was another one saying, *Save our Village!* She'd passed larger ones with similar messages along the road leading in from the highway and wondered what was going on. Something had clearly gotten up the locals' noses.

She turned into her old street and drove along the familiar, narrow road to the lookout at the end of the small cul-de-sac. There were no cars parked there today, so she had plenty of room to turn into her driveway. In a few weeks' time, tourists would be parked all along the little street as they stopped to take photographs or check out the surf. She hoped that wouldn't be her problem—she wasn't planning on being here that long. If everything went according to plan, she'd go through her father's belongings and throw most of them out before giving the place a good clean and putting it on the market. It should only take four days—five, max, she decided. She planned on spending the rest of her three-week holiday somewhere relaxing, maybe a resort further north, before returning to the UK. She hadn't had a proper relaxing holiday in years. She wasn't even sure she *remembered* how to relax, to be honest, but it was high time she did.

The car air conditioner had lulled her into a false sense of security and the humid air raced in to slap her across the face as she opened the door. This was bullcrap. If there was one thing she'd never been able to handle, it was humidity. She'd become acclimatised to the UK weather during the six years she'd been working for the Department of Foreign Affairs in London, and she preferred it. Alex had moved around a lot over the last eighteen years, never really settling down; there were too many adventures yet to have to stay in one place too long, too many things to see and explore. But now she'd found a place she wanted to settle and the only thing standing between her and buying the little cottage of her dreams was this place.

Four Winds had been in her father's family for five generations. Her great-grandfather had been given the piece of land on the top of the headland by *his* father and it was passed down to her grandfather then her father before coming to her. Not that she'd wanted it. She wasn't ungrateful, not really. It was . . . complicated.

She stood in the overgrown front yard of the white-clad house and sighed deeply. The front of the house hadn't changed in the last eighty-odd years apart from her father installing the cladding over the original weatherboards. Built in the early nineteen forties, the cottage had replaced an older tin shed. Her grandfather had added on the back section of the house, sunken slightly so it formed a downstairs area with large, curved windows to take in the endless blue ocean below. The weight of all that family history was a heavy burden. Alex had always been proud of her heritage. She had roots here—she was connected to the land and to the ocean. Her ancestors were buried in the small, white picket–fenced cemetery situated on the next headland over. She belonged here and yet . . . she didn't. Not anymore. She hadn't in a very long time.

Alex inserted the key into the front door and pushed it open, breathing in the familiar scent of the house and feeling as though she had been thrown back in time. She could almost be stepping through the front door after coming home from school. The only thing missing was the smell of her mother's baking or dinner cooking on the stove. She swallowed past an unexpectedly tightening throat and blinked rapidly. She hadn't expected those memories to hit quite so hard.

Her parents had divorced when she was eighteen and she and her mother had moved to Sydney. A few years after Alex had moved overseas, her mother had decided to come on an extended holiday and it had been nice having her mum with her in London. But then, her mother had met a man who lived only a few houses down from Alex, and within six months, they'd married.

She didn't like to sound like a jealous daughter—because she wasn't, she was thrilled to see her mother so happy after a long time being on her own—it was just that Bart came with three daughters of his own, who were all married with babies. And now her mother had grandchildren she loved to spoil, Alex felt she didn't seem to spend much time alone with her anymore.

Alex really liked her new stepsisters and they'd welcomed her into the family from the very first time they'd all met, but she had nothing in common with any of them when so many of the conversations and activities were centred around babies and small children. There was only so much Wiggles a person without their own kids could handle.

She ran her fingers along the top of the lounge. There wasn't much left in the way of furniture or homewares from when she'd lived here; that had all either been sold or donated to charity after her father died eight years ago. She'd replaced it with trendy-looking coastal chic furniture to better suit the holiday rental the house had become. It had been a nice little earner, too, in the last few years. It rarely sat empty, providing her with a side income that had allowed her the luxury of travel.

She let her gaze wander to the large windows that framed a magnificent view of the ocean. She'd grown up with this view and yet she couldn't remember if she'd ever stopped to simply admire it. She'd probably assumed everyone had uninterrupted ocean views from their lounge-room window, and as she grew older she would have been too wrapped up in the latest schoolyard drama to pay it much attention. It seemed a waste to take something so beautiful for granted. *And yet you walked away from it*, she could almost hear her father's gruff voice whisper. She hadn't walked—she'd run, as fast and as far as she could, desperate to leave all the bad memories behind her.

Alex turned away from the window and headed back outside to the car to bring in her suitcase. The sooner she got started, the sooner she could leave.

Sullivan McCoy—Sully to his friends—waved the last guest off the boat before starting the clean-up. It'd been a great trip, the weather had been perfect, and he always felt good when his customers left with a camera full of memories and a couple of fishing yarns to tell family and friends when they got back home. These fishing tours had begun as a side gig for the off season when trawling was slow and had become so popular that it'd pretty much become his full-time job.

The success of his venture gave him the perfect excuse to step back from the trawling side of the business and take a well-earned break from the hectic life that went along with being a professional commercial fisherman. He'd spent years working twenty-hour days, weeks at a time out at sea, which had messed up his relationships and family life. Of course, he still went out on the boat during the crazy season that led up to Easter and Christmas when they earned the big bucks—it was all hands on deck during those times. It usually made up for the less profitable times throughout the year. Regardless of what size catch you came back with, the crew still needed to be paid along with fuel and food and equipment. It wasn't always a great pay day when you owned fishing boats—not like the old days.

The McCoy name had been synonymous with the fishing industry around here for generations. It had also been very well acquainted with the law—and not necessarily on the right side of it, either. In his father's and grandfathers' days, the industry had still been the wild west, where pretty much anything went: no species was off limits, no haul too big.

Sully felt his jaw clench slightly and concentrated on relaxing it. His father had been old-school and, had he still been alive, he'd no doubt be giving Sully an earful about how *he'd* be doing things. 'No bunch of greenie, degree-toting uni students are gonna tell me what I can and cannot catch,' Sully could hear him say. Theo McCoy had been a hard man in every sense of the word. He was tough as old leather and had no time for weakness of any kind. Sully's hadn't been the easiest childhood—his mother had shot through when he was in primary school, taking his older sister with her. She'd died a few years back and he and his sister had only recently reconnected but they were pretty much strangers with nothing but genetics in common.

Nowadays it was only Sully running the fishing side of things—since his dad and two uncles had all passed. There were a few aunties and a couple of cousins in town, but the majority had moved on to other parts of the country—got out of town to try and distance themselves from the trouble that the McCoy name used to bring around here. Sully too had spent his entire adult life trying to wash his name free of the stains his father had left behind. He'd worked his arse off to ensure his business would be known as the respectable company it was today—a legitimate one that made money legally.

Sully shook off the dismal mood that had descended and began the clean-up. The routine was almost therapeutic. The boat had just spent three days out at sea as a team-building exercise for a group of businessmen. Sully wasn't sure what kind of business they were in, but if three days of fishing, drinking and eating was considered team building, then he was tempted to switch professions.

He glanced up as he heard his daughter call his name as she walked down the pier towards the boat. He smiled. It was hard to believe his baby was nearly eighteen. Where the hell had that time gone? One minute he was being handed a tiny, red-skinned, screaming newborn that he had no idea what to do with, and the next, here she was, a beautiful young woman, all grown up and planning to leave home at the end of January.

Gabby had always been his ray of sunshine in a somewhat less-than-sunshiny life. Even now, with the threat of an afternoon thunderstorm approaching on the horizon, she brought with her a glow. Her dark hair, pulled back in a ponytail, swung with a jauntiness that perfectly reflected her energetic personality, and her wide smile filled him with love and pride. It still stunned him that he'd somehow helped create this amazing kid.

'Hey, kiddo,' he said, hugging Gabby tightly as she stepped on deck and lowered the bucket of cleaning supplies.

'Hey, Dad. How was the trip?'

'Pretty good. Managed to catch a few decent wahoo and a marlin. How was everything back here?'

'All good. Nothing too exciting.'

Gabby had been working the boat hire and bait shop they ran from the booking office at the marina after school, on weekends and during holidays since she was fourteen years old. She handled customers with a friendly yet competent manner and had saved her wages to buy her own car when she was sixteen. Over the years she'd learned the workings of the entire business: his fleet of trawlers, as well as the boat hire and bait shop that tapped into the area's tourism industry. She knew as much about the business as Sully did and could probably run the entire operation without him if she had to. He hoped she wouldn't ever have to, though—he wanted more for his little girl than to work in the fishing industry.

They chatted about what had been happening while he'd been away as they fell into the cleaning routine. He paid her extra for cleaning and Gabby had jumped at the chance to earn some more cash before she left home. His heart sank a little as he realised she wouldn't be around to do any of this soon. He'd miss their time together. He knew he was being selfish by wishing she'd change her mind about leaving—after all, he was the one who'd always planted the idea in her head that she could do better than her old man and fishing for a job—but part of him wanted to ground her forever just so she didn't have to leave. Once people left Rockne Heads, they never came back.

He knew from experience.

'So, Dad,' Gabby said a little too calmly as Sully heaved the last of the garbage bags onto the pier. He turned to face her with a guarded expression. 'There's going to be this party on the weekend—'

Sully was shaking his head before she even finished the sentence.

'Dad! Just listen.'

'You know the rule. No beach parties.'

'I'm almost eighteen,' Gabby reminded him, planting her hands on her hips, undaunted by his stern frown.

'I don't care if you're a hundred and five. No. Beach. Parties.'

'You do realise you're being completely unreasonable, don't you?'

'So you've said every time you've ever asked the same question.'

'I wasn't asking a question,' she said flatly. 'I was stating a fact. Dad, I missed out on the Year Twelve afterparty at the formal. That was bad enough, but this is probably the last time I'll get to be with all of my friends at once before they all start heading off on Christmas holidays.'

'So go out to dinner or something. Have a sleepover,' he said with a shrug.

'A sleep—' Gabby stared at her father, exasperated. 'Dad, I'm not twelve! I'm an adult.'

'You're still living under my roof and the rules you grew up with will be enforced until you leave.'

'This place is a prison!' she snapped, storming off, before stopping and turning quickly. 'I don't understand you. I get that there was some stupid tragedy around here a thousand years ago, but it makes no sense whatsoever that I should be punished for something that happened before I was even born!'

'It's not about that,' Sully said firmly, reining in his anger.

'It's exactly about that. You said it yourself last year when I wanted to go to Connor Biscoe's eighteenth,' she said.

'It's about a bunch of hormone-ridden teenage boys sniffing about. No beach parties. End of discussion.'

'Discussion?' Gabby snapped. 'It's never a discussion with you. It's just you saying no to everything fun!'

'That's my job.'

'You make me so mad!' Gabby yelled, stomping away.

Sully watched her walk to her car. She slammed the door and he winced slightly as he imagined having to replace the rubber seals.

He let out an indiscernible sigh after Gabby reversed her little Mazda and drove away. He knew he was overreacting, and yet every time he tried to force himself to be open-minded about parties, that same, gut-wrenching helplessness filled him. There was no way he was going to risk his daughter going through that. It may have been almost twenty years ago but the ghosts of that night still lurked around their little town, refusing to stay dead.

Two

Alex pushed open the glass door and stepped outside onto the covered deck, carrying her cup of coffee. The morning air was cool, but it wouldn't stay that way for long. She'd just missed the sunrise; the intense orange had faded into a paler shade of peach and the sky was turning a vivid blue that promised another hot day to follow. The subtle smell of the ocean filled her lungs and the sound of waves crashing onto the rocks below the headland not far from the house seemed extra loud. Being back in the old house for the first time in so long, she hadn't thought she'd be able to sleep but, surprisingly, when she woke this morning, she didn't even remember falling asleep. When she'd carried her suitcase in yesterday afternoon she'd automatically turned left in the hallway and claimed her old bedroom. Of course, it had changed since then—she'd had the entire house painted when she'd inherited it, and now the candy pink walls she'd so loved as a seven-year-old were a much more grown-up white on white.

A sudden, rhythmic banging interrupted the peace and Alex gave an irritated frown. Out here, with nothing other than the ocean to look at, it was easy to forget you had neighbours behind high fences on either side.

Curiosity eventually got the better of her when the banging continued and seemed to be getting closer so she stood up from where she'd been sitting and walked around the side of the house.

Two women and a man were at the front of her house, juggling what looked like a bunch of signs. The man picked up a hammer and positioned one of the signs, preparing to hit it into the ground.

'Excuse me,' Alex called, causing all three to whirl around to face her. 'What are you doing?'

'Alex Kelly? Is that you?' one of the women asked, shading her eyes from the glare as she peered at where Alex stood.

'Yes,' Alex said, recognising the woman and the other two people with a silent groan. Of all the people she had to bump into on her first day in town, it had to be Murna Battalex. Everyone referred to Murna as the mayor of Rockne Heads. Not to her face of course, although Alex suspected she'd heard the term and secretly enjoyed it. There were a few other not so polite terms given to her, the most notable being the Old Battle Axe.

'Well, I'll be! Goodness, it must be years since I last saw you home.'

'It's been a while,' Alex said, reluctantly crossing the yard to the picket fence.

'You look exactly like your mother,' Thelma Grant said, shaking her head in amazement. 'Doesn't she, Jonah?'

The man gave an obligatory nod and a small grunt, still holding his big mallet, clearly just wanting to finish his job and go home.

'Can I help you with something?' Alex prompted as three pairs of eyes studied her much like a bug under a microscope. She couldn't really blame them, they were probably quite shocked to see the kid they'd once known suddenly reappear as a thirty-five-year-old woman.

'We're just putting up some signage, dear. We didn't know anyone was here,' Murna said, nodding at the plastic sign at her feet.

SAVE OUR VILLAGE. SAY NO TO ERMON NICHOLADES, the signs read.

'I'm not sure what this is all about,' Alex said slowly.

'They're trying to ruin our way of life, that's what this is about,' Murna snapped.

'We're under attack,' Thelma added, and Alex felt her eyebrows rise slightly.

'From whom?' Alex asked.

'From big corporations trying to buy their way into our valley and destroy our village. They want to make it into the next Surfers Paradise.'

Surely that was going a bit far? Although going by the look on Murna's face, she believed it.

'What are they proposing?' Alex asked. She suspected that, sooner or later, she was going to be hearing about it, so she may as well be properly armed.

'They want to buy up all that bushland on the way into town and tear all the trees down to build a bunch of new houses for a retirement village. They're saying they want to put in over two hundred new homes. Can you believe that? All those new people coming into town? Into our tiny village? Where are they going to park their cars, for starters?'

Alex was still trying to digest the information but found it curious that out of everything she'd just mentioned, parking was Murna's major concern.

'We won't stand for it, I'm telling you! We will fight them to the bitter end!' Thelma said firmly and not without a hint of malice. 'There's a town meeting planned for next week. I trust we can count on your support dear?'

'It's really got nothing to do with me. I'm not a local anymore,' Alex protested. She hoped this property developer knew what he was up against. Listening to a pissed-off Murna and her protest buddies would not be a pleasant way to spend an evening.

'It's got everything to do with you,' Murna said, sounding shocked. 'This is where you grew up, where your family has lived for generations.'

'Yes, well . . . I'm actually back here to put the place on the market.'

Stunned silence greeted her words and for a moment, Alex felt uncomfortable. Then she straightened her shoulders. She had nothing to feel uncomfortable about; this was her house to do with as she wished. If she wanted to sell it, she could bloody well sell it.

'What would your father think about that?' Thelma asked with a wide-eyed look.

Alex clamped down on the swell of disappointment doing its best to rise inside her at the mention of her father. He would hate it. 'It really doesn't matter now, does it?' she replied briskly, feeling bad for speaking back to one of her elders, as though she was still a kid and not a grown-arsed woman who had every right to point out how rude they were being. Old habits and good manners died hard, it seemed.

Murna gave a delicate sniff before nodding at Jonah to continue putting up the sign.

'Actually, I'd rather you didn't put one of those in front of my place,' Alex said, feeling the further cooling of the air between herself and the others. Frostbite was becoming a distinct possibility. 'I don't want to get involved in local politics—you know, what with trying to sell and everything.'

Murna held her gaze for a moment and Alex thought she might ignore her request and put the sign up anyway, but the woman turned and, with a wave of her hand, beckoned her two lackies to follow. 'I'm very disappointed, Alex Kelly. Very disappointed indeed.'

Alex headed back inside the house, fighting the urge to run after the trio and defend herself. Why should she care what they thought? Their opinion didn't matter to her.

And yet she couldn't shake the icky feeling their judgy looks had left behind. It wasn't like her reputation around here had

been anything to be proud of—half the town had made their
opinions loud and clear eighteen years ago.

Sully pushed open the door of the bakery and walked inside
to buy his usual order of fresh bread. The owner, Mitch,
glanced up from the newspaper he was reading and called a
greeting. Sully nodded to two people perched on bar stools
at the window bench, eating Mitch's famous pies. Tourists,
he instantly thought, not recognising their faces. Once upon
a time, you only saw tourists during the Christmas holidays.
Nowadays it was pretty much year-round. The caravan park
across the street was always booked out and the beach packed
with out-of-towners. Not that he was complaining. Tourism
had been the thing that had saved his business. Without it,
he'd still be stuck doing weeks out at sea catching fish and
hoping the market wasn't inundated with whatever he caught,
barely breaking even most weeks. It was even worse now that
fuel prices had reached an all-time high. Nope—give him a
town full of new faces any day.

'Have you heard who's back?' Mitch asked, eyeing his friend
carefully.

'No,' Sully said. 'Who?'

'Alex. *Kelly*,' Mitch said.

Sully felt his stomach drop then clench abruptly. He tried
to keep his face expressionless. 'No. I hadn't heard.'

'Apparently she's back to sell her old man's house.'

'Really?' That *did* surprise him. The Kellys' beach house
was part of local history. It had always been known as the

Kelly house, even when Alex had put it up as a holiday rental and named it Four Winds Beach Accommodation.

'Heard it straight from Murna's mouth just a few minutes ago.' Mitch gave a low whistle. 'And she was *not* a happy camper.'

'Who? Murna?' Then again, silly question, Murna was *never* happy—she was always complaining about something around town.

'Yeah. Apparently,' Mitch said, lowering his voice, 'Alex told them to piss off and refused to have a sign in front of the house.' As Sully raised his eyebrows, Mitch hurried to add, 'Or words to that effect.'

'No wonder Murna isn't happy. I'm pretty sure she's the first person who's said no to a sign.'

'I can't work out if she's brave or stupid. Maybe she's just been away so long she's forgotten the golden rule: Don't get on the bad side of Murna Battle Axe.'

'Maybe.'

'Anyway, how was the latest trip?'

'Great. Came back with the same number of people I went out there with, so that's always a good thing. I gotta go, I'll see you tomorrow,' Sully said, collecting his bread and saluting his friend as he headed out.

His gaze automatically went up the road from the shop to the furthest headland where the little white house sat. He wondered if Alex had changed much. He hadn't seen her in almost eight years, not since her father's funeral, and even then, they hadn't spoken. He'd wondered if she'd sell the old house, but a few weeks later it was put up as a holiday let. Part of him was relieved—that meant that there was the possibility of her coming back one day. He had to admit he'd pretty much given up on that.

Now that he knew Alex was literally only a few hundred or so metres away, he wasn't sure what to do. Had time eased some of the pain between them now that they were both adults with a hefty chunk of life experience under their belts? Or would she still hate him the way she had eighteen years ago? He wanted to march up the headland and knock on her door right now, but a saner, far more cautious part of him advised against the urge. *Let it be for a few days*, it said calmly. *You've gone this long without seeing her—a few more days won't hurt.*

It made sense—after all, for all he knew she could be happily married and the last thing she'd want was for her high school boyfriend to turn up on her doorstep unannounced. No, it was better to hang back and wait, see what he could find out about her situation before he got too excited. After all, it was entirely possible she still hated his guts.

To be honest, he really couldn't blame her, after what he'd done.